ALISON's WONDERLAND

ALISON's WONDERLAND

AN
EROTIC
COLLECTION
EDITED BY

ALISON TYLER

Spice

If you purchased this book without a cover you should be aware
that this book is stolen property. It was reported as "unsold and
destroyed" to the publisher, and neither the author nor the
publisher has received any payment for this "stripped book."

Recycling programs
for this product may
not exist in your area.

Spice

ALISON'S WONDERLAND

ISBN-13: 978-0-373-60545-3

Copyright © 2010 by Alison Tyler.

The publisher acknowledges the individual stories in this collection are
copyright © 2010 by their respective authors.

All rights reserved. Except for use in any review, the reproduction or
utilization of this work in whole or in part in any form by any electronic,
mechanical or other means, now known or hereafter invented, including
xerography, photography and recording, or in any information storage
or retrieval system, is forbidden without the written permission of the
publisher, Spice Books, 225 Duncan Mill Road, Don Mills, Ontario,
Canada M3B 3K9.

This is a work of fiction. Names, characters, places and incidents are
either the product of the author's imagination or are used fictitiously,
and any resemblance to actual persons, living or dead, business
establishments, events or locales is entirely coincidental.

Spice and the Colophon are trademarks used under license and
registered in Australia, New Zealand, Philippines, United States Patent
and Trademark Office and in other countries.

For questions and comments about the quality of this book
please contact us at Customer_eCare@Harlequin.ca.

www.Spice-Books.com

Printed in U.S.A.

For Sam.

Contents

ᐸ᠎introduction᠎ᐳ

Down the rabbit hole I go, in search of fractured fairy tales and manhandled myths, the type that would make Snow White blush Rose Red. Why fables and rhymes and stories of years gone by? Because the familiar cadence of these magical tales clings to us like the fabric of dreams. The *once upon a time* is already in place—the *happily-ever-after* is waiting for us. It's the part in the middle that's rich with promise, the sticky-sweet candy-colored goodness of a whole new type of "Hansel and Gretel" story.

The truth is that we all love a happy ending (traditional or otherwise), especially when the characters turn out to be kinky. To that end, I've compiled twenty-seven brand-spanking-new stories from such popular erotic writers as Thomas S. Roche, Tsaurah Litzky and Shanna Germain.

Many fables are immediately recognizable. Sommer Marsden's "The Three Billys" is neatly spotted as a modern-day goat story, although the gruffest of the Billys has a far dirtier method of dealing with (Ms.) Troll than in the original tale. Kristina Lloyd's "David" riffs on "Sleeping Beauty" in a myriad of ways. A surreal vampire yarn, her Beauty not only wakes up to her deep sexual submission, but she awakens her very own handsome prince. Bella Dean's "Wolff's Tavern" turns the tale of "Little Red Riding Hood" inside out—this Wolff comes to Ruby's rescue. Sophia Valenti's "The Cougar of Cobble Hill" is based firmly on the sole of "The Old Woman Who Lived in a Shoe," while Jacqueline Applebee's "Slutty Cinderella" features the only wannabe princess I know who needs a shave. T. C. Calligari spins the Grimms' somewhat obscure fable "The Magic Table, the Golden Donkey and the Club in the Sack" into "A Taste for Treasure," featuring a magical stick, crop and cot.

Several writers approached the same story, but with wickedly different results. "Fool's Gold" by Shanna Germain retells "Rumpelstiltskin" from the point of view of a woman so tightly bound by her own desires she doesn't know what she wants. Georgia E. Jones tackles the same fairy tale from more than five hundred years in the past, in the boisterous court of King Edward V. Ms. Jones's story shows that no matter what the date, love is always in fashion. Nikki Magennis's darkly beautiful "Red Shoes (Redux)" contrasts deliciously with Tsaurah Litzky's "Dancing Shoes," which features an older (but just as intriguing) protagonist, with a little bit of Cinderella for good measure.

Other creations in this collection are magical stories in their own right: Portia Da Costa's "Unveiling His Muse" reads like a brand-new fairy tale, and Andrea Dale's "The Broken Fiddle" has the cadence of an old Irish legend. In "The Midas F★ck," Erica DeQuaya delves into what might happen if a woman's secret wish came true. A. D. R. Forte's "Moonset" begs the question "Is that a werewolf in my bed, or are you just happy to see me?" In "Managers and Mermen," Donna George Storey's fantasy mermaid lives only in her main character's mind—or *does* she? In Lana Fox's "Always Break the Spines," a naughty coed learns that fairy tales can hurt. Literally. Her lover punishes her with a leather-bound book.

What ingredients are required to create a modern-day fairy tale? Sometimes all that's needed is a little magic dust—and a bit of lube. Bryn Haniver's ever-so-dirty "Mastering Their Dungeons" draws on a familiar game, but not everyone could turn a dorm room into a setting for a modern-day myth. Benjamin Eliot has conjured his own version of Sisyphus, with a protagonist forced to fix the same facility for what appears to be an eternity in "An Uphill Battle." Rachel Kramer Bussel's "Let Down Your Libido" features a completely different type of prison for a Rapunzel of the new millennium. And Thomas S. Roche's "Cupid Has Signed Off" takes us from sex play in the online universe to a sizzling scenario IRL (in real life). My own "Rings on My Fingers" features dusky Los Angeles, a shy bookstore clerk and the universal desire for a happy ending, even with a tattooed prince.

Three wishes are all one girl requires when offered to choose in Saskia Walker's "Kiss It." What exactly does the protagonist kiss? Well, he's definitely not a frog. Janine Ashbless's "Gold, On Snow" tackles "Snow White" from the queen's point of view. Allison Wonderland's "Sleeping with Beauty" delves into the bubblegum-pink universe of two princesses who forgo princes (and frogs) in favor of each other. And what if one of those handsome fairy-tale studs liked men?

Are the endings always happy? That's for the reader to decide. "The Clean-Shaven Type" by N. T. Morley, is a version of "Beauty and the Beast" with quite unexpected results for the Beast. "*After* the Happily-Ever-After," by Heidi Champa, describes what happens to poor Cinderella once the sparkle fades from her fairy-tale wedding. The collection rides off into the sunset with a fairy tale told in a hundred words. If you don't think that's possible, check out Elspeth Potter's "The Princess."

With a combination of retold tales and brand-new fables, Alison's Wonderland is the perfect naughty bedtime storybook to share with a partner (or enjoy solo style) for your own X-rated Happily-Ever-After.

XXX,
Alison Tyler

It is only possible

to live happily ever after

on a day-to-day basis.

— *Margaret Bonnano*

...don't forget about

what happened to the man

who got everything he ever wanted.

He lived happily ever after.

— *Roald Dahl*

The Red Shoes (Redux)

Nikki Magennis

Lily had walked past the shoe shop a hundred times. On her way to work at the flower shop early every morning, wearing shabby jeans and baseball boots that were worn the same color as the pavement, she'd walk fast and barely glance at the shiny, chichi window display. She didn't need to see heart-breaker heels and designer bags that would cost her a month's wages.

For the past six weeks, though, she'd found herself swiveling on her heel and turning to look at a particular display.

The window stretched high above her head, the plate glass polished so bright it reflected her image like a mirror. But Lily wasn't looking at herself. Her gaze was totally transfixed on the shoes. Glossy, cherry-red, skyscraper-high, patent-leather fuck-me shoes that made her heart beat faster just looking at them. They had deep curves and a dangerous heel and they stood center stage on a podium by themselves, proud, shockingly beautiful and insanely unaffordable. They made Lily's mouth water. She could almost taste the red of them.

Once, she'd approached the door, got close enough to feel the cool hum of air-conditioned air on her face. And then she'd checked herself. Girls with ratty hair and dirt under their chipped–varnish nails didn't enter shops like that. Not without a motorcycle helmet and a package under their arm. Not in a million years.

While she was at work, emptying buckets of stinking slime-water and slicing the stems of stargazer lilies, Lily let her imagination wander. In those shoes, she'd be able to walk anywhere—up red carpets and through gilded palaces, across Hollywood Boulevard and down the Champs-Élysées. She'd be a shameless scarlet bombshell, and take no shit from anyone. Her hips would swing and her lips would pout and men would fall at her feet.

And then her boss, Margie, yelled at her for daydreaming, and Lily snapped out of it and got on with the cold, dirty, green–stained work of the day.

It was the first Saturday in May. The city was full of mist that crawled lazily up the streets and muffled the edges of the morning. Dragging herself reluctantly to work, Lily walked past the siren-red shine of the shoes, and drifted to the window to gaze at her unreachable dreams through half an inch of bulletproof glass.

"You like them."

Lily nearly fell on her ass. A man had appeared, silently, in the shop doorway. He wore a black shirt and trousers the color of champagne. His face was taut and unlined, and his smile barely tweaked the corners of his mouth.

"I was just looking," Lily said, backing away.

"I see you," the man continued, fixing her with fathom-less gray eyes, "every morning. You look at my shoes like you're starving."

"Your shoes?"

"I design them," he said.

"No shit," said Lily.

"For women," he said, "like you."

"Oh," Lily said, and looked down at her faded, raggedy Ramones T-shirt.

A smile snaked across the man's face.

"It's what's underneath that matters," he said, his eyes hooking on Lily's chest.

If Lily had seen herself in the plate glass, she'd have seen her cheeks flare as red as the shoes. She looked down at the paving slabs and tried to think of a witty comeback.

"Come in," the man said, pushing the door open.

Lily's eyes flicked from the shoes to the man and back again. In her mind's eye, she pictured the flower shop's shutters rolling open and Margie cursing the empty street. And then, although she knew it was crazy and although she couldn't afford to get fired from another job and although everything about the man made her feel she had sleepwalked into some surreal stage play, she followed him into the cool, palatial interior.

The whole place must have been polished by an army of women on their hands and knees, Lily thought. Every damn surface shone like a mirror. Even the light shafts that fell across the room looked glossy. The air smelt faintly of a sweet, spicy perfume, and the shop was silent. There was no sound other than the click of the man's shoes as he walked across the marble floor to the window display.

He lifted the shoes by the straps and brought them to Lily, dangling them from his hand like a bunch of grapes he didn't want to bruise.

"See," he said. "Aren't they beautiful?"

But as Lily reached out, he swung the shoes away and shook his head. He gave her a smile that made her feel dizzy.

"Not yet. You can wear them tonight. When I take you out."

When Lily finally turned up to work half an hour late, she was clumsy and preoccupied. She knocked over a display and broke an orchid stem, gave the delivery driver a funeral wreath instead of a get-well-soon bouquet and ruined a hundred silk roses by dropping them in water.

"What is going on?" Margie bellowed. "Lily Spink, get a hold of yourself!"

By six o'clock, Lily was wired. She stood by the door of the shop, stepping from foot to foot anxiously while she waited for Hans. That was his name—the shoe man. It was about all she knew. But she'd guessed he was rich. She had an inkling he'd take her somewhere fancy, and so she'd stripped down to her spaghetti-strap vest and tried to scrub the green stains off her jeans. Her outfit wasn't Chanel, but it was the best she could do at short notice.

When his car pulled up outside, dark, sleek and quiet, Lily whistled under her breath. It looked like a cruise ship.

"Hold on!"

Lily rolled her eyes as Margie's foghorn voice called her back. Her boss nodded at her. "Take this, honey."

She pressed something into Lily's hand—a sprig of little bell-shaped white flowers nodding on a stem, tied in ribbon— and gave a tight smile.

"Lily of the valley. Your namesake."

He drove straight to a club downtown, tucked behind the old merchants' quarter. Hans climbed out of the car and walked around to Lily's door to open it. When she swung her feet out, he bent forward and stilled her with one hand on her knee. Lily swallowed. Hans crouched at the curb. His hands slid down her calves and looped around her ankles. Slowly, almost daintily, he unlaced her baseball boots. When he tossed the battered boots in the gutter, Lily nearly cried out, but then she saw the hot glimmer of the red shoes and caught her breath.

Hans laid them at her feet.

"Put them on."

As she stepped, at last, into the arched shoes, they clasped her feet like the hands of a lover, and Lily knew she was beautiful. When she climbed out of the car, her spine unrolled and her hips tipped forward, until her body was an S that leaned toward Hans. Even in her frayed old jeans and with her hair loose and tangled, Lily felt like a queen.

She'd tied Margie's posy to the strap of her vest, and Hans's eye caught on it as they climbed the steps.

He raised an eyebrow. "An unusual corsage."

Lily didn't answer. She felt a bit dazzled.

They entered the club arm in arm. Every head turned to look at them. The men's faces were lustful and the women looked as if they'd sucked sour plums. Damn, Lily thought. These shoes *work*. She swayed across the marble floor, hanging from Hans's arm. The shoes were so high they gave her vertigo, but there was also a zing and a shiver creeping through her veins. Lily's tits tingled like they had lithium batteries attached to the nipples.

Hans led her past the jealous crowd and through a pair of long velvet curtains at the back of the club. They entered a dark, cavelike room with black walls and black marble floors, a vast glittering chandelier hanging overhead the only decor.

"Want something to drink?" Hans said, his lips brushing her ear, and Lily shivered. Everything he said made her feel as though she were swimming in syrup.

"Or shall we dance?" Hans slipped an arm around her and let his hand trip over the curve of her buttocks. Lily's heartbeat seemed to follow his touch, and she had to force herself to breathe out. When he pulled her onto the edge of the dance floor, her feet started to twitch. Lily was restless. Antsy. She felt like there was a swarm of bees in her belly, and it was part sweet torture, part agony as the thrills spilled over and trickled through her veins.

Hans watched her. His gaze stroked down her curves, and Lily felt as though she were being wrapped in hot, wet silk. Delicious shivers ran up and down her legs, and she twisted from side to side to let the tingles travel right to the end of her fingertips. What was going on? She dropped her eyes to her feet. Was it some kind of weird acupuncture?

"Oh, God," she said. "These shoes—these shoes are… fantastic."

Hans circled her, still observing her body with intense interest. As she pointed her toes and flexed, like a cat trying to shake an itch out of its fur, he put his mouth to her ear.

"Dance," he whispered, and gave her a sharp slap on the rounded cheek of her ass. The sting made her leap, and Lily whirled around, her mouth open wide in surprise. Before she could say a word, though, her attention was distracted by a low, pulsing sound. It could have been her heartbeat thumping in her ears or it could have been music, but whatever it was, the rhythm spoke directly to her body, to her hips and belly and the sweet wetness gathering between her legs.

Lily danced. She rolled back and forth and stroked herself, balancing on her tiptoes in the towering shoes. As Hans watched, she danced for him and toward him, winding around his body and rocking against him. The complex, noiseless music continued and grew louder as she ground into his crotch, lifted up tall enough on the shoes to meet the stiff length of his cock as it pressed against her, hot even through the layers of their clothes.

Deep in Lily's thoughts, a glimmer of apprehension flared. Weren't there any waiters, any other people wandering into the hidden ballroom? She hunted the dark corners of the room, but found nothing in the shadows except more shadows, deep and thickly layered, and the sensation she was floating underwater, drifting down beyond the depths to a place where no light would reach her. She felt caressed by the dark, just as Hans gently stroked her hips and slid his long fingers inside the waistband of her jeans, reaching down to tickle the top of her ass.

When he kissed her, it was like drinking very fine brandy—smooth and strong and dark gold. Lily smelled the perfume on his neck—civet and patchouli, something dense and elusive—as he deftly unbuttoned and pushed her jeans to her knees. Any shame she might have felt evaporated like smoke, and she closed her eyes as his swaying movements helped them dance closer to each other, until there was nothing between their skin but heat and a damp slick of perspiration.

Perhaps he slid his trousers aside as swiftly as he'd undressed her, or perhaps his clothes somehow melted away, because now Lily felt Hans's cock, hot and hard, slide between her thighs and nudge at the seam of her pussy. She was molten wax, all liquid heat, and Hans was flowing into her like a knife into butter.

His hands circled her hips and held her fast as he pinned her on his prick, pulling her down slowly until he filled her right. But Lily couldn't stop moving, like the beat wouldn't leave her alone, and she squirmed against him, working herself closer and closer.

She no longer knew if she was trying to dance or fuck or swim. Her feet slid around to get purchase on the floor as he took her and lifted her up with each stroke. Lily heard moans, and wondered if they came from her mouth. Her body was wildly restless, insatiable even as she felt the blissful ache of his cock thrumming inside her.

As they worked against each other, his hands moved everywhere at once—cupping her breast, slipping over the fuzz of her pussy, pinching her clit and molding her ass. Gripped in his rough embrace and tugged and dazzled by whatever the shoes were doing to her, Lily's head started to spin.

"You like that?" he asked, and she heard a dark thread of menace running in his voice.

"Don't want me to stop, do you?" he asked, while his fingers strummed and rubbed and tweaked at her. She crawled upward, like she was trying to climb his body.

A voice in her head chanted a mantra she was only half aware of. *More, more, more.* Lily didn't know what she wanted more of—his cock, his fingers, his voice slithering into her ear like a trance, the brandy kiss or the wet shine of the shoes that clung to her feet. The feeling, the thick, dark, urgent and sweet feeling. The beat of the music rolling into her. Everything, everything.

Lily started to shiver. Hans fucked her steadily, decisively. She had to fight to breathe. The polished floor was slippery under her feet and she felt herself tumbling, slipping, falling as the burn of orgasm rose up through her body.

It started in her feet, red flares of sensation that burned in her veins and swarmed around her thighs, a hot crush inside her that uncurled and licked over her clit, clutched at her heart and sparked in her nipples as the man pinched them tightly. And then it was everywhere.

She closed her eyes and saw crimson, opened her mouth and screamed scarlet, felt the red crash over her and through her and shake her until there was no world anymore, no ballroom, no Lily.

The red splashed across her heart and sizzled in her fingertips.

The waves rocked her back and forth, swaying her until she was seasick. Lily unraveled and spun out like a ribbon caught in the ocean's deep currents. She was limp, her body shaky. Ready to climb down now, to find air, to break the surface.

But Hans's arms circled her waist and the shoes were tight on her feet. Although she was flinching, oversensitive, the cock inside her was harder and stronger than ever and her body wouldn't stop moving against it.

"Hans," she said, almost ready to beg for a moment's pause. She was ignored. He rubbed relentlessly at her aching nipples, making her flinch as the too-strong sensation shot through her. She was bathed in sweat, cooling now and slick over the surface of her skin.

She tried to pull away. But she found herself tugged toward Hans, as though there were a strong magnet in her stomach. And her hips—though they ached, they kept on moving. Her body seemed possessed—though she frowned and blinked she couldn't seem to see clearly.

"Yes," Hans said, and his smile curdled. "Dance with me."

"Oh," Lily said. Her voice was faint. "I think I need a glass of water."

Hans put his mouth to her ear.

"All you need is this. All you need is me."

He nodded his head.

"You're mine."

Lily's heart lurched. The music had become dark and hard now, it beat against her skull. Hans let his eyes drop to her shoes. He smiled, and the skin pulled taut over his cheekbones.

"The shoes belong to me. And now you belong to the shoes."

Lily's feet twitched and throbbed, and she realized in a split second that she was bewitched. The shoes were a poisoned chalice, a glittering prison, two seductive traps that she'd walked straight into. She pushed Hans away and dropped to a crouch, tugging at the straps on her ankles. It was as though the buckles were soldered shut. Her feet were burning now, and her breath was fighting in her throat. She looked up at Hans and saw twin fires in his eyes, a terrible, cold desire. The tip of his tongue flickered over his lips.

"Mine," he said.

Desperate and confused, Lily reached to her throat. Her hand brushed the wilted corsage pinned to her breast, and she clutched at the stems. A burst of sweet, green perfume floated from it. Hardly aware of what she was doing, Lily gripped hold of the flowers and held on to them tight. Her head hurt. Her eyes were bleary. With fingers wet from sap, she rubbed at her eyelids.

It was like the sky opened up. A fresh breeze cut through the thick atmosphere of the ballroom, smelling of cut grass and brine and newly dug earth. Lily looked around.

Hans was a few feet from her, but he seemed to shrink as she looked at him. Her eyes were clear. There was dandruff on his shoulder and dust on the chandelier. The music faded. Lily felt an insistent pain in her feet, and looked down at the red shoes. Irritated, she kicked a shoe across the dance floor, and stepped lightly out of the other.

The floor was dusty and small pieces of grit dug into the soles of her feet, but it felt good. She flexed her toes. Lily heaved a deep sigh.

"Well, Hans, you know that was fun, but I think it's time I got going."

He didn't answer, but instead made a hissing sound, like a balloon when the air is let out of it.

"No, don't fuss, I don't need a ride home," Lily continued, rubbing mascara from under her eyes. "It's been a great night. Really interesting. Although—" Lily leaned toward Hans and whispered loudly across the empty dance floor, "You might want to lay off the Viagra. Too much of a good thing, you know?"

With that, she blew him a light kiss off the end of her fingertips, turned and left.

Fool's Gold

Shanna Germain

Spin a Yarn

It was a random boast. Too many gin and tonics, too aware of how my ass looked in a new pair of dark jeans. Far too aware of how he'd been watching me across the loud space of a bar table all night, long fingers reaching up to push a few strands of dark hair away from his blue eyes. Not a close friend, but still a friend. And for long enough you'd think I'd have noticed him that way before. But sometimes that's how it happens, a flip switches, and the guy at the edge slips into the center. He is suddenly all you can see.

This flip was the conversation that turned from usual drunken rants to sex. Specifically to bondage sex. After a few minutes of the boys around the table laughing and the girls not really saying much, I pushed the lime into my gin and tonic with the end of my stir stick. "I don't know what the big deal is." I imagined being stuck somewhere, seat-belted in, unable to reach the drink holders or turn the knobs on the dashboard. "I like to move when I have sex. Why be tied down?"

Suddenly, the quiet man that I mostly knew from group nights out was leaning across the table, creating near-perfect paper strips from the bar napkin, talking about ropes and twine and knots in a power voice, a low light flickering in his eyes. He wasn't talking to me, not specifically, but his gaze flicked to my wrists as he talked. "There's freedom in constraints."

I curled my hands around my glass, the bones feeling exposed, the pulse thump-thumping beneath the skin. "There's constraint in constraints." My words had made more sense in my head.

He followed the movement of my hand with his eyes, tearing another near-perfect strip from the edge of his napkin as he waved my comment away. "But it's not really about what you use to tie someone down. At least, not the physical thing you use to tie someone."

He laid the thin strip of torn napkin over my wrist, holding the edges with a few fingers to the table, as though paper and pressure was enough to keep me there.

"It's other things. Isn't it, Elly?" His eyes settled on mine. Such intense blue, like a weight all their own, trying to keep me against the overly warm bar seat.

I dropped my gaze to watch the lime floating in my drink, raising both shoulders in a shrug, my wrist slipping along beneath the paper. "You're asking the wrong girl," I said, when I could finally meet his eyes again.

He arched a brow, the low bar lights flaring in his gaze as he shifted his head. "Am I?"

"Yes." The others faded away. Did they grow quiet on their own or just slip into the edges of my vision, sliding into the place he'd occupied so recently? "I've never been bound to anything. Man or bed or chair. And I don't intend to be."

He stood suddenly, the lean movement of predator, still holding the napkin strip across my wrist with one hand. His other hand snaked forward to tighten into the length of my blond hair, fisting his fingers at the nape of my neck to pull my head back slightly. My mouth gasped open—I couldn't help it—and then I was looking up at those blue eyes. Darkening to near black on the edges. "No?"

A single word. A challenge. Something that I would have ignored most times. If not for the drinks. Or for the fact that his fingers were still on either side of my wrist, tightening in, capturing my skin between them. If not for the way my body suddenly responded, a dizzy spin of want that left me hollow and wet.

"No." Fingers digging into my head, holding me. I tugged my head forward, but his grip only tightened. So tight I saw threads of black and gold through my vision, and still the blue of his eyes through it all.

"You've never..." I didn't know if the others could hear him, even though he was leaning down slightly, the press of his fingers keeping me there. "...called someone master?"

I pulled my body away although my hand, inexplicably, didn't follow. I was sure I'd meant it to. "Hell, no. And I never will."

"Shall we bet on that?" he asked. I was sure the others could hear him now, as well as my own bitten-back moan in response. What was my body doing to me? Betrayer.

Still, I suddenly and desperately wanted to prove this man wrong. I didn't know if it was to knock his ego a notch or soothe my own pulse, which was thumping hard beneath my skin.

I took a deep, unsteady inhale. "What do I get if I win?"

"You won't," he said.

"Then there's no reason to bet, is there?"

He laughed and let go of my hair, touching a single finger to the corner of my mouth as he bent and said softly, his lips whispering along the curve of my ear, "What's my name, Elly?"

I'm sure I looked at him like he was stupid. How long had we been friends? Of course I knew his name.

"Jackson," I said. At the same time, I pulled my wrist up, breaking the napkin.

As the paper split, releasing my wrist, he bowed down again to drag his teeth along the curve of my ear. "That's one."

Spinning Round

Time goes, as it does. I didn't see him for nearly six months. I'm sure I didn't think of him. Or his bet. Or the way I sometimes thought I felt his fingers in my hair, tangling me up.

And then, at a wedding, there he was. Tuxed up in a way that changed him once again. Prince maybe. Or young king, before he leans old and weary. He turned, halfway through the ceremony, looked into me with those blue eyes, and I forgot his name. Forgot my own. I had an image of my wrist held to the table with no more than a paper strip, remembered his fingers threaded in my hair. The heat that filled my cheeks—I knew I was turning the same color as the blood-red dress I wore, and I dropped my head, my blond hair falling forward around me. Closing my eyes for so long, I missed the bride coming up the aisle.

At the reception, he stepped beside me near the dance floor, keeping a careful distance. He touched me lightly on the inside of my arm. Even his voice was soft.

"Come and dance?"

Soft hands, safe hands around my back, careful how he touched me. He brushed a few strands of my hair from my face, his fingertips barely touching my skin, soft as silk. I looked in his eyes, waiting for him to say something like he did before.

"How have you been?" is what he asked.

So formal, so regal and considerate, I wanted to scream. I wanted to arch my hips against him and beg him for…what? I didn't know. I wanted to see what he would do with a paper napkin, a wedding streamer, the straps of my dress, the bride's veil.

I bit my lip instead, answered with the one word I could find. "Fine."

I couldn't think how to turn the conversation, so I danced with him, aching. I draped my wrists along his shoulders, turning them softly, just to see. I let my long blond hair brush his shoulders. My eyes on him, silent desire, but he merely tucked my cheek to his chest lightly, swayed to the bad music without touching his hips to mine. Every touch so soft, I couldn't help but bend my body toward it. By the end of the song, I decided I must have confused that night. Or his comments. He'd been drunk. So had I. Perhaps our conversation had been something for only the dark of a backlit bar. Perhaps he'd forgotten our bet.

Besides, I told myself as he maneuvered me around the floor, I hadn't wanted that, right? No bondage. No stupid calling someone master. Why did I care? I chalked it up to the soft whisper of fabric as his hips edged along mine and to the feel of his breath along my cheek.

As the dance ended, he stepped away with a gentle smile. The quiet press of his hand to my shoulder was so formal that I again thought of kings and royalty. Then he reached and curled a hand to the back of my neck, the blue of his gaze hardening as his eyes settled on mine. His hold was so strong and sudden that I yanked my head forward, pulling it from his grip. Too late, I realized what I'd done.

He dropped his head, mouth edging to the curl of my ear as he laughed quietly along my skin. "What's my name, sweet Elly?"

"Prick," I sputtered, so in want and confused that I was sure the dance floor was swaying beneath me.

He winked at me before he pulled away and left me standing in the middle of the floor by myself, only his words remaining. "That's two."

Spun to Gold

I spent two weeks arguing with myself. Wearing my seat belt extra tight in the car to remind myself why I didn't want it. Didn't want him. But all I could see were his blue eyes reflected in the sky of my windshield.

I called him. Some faltering tone in my voice about dinner, or drinks. I looked at my wrists while I held the phone, their fine bones, the thin length of them. I bent my head forward and touched a few fingers to the nape of my neck.

"Tell me where you live," he said, and I did.

I slipped into jeans. Then a sundress. Then a T-shirt and a soft yellow skirt that swirled around my thighs. I paced, touching things, asking myself what I wanted. Unable to say the answer aloud.

When he got there, I opened the door, unsure whether I'd find predator or king. Or perhaps just the man I'd known for so long, before that night at the bar.

He was neither. And all three. Leaning against my door frame in jeans and a shirt that fit his wide shoulders. Arms crossed, those long fingers hidden from view, he slid in through the door finally, gesturing to the couch without a word.

I sat, fiddling with my skirt. Wishing I was anywhere else.

"Hold still," he said, reaching for my head.

The pain was small and short, the backward prick of a needle, and then he was holding one of my long hairs in his fingers. "Golden thread," he said, "to bind you with."

I laughed. I couldn't help it. The sound eased the nervousness in my stomach and made me feel sick and stupid at the same time. "That? A hair?"

Without saying anything, he pushed the coffee table out of the way, then pressed both hands to my shoulders, easing me back. Scooting my hips forward as though I was a mannequin. With just his fingertips, he pushed my shirt up, then laid the hair across my stomach, the thinnest of gold threads. A breath would blow it away.

Down on his knees, he looked up at me, sending me swimming in blue. "Last chance, Elly," he said, and his teeth were big when he smiled. "You decide."

He didn't wait, just curled his fingers beneath my skirt and hooked them into my panties, began to ease them down my thighs with tiny pulls. Bit by bit, until he caught them and pulled them over my knees. His tongue curled along the inside of my thighs, meaningless circles that echoed the turns of my stomach, the spinning ache that made me want to push my hips up from the couch.

With the very tips of his fingers, he pushed the fabric of the skirt up along my thighs, watching me with every inch of skin he exposed. Until I was naked and he was dipping his head between my thighs, glossing his tongue along the heated space between. And still I let him do all these things. I wanted him to do all these things. Only a thread, a hair, nearly invisible, holding me still.

"Wait…" I said. But he didn't. He dragged his tongue like a cat along me until I was panting, the hair across my stomach rising and falling with each breath. So much as a movement would send it curling and spinning, off into nowhere.

His eyes stayed on the hair even as he slipped a finger inside me, then two, curling them upward, pulling me forward with that small gesture that made me cry out and reach forward to thread my fingers lightly into his hair. I breathed and breathed, careful not to aim my exhales at the hair that lay across my stomach. His thumb touched my clit, and I rose and jerked, the hair slipping just a bit. Settling into a slow, rhythmic circle, his thumb made me want to call his name, to beg him not to stop. I bit the sound back, my teeth hard over my lips.

He laughed, the sound vibrating along my skin. He lapped me between words, until each draw of his tongue sounded like language and each sound felt his tongue. "Don't... move...."

I didn't. I couldn't. Trapped and yet not. My outside still enough that the inside was all I could feel, the pleasure that wove itself through me with its golden promise of release.

"Please..." I begged. I wasn't ashamed. I wasn't caught. I arched my body—not the outside, not my skin and bones, but the desire that rose in me, uncoiled itself into a long thread of pleasure. Asking for more, keeping my stomach perfectly still beneath the length of golden hair, while the rest of me spun and spun and spun.

"My name, Elly," he said.

"Oh..." I clenched my teeth, trying to keep my movements still. "Please..."

He began to pull his thumb away from me, slowing his circles. Sliding his fingers from me. His retreat left me already empty. I wanted to shove myself over him, then sink his fingers inside me with a fast, hard pierce. But I couldn't move. Couldn't.

"Name," he said softly, flicking his thumbnail along the hardened point of me until my breath caught in my throat.

"M-master," I called out, my rasped voice rising in the air between us.

He grinned that dangerous grin of his, making me want to take it back, but it was too late. He was tightening his thumb back to my skin, cocking his fingers inside, his tongue curling over and over my skin until I was sure I was melting beneath the soft spin of his touch, turning liquid, turning gold.

The Three Billys

Sommer Marsden

"Philomena Fitzpatrick Troll," she said. She said it louder than necessary because they stood there with their buckets, tarps and ladders looking like a ragtag bunch if there ever was one. And they had dirt on their boots. Dirt that crumbled into little brown piles on her perfect black-and-white tiles. What had Harry been thinking? They were a wreck. All three of them. And what kind of name was Three Billys Building anyway?

"Nice to meet you, but we just need to get access to the second floor and—"

"I understand," Philomena interrupted. Rude but necessary. The big one did the talking. He had the beginnings of a goatee, which almost made her laugh because she was thinking of the fairy tale. Instead, she smoothed her brown dress and squared her shoulders. "In the future, please use the service entrance so as not to..." She let the sentence trail off as she raked a disapproving gaze over her now-marred floor.

"Sorry about that. First day and all. We weren't sure, Philomena."

"Ms. Troll."

"How unfortunate," he thrust.

"How clever," she parried.

He grinned. This big Billy. Philomena felt a blush start at her cheekbones and burn a blazing trail well south of her cheeks. "This way," she said. She took off at a smart pace before he could see her face coloring and her breath quicken. The big one was going to be a problem. Staggeringly tall and broad with nearly black hair, and eyes that flashed an emerald-green. Philomena had noticed those eyes right off the bat. A bad sign for her.

Usually, she could focus at work. It took an act of God to pull her from her head librarian duties. More than a few men had come along thinking she would be some fantasy, like in the music videos and movies. They flirted and waited for her to come undone for them and turn into a bookish wet dream. But Philomena kept her focus. When she was at work, she was all about work. And these days, work rated number one with a bullet in her life. Because she didn't have much more.

Now he pinned her with those haunting green eyes and she had to put more swagger in her walk than she felt. They clomped behind her. Oafish and messy. Oh, she could just picture the debris sifting from their boots and that horrible paint-splattered ladder leaving gouges in her impeccable walls. It did not occur to her until halfway up the staircase that three pairs of male eyes were now pinned to her swaying bottom. The thought almost felled her, nearly brought her down like a dry tree in a February ice storm. She stilled and someone chuckled, a small knowing laugh. Had she been a betting woman, Philomena would have laid easy money on the big Billy. She closed her eyes, wrangled a deep breath and forced her sensible square-toed work heels to continue.

At the second floor, she surveyed the water damage. The rugs had already been torn up by maintenance. A pipe had ruptured in the ceiling, the water raining down from overhead, not from the sprinklers, but from the water pipes that ran under the third floor. She tried to remind herself (yet again) that the situation could have been worse. There could have been damage to the third floor—the archival floor. She blew out a sigh and indicated the mess. "Here we are, gentlemen."

"The man who hired us," said the middle one, "where's he?"

"Harry is off today. He'll be here tomorrow. As, I trust, will you." Philomena had nightmares about contractors who showed once and then never came back. She'd heard horror stories.

"Bummer. He's a nice one." The small one was a bit shifty. He had a nervous thing he did with his chin. Thrusting it forward like he was chewing cud. She found the tic mesmerizing in a completely inappropriate way.

"Now," she hurried on, trying to focus, "as you can see, there's some damage to the wall over here. And down at the checkout counter where you came in." She walked to the far wall. The floor above the checkout was metal gridwork. Wrought iron and fancy. Meant to let the patron look down to the level below. If she put her head back, she could see the domed ceiling above in the archives.

She turned, and the biggest man was right on her heels. Those gorgeous green eyes took a lazy tour of her chocolate-brown wrap dress and her sensible heels. Damn it all if she didn't start blushing all over again. He leaned in and then past her, but she felt the soft dark brush of his warm breath across her bare neck. "So the water just ran right over the edge and down the wall. And this all happened after closing time?" He turned his head but kept his body angled, his generous mouth a bare two inches from hers.

In her mind's eye, Philomena could see those big dusty hands with the ragged nails settle on her hips. She could see the busted knuckles flex as big bad Billy's powerful palms hauled her in and pulled her flush to his hard angles. She imagined with bizarre clarity what those full pink lips would feel like crushing down on hers and how hot his tongue would be working past her own swollen lips. The raspy sound his calluses would make as he pushed her dress up, dragging his work-abused hands up her stockings until—

"Right?"

"Calluses," she blurted, and then bit her tongue so hard her eyes blurred. How asinine. "I meant 'correct.' That is *correct*. The mess sat all night long. And it was during a heat wave. The water shorted the air-conditioning unit, creating mold and mess and more water." Her tongue tripped over the words as if it had never formed such things before.

The towering Billy touched her forearm and the sensation of his skin on hers made her shiver like she was cold. "You okay?"

"I am fine, Mr....um, Billy..."

"Benjamin."

"I thought you said your names were all Billy," Philomena squeaked.

"Billy Benjamin. The little one is Billy Samuels and then there's Billy Midlin."

"Ah. Thank you for the introductions. Now, about the floor."

His breath stroked her skin again as he leaned in to hear. Philomena felt her mouth sag open just a little, her heart did a little flip-flop in her chest and she felt intense moisture between her legs. This was the point where men started doing math in their heads, she thought. What did women do?

"What about it? This seems to be the only part of the floor up here unharmed."

"What I am trying to say is, during operating hours, people will be passing through on the first floor. Please refrain from walking over this section during work hours. There might be…" She pointed to his shoes.

Billy Benjamin laughed and clomped his chunky boot on the floor until a small chunk of mud flaked off. Why? She wanted to grab him and shake him and demand to know why! But then her gaze returned to his mouth and her mind turned from mud to mush. And her insides turned molten hot and her pussy followed suit. Work. She was at work.

"You have a thing about dirt, don't you?"

Philomena could only nod. The other two men were placing drop cloths and making a horrible racket. Big Billy— Billy Benjamin—had eyes only for her. He moved in farther and Philomena took a staggering step back as her heel went to war with the wrought iron gridwork. It gave him an excuse. He reached out, his hands latching on to her forearms. No. *Swallowing* her forearms right up.

"I do." Her voice was strangled and not at all as authoritative as she wanted. Even though her mind went down a verdant dirty path the moment he touched her, she tried to hold on to her head librarian persona. "I also have a thing about being manhandled. Please let me go and keep yourself and your men from walking over this section during patron hours. Thank you."

He leaned in, his mouth so close. He smelled of cinnamon and mint and coffee. A very yummy, very warm smell. "No problem, boss lady Troll."

"Yes. Right." From below came the *ding, ding, ding* of someone pressing the red button for assistance. Saved by the bell. Literally. "I'd better go answer that."

"Hurry, scary boss lady. Get back down below." He winked when he said it and the wink sent a fireball of attraction rushing from the deepest pit of her stomach to the warmest recesses of her body. She straightened her spine so hard her whole body clenched. Bad move. The clenching made the desire run amok and she nearly, *nearly,* mind you, leaned in and kissed him before her brain could even think it over. Thank goodness, she managed not to do that.

Thank goodness. Right?

"I would suggest you get to work now, Big Billy."

Time stood still then. Everything froze, including her unstably beating heart. Had she just called this colossal, handsome, green-eyed man...Big Billy? To his face?

He barked laughter, green eyes dancing, narrowing and darkening a bit with predatory glee. He looked her over and the gaze itself was like strong fingers sliding over her skin.

"*Big* Billy?"

Yes. Yes, she had said it out loud.

"Sorry. My apologies," she choked out, and ran on her unsteady heels from the scene of the crime. On the first floor, safe behind her library counter, Philomena prayed for death. It did not come.

Right after lunch as she was checking out a gentleman with a substantial stack of books on the practice of Wicca, the first dirt shower came. A small clod rested on *The Layman's Grimoire,* then a faint sifting decorated *Everyone Witchcraft.* Philomena steeled herself, looked up and got a nice piece of silt in her eye for her efforts. "Please, Billy! Please, I asked you three not to walk over me during patron hours."

She mumbled her apologies and wiped the books clean and got the somewhat bemused customer on his way. Then she threw her head back, hands on hips, blood boiling as the boots did another pass overhead. It was the little Billy. The jaw thruster. But damn, what was his name? "*Helloooo!* Do you hear me?"

He paused, looked down into her eyes, grinned, jaw moving a mile a minute. "Sorry. Billy. *Big* Billy told me to hit the switch and the switch plate is over there, lady."

"Ms. Troll," she corrected.

"Right."

Philomena bit her lip and steamed. She couldn't argue, though. The switch plate for the main bank of lights was on the far wall. Which meant walking over her. "Fine. But that's it. Please!"

"I'll give it my best. Otherwise, take it up with Benjamin."

"Ri–ight," Philomena growled and wiped down her counter with some cleaner and a paper towel. This would not do. Not at all. But she knew that she would just have to soldier on. The more hours the three Billys could get during the day, the faster they would be done. And then they would be out. Them and their mess!

Next was a regular, and Philomena knew exactly what would be in his stack when he started self-checkout. Second World War, civil war, Korean War. War buff. Mr. Sinclair was his name, and he flirted shamelessly, but was 110 percent harmless. "Are they getting the upstairs all squared away then, Ms. Troll?" His voice was a mellifluous balm after the rattle and racket from the second floor.

"Not soon enough, Mr. Sinclair."

He slid his stack over her way and cleaned his glasses with his shirttail. "I can tell you're a wee bit worked up over the upheaval."

Some insistent buzzing thump came from above her head and she cringed. "Yes, well…" More dirt! Right into her keyboard and right on top of Mr. Sinclair's bald pate. A rage of blush fired her cheeks and she bit her tongue to keep from screaming. Still, Philomena threw back her head and though she tried not to, she howled, "Why are you walking over my head, Billy…the middle one!"

The middle Billy—dark blond hair with snowy-blue eyes—stopped and squatted. He gazed down at her, a mischievous grin split his rugged features. "Sorry, there, Philomena."

"Ms. Troll!" The words ripped out so fiercely that her throat hurt. Mr. Sinclair's watery brown eyes flew wide. The dirt on his scalp slid to the left. "So sorry, Mr. Sinclair. My deepest apologies."

"Ms. Troll, I was told to plug in the sander, and the three-pronged outlet is right under the switch plate. So..." He shrugged, eyes twinkling. "A man's gotta do what a man's gotta do. If it's a problem, I can send Billy. *Big* Billy." He chuckled, stood and his boots threw off more ick as he went. She dodged, and Mr. Sinclair scuttled off with his goods.

What could she say? Nothing. And she most certainly did not want to deal with Big Billy any more than necessary since he seemed to scramble her brain faster than a martini. Philomena wasn't much of a drinker, and she didn't seem to be much in the way of handling big handsome contractors with flashing green eyes.

Again with the cleaner and towels. Philomena kept looking up. She felt watched. Maybe it was simply the bizarre and overtly steamy mental movie playing in her head that had her on edge. No matter how hard she scrubbed the counter, she could imagine kissing him. That big, huge, irritating man. Kissing him on the lips and down over the stubbly jut of his jaw. Biting just below where his pulse jumped in a steady beat and down along his broad throat. Over the swell of his Adam's apple, and then her kisses, in her head at least, went due south and she had to take a deep breath to steady herself. She could shut her eyes and feel the heat of his mouth closing over her nipple, tracing her hipbone and then lower still. Parting her legs and then feeling his lips, so close to where she wanted him, kissing the very top of her thighs. How would it feel to have his lips on her clit, probing her? How would his kisses feel when his heat closed over her willing pussy and licked her until she clutched the bedsheets in her trembling hands and—

Something hit Philomena on the head. Something hard. Definitely not dirt. Her eyes flew wide. "What the hell!" The words slipped out before she could stop herself. She ran her fingers over her scalp. Then she spotted the weapon. A blue ballpoint pen on the floor. "Simon! Simon?" One of the assistants came scuttling out.

"Yes, Ms. Troll?"

"Watch the counter." Her eyes had found him. Over her. Hovering. Smiling!

"Oops! Sorry, Ms. Troll. I had to hook up the—"

Big Billy. The main man. The head honcho. The thorn in her side. The burr in her ass. Philomena pointed a finger at him and glared. "Stay. Right. There. Mr. Benjamin, I am coming."

"I look forward to it."

She blinked and her body responded with a warm flickering wave of excitement. "Do not be crude! Do. Not. Move."

Simon looked as if he wanted to die on the spot. Instead, he wiped the counter again. Hers would be the cleanest counter in the land when all was said and done. Philomena stormed up the wide, stone steps, trying so hard to force aside the mental images that had her melting hot so that the anger that had her equally hot could emerge.

He had listened. There he stood, poised on the intricate floor, dirty work boots in a defiant stance. He held an industrial yellow three-pronged plug in one hand. His beat-up, faded jeans slung low on his hips and his cocky smile spread on his lips. "Mr. Benjamin!"

"Ma'am?"

"I…" Philomena blinked. What? You must work but you cannot plug that in? How dare you try for electricity? A grounded outlet? What?

"Yes?" He took a step toward her just as one of the other

Billys, unseen at this point, fired some big machine in the rear of the stacks.

"I…I am very concerned because…" Damn. There she went again, trailing off. Her mind taking a right turn and putting her on her back with this big, dusty, cocky man climbing on top of her. Somewhere in the mental scenario he had lost his shirt. How had that happened? And a hard ridge of male excitement pressed the faded cotton of his fly.

"Because I didn't obey?"

"Well, yes. I am the—"

"The boss. You are the boss. You're used to being the boss, aren't you, Troll?" He took three big steps and there he was again, in her personal space. Invading her turf. Setting her on edge. But in the most bizarre way. Her nose tingled with the dark and spicy scent of him. Her nipples peaked, and between her legs she went hot and wet in the blink of an eye. Her hands turned to fists and her heart felt as though it would pound its way right out of her chest.

"I…I…"

Billy Benjamin leaned in so that only the smallest slice of air rested between their lips. "You might write the checks, but you are not the boss of me, Troll."

"*Ms.* Troll."

He leaned in farther still and Philomena heard her heart over all of it. Over what sounded like a sander and someone hammering and the rain on the skylight in the archives above them. Thunder boomed outside, and inside the cage of her chest.

"I…" She smacked him. That fast, out of nowhere. Her hand landed and they both made surprised noises at once. His low and guttural, hers high and breathy. "Oh, my God. I am so, so very sor—"

He didn't let her finish. He grabbed both of her fluttering wrists in his harsh grip and dropped the thick yellow snake of cord. "You think you rule the world down there under the fancy floor. Barking up orders and making our job that much harder. You think you are so scary, Philomena. But you're not. My God, look how small you are! And you do a piss-poor job of handling sexual tension."

He pushed her into a small storage room and shut the door. Philomena did her best to bark out a sarcastic laugh as if to say, *You don't scare me, you dirty labor person!* Instead, the noise became some kind of sultry sigh that made even Billy Benjamin pause. She caught herself then. "There *is* no sexual tension. You are clearly insane."

"Yeah?" He stepped into her then. His belly to hers. The fly of his jeans to the skirt of her dress. His broad hard chest to her wildly struggling breast. Her body tried so hard to suck in air, but all she managed to take in was more and more of the scent of him.

"Mr. Benjamin—" That was as far as she got when his hands clamped down on her hips. Without thinking, Philomena pushed her pelvis to his pelvis. She slid her body against his, feeling his hard cock between her legs. Wishing she was feeling it sans fabric and panties. He seemed to read her mind, because his hands bunched the fabric of her dress in his hands, hiking it up, drawing the dress up slowly like a curtain. Then he lost his patience and shoved his hands under the hem. Fingers on her hosiery. She started to wiggle to help them down, but Billy had other plans. The sound of her nylons tearing filled the teeny, tiny closet.

"Those were new!" She said the words with wild displeasure, but her legs fell open for him and she shivered with fresh whorish delight.

"Tough shit. I'll buy you another pair," he responded, his mouth buried between her breasts. His tongue darting into her cleavage until she held his head to her chest like she was drowning. "I can't breathe," he said.

"Right. Sorry." She let him go as he dropped to his knees, growling and grumbling about her bitchy nature all the way down. Her fingers flitted over his soft flannel shirt as he put his mouth to her thigh and began kissing. It was as if all her dirty fantasies had come true. "You smell nice and sweet for such a bossy prude," he growled, and put his mouth over her small satin panties. The heat of his mouth bled into the fabric like a stain.

"I'm not a prude," she managed to say, plucking at his wide shoulders.

"Yeah?"

She nodded, silent but gasping for air. He tugged her panties and she arched her hips for him. Would her heart give out before his mouth finally touched her? No. Because there it was. On her pussy, licking and pushing at her until she threw her head back and let him eat her any way he pleased. This was better than being in control.

"You don't scare me." He pushed his fingers deep inside her and curled them. The room swayed a bit.

"I know."

"You're bossy but not scary. At least to me." *Curl, curl, curl* went his fingers. *Flick, flick, flick* went her cunt. Heat flooded her limbs, her hair swished.

Close. So very close.

"You don't need to be that way so much. Calm down a little. Unwind." Oh, she would unwind, all right. Right here. Right now.

"Yes, you're right. Yes, yes, yes!" Philomena cried. She did not need to be so rigid. Looser and more relaxed could be good.

She tugged this big Billy up and attacked his zipper. "Look, I'm not a closet sex person."

He nodded. Helped her trembling hands.

"But you… You are…what? Magical? Brave? Maddening? Whatever. I've been having dirty fantasies about you, and now…" The pants were down and she took him in hand. Big, hard, warm.

"And now what?"

"Now let's do this."

He laughed softly and kissed her again. His mouth tasted like vanilla and mint and her. He moved between her thighs, pushed at her, hooked her leg around his waist. Slid in effortlessly and started to move. Philomena had to grit her teeth not to come right there. "See how soft you can be?" He pushed into her harder.

"Yes."

"See how flexible you can be?" He thrust higher, faster, holding her bottom in his big hands. He angled her, and the head of his cock bumped her G-spot perfectly. Philomena was grateful for his size, because her knees sagged and he held her up.

"Yes, I can be. I do see. I need to…"

"What?"

"…ask you…"

"What?" His mouth settled on her—kissed her, bit her just a bit too hard and in the perfect way.

"Can you fuck me harder?"

"That I can do, Ms. Troll." And he did. Harder, faster. He drove into her until she scratched at flannel and stubble and man and came hard. Again. Heart racing, lips kissing.

"Philomena," she said.

Philomena did not care that her dress was crooked or her hose were ruined when she left the closet. She did not care when a clod of dirt fell on Mrs. Tasselmeyer and her knitting books. She did not care when Small Billy walked over her. Or Middle Billy. Or Big Billy, who stopped to smile down at her and wink. Tapped his watch. A few hours and they'd go out for drinks. And then maybe food at her place. Or him at her place.

When they started the sander directly overhead and her patrons complained, Philomena just smiled her secret smile, because she might not be scary and she might be small, but *big* had definitely been the right word for Billy. *Big* Billy.

David

Kristina Lloyd

It's hot today. I have a problem with the heat because I sweat and my sweat is pink. Pink sweat attracts notice, forcing me to flee to another town to preserve my secret. But damn it, I like this place and I want to stay.

When I was mortal over forty years ago, I was a woman who lived for parties, sunshine and attention. I would dance barefoot on beaches on warm summer evenings, and late at night I'd still be there, laughing around a campfire with my beautiful friends, hippies in beads hoping to save the world through sex, love, peace and hashish. I look at my generation now and wonder if we couldn't have tried a little harder.

But no matter. They're not my generation anymore.

My sweat is pink and it's a problem.

A passerby tosses a coin onto the cloth at my feet. Quite a pile I'm getting today. It's the sun, you see. It brings people out, makes them loose with their cash. And this loose cash is making me feel loose with my morals.

I stare blankly ahead. I'm coated in white body paint and wreathed in a toga, my hair coiled high and dyed a bright chemical pink. My arms are held in an elegant curve, chin angled to the left. I am a busker, a living statue, and I'm very good at my job. Crowds gather. They stare and smile. A few will move tentatively closer. "It's like she isn't even breathing," they'll whisper.

And of course, I'm not. I am dead.

My hairline starts to prickle. If it weren't for my pink sweat, I'd still adore the sun, though I realize that makes me atypical. The heat clings like memories, taking me back to those sticky nights of tangled sheets when my cunt would throb with lust for another. Oh, to be vital again! To be fucking someone for the sake of fuck alone, not fucking them with thoughts of their blood in my throat. Or, best of all, to have someone fucking *me,* to have them holding me down, fearless, brutal and strong.

Because, to my shame, that's what I crave: a man to overpower me. Once when I was alive, I asked a boyfriend to act as my kidnapper. "Tie me up and gag me," I explained. "Use me as your plaything. Take no notice of my screams." But he said he couldn't do that because sexual expression through violence contravened his pacifism and he viewed our lovemaking as a cosmic union of souls and in this I was his sister. Sister? If you ask me, that's far worse than what I was suggesting.

A bead of sweat trickles down my back. That's fine. They can't see under my robes. To my right, I hear the soft click of a camera. More money clinks into the collection. Two hundred seconds later (Christ, it's boring being on a pedestal), I twist my shoulders and turn my head several degrees. A murmur of delight ripples across the crowd.

He's mesmerized as if my stillness is infectious. He's big, beautiful and rough looking, an arrogant young bruiser with his hands stuffed in his pockets. He's wearing a suit, but he's no businessman. His tie is askew and he clearly doesn't care about preserving any neat lines of tailoring. He watches, fascinated, contempt curling his lip as if he's thinking of all the sordid things he could do to me, irrespective of my wishes.

I cast him a glance, wondering if I can snare him. Unfortunately, I attract the wrong sort of guy. Maybe that's inevitable. I know my place in popular culture and the assumption goes because I'm a monster, I must also be an aggressor and a sadist. But the truth is, I'm a sexually submissive vampire and, if you'll forgive the pun, that sucks.

It sucks because I feel I'm letting the team down. My kind are predators and they tend to be on the toppy side. But it's not as if I was ever going to fit in anyway. Ever since my sweat turned pink, I've been shunned by my peers. I was once an ordinary monster, happy to get along, but then something went wrong inside me. When I feed, I can't use all the blood. It seeps out through my pores, making me a liability, a freak in danger of exposing the community. I've no choice but to be itinerant, keeping my head low, because there are many who would rather see me dead. Truly dead, not undead-dead.

But being submissive sucks mainly because I'm just not getting any. I guess I come across as scary, and I'm aware my inability to form lasting relationships has engendered a certain aloofness. Maybe that's why I'm often propositioned by men who offer money to call me Mistress. Or maybe it's because I earn my living from being bored on a pedestal. Perhaps they see their proposal as promotion.

But being on top leaves me cold. I want a man who'll bring me down, do terrible things to me and take away my power. I want him to debase me, bind me, fuck my face and force me into sex, perhaps with a little help from his friends. And if this ever happened and I were to kill them all afterward, I can honestly say, hand on my unbeating heart, it would be done in a spirit of regret not revenge.

Because I can't help who I am. I need blood to survive. Perhaps there's a murderous streak sparkling in my eyes. Whatever the reason, I don't get the right guys and for too many years, my submission has lain dormant, existing purely in my own warped fantasies. It's not enough. I want to play passive. I want a man who'll bring my dark desires to life again.

I lay a hand below my throat in an attitude of piety or mild shock. He's still watching me, that rapt and cunning expression on his face. Gazing beyond my audience, I focus on a faux-Victorian lamppost in the shopping plaza. A droplet of sweat dribbles past my ear. No one will see that, I'm sure. But it's only a matter of time and before long, I feel moisture stippling my painted face. I'm corpse-white already, so the paint is merely for texture and sunblock. It can't hide perspiration. A single bead of sweat slides down my forehead and, horrified, I picture it as an enormous globule of shimmering liquid, pink as a strawberry milk shake. They're all staring. Seconds later, the droplet spills and splashes from the ledge of a white-coated eyebrow.

Nothing happens. There's no muttering or shifting among my audience. I reckon I've got away with it. But then a second droplet emerges from my hairline, a third and fourth. I don't like to come alive when the crowds are large. I prefer to let the numbers dwindle, but it's too hot today. This isn't going to work. My secret isn't safe.

"Oi!" calls a voice. "Yer wig's melting!"

Their laughter is nasty. Sweat is running freely down my face now. A patch of uncertain applause lifts and dies and coins clatter brightly at my feet.

"How does she do it?"

"Ugh, that's well creepy."

"My God, she looks rotten. She was so pretty before."

Droplets trickle toward my eyes, making me weep pale red tears. I stand like a parodic Jesus Christ, my candy-pink hair my crown of thorns, my face streaked with sweat that has the taint of death.

Money tumbles and cameras click. Carefully, I step down from my pedestal. I keep my head low, my movements soft. I bend and crouch then I lie on my money, curling into a ball. The money smells bitter. Some people walk away. All I want to do is stay here till it's pitch-black, the shops have shut and everyone's gone home. Moments later, a shadow falls across my face. He squats and clasps me by the wrist, making my arm twist awkwardly. Jewelry glints on his hand.

"I'll look after you," he says, and his voice is laced with threat.

His hair is shorn, his eyes are hard and a small graze on a cheekbone hints at ruby-red blood. He has the corrupted beauty of a handsome man who's too fond of danger. I wonder if he's a dealer or a pimp. He jerks my arm, urging me to stand.

"Thank you," I reply, and I know I have him: my victim, my prince.

I leave my pedestal and cash in a locker at the train station and, as the light fades, we walk through town. I pat my sweat dry but don't bother changing. I've loosened my hair and it tumbles past my shoulders in crazy pink tails. I hook the drapes of my toga over one arm and walk barefoot. My soles are as tough as old boots, a legacy from my hippie days, and I shun shoes whenever I can. I look like a cerise Medusa and beside me is David, worthy of Michelangelo, eating a burger from a polystyrene tray.

"There are more lucrative ways to earn money on the streets," he says through a mouthful of food. "I could show you where to start. Pretty girl like you is wasted as a statue. Plenty of men who'd appreciate your charms. Trust me, you could make a fortune."

"Are you trying to make me your sex slave?" I ask hopefully.

David laughs, throws his burger box into a bin and wipes the back of his hand across his mouth. A chunky wristwatch peeps from the sleeve of his suit. He's very flash.

"Because I'd like that," I continue. "I'd like to be your whore." Saying the words is easier than I'd anticipated. I've kept my desires to myself for so long that voicing them is a leap of faith, but once I've started, the words simply flow. "You could do whatever you want to me," I say. "Let other men use me, as well. But I've never been a whore before. I might need some practice."

"Nah, it's a doddle," says David. "All you have to do is open your legs."

I don't think he's quite understood. "I think you should give me a test run," I reply. "Make sure I'm good enough. And I think I should know what it's like to meet a punter who wants to do terrible things to me."

"Uh-huh? What sort of terrible things?"

"Call me names," I say. "And, um, maybe I need to know how it is to go with a guy who gets off on kidnapping women, someone who wants to tie me up and gag me, who wants to use me as his plaything. A guy who won't take any notice of my screams. A guy—"

David swings to face me, grabs me around the arms, then bundles me backward into an alley. A few people glance our way, but nobody intervenes. Given that I'm chalk-white in a toga and David's in a suit, they probably think we're performance artists or actors. He slams me up against the wall, a hand clamped to my mouth. He glares at me, eyes full of glee.

"Dirty little bitch," he says, and he shoves a hand between my legs, bunching up the folds of my toga. "Gagging for it, aren't you?" He rubs the cotton hard against my cunt. "Aren't you, slut?"

And I moan that I am, while thinking how times have changed since the sixties.

"Come on," he says. "I'll give you a test run." He grabs a fistful of my hair and frog-marches me deeper into the alley. He turns left, and I stumble ahead of him into a wider back-street bordered by higgledy-piggledy buildings with narrow fire escapes zigzagging up their brickwork. Small, grimy windows cast smudges of light into the dusk of evening, steam plumes from vents, and clanging saucepans and barked orders punctuate the seedy calm of this hidden street. We are behind a stretch of restaurants and cheap hotels, stumbling through the grubby reality that feeds and fuels the tourist trade.

It's quieter here. David seems to know where he's going and that makes me nervous. I start to wonder if this is what I really want. Oh, I know I'll win, I always do, but as David shoves me into a recess, I have to ask myself: At what cost? I'll escape with my life—if you can call it that—but what might this do to my mind?

In the recess is a fire door partially blocked by a stack of wooden pallets, and the lilac of a UV insect zapper glows from a small, wire-mesh window. David presses me against a narrow wall, his forearm across my neck, pushing my chin high. He's breathing fast, his eyes are wild, and that faint scab on his cheekbone gleams in the purplish half-light.

"Test run, eh?" He covers my breast with his free hand, pummeling through my toga. "You like that?" he asks. "You like it when guys touch you there?"

"Yes," I whisper.

David grins and I note he has excellent teeth. "Well, listen up," he says. "It's not about what *you* want. You're a whore, see? Just a cheap little whore, so no one gives a fuck whether you like it or not." His eyes are fixed on mine and he fluffs up the skirts of my gown, pinning the folds back with a thigh until he can reach between my legs. "Okay?"

I nod. David rubs briskly at my underwear, fingers sawing before he pushes the fabric deeper into my wet split, separating me there. His forearm leans harder against my neck and he moves his face closer to mine as if to better gauge my response. I feel weak in every limb, so aroused I might melt to the floor. After all those hours on my pedestal, a remote and frozen beauty, untouchable and on display, it's wonderful to know the hot press of desire in a dingy backstreet. It feels like the closest thing to life—life in all its murky, messy, furtive glory—that I've known for such a long time.

Sweat prickles under my arms and I hope I don't turn too pink too soon. When I groan my pleasure, David slips two thick fingers past my underwear. "You're not meant to be enjoying this," he says, and he hooks his fingers inside me, rubbing so perfectly I can't help but groan again. "Hot little slut," he says approvingly.

He steps back, releasing me with his hands but not his eyes. He whips off his tie, his gaze never once leaving mine. Sneering, he cracks the strip of cloth in the air, clearly relishing his own brutal purpose. I can see strength flex in his torso beneath his shirt and his sweat smells good and manly.

"Turn around," he says. His voice is scarily tender. For decades I've wanted someone to talk to me like that.

"No," I whisper.

In the small silence that follows, I wonder if I've gone too far. If I had a living heart, it would be thumping in fear and excitement right now. Anger darkens his brow and I know I said the right thing because he doesn't tell me again. Instead, he spins me around, hissing that it wasn't a fucking question, it was an order. He twists my arm, pushing me face forward over the stack of pallets. His thighs press against mine, holding me still as he clasps my wrists behind my back. I wriggle and kick, knowing it's futile.

"Get off me!" I say as I feel his looped tie tightening on my wrists. He tugs, binds and knots, deftly trapping my hands. Grabbing a bunch of my hair, he arches my neck backward.

"It wasn't a fucking question," he says again, and I hear the rasp of him unzipping. With one hand, he pushes my toga up, then yanks my underwear down, exposing my cunt and cheeks. The tip of his cock is stout at my entrance, then he surges in, packing my wetness with his solidity. His thrusts are ruthless. "Not. A fucking. Question," he snarls, pumping away at me.

I protest and he immediately makes a gag of my hair, ramming pink snaky lengths across my mouth. He pulls as if my hair's a bridle and I splutter and cry, hating the texture and the taste.

"Shut up," he hisses. "No one's gonna take any notice of your screams."

And I come so hard, my clit nudging at a hump of fabric as decades of wanting shiver and clutch. I'm left feeling as limp as a rag doll, and all I want to do is take it as he rams on and on into my soft swollen hole. I let him come—I think it's only fair—then I do what I always do: kill.

Or at least, that's my intention. As my strength swells, I break free of my bondage and whirl around, attacking so fast he barely sees it. I slam him against the wall, my toga unraveling, and latch on to his neck. It's bristly with stubble and when I puncture his skin, that familiar coppery warmth floods my mouth. I'm almost lost to joy until sanity pricks my greed: the sex was incredible, I want more from him.

So as his pulse fades in my veins, I snick my wrist and press the wound to his lips, giving him a new kind of life. I don't know if his sweat will be pink, but if it is, so what? We will unite, defective or not, and in our monstrous limbo, we'll face the world together. When I take away my wrist, David smiles, the pallor of death already lightening his skin. And I know at once how we'll survive. He will join me as a living statue, David in a fig leaf, the beautiful brute I turned to stone.

Managers and Mermen

Donna George Storey

"Do you want to go for a ride?"

Her liquid warble makes it sound like an invitation, but the glint in her green eyes tells me it's really an order.

There will be consequences if I don't obey.

And so I straddle her tail at the widest part—where a human girl's hips would be—and squeeze my thighs around her. It's not so different from riding bareback, except her scales aren't warm like horseflesh. They're cool and slippery and they tickle my tender parts through the crotch of my swimsuit. I wriggle a bit, trying to get comfortable, but it only makes the tingling sensation more intense.

"Hold on tight," she warns, and immediately shoots off through the water. My upper body rocks like a broncobuster's as we speed through the swaying seaweed. I have to grip her with all my might to stay on. My legs are aching and I can feel the powerful muscles of her tail rippling between my thighs. Soon her once-cool skin is plumped and warm, pulsing faintly. Or is it just me?

She swoops into a grotto and rears up to a stop. I fall forward and clutch her shoulders, panting. My veins sing with adrenaline.

In one swift movement, she twists around to face me. The slick twirl of her tail between my legs sends electric jolts through my body.

"Keep those pretty legs squeezed tight," she says, her eyes boring into me. "You don't want our ride to end yet, do you?"

I shake my head. What else can I do? She has me trapped in her lair, under her spell. I watch, enchanted, as she hooks her fingers under the kelp straps of her seashell bra and rips them away to expose her full breasts. Her skin is creamy, like a human girl's, but the nipples are strange—a luminous jade-green.

"Kiss them," she commands, lifting her breasts in offering. Again, I have no choice. This is her realm, her laws.

I bend forward and take one shimmering nipple between my lips. The salty tang of nori fills my mouth. Suddenly I'm ravenously hungry. I tug on her, harder, as if I can satisfy the growing ache in my belly that way.

"That's lovely, keep up the good work," she sighs, but then her voice takes on a sterner tone. "Except it's not really work for you, is it? I can feel what's going on *down there*. Your secret muscles are all fluttery and you're wet inside, too. You like playing with another girl's breasts, don't you?"

Still suckling, I nod. I must always agree, always do her bidding. But she's telling the truth, too. I do like this.

"You are a naughty girl, but you're making me all fluttery, too."

Indeed, her tail is gyrating gently, pressing up against my clit, then circling away. I can tell from the way her eyes glow that she's enjoying every second.

What comes next takes me completely by surprise.

I hear it before I feel it, her leathery tail fin landing a perfect blow on my ass cheeks. I stiffen and cry out.

She smiles.

The second time is more of a caress, as she slides the tip of her fin under my swimsuit and tears it smoothly away from my flesh.

My jaw still gaping in shock, I meet her gaze. Her eyes seem to reach down inside me. I feel a tugging deep in my belly, rising up my spine as if she's sucking down all my soft, secret parts like an oyster. As my body grows lighter, she seems to take on more substance. Her cheeks grow rounder and ruddy, her lips plump and full. I realize it is not my flesh that nourishes her. She is feasting on my mind, every dirty fantasy that has ever floated through my brain. She knows me. No other being has ever known me so well.

"That's right, I do know what you want," she says, her voice echoing through the water. "You want to suck my tits while I spank your ass until your cheeks are all red and tingly. You want me to spank you until you come."

I'm so weak with lust that I can't even manage a nod in reply. But a moan seems to suffice as I bend to take her nipple in my mouth again. I grope for her other breast with one hand and cup my own with the other, my thumb flicking the tip, already sensitive and tingly from the salt water.

I'm ready. Now.

Smack.

I swallow down a yelp as her stiff paddle meets my buttocks. My bare cunt skids over her scaly skin, and the prickling sensation ignites into a steady burn.

She punishes me again. And again. The fin makes an obscene slurping sound as it strikes, like a pussy being fingered fast and hard. I grind my clit into her, my whole body shaking, a sob rising in my throat. I'm close. Very close. The next one will take me over the edge. I know it. She knows it.

Which is why she pauses at that very moment. I'll have to beg for it. I always do.

Suddenly a car door slams in the driveway right outside the bedroom window.

I freeze, a bullet of fear piercing my belly. A moment later, I hear a key in the lock of the front door.

Fuck, it must be Anton, even though he's not due back from work until six or seven. It's either my husband or a burglar, and in my panic I almost wish it were a break-in. I wouldn't owe a criminal any explanation for why I spent the afternoon with my hand down my pants while he had to sit through endless seminars on effective management techniques at his new company.

My chest heaving like a fish out of water, I yank up my shorts and pull my T-shirt chastely over my breasts. Too late to hook my bra or do the zipper. The footsteps have reached the bedroom door.

I stretch and sigh, feigning the yawn of a woman just waking from a nap.

"Ah, the lazy life of a masseuse." Anton bends over me for a quick kiss. He fishes his wallet and keys from his trousers and tosses them on his dresser, then takes off his watch, the things he does every day when he comes home from work. He has no clue that his wife has spent the last hour cavorting with a piscine dominatrix.

I exhale with relief. I might just get away with my little afternoon infidelity.

"Shiatsu classes don't start for three weeks," I remind him. "Until then my only job is to be your love slave, right?"

It's a risky move, but I'm feeling bold. And horny. If he has to come and interrupt me just when things are getting hot, the least he can do is help finish the job.

He pauses, fingers at his shirt buttons, eyebrows lifted hopefully. "Love slave, huh? As a matter of fact, that is my preferred job description for you. Lucky for us the seminar finished early today. The facilitator had that Friday-afternoon golfer's gleam in his eye." Anton's eyes gleam, too, as he looks down at me.

I'm expecting he'll go into the walk-in closet to hang up his suit, so I can at least zip my shorts, but unfortunately, my come-on line was a little too successful. He undresses quickly, draping his suit and shirt on the armchair, then peels off his briefs. I can't stop staring at his hard-on, a thick, red baton, floating in air as if by magic. My mouth starts to water. On summer days his dick tastes saltier, like a big pretzel stick.

He slips into bed beside me, and I press myself against him, hoping he'll be too distracted to notice I'm already partially undressed.

It seems, however, that my luck has run out.

He's already reached under my T-shirt. "Hey, what's with your bra?"

"I unhook it when I nap," I answer quickly. "It's less constrictive."

His hand drops to my shorts and slithers through the gaping fly. I know my panties are damp. Sopping, actually. And there's no mistaking that briny fragrance of aroused female.

"Okay, Stef, what were you really doing when I got home?"

My stomach clenches with guilt and a touch of fear. Which is stupid because he knows I masturbate when he goes on business trips. He certainly wanks when he's away. But it's different to be caught in the act with no excuse except the old saying "Idle hands do the devil's work."

"I was just doing what you do in those hotel rooms while you're watching porn movies," I say, trying my best to sound cool.

"Actually, I don't waste money on stupid movies. There's plenty of good stuff for free on the Internet."

Anton laughs and I join in, a touch too heartily.

Then I ask shyly, "Do you mind?"

I'm not sure why I feel so guilty about this. As if I'd actually cheated on him with another woman.

"Not at all. I'm sorry I missed the show."

"I think we can put on a better one together," I whisper as I turn toward him. I cup his balls and walk my fingers back to the sensitive strip of flesh between his legs. Stroking him there always stops any conversation short.

He sighs and his thighs ease open. "So, what were you thinking about when you were doing it?"

My fingertips pause on their journey back to tease his ass crack—which would surely have distracted him from unwanted questions. What do I say now? Of course, I've shared a few fantasies with him before. Crushes on movie stars. Doing it on the beach. But getting an ass-searing spanking from a lesbian mermaid was something else altogether. Besides, Anton was a swimmer in high school—his team came in third in the state finals. If he knew his doggie-paddling wife had nautical yearnings, he'd probably laugh himself silly.

"I wasn't thinking about anything," I say. Even I know it sounds unconvincing.

"Come on."

"It's true."

Anton closes his legs, forcing me to pull my hand away. "You know, we had a presentation about people like you in the seminar today."

His tone is playful, but I feel my body tense. "What do you mean?"

"Difficult employees. They're a challenge. And I have to say your performance as my love slave leaves a lot to be desired right now. But the facilitator explained that each employee has a different working style and if the manager modifies his communication tactics to meet those needs, the result can be a mutually beneficial outcome."

I can't restrain a derisive snort. "You've lost me there, honey. Can you put that in words your more simpleminded workers can understand?"

What happens next catches me totally unawares. Anton plants a nice smarting slap right on my ass. Which is not nearly as surprising as what follows: an embarrassing gush of wetness between my legs and my involuntary cry of pure arousal.

I swallow hard and look away, struggling to pull myself together. "Is this what they're teaching you in that seminar?" It's meant as a clever comeback, but my voice is husky and my heart is pounding.

Anton tilts my chin up. Our gazes lock. *He knows.* My whole body blushes with arousal and shame.

"Were you thinking about having sex with someone else?"

It's my chance to confess and come clean, but perversely, I shake my head.

He slaps my ass again.

"Tell me the truth."

I wonder, fleetingly, if this new managerial tone will have the same effect on his employees as it has on me. By now I'm so aroused I can barely breathe.

"I…can't do that," I stutter.

"Then," he replies, his voice calm, "we can both agree that you need serious disciplinary measures. Pull down your pants and lie on your stomach."

I'm his love slave, I have to obey. Hands shaking, I struggle out of my shorts and panties and position myself as instructed. He reaches under my T-shirt and takes my nipple between his fingers. In a perfectly timed motion, he tweaks my nipple just as the first smack lands square on my ass.

I grind my pelvis into the mattress and groan.

He spanks me again. A wave of heat rolls from my cunt to

my nipple and back again. The bed is already soaked and my ass cheeks burn, as if they've been baked under the glowing orange coils of a toaster oven.

Instinctively I push my buttocks up for another.

"Forget it," Anton says. "No more until you tell me what you were thinking about while you were fingering your pussy. In detail."

I gulp. I'm too worked up to think of a good lie now. But what would he do if he knew what really went on in my head?

"It's kind of…kinky."

"All the more reason I should know. Girls who think about kinky things need a spanking to teach them a lesson," he insists.

Well, if he's going to put it that way, what else can I do?

"It was sort of a lesbian fantasy."

"You were doing it with another girl?" His tone is even, utterly professional. I have no clue what his real reaction is.

"Not a girl exactly. A mermaid. And she made me wrap my legs around her slippery hips and suck her nipples while she…she…"

"Spit it out, Stef."

"She spanked me with her tail and…she said she wouldn't stop until I came."

He sucks in his breath. "Well, I think we already know the appropriate method to deal with a fantasy like that. I just want to make sure we're on the same page. That's key for good manager-employee relations. Do you know what I'm going to do next?"

"Spank me?" I whisper.

"Yes. More specifically, I will spank you while you straddle me just like you did with your girlfriend. But of course, instead of a fish tail, I've got a very hard cock here and I have to figure out what to do with it. Do you have any ideas?"

"Fuck me?"

Anton chuckles. "You know, honey, you're turning into a very cooperative worker after all. Climb on."

I swing a leg over him and settle onto him. My flesh makes a soft sucking sound as he slides in. His thick cock feels so good pressing against my swollen walls that in spite of my hunger for new and sharper pleasures, I start to ride him in the usual way, with quick thrusts of my hips.

But things quickly take an unusual turn. He aims his first slap right into my sensitive ass crack.

I cry out, my muscles gripping him convulsively.

He makes a low grunt of approval. "Good work. Let's try that again."

The next blow is harder, driving my clit against the rough hairs on his belly. I grit my teeth and clutch him tighter.

"Did you suck her nipples while you rubbed your cunt on her?"

"Yes," I admit breathlessly.

Smack.

"Bad girl. You deserve to have your ass spanked until you come."

I feel no shame now. With each slap, I grind my clit on him and then push my ass out again for another sweet shot of that intoxicating cocktail of pleasure and pain.

"Do you like this? Is it as good as it was with her?"

"It's better," I confess. And it's the truth.

Anton grins up at me. "Well, that's the response I was looking for. I guess I can stop spanking you now."

"No, don't stop," I plead before I'm really aware of what I'm saying.

"Oh? You mean, you want me to keep spanking your ass?"

I nod.

"Then beg me."

Back in my other life, I'm too proud to beg for anything, but all the rules are different now. I'm different. In this slip-sliding underworld of lust, I'll do anything to feel the delicious sting of his hand stoking the fire in my flesh.

"Please, Anton, spank my ass while you fuck me." I'm almost crying, and my pussy, too, is weeping, the juices pooling on his belly.

Anton starts bucking, a butterfly-stroke dolphin kick, mattress style. "Say it again. Tell me how much you want it," he orders, his voice hoarse and thick.

"Please spank me. I need it. I'll die without it. Please, boss, please."

With those magic words, I finally earn my employee bonus, a flurry of slaps on the ass that drive me up and over the edge. A voice screams, "God, I'm coming"—I think it's mine—and another, lower one joins in with a "Fuck-oh-fuck-oh-fuck," and I have to grip my thighs as tightly as I can to stay on as he empties himself into me.

Afterward we snuggle, wrapped around each other like fronds of seaweed, not even bothering to mop up the sticky wetness.

"Do you think I'm a pervert?" I say softly, into his shoulder.

"I think you're hot," he replies, stroking my hair.

I smile. "So what do you like to think about when you...you know...?"

Anton laughs. "Funny you should ask. One of my old favorites is that I'm spying on two sexy women doing it in a pool and they catch me and beg me to fuck them."

I laugh, too, with pleasure and relief. "Really? Do you spank them?"

"No, but I will next time."

He tilts my chin up. Our eyes meet. His are green and liquid and seem to reach down inside me to touch all my soft, secret places. I hear a voice, too, echoing faintly in my head— his or mine, I'm not quite sure.

Thanks for the ride.

The Clean-Shaven Type

N.T. Morley

Belle arrived at the castle at midnight, soaked through to the bone. The rain had been pouring down amid lightning and howling winds for hours, turning the road into mud and making the mountain passes all but impassable. It was a miracle that she made it through—even more of a miracle given that the carriage she rode in did not have a driver, but was steered in and of itself, or perhaps by forces unseen—while Belle shivered and stewed in the velvet-furnished compartment.

Belle's carriage was greeted by a tall handsome servant dressed in short breeches and a close-fitting top, a muscular man with a handsome face. He helped Belle down from the carriage with a chivalric hand and a respectful gaze.

"It is a pleasure to welcome you to the castle, Madame Belle." That title sounded strange to Belle's ears; she was not used to being called *Madame*. "I am Andrew, the majordomo. All the castle's servants are pleased to be at your disposal, Ma'am. Please say the word and anything you wish will be yours."

Dripping, Belle followed Andrew down long corridors and up great sweeping spiral staircases. The castle was cold and dark, this being well after midnight; wall sconces held candles that lit as they passed, but the chill was oppressive. As soon as Belle entered her chambers, the warmth comforted her; a fire burned, creating a comfortable and cozy temperature. The room was enormous and lavishly furnished, with divans of silk and a great four-poster bed fitted with luxurious bedding and silk sheets that had already been turned down. The fixtures of the room were of gold and silver and even more precious metals, and a small table had already been set with glittering dinnerware and a meal of cold turkey and fruit, with great flagons of wine.

"Shall I help you out of your things, Madame Belle?"

Standing before the fire, Belle turned and looked him up and down, puzzled.

"Isn't there a maidservant?" she asked haughtily.

"I'm afraid not," said Andrew.

A pool of rainwater was growing around her as she dripped.

"May I help you get undressed, Madame Belle?" Andrew asked again after a pause.

The honorific reminded Belle that she was not here to serve; she was here for another reason entirely. Her old life on her knees was through, at least until she accepted the Beast's proposal.

Belle nodded imperiously.

Andrew knelt behind her and unlaced Belle's corset. She took a series of deep heaving breaths as her aching back relaxed. Andrew unfastened the laces down the rear of Belle's dress and she shrugged the thing off, covering her bare breasts with her arms. Her flesh was goose-bumped and her nipples almost painfully erect. Still on his knees, Andrew obediently slipped Belle's dress over her hips and the garment fell around her feet. She stepped out of the fabric and turned and stood facing Andrew, nude but for her knee-high, spike-heeled boots.

"Are my clothes being sent up?"

"No, Ma'am." Andrew did not elaborate, which irritated her.

She took a step closer to him, savoring his evident discomfort as he attempted to position his body to conceal from her his still-growing erection.

"Put your shoulders back."

Andrew flushed still deeper. "I'm sorry?"

"I said, *put your shoulders back,*" Belle repeated, lifting the toe of one pointy boot and deftly placing it on the kneeling Andrew's shoulder, pushing. This was not easy given Andrew's stature, but Belle was a tall and flexible woman. Doing so placed her sex in close proximity to Andrew's face, which caused him to draw a sharp breath as he went slipping back at the pressure of Belle's toe. Catching himself on his hands, Andrew remained there looking up at Belle, his face level with her sex. The position was awkward for Andrew, requiring him to support his body with the muscles of his arms and thighs and ass. She could see his chest rising as the scent of her intoxicated him and the effort to maintain the posture grew.

His cock was quite evident in his pants.

"May I help you off with your boots, Madame Belle?" asked Andrew suddenly. In the culture that had born both Andrew and Belle, such a suggestion was a colloquial way of suggesting intimate relations, the implication being, of course, that people fucked with their boots off—something that was very rarely true in Belle's experience.

Belle realized that upon uttering this rude innuendo, Andrew had inclined his head slightly, as if to present his face to her, all but begging for her to slap him.

Belle was unfamiliar with having the power to slap someone. She was surprised to find that it excited her immensely to see Andrew on his knees, offering his face to be slapped. And such a pretty face it was.

This was exactly what made Belle go wet and hot inside when she was the one on her knees, in Andrew's position. But she was really more interested in other pleasures at that particular moment, and in fact was quite eager to have Andrew "remove her boots."

Instead of slapping him, Belle caressed his beautiful pink cheeks with her fingers and said, "What did you ask me?"

"I asked if I could remove your boots," Andrew said brashly, all but daring her to slap him. "Madame Belle, may I please remove your boots? I would *love* to remove them and...take them *all* the way off."

"Hold that thought," she said. "And don't move."

Belle stalked to the table, where cold turkey and wine awaited her. She sat at the table nude except for her boots and, at her leisure, she took slim savory morsels of turkey and poured herself a glass of wine.

"May I serve you?" asked Andrew.

"No, you may not," she said absently, without looking back at him. "If there's one thing I've learned in a dozen years of sleeping with men—" she laughed "—it's how to serve myself."

She could not see him, but she could feel the sting of her words.

"As you wish, Madame."

Belle could also hear the strain in Andrew's voice; it was becoming hard for him to hold that position, resting with his hands back on his ankles and his cock bulging forth. She did not glance behind her to see the stress in his body; just knowing it was there made her meal that much sweeter.

Belle took her time eating. The turkey was delicious and the wine was excellent. She had several pieces of fruit, including a few varieties she'd never tasted before—they did not have them in her region.

Belle rose and walked back to Andrew, who was biting his lower lip quite fetchingly, struggling to maintain his posture.

Belle stood before him, taking a long minute to lick her fingers—which were greasy with turkey and sugary with fruit—and her lips, red with wine. Her order not to move, which by now had caused intense pain to the muscles of Andrew's arms and thighs and ass, had not diminished his erection. Belle could relate.

She licked her fruit-sweet fingers as she spoke. "Andrew, I think you asked me something," she said innocently.

Andrew spoke with great effort, his brow moist with the tension in his muscles.

"I asked if I could remove your boots, Mistress," he said, his voice conveying a great humility. "It was impolite for me to ask. I apologize."

Belle reached out and ran her slick fingers across Andrew's throat, teasing him. She leaned close.

"They're the most beautiful boots I've ever seen," he blurted.

He looked up at her, his eyes succulent with adoration of her for the ordeal she'd just put him through, and particularly for the obvious pleasure she'd taken in it. Belle looked down into those gorgeous eyes and laughed.

"My boots are filthy from the ride. I wouldn't wish you to remove them until you've cleaned them—*very* well."

Belle turned and stalked the few feet to a large armchair, feeling the soft silk embrace her bare body as she sat down. She stretched her legs out and presented her high-heeled, pointy-toed black leather boots, which were soaked through and muddy.

Andrew crawled to her and lowered his face to her filthy boots. Belle caught him before his mouth met the muddy leather. Her hand went into his long blond hair and she pulled.

"You have me at a disadvantage," she said. "Is that fair, Andrew?"

"No, Madame," he said. She released his hair. He went to get up as he reached for the fastening of his breeches; again, Belle shook her head.

With some difficulty, Andrew undressed on his knees, kicking off his own footwear first and then removing his breeches to reveal his ample erection, which was even larger than Belle had first thought. When Andrew's tight top finally made it over his head, he discovered that Madame Belle's knees were now folded neatly over the great pillowed arms of the chair, her thighs spread wide and her sex blatantly revealed, the smooth flesh pink with want and the center of her glistening and aromatic. Struggling to contain his hunger, Andrew bent sideways toward one of Madame Belle's muddy boots.

"Please," she said, slipping her hand into his hair again. "Please don't play dumb. You know what you were asking— oh!" She guided his mouth to her sex and pulled his hair firmly as, obediently, Andrew began to lick.

He serviced Belle's sex ably, licking from the sweet center of her opening up to the swollen bud of her clitoris, which drew great sighing moans from her, and later great shuddering gasps, as his tongue skillfully caressed it. His lips closed gently around her clitoris and he worked it eagerly with his tongue as her pleasure mounted.

"I wonder if you think you're going to get that thing inside me?" she panted as she neared her orgasm. "I've never had a boy to play with before. I've always been on the bottom, Andrew. Do you think I'm still dying to get fucked, boy? Andrew, I asked you a question."

She had timed it right, so that his mouth's withdrawal from her sex to answer bought her several more seconds of pleasure.

She did not want to climax too quickly; to do so would be to all but waste the subtle caresses of a very submissive man. Belle had never enjoyed such things before, and planned to savor them as long as she could.

"I believe Madame will do what she wishes," said Andrew obediently. His mouth returned to its ministrations on her clitoris, and Belle pushed him back.

"Of course," said Belle. "But do you think I want to get fucked? Andrew! I asked you a fucking question."

Andrew drew back, his mouth dripping with Belle's juices.

"Yes, Madame. I believe you do want to get fucked."

"Mmmmmm." Belle sighed. She laughed. "Just like a man... He thinks his cock rules the universe. Get me off, boy." She was very close at that moment, and almost no malfeasance on Andrew's part could have prevented an intense orgasm by Belle, but it gave her pleasure to order him to finish her. So often, as a bottom, she had been denied orgasm at the last minute. It invigorated her, now, to take as she wished.

Andrew obediently returned his mouth to her sex, and Belle relaxed into the strokes of his tongue as he serviced her clit. She pushed off her climax as long as she could, savoring the pleasure, but finally Andrew's skills were more than she could resist. She came fiercely. One hand clawed her own thighs until she left great pink furrows; the other went snaking into Andrew's hair and gripped him, forcing his head roughly against her sex as her pleasure mounted and her hips started to move. Andrew continued his service as the Madame, essentially, used him. Belle had never fucked a man's face like that before. She came harder than she ever had.

As she relaxed into the succulent, warm afterglow of her orgasm, Belle was surprised to discover that Andrew continued servicing her, his tongue working even as the pleasure in her clitoris turned to a sudden ache. The pleasure mounted to discomfort momentarily and then, as Andrew slowed his strokes and gave her a minute to recover, it merged back into pleasure, and Belle felt a new sensation growing.

For all her unexpected lust for domination, Belle was still naive in many things.

"Why aren't you stopping?" she panted.

Andrew only drew his tongue away from her for a moment.

"You did not instruct me to," he said, and returned to licking her clit.

Belle went slack into the deep armchair, her eyes glassy with unexpected pleasure. Once, Belle had been bound over a Master's lap as he used a vibrator on her until she succumbed to the onrushing pleasure-pain of a second and a third orgasm. But usually, when she was fucked, she was allowed one—if she was lucky enough to be allowed that at all. This was wholly different, the pleasure mounting as stimulation continued; she felt a momentary flash of guilt, feeling she should instruct Andrew to stop. She was very close to her second orgasm, unexpectedly shuddering all over with increasing pleasure, when, quite to her own surprise, she blurted: "You don't have to."

Andrew looked up at Belle in confusion, the expression on his face going from rapt excitement and pleasured acceptance to something akin to panic. It was the first time Belle had ever seen the ecstasy of total submission on the face of another person. It gave her, simultaneously, a thundering sensation of happiness and the sharp taste of guilt for her own doubts.

"Madame?"

"You don't have to stop when I come," she said quickly, making her voice as sarcastic as possible. "You men always want to finish after you get us off a couple of times. I'm going to come till I'm finished, do you understand?"

"Of course," said Andrew breathlessly. "I would never stop until ordered to, Madame." His eyes went hot as he looked up at her. "If I did, you'd be well within your rights to punish me."

Belle's breath was coming short; she felt the buzzing high of power. Andrew was depending on her; as much as she desired to be bent and stretched and spread on her Master's lap and bed and rack, Andrew wished to be here on his knees, servicing her until he was ordered to stop.

She brought her leg down and tucked it between Andrew's legs, pushing hard on his erect cock with her muddy spike heel.

"I'll already be punishing you," she growled. "For enjoying yourself too much. Now, get me off again, boy, I'm far from finished with you." To hear her own voice uttering such aggressive statements was unfamiliar and deeply erotic to Belle, and she realized perhaps for the first time that she was no longer a sexual servant, as she had been for some years, but something else entirely—or becoming something else, with every stroke of Andrew's tongue.

"Yes, Madame," he said breathlessly, and lowered his face back to her sex.

Belle cried out as she came for a second time, and a third. Only then did she let him enact the ritual of cleaning her boots, from top to toe to spike heel, before he removed them. And then, with her appetite whetted, Madame Belle took her servant to bed.

As it turned out, she did let Andrew's cock inside her—and a mammoth thing it was, sliding into her at a variety of angles as she instructed him to raise and lower himself for her exact satisfaction based not on his desires, or his pleasure or even his physical capacity—she pushed his thigh muscles almost to the breaking point, multiple times—but on the angle at which Madame most eagerly wished to enjoy Andrew's cock.

Good Lord, she discovered, she really did have a G-spot! And Andrew's cock hit it perfectly, provided he stood at the edge of the four-poster bed with one foot on the mattress and one on the floor, and Belle reclined with one leg over his shoulder. She used him that way, commanding him not to come, until his face went red and his thigh muscles rubbery. Only then, when she'd exhausted both herself and her slave, did Madame Belle relax alongside her servant, relishing the feel of his naked body against her and the hardness of his cock, still moist from her, in her hand. She stroked it rhythmically and caressed it with her long, slender fingers.

Perhaps it was the very late hour and the long journey and her own physical satisfaction that made her feel so drunk with excitement.

Or perhaps it was the pleasure of power over her servant that made Madame Belle say to Andrew: "I *could* let you come."

"Yes, Mistress," he said, his voice thick with hunger and weak with submission. "If you wished to do so."

She stroked her fingers up and down his wet cock, alternately caressing and gripping it, showing the extensive skills at manual pleasuring she had gained from her long, long time on her knees. So many times she'd been engaged to pleasure a man with her hands, and she knew Andrew was very, very close. Her habit was, unquestionably, to satisfy the man immediately, per her role in life. But now she felt differently. It would have taken a few firm strokes of her hand, or the permission for Andrew to mount her again and fuck her for his pleasure, or a few quick slurps of her mouth—which was even now watering. She could even just issue a dismissive word that would allow Andrew to satisfy himself: "Stroke," or "Jerk," or "Finish" or, most simply, "Come."

But she did not say any of these words, or pump Andrew's cock with her hand, or order him back into her or go down to suck him, though she very badly wanted to. It was the first time she had ever been with a man without going down on him. It would be the first time, she decided, that she had ever been with a man when he did not come.

Belle sighed and laughed musically. She removed her hand from Andrew's cock and stretched her naked body out across the great expanse of the bed. She'd like it all to herself, she decided, and as delicious as Andrew was, she was finished with him.

"I don't think so," she told him. "Go now. Wake me in the morning."

"Yes, Madame," said Andrew. "May I kiss you goodbye?"

She looked at him pleasantly.

"No," she said.

"Yes, Madame." He got out of her bed and stood beside her, his cock erect and pink with effort, still glistening with her. Belle yawned and closed her eyes.

"May I ask a question?"

"What is it?" said Belle flatly, without opening her eyes.

"Did Madame enjoy herself?"

Belle's eyes popped open; she looked Andrew up and down.

She had enjoyed herself very much; she was almost terrified by the pleasure. She'd had more orgasms than she'd ever been allowed during any other tryst throughout her long life as a submissive, or before, when she'd gone to bed with men on equal footing, when she'd had, in fact, very few orgasms. But the vast physical pleasure she'd experienced was as nothing compared to the overwhelming intoxication of power. She felt ecstatic over the fact that she was being asked—and could answer as she wished, something she'd never been able to do the dozens of times she'd been asked before she became kinky, when she'd always said yes out of politeness, often elaborating with great vigor despite being vaguely dissatisfied.

Now, her body soft and relaxed with many orgasms, her satisfaction overpowering, she could answer as it pleased her to do so, and she realized she did not know how best to use this new tool for her amusement.

"Not nearly enough," said Belle coldly. "You'll have to try harder next time." She felt a surge of excitement at the look of deep submission on Andrew's face. His cock remained hard. She closed her eyes.

"Madame, am I allowed to masturbate?" he asked.

She opened her mouth to ask, "Is that my decision to make?" but stopped herself before she uttered the question.

Instead, she looked at him pleasantly, so she could feel the hot wave of his submission when she told him:

"No. You may not masturbate. And have my clothes sent up."

"They've been confiscated," said Andrew.

Belle frowned.

"Then clean my boots," she said. "For real this time."

"Thank you, Madame. I shall wake you in the morning."

"Just try." Belle laughed, and went to sleep.

Belle slept deep and long, and refused to be roused when Andrew came to wake her in the morning.

"The Master wishes to lunch with you, Madame," said Andrew.

Belle sighed, yawned and cast aside the blankets. She slipped her legs over the edge of the bed, spread her legs and crooked a finger at Andrew.

"Madame, he's waiting."

"Let him wait," she said, and grabbed Andrew's hair. She pulled him onto her, then threw him on his back, riding him with excruciating slowness. Each time he bit his lip and struggled not to come, it made Belle's excitement sore higher.

Three hours later, she still had not granted Andrew leave, and she laughed as she bade the poor man lace her boots up, seeing his trembling from head to toe as his desperate sexual need pulsed through him.

"Just a stroke or two of my hand, wouldn't it?"

"Madame?"

"That's all it would take." She sighed. "Just a soft little stroke, and I could give you everything you ever wanted. Or maybe—" she bent down low and ran her fingers over the back of Andrew's neck "—I could use my mouth. Would you like to come in my mouth, Andrew?"

The servant let out a faint, desperate squealing noise before he finally managed to rasp, "As...Madame...wishes."

Belle laughed.

When she finally let Andrew lead her into the banquet hall, it was very late in the day. Sitting at the head of the table was the man whom submissives from France to Russia called the Beast, his face red with anger.

Entering the room ahead of Belle, Andrew announced her. Then he said, "I'm sorry for the delay, sir, Madame Belle—"

The Beast cut him off with a savage wordless growl and slammed his fist down on the table. Andrew paled and stood stock-still. But then Beast rose as Belle entered the room, and his face was transformed into an expression of gentleness.

He hurried to greet Belle, going down on one knee and kissing her hand as she extended it. "It is a pleasure to meet you, Madame Belle," said the man they called the Beast. He was not a bad-looking man, though Belle had always preferred those without the long bushy beard the Beast favored. Her own Master was clean-shaven. In just the last twelve hours, she'd come to very much appreciate the long hair of Andrew—

it provided quite a useful handhold when she wished to direct the location of his mouth. Beast had the same long hair, though he was not nearly as blond—gray shot through his hair even more than through his beard.

Belle took a long moment to savor the Beast on his knees; were she to remain here, it would be the last time she saw it for quite a while. She did not withdraw her hand or respond for a time, and the Beast remained on one knee looking up at her in growing irritation.

"It is a pleasure to meet you, Master. Your servant has been showing me quite evident hospitality."

She saw the color come quickly to Beast's face, and felt a sudden charge. She took her seat and the Beast returned to his, his eyes shifting nervously back and forth, as if he were stealing glances at Belle's naked body. Certainly a Master like him had to be quite accustomed to taking his pleasure with a slave, both visually and otherwise. But here, before the final negotiation had taken place, the Beast was like a sneaky schoolboy, stealing clandestine looks at Belle's perfect tits. Not a week before she was nothing more than a slave whose breasts were on display whenever her Master wished them to be; now, this Beast seemed almost ashamed to look at them.

Belle felt a great thrill of power, and did not wish to give that up.

"Shall we eat?" asked Beast.

"Of course," said Belle. "I've worked up quite an appetite."

Beast's lips pulled back and he glared at Andrew with a savage fury. The servant retreated from the room.

Unseen hands served the meal, with the great silver domes of the serving dishes receding at the wave of the Beast's hand. Underneath were steaming plates of roast beef and vegetables, and Belle had only to look at something and desire it, and invisible forces would seize utensils, slice or spoon her up what she wished and carry them unbidden to her plate. The same was true of wine; each flagon was poured whenever she noticed that her glass was getting partially empty, and when the main course was finished she enjoyed the same magical dispensing of rich sweets and coffee.

"Well, then—it's time," said the Beast when steaming mugs were before them. "Shall we talk business?"

"Most certainly," purred the very naked Belle. "I like nothing at all so much as I like business."

"Yes, well—as you know, you were sold to me by your Master, or your *former* Master, since at this very moment you are in transition—"

"Yes, of course," said Belle. "You're stating the obvious, Beast."

The Beast bristled. "Must you call me that?"

She smiled. "I'm sorry, I meant no offense. You must know the submissives all call you that."

"For what reason?" he said bitterly, as if he already knew the answer. Belle could see the sadness in the Beast's eyes.

She felt a heady thrill of excitement, and with her new-found candor she just began talking: "They say you're very rough, Sir. Quite a savage fuck. They say you're like a mad wild animal, that you've claws and teeth and a cock not at all shaped like a normal one—a human cock. Some say you've four or five of them secreted at different parts of your body. They say you love to do horrible things—to pull a slave's hair, to slap her face, to spank her, whip her, cane her, to fuck her ass with a wicked ardor—"

Beast rose from his seat, the heavy chair tumbling back and crashing to the floor. He smacked his palm against the table.

He bellowed: "Is that not what she desires? Does a submissive not beg for such treatment? Each girl begged—"

"Please, Sir," purred Belle, her soft voice cutting through the Beast's very loud one despite his excitement. "I meant no offense. I'm merely telling what I've heard about you...if I'm going to kneel before you, Sir, I believe frankness is called for."

The Beast looked ashamed. He righted his chair and sat again.

"I'm sorry."

"Of course you are," said Belle with a soft smile. "You were saying something, I believe, Sir?"

The Beast stared at his coffee. "No, not at all, Madame...if the lady wishes to speak, then——"

"I'd prefer to hear what the Beast has to say for himself," Belle told him. "Such a bad, bad man...frightening submissives from Tuktoyaktuk to Timbuktu...you're like the bogeyman that Masters tell their girl slaves about. And here you've purchased me, and so soon I'll be on my knees before you...sucking your cock, Sir, and begging you not to spank me." She made sure she had his eye, and gave him a dirty wink, brushing her hand across her bosom as she did so. "But secretly hoping that you do, Sir. Why should I relish this?"

The Beast went red, hot, his breath coming short. He tried to look at Belle, but could not; her beauty had frozen him. He tried to speak, but no words came out. Finally, he stammered, "W-we met," he said. "I fucked you."

"I'm sorry?" Belle said, puzzled.

The Beast's words came in a torrent, his nervousness showing. "It was at the New Year's party at your Master's house," he said. "He...he provided you to me. You were hooded, I was masked. Your hood did not have eyeholes. You were bound on your back, with your arms over your head and your holes—forgive me, Madame... I used you quite savagely...as you say, befitting my reputation. You seemed to like it." The Beast could not look at her; he stared into his coffee.

Belle caught her breath; she remembered it well—very well. She felt her nipples stiffen almost painfully. For a moment she could not speak. She covered her discomfort with an imperious air.

"I did," she said. "I enjoy everything my Master orders me to."

"Your *former* Master," the Beast said coolly.

"Of course."

"Your…your body, Belle—*Madame* Belle—it was…it was exquisite. I had never seen a naked slave so beautiful, bound as you were…but it was more than that, Madame. The way you reacted, the way you relished the sensation. The way you answered to my hand and my whip and my cane and my cock—not just your body, Madame, but your mind. I…I believe I fell in love with you that night, Belle. *Madame* Belle." The Beast stood up again, quite unexpectedly, and his chair again slammed into the ground with an explosive sound. He slammed both fists into the table, tipping his wine flagon.

He cried, "*Madame* Belle—I hate that word! God, but I hope you'll come and kneel before me so I can stop calling you *Madame*…and call you things that make you wet—whore, slut—"

"Stop!" cried Belle, her head spinning. She felt drunk; she had not consumed nearly enough wine to make her as intoxicated as she felt. She breathed hard, looking at the Beast and feeling her own sexual needs pulsing hot in her naked body.

"Right your chair," she told him.

"Of course," he said. "My apologies, Madame. I did not mean disrespect. Of course I would never call you—"

"First," said Belle, her breath coming short, "I would like to summon Andrew."

"Why?" asked Beast, looking cowed. "Do you fear me? Do you—" His shame turned to anger, evident on his face. "Do you think he'll protect you if I *do* wish to hurt you?"

Belle felt her stomach swirling as she made her decision.

"I wish to have him here."

"All right," said Beast, and called Andrew's name.

The servant arrived, and with a gesture from Beast, he stood next to Belle's chair. Belle immediately reached out and unfastened his breeches.

Beast's eyes went wide in horror. "What are you doing?"

"I've some business to finish up," said Belle. "This man's been positively a saint to me."

Andrew's eyes were darting about with a violent conflagration of confused dismay, shock and pleasure as Belle undid his breeches and pulled out his good-size cock. He was mostly soft, but that did not last more than the ten seconds during which Belle bent forward and applied her swirling tongue to his shaft and head.

Beast watched, eyes wide, mouth open, as Belle slicked up her fingers with olive oil from the dish and began to stroke Andrew's cock.

"I'm a bit confused," Beast said.

Andrew let out a desperate squeaking sound as Belle took time to caress his balls with one hand while applying the palm of her other hand to the underside of his head.

Belle twisted her naked body awkwardly so she could face Beast while using both hands to beat off Andrew. She said, "I'm sorry, I don't mean to be rude—I'll face you as I talk to you."

"I'd very much appreciate it," said Beast, his expression one of utter disbelief.

"So, I'll try to be frank, Sir… I'll not call you Beast any longer, Sir, because I believe that is a sorely misapplied nickname."

At once, Beast bristled and glowed. He nodded.

"You know, as I do, that when my Master sold me, for quite a healthy price, I know—all he was selling was the right to first negotiation. You own me insofar as I allow you to own me…Master."

Belle had used that word quite carefully, savoring the look of warm surrender on Beast's face as he heard her directing it toward him—along with the heat that rose from seeing her stroking Andrew. The servant, for his part, was biting his lower lip, struggling against his mounting pleasure. Belle looked up at him as she stroked and whispered to him, "It's all right, baby, I'm going to let you come this time…but not yet, baby, just give me a few minutes. Does that feel good, baby? Do you want to come all over my tits? Good, darling, I'm going to get you off, but you have to be strong for me. Promise? Good boy. Good Andrew. Good *slave*."

The Beast was staring gape-mouthed as Belle dirty-talked his slave in front of him. She was a guest in his house; she had every right to do so. Until the moment she submitted to the Beast, Belle was privileged to use Andrew as she saw fit, and intended to do so—if only, now, to illustrate her point.

"Any girl worth her salt would beg to kneel before you, Sir," purred Belle. "You're rich, you're sexy, you have a terrible reputation for doing awful things to helpless, tied-up girls—"

"Unearned!" he bleated. "I swear to you, Belle, I only do what—"

"Of course you do," she interrupted him, her voice rising quickly. "Submissives are like drama critics…everything's a masterpiece in the newspaper Friday morning, but a travesty in the salons on Saturday night. You're everything I'd want in a Master, Sir… You see, I've got a bit of a reputation myself." She winked at him.

"Understood," said Beast, and it was evident from the look on his face—Andrew's in-progress stroke job notwithstanding— that Beast knew quite well what reputation the insatiably ravenous and fantastically difficult-to-sate Belle possessed. Why else would her own Master elect to relinquish her? "I consider that a major selling point."

"I'm sure you do," said Belle, and took great pleasure in making the Beast wait while she bent forward and applied her skilled mouth to slurping much of the olive oil off Andrew's cock. It was a delicious vintage, probably northern Italian, but possibly—just possibly—Spanish. Or maybe a blend.

Belle had to pause halfway through to say, "Don't come yet, baby. I'll get you off, but you've got to be strong for me. Can you wait?" Andrew was sweating, his face red and his muscles clenched tight.

"Yes, Mistress," he gasped, and Belle slurped him back into her mouth, her lips and tongue gliding up and down on his impressive shaft, as Beast watched with increasing desperation.

"Madame Belle, if you'll forgive me—"

Belle withdrew her wet mouth from Andrew's cock. She shook her head and cut Beast off. "Uh-uh," she said. "I'll never, ever forgive you. You'll earn each dose of penance, Sir, mark my words."

"What?" asked Beast.

Belle laughed musically, and continued beating off Andrew as she talked.

"You see, I've been a slave for ten years, Sir…and in the last twelve hours I've learned to like it on the other side."

"That's how I run my house!" cried Beast. "I'm a different man entirely from your Master. He believes all slaves are servants, whereas I believe all servants are slaves! And slaves, Belle…a slave has privileges in my house that no other Master would give her! Please, Belle…kneel for me, and you'll be a powerful lady, and kneel to no man…no man but me."

"I want that—" Belle smiled "—minus the kneeling part. I remember how it was that one night. You dominated me, but you…well, Sir, part of you surrendered. Didn't you?"

Beast was out of his seat again, the chair crashing, his fury erupting as he swept plates and bowls and flagons off the table in a great horrible mess.

He stopped, however, leaning over the table to scream something, with his mouth wide-open—because he'd discovered that he had nothing to scream.

"I thought so." Belle sighed, looking up at Andrew and stroking his cock. "I believe you did fall in love with me, Sir, and love makes whores of all men. And a whore is just a slut who gets paid, and…you know it, don't you, Beast? All slaves get paid. Surely you catch my meaning, Sir."

Beast was panting. He trembled all over and bit his lower lip. "I think so," he finally said.

"Good," whispered Belle. "You see how I'm treating Andrew? That's what you can expect…the same cruel kindness. Surely you know what we did all night, don't you, baby? Sir?"

Beast reddened.

"He was watching through a knothole," said Andrew boldly. "He saw everything."

Beast gasped and looked down in shame.

"Good slave," said Belle, and in that moment neither man was sure to whom she was referring. It was a telling moment for both men.

Belle turned her eyes up to Andrew. "All right, baby. I'm going to let you do it. Just surrender. Come for me, but keep eye contact." Both slick hands worked steadily on Andrew's cock, aiming it at her breasts while she held Andrew's eyes in hers.

Andrew let out a great cry and shook all over as he came. He never broke eye contact with Belle, and her soft moans and cooing sounds coaxed him on to greater heights of eruption. Soon her perfect breasts were anointed—the baptismal male orgasm of Belle's life as a dominant.

She released Andrew's cock.

"Thank you, baby." She sighed. "You can go. I'll spank you later."

"As…Mistress…wishes," gasped Andrew, and limped out of the room.

Belle turned her attention to Beast, who leaned heavily on the far end of the table, staring at her, enraptured.

Belle pushed her chair back from the table, running her fingers through the warm liquid on her breasts. The feel of it was intoxicating, the liquor of power. She licked her fingers and remembered the taste of so many men while she rested on her knees—this taste was different, so different. A different beast entirely.

"Surely you catch my drift, Sir?" she asked him. "I believe you're in love…and these are my terms, Sir. Take it or leave it." She lifted her legs, draping each knee over the arms of the wooden chair, her high-heeled, pointy-toed boots dangling fetchingly where Beast could easily see them.

Belle smiled. She could see the Beast's eyes roving over her naked body, and particularly lingering on her boots. Beast came around the table, walking through the detritus of his fury, his boots crunching on crackers and squishing on poultry. He walked to Belle's chair and stood before her, stealing glances at her naked, spread body as he tried, without much success, to keep his eyes on the floor.

"I'll take it," said Beast. "Mistress."

Belle laughed musically. "Good slave," she said. "Why don't you take my boots off?"

Beast lowered himself to his knees and reached for Belle's laces.

"But clean them first," she told him. "It's such a long, filthy trip from my chambers."

"Of course, Mistress," said Beast, bending forward to apply his tongue to the already immaculately clean leather of Belle's tall boots.

She almost reached out and, seizing Beast's long hair, guided him where she *really* wanted his mouth to go.

But she relented, at the last moment, and decided to let him actually clean her boots. She was more than satisfied, for now—and the first order of business, anyway, was to shave that epic beard. When it came down to it, Belle really preferred the clean-shaven type.

The Midas F*ck
(or *The Look of Love*)

Erica DeQuaya

"You're kidding."

Laura took a sip from her drink, restraining the impulse to chug. The liquid slithered down, warming her. She'd ordered a double and a double is what she got. Goodwin's Gulch never watered down its drinks.

"I'm not," Laura said.

Carolyn frowned, toying with her own drink. "Laura, I think you're a wonderful human being. You've been my best friend for years. But one thing you ain't is irresistible to guys."

Laura sighed. She had really hoped it wouldn't come to this, but Carolyn obviously needed proof.

"Look at the bar," she said. "The hunka-hunka burning love there."

Carolyn turned slightly to look while Laura indulged in another gulp of liquid comfort. She knew what her friend would see. Tall, broad-shouldered, to-die-for guy leaning against the bar, tossing comments to Rick Goodwin, who stood behind the bar, making drinks and watching the Chicago Bears on the television. Every so often, hunka-hunka would scope the scenery. Not that there was much right now. The action in this Chicago bar didn't heat up until after 10:00 p.m. on Fridays and Saturdays. Sundays at 4:00 p.m. only brought out the regulars like herself.

"Cute," Carolyn said, turning back to her.

"Watch," Laura said.

She pulled off her sunglasses and waited until hunka-hunka's glance slithered in their direction. When their eyes met, hunka-hunka's jaw dropped and even from a distance, Laura saw desire flare in his eyes. As Laura dropped the sunglasses over her eyes, hunka-hunka moved toward their table, oozing seduction. He was good-looking, all right, with dark hair long enough to touch his collar. Sensual lips. Deep blue eyes that promised all sorts of bedroom pleasure.

Laura felt nothing.

"Can I buy you ladies a drink?"

Translation: Can I get you into bed? Namely, the fat one there in the gray dress?

Laura treated him to an artificial smile. "We're fine, thanks."

"I could use a drink," Carolyn said, longing heavy in her voice.

"Your friend said you were fine," Hunka-hunka said, his eyes not leaving Laura.

Translation: I don't give two craps about you. I want to fuck your friend. The fat one in the gray dress.

Laura wished she hadn't started things. "Maybe in a few minutes," she told him.

He treated her to an intimate smile. "Later then," he said softly, then sauntered away.

Carolyn stared after him, then turned on Laura. "You weren't affected by *that?* Jesus, I'm creaming in my pants!"

"I know," Laura said gloomily.

"It still doesn't prove anything."

Laura gritted her teeth. Her friend would need a little more convincing.

"The table near the door. The guy in the business suit, working away at the laptop," she said.

Carolyn looked, then shrugged. "He's married. Gold band on the left hand and all."

"It doesn't matter." Laura removed her glasses and stared hard at the man. He wasn't as good-looking as hunka-hunka, who was still eyeing her longingly. But he'd pass. After a few moments, married guy looked around as though feeling her gaze. As his glance met Laura's, he straightened up. She could see the internal struggle: remain faithful to wifey or try to go for a fast fuck with the fat chick?

Wifey apparently went out the window. The man stood, and Laura half expected him to come to their table. Instead, he went to the bar and conferred with Rick, who glanced at them, then nodded. As the guy returned to his table, he stared at Laura, a knowing smile creasing his lips.

Rick came to them, drink in one hand, note in the other, and Laura hurriedly put her sunglasses in place. "Compliments of Chris, there," Rick said dryly as he handed Laura the drink and note. Laura opened it. It contained a room number at a nearby hotel and a sentence: *Stop by later, if you have time. Chris.*

Laura passed the note to Carolyn. "Thanks, Rick," she said.

"Sure thing, Laura." He seemed about to say something, then went back behind the bar.

Carolyn blew a breath and passed the note back. "Okay, explain this to me again."

Laura gazed morosely into her drink. "Ken and I broke up about six weeks ago. I caught him cheating and threw his sorry ass out the door."

"I remember," Carolyn said, nodding.

"I was so miserable, I wanted to be more attractive to men. I cried myself to sleep and then this—this angel came to me in a dream. Tall guy. Long, blond hair, with wings. Clutching a bow and arrow."

"Sounds like Cupid." Carolyn finished her drink.

"Whatever. He told me my wish was granted. Since then, I've been irresistible to men. All I have to do is look at them and—and they become sexually aroused. They won't leave me alone," Laura said miserably.

"Why is this a problem?" Carolyn said impatiently. Laura buried herself in her drink. She'd never win an award for Raving Beauty of the Year, especially carrying thirty extra pounds. Being the sexual target of men had been a heady experience. At first. "The problem is—" She stopped, felt herself turn red. "I don't get any enjoyment out of it."

Carolyn shrugged. "Lots of women don't have an orgasm—"

"I can't get turned on."

"Ever?"

"Ever."

"That's a problem. There has to be a way out," Carolyn said practically. "Maybe you can—uh—dream up that long-haired cutie again?"

"I've tried."

At the nearby table, Chris stood and ran his eyes over Laura, clearly undressing her in his mind. He put the laptop in his briefcase, blew a kiss and left.

"Unbelievable," Carolyn said. "It's kind of like whoseewhats. You know, Midas. The golden touch. Everything he touched turned to gold. Even his daughter."

"I don't have to worry about that. At this rate, I'll never *have* a daughter."

"Hey." Hunka-hunka was back. He grabbed a chair, placed it next to Laura and sat, sliding an arm around her shoulders. Ignoring Carolyn, he pulled Laura close.

"Not to rush you, sweetheart, but I'm rock hard for you,"

he whispered in her ear. As he ran his tongue over her earlobe, he took her hand and placed it on his crotch.

Laura removed her hand and forced a smile. "My friend's over there," she murmured. "Just give me a few more minutes, okay?"

"Anything you want." His hand moved across her breasts and slid over her hip to her upper thigh, where it lingered. Then he pulled away, stood and sauntered off.

Carolyn stared at her. "I can't believe you didn't feel anything from *that*."

Carolyn had a point. There was something raunchy and exciting about being felt up by a guy before her friend. But Laura felt nothing.

"If you were a real friend, you'd take him off my hands," she said. "I'm exhausted. I can't take much more of this."

"Well—" Carolyn glanced at hunka-hunka and grinned.

"Thanks." Laura stood. "I'm going to the bathroom. How long will you need?"

Carolyn studied hunka-hunka for a moment, who was still staring at Laura. "Five minutes," she said. "Assuming he won't be lusting after you."

Laura shook her head. "Once I'm gone, they forget about me."

"Okay. I'll tell you how it works out."

Laura nodded and went into the bathroom, hoping hunka-hunka wouldn't follow her. It wouldn't have been the first time some guy trailed her into the ladies' loo. But thankfully, he didn't seem to be into bathroom trysts.

Laura perched her sunglasses on her head, taking stock of her reflection in the mirror. The gray dress hid her ample curves. Her long, dark hair was parted in the middle and pulled back into a ponytail. Her round face with her bow-shaped lips and dark brown eyes was free of makeup. No way was she any guy's fantasy. But tell the guys that.

Sighing, she turned from the mirror, washed her hands perfunctorily and glanced at her watch. Hopefully Carolyn had wooed hunka-hunka away and she could enjoy another drink, or two, or three or more, in peace. When she emerged from the bathroom, Laura saw the bar was empty. Carolyn had cleared out with her hot stud.

"Your girlfriend left with your boyfrien," Rick said. Laura slid onto a bar stool and glanced at the television. The Bears were losing. Nothing new there.

"I asked her to," she told him. At Rick's curious look, she shook her head. "Just get me another bourbon, please. Make it a double."

Rick grabbed a bottle and poured. "Why the dark glasses?" He touched the glasses perched on her head and Laura looked at him, startled, then cursed herself. She'd forgotten to cover her eyes. By all rights, Rick should have been all over her.

She looked at him again, and he winked at her. It seemed as though she had no effect on this man. Probably a good thing; he wasn't her type. Still, he was cute, with short blond hair contrasting nicely with intelligent, humorous gray eyes. He topped out at around five-nine, and was nicely proportioned. He had his share of women lusting after him, but Laura was relieved she could look one guy in the eye without getting him hard.

"Tell Uncle Rick all about it, okay? You can trust me."

He took her hand in what was clearly meant to be a friendly gesture. But Laura yanked it back, a bolt of sudden and unexpected desire slamming through her. She stared at Rick, noticing the sudden spear of lust moving across his face before disappearing into astonishment. They stared at each other for a long moment before Laura found her voice.

"Rick—?"

"Office, Laura," he whispered harshly. "In the back. I'll be there in a minute."

He slid from behind the bar and made his way to the front door to lock it. Laura didn't hesitate, but went to Rick's office and opened the door. It was a small room, containing a desk and some boxes stacked near the door. But it was the sofa that caught her attention. As she yanked the elastic band from her hair and undid the zipper of her dress, Laura saw herself and Rick indulging in carnal delights on that piece of furniture. The image was so vivid, her body throbbed, and she groaned.

A moment later, the master of her fantasies came through the door, slammed it shut and pinned her against the wood, kissing her with a hard passion. His tongue danced with hers and Laura clung to him breathlessly. She moved her hips against him, feeling his cock press through their clothes against the juncture of her thighs, and she moaned.

"Jesus," he said breathlessly in her ear. "One minute I'm talking to you, the next minute, I want to fuck you…I haven't gotten hard in weeks…"

Feeling desire rampant through her body, Laura ran her hand between his legs, playing with his rigid penis through the fabric of his jeans. She unzipped him, slipped her hand into his underwear and trembled at the feel of his hard, pulsing flesh against her palm.

Rick removed her hand. "No. Get undressed and lie down on the sofa."

Laura backed away from him, removing her dress and yanking off her bra, tearing her stockings in her haste to get out of them. She lay on the sofa, closing her eyes, slippery warmth throbbing between her legs as she grew wetter. It was as though weeks of numbness were melting away, her pent-up lust unleashed at the hands of this acquaintance-lover.

Laura's eyes flew open at the touch of cloth on her arms and she saw Rick, half-naked, face intent, as he leaned over her and tied her wrists together. For a moment she quailed— she'd never been bound during sex. But the thought of herself naked and helpless boosted her excitement and she caught her breath.

"Rick," she whispered. "Do me. Jesus, I'm so hot for you…"

"Patience." His voice was hoarse. He smiled at her and, taking a bottle from his desk, poured some of the contents in his palms. The smell of raspberries permeated the room as he came forward, rubbing his hands.

"Massage oil," he said huskily. "Something told me to buy it. I'm glad I did."

He placed his hands on her shoulders, then moved them smoothly over her breasts, the oil on his palms warming as it penetrated her flesh. Wrists bound above her head, Laura was helpless as he stroked her stomach, then moved to caress her breasts.

"My nipples," she gasped. "Lick them, Rick. Please."

He took one of the hardened peaks in his mouth and tongued it before moving to the other. Laura groaned and arched her back, lust spearing a path to her groin. She was dimly aware she was pleading with him as his lips and hands moved from her breasts to trace patterns across her stomach before going lower.

Breath hot in her throat, Laura arched her back again, wanting him to caress the tender flesh between her swollen nether lips. But Rick continued teasing her, his lotion-laden hands moving silkily over the flesh between her legs. His lips followed, laying tiny kisses on the skin of her inner thighs, moving close to her pussy before retreating downward again.

Laura pounded her bound wrists on the sofa, unable to take much more of this erotic torture. Then Rick's mouth was on her lower lips, French-kissing them, his tongue darting out to caress her swollen clitoris. He lapped slowly at her engorged folds and Laura screamed, the heat of her climax engulfing

her, submerging her in almost unbearable passion. Rick continued tonguing her, and she was hit broadside by a second
orgasm, her body spasming in unspeakable pleasure.

Rick released her when her voice was little more than a
choked-out whimper. He left her for a moment and she heard
him slide off his clothes.

"I want to fuck you," he said softly. "I'm so damn hard for
you, I can't stand it…"

Unable to speak, still trembling, Laura watched as Rick
knelt between her open legs, stroking his enlarged penis, his
glance catching hers. She nodded, her body tensed in anticipation of his entry. He slid into her and Laura moaned at the
touch of his hard flesh moving against her swollen walls. She
wrapped her legs around him as he set a steady rhythm, her
hips moving involuntarily. Astonishingly, she felt the warmth
of a pending orgasm begin to flood her body again, and she
gazed at Rick.

"I'm going to come," she said, gasping.

"Do it," he said hoarsely. "Oh, sweet Jesus…"

Laura felt his release a split second before her own. She
cried out, giving in to her climax and when it was over, collapsed beneath him, her breath coming out in sobs.

Rick slowly reached to untie the cloth binding her wrists.
He sat up and drew her into his arms. Laura lay against him
for a long moment, the smell of sex and raspberries enhanc-
ing the afterglow.

"That was incredible," he whispered in her hair.

She nodded, her eyes closed. Incredible described it. "That
was a first for me," she said. "I've never really received pleasure
in bed. I was the one who gave it."

"Men like to give pleasure, too." He spoke as though a reve-
lation had just come to him. "Maybe that's what the long-
haired dude with the wings was talking about in a dream I
had." He laughed a little. "He said I was a selfish bastard in

bed. Maybe it's the reason I haven't been able to get it up. For anyone. Until today. Until I gave pleasure."

Laura sat up suddenly, and turned to him. "You—you had the dream about that long-haired guy, too? About six weeks ago?" At his nod, she shook her head. "So did I. Carolyn thought it might have been Cupid." She felt stupid as she said it, but Rick regarded her thoughtfully.

"The god of love?"

"I know it sounds strange, but hear me out. Ken and I broke up," Laura said. "I wanted to be more attractive to men. It's like—I got my wish. I attracted guys, but couldn't get aroused."

Rick considered her. "You haven't received pleasure in bed and I haven't given it."

"Until now," Laura said softly.

"Until now," he affirmed. They were both silent for a moment.

"Maybe this long-haired dude—Cupid?—had a reason for invading both our dreams," Rick finally said. "It makes a weird sort of sense that—that maybe we were brought together like this to learn something."

Laura sighed. "It's no weirder than what's been happening to me these past few weeks."

Rick stood, hunted for his clothes and found them. As he slid them on, he found her glasses on his desk.

"You may not need these again," he said with a grin.

"Hopefully not," she responded, smiling back.

He tossed the glasses back on the desk. "I'd better open up. You might want to get dressed or I'll want a repeat of what just happened."

Laura thrilled at his words. "Later. I'll give you all the pleasure you can handle later on."

Rick came back to her and gave her a quick kiss. "I'll hold you to that," he said, then left.

Smiling a little, she pulled her clothes on then left the office.

Rick was behind the bar, the Bears game was on again. They'd tied the score, and had possession of the ball. Rick waved at her, and she returned it.

The two guys at the bar turned to look at her. One nodded politely, and they both turned their attention back to the game. No lingering glances, no come-on smirks. Just two guys watching the Bears.

Vastly relieved, Laura gave a thumbs-up to Rick, who returned her smile.

Sleeping with Beauty

Allison Wonderland

You know how the saying goes: You have to kiss a lot of frogs before you find your princess.

All right, so in all fairness, that's not exactly how the saying goes—I had to modify it slightly for personal reasons—but the sentiment is still pretty much the same.

I've kissed my share of web-footed amphibians, not to mention a handful of horny toads. But none ever slipped out of its shiny green skin and into a garish gown and polished pumps.

My princess will come someday. She could have come yesterday, but she didn't. (She must have overslept.) She could still come today, but she won't. (Too bad she's not an insomniac like me.) She might come tomorrow, but I seriously doubt it. (You know, most people function just fine with only eight hours of shut-eye.)

Well, there's always the day after next. (Provided she doesn't sleep the day away, of course.)

With his drooping eyelids and sonorous yawns, Prince Charming looks more like Sleepy the dwarf than the handsome hunk of heroism he's supposed to be impersonating.

I really have to wonder about his qualifications for this line of work. I realize he's new on the job, but still, he's supposed to be portraying an animated character. The least he could do is try to look alive.

Like Kendall.

Kendall is one of the other neophytes, joining the plethora of theme-park princes and princesses just two days ago.

I'd like to say she had me at hello, except she didn't have me at hello, because hello isn't the first thing she said to me. Instead, she opted to open with: "That is the cutest pair of panties I have ever seen."

I looked in the mirror affixed to my locker door, waiting to catch a glimpse of the blush that would soon be peeking through my concealer.

The cutest pair of panties that she has ever seen were fashioned from preshrunk white cotton, freckled with bitty blue hearts, and adorned with the visage of Snow White, my character's cartoon counterpart.

"I didn't know they made those in grown-up sizes," she continued, setting a tie-dyed tote bag onto the bench.

I examined my reflection, noting, with a mortified moan, that my face and hair were now color coordinated. "They don't," I said, and pretended to search for something inside my locker. "They're, um, kids' ones. I just figured they would help me get into character."

I just figured they would help me get into character?

I did not just say that.

She smiled. "I'm Sleeping Beauty," she said, extending her hand. "And my alter ego is Kendall."

As she unzipped the dress bag containing her costume, it occurred to me that I should probably reciprocate the formality, but my mouth felt parched and my lips seemed to have fused together.

"I love this place," Kendall shared, pulling her T-shirt over her head. "My parents used to bring me and my brother here every summer, although I never understood why we went someplace in the summer that's warm all year-round when we lived someplace else that's *not* warm all year-round. We should have gone in the winter, know what I mean?"

I nodded, with more exuberance than the comment called for, and hoped that she would find my imitation of a bob-blehead doll endearing, or at least entertaining.

"So, what's your name?" Kendall asked.

"Carla," I answered, and watched her wriggle into her flesh-tone panty hose.

"How long have you been working here, Carla?"

I lowered myself onto the bench, sliding my bobbed black wig toward her pouffy platinum one. "About seven months."

"Not quite a rookie, but not exactly a seasoned veteran, either," Kendall murmured, then paused to roll antiperspirant under her arms. "Have you ever seen a princess with pit stains?" she quipped, and swatted my thigh playfully, the kind of camaraderie that's usually reserved for good friends.

We continued to chat while we changed. I made a greater effort to listen as Kendall talked and to respond instead of gawk.

As a reward for being so attentive, I allowed myself a brief gratification, letting my gaze rove the silhouette of her shape. Her curves are subtle in some places, prominent in others. Her breasts are modest, their peaks contiguous with her chest. Her waist glides into her hips, their rounded corners enticing my eyes to her thighs, and below them, her calves.

It wasn't just her body that I found so enchanting. It was her personality, too, what little of it she'd revealed. I generally decide if I like—or dislike—someone within the first few minutes of meeting them. I guess you could say I make snap judgments about people, which, if I'm willing to admit it, probably accounts for my botched-up love life.

In any event, within the first few minutes of meeting Kendall, I decided that I liked her. She seemed so charming and...I hesitate to use the word *perky,* but it's really the most accurate descriptor I can think of. But she's perky in that way that's genuine, not pretentious. Not like those contestants in beauty pageants, for instance, who *have* to put on a happy face, usually with the aid of petroleum jelly.

Did my princess come? Finally? Am I through kissing frogs?

No, I'm getting ahead of myself. She could have a boyfriend. Or want to have a boyfriend.

I studied the inside of my locker door, regretting the lack of decorations. I should have tacked up some sort of gay-pride paraphernalia. Maybe one of those stickers that says, *Let's get one thing straight: I'm not.*

Is she?

Although our shifts coincided, Kendall and I didn't work together. But our paths crossed frequently. I'd wave at her, Miss America–style, from the Snow White float in the parade. I'd wink at her, conspirator-style, from my post outside Cinderella's castle, which sparked a few tiffs over territory with Cinderella. I'd smile at her, starstruck-style, from my seat in the commissary, where she sometimes entered flanked by fairies, who fluttered their wands and fawned over her as if she were the real thing. I'm not entirely sure what kind of signals I was sending, but Kendall seemed responsive, so I figured I was doing something right.

Over the next few weeks, Kendall and I got better acquainted. I discovered that we had a lot of mutual interests. However, I didn't discover if we shared the one interest that mattered most of all. She offered clues, at least, which made me hopeful. She never mentioned men. She never suggested that we go anyplace where we would be mingling with men.

She never talked about sex with men. But then, she never talked about sex with women, either.

After work, we socialized—dinner and a movie, as if we were courting. Then we'd hug and say good-night, and I'd continue the evening alone, in my head, with my hand.

The more time I spent with Kendall, the more I became imbued with longing, riven with desire. I'd envision her body lying supine on my jersey sheets, the ones that are bright pink, like bubble gum. Like her Sleeping Beauty gown. Except she isn't wearing her Sleeping Beauty gown while lying supine on my jersey sheets, the ones that are bright pink, like bubble gum.

Kendall squeezes my thigh and laughs, tilting her head back. "You're such a character," she says, and crumples her straw wrapper into a ball. "*That's* what you consider the downside of the job? The ban on nail polish?"

"It's not a ban exactly," I reply, shaking salt sprinkles onto my mashed potatoes. "It's more of a regulation. We're only allowed to wear certain shades. I used to put on all these really crazy colors, like Gator Green and Candy-Corn Orange. I miss that."

Kendall shakes her head, her eyes wide, as if she finds this fascinating, or maybe just frightening. "You're really unusual."

"Thank you," I return, sounding at once arrogant and in-dignant. "What about you, Kenny? What do you consider the downside of the job?"

Kendall leans back against the speckled silver vinyl of the booth. "I would have to say it's the role-model aspect," she answers. "I'll admit, it's fun having all these little girls worship me, even though it's not really me that they're worshipping. But then I feel bad about it, know what I mean? Like I'm sending this really awful message about romance and relation-ships and femininity and all that. I feel like I'm corrupting them in a way. A princess is supposed to be the epitome of elegance and grace and sophistication, right? But we're really just sex symbols, aren't we? We teach little girls that being a princess means looking pretty and wearing pretty clothes and dating pretty boys. Well, not dating, even. Marrying. They meet, they smooch, they tie the knot, the end."

"Kind of like a shotgun wedding, except without the bun in the oven."

"Exactly. And what's up with all the little animals, those little woodland creatures running around all over the place? Is that some sort of prerequisite for princesshood? Bonding with woodland creatures?"

"Actually, I think it's only a prerequisite if you're a Caucasian princess," I surmise. "If you're Asian, let's say, you have to bond with a dragon and a cricket. Now, I don't know about you, Kenny, but personally, I much prefer dragons and crickets to chipmunks and skunks."

Kendall laughs and nudges my foot under the table, the wedge heel of her espadrille sandal connecting lightly with my calf. "It's funny," she says, reaching into her purse. "We don't practice what we preach."

I want to know what she means by that, but she anticipates the question and answers before I even ask.

"Well, for one thing," she elaborates, sliding her plate toward the edge of the table, "we're not superficial. We care about other things besides our appearance. And for another thing, we're not straight. We don't care about guys."

I should probably say something, at least acknowledge her statement, but my mouth feels parched and my lips seem to have fused together.

Kendall smirks and leans toward me, elbows perched on the wooden surface of the table. "You think I never noticed you checking me out, Carla?" she queries, her pitch slightly deeper than normal.

"Um, no, not really."

"Did you ever notice *me* checking *you* out?"

"Um, no, not really."

"Well, I guess you were just too busy checking me out to notice me checking you out. I believe the word for that is *oblivious*." Kendall angles her head to the side, scrutinizing me as though she's suddenly noticed something that she never noticed before. "Let's get one thing straight, Carla, okay? I'm not."

Kendall's eyes move closer.

Her smile, too.

Her lips.

Close enough to—

I don't have time to react, only to respond, to touch her lips the way that her lips are touching mine.

"I've been waiting almost two months to kiss you," Kendall shares when we separate. "But I didn't want to rush things. I'm a very patient person. Patience is a virtue."

"Trite but true," I concede, relishing the zest of her kiss. "And what is a princess if not virtuous?"

"Ravenous," she replies, sounding and looking the part. I peer into her eyes, a glittery, glistening gray. They seem larger than I remember.

"That was, um, that was a rhetorical question," I stammer, the pulse of my pussy racing.

Kendall winks at me, conspirator-style, from her seat across the table. "I can't say the same for the answer."

"Oh, I see you're wearing your princess panties. May I partake of the royal pussy, Your Highness?"

"Please, be my guest," I enthuse, punctuating the invitation with a curtsy.

Kendall's fingers flirt with the lace of my panties, trailing the pale yellow netting along the waistband. I close my eyes just as her digits disappear inside the fabric, like a hand tucked into a pocket, the elastic expanding to accommodate her entry.

My body quivers as she approaches the stretch of cotton safeguarding my cunt, then deftly peels the panties from my torso. My body shivers as she kisses my navel, then teases the tiny knot with the tip of her tongue, shooting jolts and tingles to my clit.

I coax my eyes open, my head abandoning the pillow as I recline on my elbows. Kendall stamps kisses along my abdomen. The tint of her lipstick leaves rosy-red stains on my flesh, each a littler paler than the last.

Her lips melt into my cunt, her hands anchoring my tremulous thighs. She embarks on an odyssey from cleft to clit, etching hearts and spirals and crescent moons into the slippery ripples, singeing my cunt, tongue quick and slick.

My legs begin to twitch. I fan my thighs, moans gushing through my gaping mouth. Fluorescent colors coalesce behind my eyelids. Spurts of pink and blue, bursts of silver and gold. I seize the sheets between my fists as my climax detonates, propelling my hips into the air, curving my spine into an arch, like a stream of water exploding from a fountain.

I smile at Kendall, starstruck-style. Suffused with lust, I don't stop to catch my breath or give Kendall a chance to breathe. (After all, what is a princess if not ravenous?)

I wedge my hand between her thighs, my palm nearly mashing her clit into the pulpy pink flesh of her labia. Her limbs jerk. Her juices drizzle down my hand, slinking through the spaces between my fingers.

I angle my head to the side, scrutinizing her as though I've suddenly noticed something that I never noticed before.

My eyes move closer.

My smile, too.

My lips.

Close enough to—

She doesn't have time to react, only to respond, to touch my lips the way that my lips are touching hers.

And then, just as I'd envisioned, Kendall is lying supine on my jersey sheets, the ones that are bright pink, like bubble gum. Like her Sleeping Beauty gown. Except she isn't wearing her Sleeping Beauty gown while lying supine on my jersey sheets, the ones that are bright pink, like bubble gum.

Kendall giggles and jiggles beneath me, her hair flaring out across the pillowcase. She is all smiles as my fingers, wet with her excitement, whet her senses, overloading, overwhelming. I can tell she is close to orgasm when the muscles in her cunt begin to constrict, strangling my fingers.

Our lovemaking segues into the customary postcoital cuddling, and we hold each other, her leg draped over mine, mine draped over hers. I nuzzle her neck and inhale the fragrance of her soap, a blend of orange and vanilla. I tease her, telling her that she smells like a Creamsicle.

Her response is equal parts silly and suggestive: "Why don't you go ahead and lick me."

I go ahead and lick her, of course, because it's bad manners to refuse the demands of a princess. I take my sweet time, being very attentive to her needs, and especially to the creamy melt trickling between her thighs.

I watch my Beauty sleep. I contemplate kissing her, waking her.

My lips move closer. They touch hers, keep touching hers until she stirs and joins me.

"You're my savior from slumber," she gushes, giggling. "I am eternally grateful, forever indebted to you, Princess, for rousing me from this wretched state of terminal hibernation."

"Don't mention it," I say, and squeeze her waist.

She kisses me again. And again. Her mouth strays from my lips and wanders to my neck. Her hair, with its gently curving tips, like the petals of princess tulips, caresses my skin as she sucks and strokes, leaving damp, salty streaks on my skin.

"Hey, Kenny?" I murmur, already traveling toward delirium. "Fairy-tale tradition dictates that the prince and the princess live happily ever after. Do those same rules apply to us?"

Kendall lifts her lips from my breast and looks up at me. "Well, we're already...subverting convention, if you will, so maybe we shouldn't tamper with tradition any further."

Nodding in agreement, I pucker my lips, then press them to her forehead, just like Snow White kissing the dwarfs.

The saying's true, you know. You have to kiss a lot of frogs before you find your princess. And now that I've found her, I can kiss those frogs goodbye.

Unveiling His Muse

Portia Da Costa

"No! Not again! I'm not having this!"

Charlie Glenister slid off his stool and adjusted the fit of his jeans. Somehow he'd managed to get an erection for what must have been the tenth time in an hour, and it was getting ridiculous.

Why was this happening? Didn't he have any self-control at all? He was bloody miles behind with a zillion deadlines and all he kept doing was getting hard-ons and frittering his days away fantasizing and tossing himself off. There were already three publishers and a magazine editor breathing hard down his neck for illustrations and cover designs he owed them, and he was going to fuck up his reputation beyond repair if he didn't get his act together.

Bills didn't pay themselves, and there was no magic fairy godmother to cover his rent, so he was going to have to move on, squelch this fixation and stop getting the horn every time he tackled one single piece of work.

Fairy godmother…huh, that was ironic.

It'd started out as one drawing for a fantasy book cover but it had turned into an obsession.

It's all your fault, you bitch!

He strode up and down the best he could in his small studio, and with a raging erection. He tried not to think of her, but failed. Astronomically.

Her. She. The Queen of the Fairies.

"She" was an "it" in actuality, begun as bold ink lines and washes of color on a commonplace sheet of art paper. Nothing more.

At least it'd started that way, once upon a time that felt like a hundred years ago but which had actually been just a couple of weeks. A commission for an urban fantasy book cover that'd somehow grabbed him by the balls and libido and made it impossible to work on anything else. It was all so bizarre and ludicrous, and the powerlessness he felt would have unmanned him if it hadn't turned him on so much. He'd always fancied slightly dominant women and even now when he glanced at his drawing board out of the corner of his eye, his cock lurched so hard in his jeans it made him gasp.

No way! No fucking way! I'm going to do something else if it kills me!

Stalking back to the board, he lifted his pen like a dagger, ready to slash it across the paper and "kill" her.

But how could he destroy the best piece of work he'd ever created? How could he kill the Queen of the Fairies? She was his muse. He adored her.

Shit, man, I'm done for.

The Fairy Queen had begun innocuously enough as a seven-ink full-color cover commission, but now she was there every time he picked up a pen or a pencil or the stylus of his drawing tablet. Each time, she looked even more exotic, more lush, more totally and completely shagable. Each time he tumbled deeper into love-hate.

His pen hand shook and his knuckles whitened. What if he *could* hack this drawing apart? Would he be free then?

Would all the other images of her he'd created lose their hold over him, too?

What would it be like to just get on with his life and draw something else?

But he couldn't do it. Letting out an indrawn breath, he set aside his pen with infinite care, with awe. She was the source of all his trouble and all his pleasure, too, nowadays. Applying his fingertip to the periphery of one area of color, he discovered she was still wet.

In more ways than one, judging by the sultry knowing look on her face. Oh God…

Charlie's own arousal gouged at him. His belly felt as if it were filled with lead, and he had an urgent desire to double over and clutch at his cock. He was already moving, already halfway to flinging himself down on his studio carpet and wanking himself senseless while he sobbed and groaned and praised her imaginary name.

Clenching his fists, he straightened up again, fighting her hold on him.

The Fairy Queen was adorable, though. An unabashed temptress, the archetype of a high-fantasy heroine in the Boris Vallejo style, but so much more. Nobody would believe how much more.

Her figure was slim and graceful, nymphlike even. But he'd also made her deliciously large breasted. Far more so, in fact, than the brief had specified. The book she was to adorn was pretty much intended for a female readership, and such overtly man-pleasing opulence might not go down too well with the publisher's art department. But when he'd first taken up his pen to sketch out the character, those full, high, rounded breasts had almost seemed to draw themselves and his loins had roused immediately to salute their spectacular splendor.

The Queen of the Fairies had other clichéd sex-bomb attributes, too. A wild mane of brilliant titian hair, slumberous almond eyes and a wide ruddy mouth with a plush lower lip. Her skin was the color of cream poured over alabaster, her teeth were pearl-white, and she had the sweetest, cutest snub nose, too. Tonight, he'd dressed her more conservatively than usual, although the neckline of her gauzy, drifting blue gown did plunge to the vicinity of her navel, and display the milky, rounded slopes of her majestic bosom. She was wearing a complicated necklace, too, but the jewels didn't hide anything. The filigree network of twinkling stars and silver chains only drew attention to her almost overspilling cleavage.

Charlie moaned as his swollen cock leaped and stiffened even harder.

And he frowned at the same time, though not from frustration, strangely. He had that creeping, lurking feeling again that despite the Fairy Queen being his best work, he couldn't really take all the credit for her.

There'd been no working out what she was to look like, no trial and error, no rubbing out and starting again as there usually was with any project. She'd just swanned like a goddess into his imagination, bringing every single detail with her onto the page, no creative angst required on his part.

And see her, want her, that'd been it. Done deal. It was a good job he had his own studio or he'd have been hiding in the bathroom all the time to conceal his constant erections.

"Shit! Fuckety-fuck-fuck!"

He picked up his pen. He put his pen down. He sighed. Around the room there were scores of Fairy Queens taped to, pinned to and propped against every available surface in his studio. He was pretty good in most media, and she'd made him good in ones he didn't usually excel in. There was an entire gallery of her in an array of abbreviated, figure-hugging outfits, most little more than a loosely assembled arrangement of transparent veils.

And there were nude studies, too. Lots of them. He wasn't sure his cock could get any harder, but it seemed to when he looked at the unveiled versions of his muse.

Lounging with her sleek legs open, she looked ripe for sex, or fresh from it, languid and satiated. He'd even done one drawing just of her pussy. And without benefit of a face or the rest of her body he still knew it was her. She was wet and wanton in shades of red, hot pink and peachy amber. He wanted to kiss her plump clitoris, and sup from her mysterious shadowy cleft.

And that was the picture that had lost him his latest girlfriend, not that they'd been getting along all that well anyway. Karen hadn't been keen on his normal workaholic ways, but she'd hit the roof when she'd seen his drawing of the Fairy Queen's sex.

"That's gross! You're sick... I've had enough of this," she'd said in a cold angry voice. Unfortunately, she'd been sort of halfway to having sex with him in the studio at the time she'd spotted the drawing. He'd been eager to distract himself from his obsession and let off the steam of his arousal.

"It's just a drawing... A commission," he'd lied, trying to distract her. But she wasn't having any of that.

"You're a liar... It's *her,* isn't it?" She'd rifled through some other drawings, and Charlie had felt like kicking himself for leaving them lying around. So much for at least trying to be partially honest as a boyfriend. It'd turned around and bitten him in the ass.

You'd understand, though, wouldn't you?

What an extraordinary thing to think. He stared down at his latest Fairy Queen, and squinted. Was he imagining things? She was as sexy as hell, but there was a gentler look in her eyes somehow. A softer expression. He rubbed his head for once, instead of his groin, wondering if he was losing it even more than he thought he was already losing it.

After flinging aside the pussy drawing in disgust, Karen had thrown on her clothes and stormed out without giving Charlie any further chance to vindicate himself. Not that he could have done that anyway.

Where was that drawing now? Sifting through the dozens of illustrations on show, Charlie assured himself it was tucked safely away. He was expecting another female visitor tomorrow, and he didn't want to piss her off with it, too. Tania Richards was a fellow artist he'd hooked up with online, someone he was hoping to collaborate with on a few projects. He'd never met her, just exchanged e-mails and IMs, but she sounded smart and interesting and on his wavelength, and the examples of her work she'd sent him were startlingly good. Some similar in style to his, others quite different. They'd make a good team, he was convinced.

Tania was dropping by tomorrow morning and no matter how smart and interesting she was, it probably wasn't wise to leave a Technicolor image of another woman's pussy lying around at their very first meeting.

Back at his board, he added more red to the Fairy Queen's tempting slightly parted lips, a feature as erotic in his opinion as her sex was. They were full, and somehow had the look that they'd been thoroughly and hungrily kissed, although all Charlie could think about at the moment was sliding his cock between them and into the hot haven of her mouth.

His erection throbbed slowly, like the beat of a heart, as he imagined her caressing him with her lips and her tongue. It'd be like being gloved by heat and wetness, teased and tormented in a deep, sweet vortex of pleasure. His semen lay heavy, heavy, heavy in his balls, and seemed to drag on his belly. He'd have to attend to himself tonight, maybe several times, or he'd be walking hunched over when his new friend Tania arrived.

God, if only you were real, my Fairy Queen!

If she could rise from the page, become a living, loving woman, he wouldn't have to resort to lonely masturbation. She'd do it for him, as well as fucking him senseless. She'd take his tormented length between her long, dainty, lacquer-tipped fingers, and play him like an instrument, and then she'd offer him her alabaster-white body for his ease. Sighing resignedly, he pressed his hand to his aggravated crotch. It was looking depressingly like another night of very little work achieved, and he'd so wanted to have a few non–Fairy Queen drawings to show Tania in the morning.

But it was the old familiar story, he suspected. A night of furious wanking then a collapse into exhausted and troubled sleep afterward.

With a sigh, he threw himself into his favorite armchair and focused on the nearest image of his tantalizing muse—a marker-pen sketch he'd been particularly pleased with. It showed her topless and with just a wisp of silky folded fabric around her hips. Imagining her unwinding it in a private show for him, he slid down the zip of his jeans, then reached inside. He cursed when the ink on his fingers smudged the white cotton of his shorts, then thought, fuck it, who the hell cared. When he pushed down the shorts, his aching, rock-hard flesh bounded up eagerly.

Even with his eyes now closed, he could still see her. She was burned into his heart, into his soul. He closed his inky fingers around his shaft and launched into the oh–so–familiar up-and-down rhythm.

Pleasure gathered quickly and he paraded his best-loved scenarios through his mind.

The Fairy Queen doing to him what he was doing to himself.

Him pushing down her head, hand buried in her curls as he urged her to suck him.

Her making him do the same to her, commanding him to sup at her divine pussy until she howled and cursed in ecstasy.

Him fucking her and possessing her in every position he could think of and some that were pushing at the boundaries of anatomical impossibility.

He was making her do the things that he wanted in these fantasies, yet somehow she seemed to relish everything with increasing enthusiasm and vigor. She wanted him. She wanted to please him. And that made every move, every nuance of her supple, athletic body multiply his pleasure. She gave back ten, twenty, a hundred, a thousand times what he gave to her, and praised his performance in a voice that was a sensuous, drawling purr.

She was just urging him to "Fuck me, lover! Fuck me! Fill me with your beautiful cock!"—or something like that—when two different things happened simultaneously.

The first was his orgasm, a breath-grabbing, heart-wrenching rush that sent a long jet of semen spurting heavily onto the carpet. The second was the strident *bing-bong* of someone ringing his doorbell.

It took him half a minute to be in a state to even move, and in those gasping, shagged-out moments of descending back to earth the doorbell chimed several times more.

"Won't be a minute! Don't go ballistic!" he called, his voice coming out strangled and squeaky. As he lurched to his feet, his jeans slid down around his knees, and he had to spend more precious seconds grappling with them and stuffing his limp and sticky penis inside his shorts.

The doorbell bonged again imperiously as he was rubbing the carpet with his bare foot, trying to work the semen into it. "All right already!" he shouted. Hopefully, the tang of semen would be lost in the pungent, solvent-laden fug that always pervaded the room when he was working.

Snatching a couple more seconds, he checked himself out

in the mirror. *Ack,* what a mess. His hair was wild, his eyes were guilty and he looked like a hobo. A hobo who'd just been wanking. He was scratching at a patch of what looked suspiciously like dried semen on his jeans, when his visitor lost patience and the door swung open.

Charlie's jaw dropped and *he* lost the power of logical thought. His hands felt as if they were flapping at his sides, disconnected from his brain and all nerve control.

For a full half minute, he just gawked at the figure who stood waiting on his threshold.

"Well, are you not going to invite me in?" remarked the Queen of the Fairies, gliding forward and compelling Charlie to back up and back up so as not to impede her regal progress. "I thought that you would be pleased to see me!"

"But—" was all Charlie could utter. His mouth still seemed to want to hang wide-open in flabbergasted amazement. The door behind his visitor closed without benefit of her hand or his own and he was faced with his imagination made flesh.

She was exactly how he had drawn her. Every line. Every detail. And yet much, much more. Her body was lusher and more full than the paper version, and the gossamer-like dress that approximated the gown he'd drawn for her was barely more than a film of heavenly blue pigment that floated translucently on the surface of her skin. She even wore the complicated necklace of pearlescent stars he'd created.

Her face was perfection. An overused word, but he couldn't think of another. A beautiful, pure, immaculate heart shape, with skin that was as white as a dove's wing, yet dewy and all a-sheen with vibrant life. Thick glossy hair seemed to hover and float around her head in a fiery mass of many different shades of crimson, auburn and terra-cotta. While her lips gleamed with precisely the same singing rose-red he'd painted on them just minutes ago.

But it was her eyes, her eyes that froze him to the spot.

Huge, slightly uptilted, lined with kohl and sparkling with all the shades *he'd* used to portray them. Ultramarine, Prussian blue, twinkling flecks of mica-flecked cerulean.

"What are you staring at, Charlie?" she inquired with a sultry smile that was so familiar it made him want to swoon like a girl. "Did I not get it all right?" She paused, then slowly ran both her hands upward over her sumptuous curves until they reached her flawless face. Once there, she delicately touched her pretty jawline, her high cheekbones and her luscious lips. "It is all here, is it not? Everything you wanted?"

"Ye-yes... But..."

"I could explain it to you, Charlie—" she closed the small distance between them "—but it would take an age, my dearest boy, and there are so many nicer things we could be doing with the time."

Even as she was reaching for him, Charlie's scanty courage reemerged and he lifted a trembling hand to touch her.

The first place he made contact with was a full, sweetly rounded breast.

"Yes, my Charlie, that is right!" Encouragingly, she cupped the firm yet soft orb herself and seemed to push it into his grip. He felt her nipple peak through silk as he held her.

This can't be happening. I designed you. What are you doing here? There is no such person...or thing...as the Queen of the Fairies.

And yet she was here. Her body was responding to his, real and living and utterly sensual.

"Why not try both?" Purring, she took his free hand and closed it around her other breast. "Caress me. I am what you want. What you need... You are nothing without me." With her head tipped back, her throat was a long ribbon of alabaster. "Have me, Charlie, and free yourself from torment. You will be able to work again...and better and more successfully than you have ever worked before."

"But you're not real!"

Yet the words were a nonsense when her deft and very tangible fingers were already unzipping his jeans.

"But what do you understand by 'real,' Charlie?" Her words were soft, barely more than a breath as he gazed down between his outstretched hands, watched her open his ink-smeared fly and slip out his rigid penis. "What is real...and what is imaginary? I venture that you do not truly know, do you? You do not believe in yourself, and therefore there is little else you *do* believe in. Am I correct?"

She was. She was right on the money. Quivering with pleasure, Charlie nodded. Almost absentmindedly stroking his cock, the Fairy Queen continued, "But you must believe in something, Charlie, or life is intolerable. So why not believe in me?" She paused, then sniffed the air and smiled right into his eyes. "Surely anything is preferable to being alone with only your right hand to pleasure you."

The Fairy Queen knew everything about him, and he didn't think it was from stains on the carpet or the sticky residue that still clung to his cock. She knew him from the inside out.

"You have been playing with yourself, have you not?" Blue as the sky's vault, her eyes controlled and teased him, yet were deep with sympathy. She flowed out of them into an aching void within him, offering not only release, but a sense of forever, of happily ever after.

"You have toyed with this lovely thing—" slipping two fingers beneath his aching flesh, she jiggled him playfully "—and you have made it spurt your essence all over the floor."

Impossible as it seemed, Charlie got harder, and he watched, his belly a-tremble, as the Fairy Queen took hold of his plump glans and worked it delicately between her finger and thumb.

"You are a naughty boy, Charlie, are you not?" Her all-knowing gaze demanded an answer, so Charlie nodded as if he was in a trance, controlled only by her. "Wasting all that sweet nectar, when I am close by...and so hungry."

As she drew a long crimson fingernail thoughtfully around the tip of his penis, Charlie moaned softly. Then moaned loudly as his numbed brain grasped her meaning.

"What in heaven's name is the matter now?" Setting both of her slender hands to the task, she held his shaft with one, whilst flicking and manipulating him wickedly with the other. She squeezed and tickled at the bulging plum, then scooped up his thin, gleaming pre-come and transferred it to her tongue as if it were ambrosia.

"Please!" Charlie gasped, his hips surging and his shorts and jeans slithering to his ankles. His hands flexed, tightening his hold on her breasts. For a moment he thought he'd hurt her and she was about to pull away, but then she sighed and her body rippled in a long, seductive undulation as she rewarded him with a sweet squeeze, too.

"Please what, my Charlie?" Her breath was perfume against his tense, sweaty face, and between his chest and her stiff-tipped breasts, his hands were squashed. All the time she still manipulated his shaft.

"I don't know! I don't know!"

Charlie couldn't breathe, he couldn't think. Purely on instinct, he released her breasts so he could crush her closer, savoring the way she rubbed and pressed her sinuous torso against him, inviting the jab of his rampant erection. The blue veils of her dress ruffled and slithered against his belly.

"Patience, my sweet." The Fairy Queen inched away from him, adjusting her grip on his erection. "Trust me, Charlie dearest, and believe." Her voice was a whisper, and so was the soft center of her palm as she cupped it around his glans while closing her other hand firmly around his shaft. "Believe!" she commanded, working him with her fine strong fingers, dragging the velvety skin of his cock up and down, up and down, up and down over its stiff, blood-filled core. Like a demon goddess she pumped him, working him to a pitch of pleasure so great it was almost agony. With a broken cry of surprise, Charlie climaxed, his semen spurting into her slender, gripping hand.

His body racked by sobs, he struggled to focus. The Queen of the Fairies lifted the hand that had caressed him, drew it to her luscious rosy mouth and lapped his essence from it as if it were honey from the slopes of some sweet promised land. Knees like rubber, he swayed and staggered, then let his dream, the insubstantial illusion he'd created from ink and paper, take the full weight of his fainting body and lower him down to the rug alongside her.

Bing-bong! Bing-bong, bing-bong, bing-bong!
"Don't go ballistic!"

Disorientated and queasy, Charlie hauled himself reluctantly back to consciousness. How the hell had he ended up on the rug? He hadn't the faintest idea how he'd got there, and the floor was hard, and he ached.

Glenister, you bleeding idiot, kindly remember to open a window when you use these!

Frowning, he struggled to his feet and shook his head, jamming on the caps of a few stray felt-tip markers that lay scattered along the pen tray of his drawing board. He'd been tripping, because the room was full of fumes.

Bing-bong!

"Won't be a minute!" he called out. Stumbling around, he was almost afraid to pull back the curtains, and when he did, he cringed at the state of chaos. The room was a disaster and so was he, and judging by the sun so high in the sky, his impatient visitor was probably Tania Richards, who he'd secretly had hopes of impressing.

Snatching up a few of the most erotic drawings of the Fairy Queen, he hid them under some less explicit ones, then groaned as he turned his attention to his own appearance.

"You're disgusting, man…you're a freak." There was ink, paint and what was unmistakably semen on his T-shirt and jeans. His heart sank. He'd been clinging to the hope that whatever obscene activity he'd indulged in last night had just been a dream, induced by accidentally inhaling solvent fumes. But judging by the amount of spunk on his clothing, at least some of it had been all too real.

Jesus, I've got to get a grip. I can't go on like this.

He'd been lost in a lovesick wet dream of fucking and sucking and grabbing. Of using his fantasy woman's every lovely orifice, and slaking his sexual frustration on her peerless elegant body.

The doorbell rang again, a triple blast this time, and with a sigh of resignation, he went to answer it.

"Hi! I guess you're Charlie?" His visitor strode confidently into the room, black leather portfolio under her arm, apparently oblivious to the rampant squalor and odor of sex. "I'm Tania Richards. Nice to meet you."

Charlie stared at her blankly, rubbing his tangled hair on auto, the breath knocked clean out of him.

Tania Richards was a redhead. She had a porcelain complexion and clear blue eyes. She was even wearing a long, flowing blue dress in some kind of soft, floaty fabric.

"Hey, are you okay?" She studied him with eyes that were brilliant with suppressed laughter. He supposed he couldn't blame her. "I don't mean to be rude or anything, but you look really out of it… Is this a bad time?"

"No, it's fine. I'm okay." His face stretched into a nervous smile, or the nearest he could approximate. Surely, it was just coincidence… The hair, the blue dress, the rest of it. Crikey, she was even wearing a similar necklace, a kind of hippy-dippy Indian silver-filigree thing with a network of twinkling little stars.

And her breasts. And that soft, full, rosy mouth, that bitable lower lip. Oh, God, she was almost as beautiful as…

"Fuck!" Taking a wary step, he'd trodden on something sharp that was jabbing into his bare instep.

"I beg your pardon?" Tania's perfectly sculpted crimson lips curved deliciously as she unzipped her portfolio, all no-nonsense and business, and started taking out sheets of white drawing paper.

"Sorry about that. I trod on something…a drawing pin or whatever." With his eyes riveted on sumptuous curves defined by a thin veil-like dress, Charlie bent down to pick up the offending object.

Then almost dropped it again.

The room seemed to speed away from him, then rush back again, like some kind of optical effect from a movie. His blood chilled and his cock went rigid in a sudden, intense, almost painful state of arousal.

No! It couldn't be. She must have dropped the thing just now. It couldn't already have been here. And *she* couldn't be who he imagined she might be…

Tania Richards was simply a pretty girl who just happened to have lush red hair, sparkling blue eyes, truly magnificent breasts…and a rather dilapidated secondhand necklace that seemed to be shedding its components.

"I believe that's mine." Long, alabaster-pale fingers, tipped with scarlet lacquer reached out for the small opalescent star. "I knew I'd lost one somewhere around."

Paralyzed by her amused and hypnotic regard, Charlie felt the room do its disorienting, retreat-advance thing again. It was like he was drowning, sinking into the well of blue in her eyes, bedazzled by the floating brilliance of her amazing hair. Everything was there. The perfect heart-shaped face…the full, breathtaking breasts, the hard, dark nipples, the cute little dink of her navel and the delicate curve of her pubic mound, barely veiled but also defined by the wispy, gauzy layers of her gown.

"Would you like to see *my* drawings, Charlie?"

As her words dropped into the room like the notes of a wind chime, she tossed the pearly star onto a blank sheet of paper. Once there, it dissolved instantly and a manlike shape, etched in dusty lines, replaced it. A quick pass of her slender fingers, and details began to appear of their own accord.

Charlie opened his mouth, tried to cry out, but couldn't utter a sound. Before him was a very good sketch of a lean, disheveled, but remarkably handsome, young man with shaggy, tangled dark hair and a bemused expression on his face. His heart lurched wildly and his cock lurched, too, swelling even harder and higher inside his shorts. He stared at the paper in awe and disbelief, seeing the very face he saw each day in his bathroom mirror.

Within seconds every last feature of the drawing was complete and utterly lifelike. He stared down at it because he didn't dare look up.

"You see, even *I* need something to believe in, my sweet Charlie," murmured the Queen of the Fairies, her words thrilling and affectionate as she cupped his aching groin.

Always Break the Spines

Lana Fox

Fairy tales hurt. Believe me.

It started in the bookshop down Stoke Street, where I'd been handling the leather-bound covers. I'd always loved leather—the feel, the smell—and once I'd started touching the covers, I never could stop. I felt someone's breath on my neck and turned to face a stranger with wolflike eyes. He snatched the book from me. I gave a little gasp.

"You're a student," he said in a stuck-up voice. "I can always tell a student." He tipped his head and stroked along the cover. That's when I noticed his hands, with their long, pale fingers, and the way he grasped that leather, as if he'd like to claw it. "This book deserves respect," he said. "Little girls know nothing of that."

"I'm *not* a little girl," I said, "and I'm certainly not a student." (This was a lie—it was my first year of college.)

"Then what *are* you?" he said, eyebrow raised.

"I'm a customer," I snapped, "and I was going to buy that book."

He drew himself closer. He was clean-shaven, with graying hair, and teeth that were smooth and white. What big eyes he had. What a dry smile. He wasn't the sort of man I'd usually crave, and yet just standing there was turning me on. It was his severity that did it, and his rudeness perhaps. "But you're *not* about to buy it," he said. "You want to abuse it. *The Complete Grimm's Fairy Tales,* but what do you care? I'd refuse to sell it to a dirty girl like you. You'd no doubt break the spine."

I was at once so angry and so totally aroused that I ripped the volume from him, as if to teach him a lesson; but, being a step ahead of me, he pushed me to the shelves, and, snatching back the book, pressed a hand against my chest. He splayed his fingers above my collarbone—cool and dry, no sweat, no strain. "I *knew* you were foul," he said.

"I know your type," I told him. "Girls for you are either whores or princesses."

Lust flared in his eyes. "Correct," he said, "and you're hardly Snow White." Slowly, he raised the leather-bound book. I thought he might make me smell it. But in fact, with the flat of it, he raised my chin. The scent of the hide filled me, the cover dug right in. He glared across the leather, right into my eyes. "Foul girls," he told me, with hot, wet breath, "need to be made right." And he grabbed my waist and turned me, so I fell against the shelf. I knew we were in a public place—that this was his bookshop. I knew there were customers browsing nearby. But when he raised my skirt and slammed the book between my thighs, so the edges pinched my flesh…and when he pulled it out again and thwacked my ready ass…I knew (oh, God, I knew) that I was going to submit and this bastard, whoever he was, would be the best I'd had.

"I guess…" I heard myself whisper. "I guess I *have* been foul!" And with that, I reached for his hand and pulled the book against me. "Punish me, then! Do it. Make me *pay.*"

He spanked me several times, saying, "Never. Make. Demands." My mouth had fallen open; every part of me was drooling. His torture stung so hard that I realized what this meant: unlike the boys I'd slept with, this man was in control—that was why he turned me on, while the others couldn't. He stopped, suddenly, and gave a breathy groan. "Keep doing it," I cried. "Yes, you'll do it again!"

I felt him pause behind me, grab my jaw and twist it back so I was looking up at him. "I will tame you," he said quietly, "exactly when I please. I won't have you saying when and how. You will come back at ten and, if I deem it fitting, I'll punish you more thoroughly." Then he raised the leather book, which was damp from my sweat, and whispered, "Now it's spoiled and you must pay. If you touch yourself, just once, before I see you next, I'll know."

"You don't scare me…" I said.

"Ernest," he said, by way of introduction. And his eyes filled with heat. "Then, sweet whore, you'll suffer."

Believe it or not, I was shy back then. I rarely got angry, never snapped at strangers, didn't borrow books for fear I might abuse them. My own books were stored in order of height, in rows upon my shelf. But somehow, Ernest brought out my inner bitch—the one who longed to spit her gum between those perfect pages.

I went home, showered and touched myself *a lot*. I came several times, thinking of him. I craved his leather beatings and, of course, he knew it. Never before had I felt like this. To trust a stranger! And then to let him spank me and screw me in his shop! This wasn't me. It wasn't. And yet, it *felt* like me. Just a darker part: a "me" I'd never met.

I wore a flared skirt with nude-colored stockings and a silky top with nothing beneath. Hard and sly, my nipples poked through. What would Mother say?

The shop was shut when I got there, and I couldn't see

Ernest. My thighs were slick, I was so turned on. I knew what this meant. If Ernest wasn't here, I'd have to sink into the shadows and thrust my fingers into myself and rub my aching clit. I'd be hard with myself, till I groaned with relief. Too bad if anyone saw! I smiled when I thought of the fairy-tale book. Was I the little girl waiting for the wolf? I leaned against the door and idly stroked my breast, before raising my skirt and dipping underneath. I reached across my stocking tops, fingers creeping. My head rolled, as I blinked and moaned.

Then I heard a noise. A snapping twig. And there, beneath the streetlight, was Ernest. "You disgust me," he said.

My sex flooded as he strode right up. Then he pulled me aside, jangled his keys and unlocked the door. Still gripping my arm, he dragged me through the shop and hurled me against the counter. I fell clumsily. How I longed to be beaten with the fairy-tale book! "You'd touch yourself in the street?" he said. His breath was fierce. "Slumped in a doorway? Dear God, the bad girls stray."

"I'll be bad if I want to! What are you going to—"

He clasped the back of my neck in a way that made me arch, then thrust me forward so I fell across the surface. My nipples hit the wood. The pain was sublime. "You need another lesson from the Brothers Grimm."

I felt him up against my ass, grinding through my skirt. His sex was hard and full. I felt him reach across me, then pull right back again. Instinctively, I knew he'd got the book. "You make me want to fuck you, whore."

"Don't call me that."

He said he'd call me what he liked.

"Then do it," I cried. "Hit me with the leather." My mouth was moist and I couldn't keep it shut, my breaths came quick and fast. I was caught between his hard-on and the counter as he yanked up my skirt. His hands were cold as they slid across my cheeks.

"No panties?" he whispered. "That's wicked." I felt him shudder. He thrust his fingers into me and I let out a groan. His words rolled on a growl: "You need a lesson in morals." Then I felt the leather, and everything went still. "These are moral tales," he said, the book against my ass, my breath trapped as I waited for the beating. "The little girls who stray get eaten by the wolves. Whores are savaged, virgins are saved." He drew back the book, ready for the swoop. "So what are you? Virgin or whore?"

I begged him to find out.

At once, I felt him move—I mean, really, really move—and I knew the blast was coming and my heart thumped loud. The first slap was fierce, the second far worse, harder and harder, so my body slammed forward. He just kept going, the leather hard and fast. What bliss to be spanked with such force!

"I'll teach you some morals!"

I rolled and moaned as the pain burned. I raised my buttocks higher, stretched out my arms. "You're savage," I moaned.

"I'm saving you," he said, and, still spanking with the book, he reached round my front and cupped my sex. His touch was hot. His fingers dug in. Desperate for pleasure, I rubbed myself against him. He paused for a moment. I stayed stiff against the counter. Then he dragged the leather spine up my inner thigh and said, "Want me to keep going?"

I sighed. "Oh, yes."

"What's the magic word?"

"Please!"

He reached the book round the front of me and pressed the spine on my sex. It dug through my wetness and rammed against my clit. I fought for friction as I heard him unzip. Then I felt him fill me from behind. Oh, the pleasure of his cock and the leather! Now Little Red Riding Hood was truly being ridden, for as he thrust into me, again and again, he spanked me with his freer hand and made me cry out. I'd never been so sore, had never been so wet. His cries were low and wild. My body bashed and pounded. I gripped him deep inside. He shoved the book into my mouth and made me gnaw the spine.

"Eat your words," he gasped, but I was too far gone. The book clattered to the floor.

When a guy doesn't care if you come, it's always the ultimate letdown. You're well oiled and ready, but a couple of thrusts and he's through. He climbs off and quits, assumes you've had your kicks, and you're left there, working your poor, damp clit. But after all that muscle, your fingers aren't enough, and you only get a flutter like a faintly dying moth.

But with Ernest it wasn't like that. I was wickedly turned on. We slammed together, flesh on flesh, my limbs jolting hard...and when, at last, I started to come, the feeling swept me up. Now. Think trampling beasts, not moth wings! Think shuddering hooves and swords tearing at thick, wet vines. Oh, Ernest's sex inside me was punishingly good, pushing me so far I flailed around. And as I heard him come, and felt him force himself within me, I splayed against the wood, my eyes upturned. I gasped some crazy words and the world seemed to shake, and I came and came and came.

Afterward he bit my neck. "Feel punished, dirty girl?"

I laughed. "What a good book that is."

"All the better to tame you with."

He ran a finger down my back and kissed the nape of my neck. "Till tomorrow, then," he said, and I felt him turn away. I pulled on my skirt in the darkness. I was soaked beneath its folds. But I knew I had to leave—else the moment would be lost.

I gave a smile that felt new on my lips: the smile of one who knows. I would come here to be punished. I would come here for adventure. I would come here every night to be saved. And in day-to-day life I'd grow more rebellious: I'd borrow books from lecturers and always break the spines.

An Uphill Battle

Benjamin Eliot

"Mr. Bowman?"

Oh God. The clock said 11:35 p.m. No, no, not again. Zeke sat up, cleared his throat. "Yes, Mrs. Sheridan?"

"Ms.," she corrected.

Zeke swallowed a mighty sigh. "Yes, Ms. Sheridan?"

"It's doing it again, Mr. Bowman."

Zeke ran a hand over his face. He swore he could hear his brain cracking from the stress and exhaustion. This woman. This beautiful, annoying, infuriating, odd woman was going to be the death of him. "Can it wait until morning?"

"No, Mr. Bowman. It cannot. I cannot sleep. And if I cannot sleep—"

"I don't get to sleep," he groaned. "I'll be there in a few minutes. You know, if you just jiggle the—"

"I have jiggled the *thing* and it is doing no good. So please do come up, Mr. Bowman."

Zeke buried his head under the pillow to hide a groan. He mashed the phone back to his ear and growled, "Yes. I'll be right there, Ms. Sheridan." Zeke pulled on his jeans. His hamstrings were singing and his calf muscles felt like rocks.

He pushed his tired feet into his boots and pulled them tight. Grabbing his toolbox (which he would not need), he started up the eight flights of steps to Pine Sheridan's apartment. His fourth—fifth?—trip of the day? He couldn't remember. All he knew was if someone wanted buns of steel all they had to do was work for Pine. Pine would make your ass as hard as titanium if she could.

"And the damn elevator is still out. Perpetually and forever out, it seems," he muttered to himself. Talking to himself on the long flights up helped. He had made up songs such as "The Devil Is a Redhead" (dedicated to *Ms.* Pine Sheridan) and "Siren's Song" (which wasn't too bad) as he climbed. He had mentally rebalanced his checkbook and plotted out his running route until 2014. And every day, many times a day, he and his trusty toolbox got to trudge the long white staircases to *Ms.* Sheridan's apartment. Most of the time for her toilet. The forever running, running, running toilet.

"I have no fucking clue what is wrong with that thing," Zeke said to himself. "How can one woman screw up a toilet over and over again? From the looks of her, she doesn't even need a toilet. I don't think she's human. Beautiful but inhuman. Some kind of demon or ethereal being. And surely they don't need to use the facilities." He laughed softly to himself and realized he was downright punchy. Punchy from the phone ringing every two hours for the running potty that would not die.

"And it's thanks to Uncle Dom," he growled. "I'll teach you a lesson, boy. I'll show you what it is to be a man. Get your head out of the clouds, stop dreaming about music. Just man up! Being a good man and earning a living is an uphill battle, just like keeping an aging building running smoothly. Something you have to tend to. Something you have to work for!" And it was true. His salary was awesome. Allowing for equipment like he never could have afforded simply working gigs at weddings and the like, but the hours were ridiculous. They were 24/7. He was on call if he was in the building. Sort of like being mother to twenty small apartments. On some days that was a downright nightmare.

And then there was Pine Sheridan. Tall and thin with skin the color of milk. She had a spattering of caramel-colored freckles over the bridge of her nose. Her eyes were green like new spring grass and her hair was so shockingly red that it resembled some mythical flame all knotted up in a sexy mess atop her head. She was maddening. And gorgeous. Truth be told (only to himself on his lonesome upward trek), Pine Sheridan had starred in more than one of his lonely, tangled wet dreams. "But she is the devil," he reminded himself.

"True," he answered.

And what did she do, anyway? I mean, my God, the woman was home at the most ungodly hours. One day the previous week, she had called at seven in the morning, eleven, one, three and then at five. Six hours later, she had called at 11:00 p.m. and made him climb all the way up to the fourth floor again. He hated her. But he thought he was slightly obsessed, as well. That night she had bent forward to examine the chain attached to the ball float. The one that Zeke was desperate to teach her to unkink so he could stop doing stair-step-a-looza every day. When she had leaned forward, her dark blue nightgown had gaped forward and one perfect, pale teacup-size breast had been visible for only a flash. The nipple, the palest pink round of flesh nearly the same color as the tea roses his uncle used to grow. In his mind, for that exhausted instant, he had imagined turning her, trapping her thin wrists in his hand and taking that nipple in his mouth and sucking it until she begged him for something other than an unkinked lift wire and a flush flapper ball.

Zeke turned the corner on the fourth flight of steps, trudging ever upward. He shook his head to shake loose the image.

The last thing he needed was to show up at her apartment with a hard-on. That would be bad and entirely useless for fixing her toilet. He rounded the landing, boots slapping on the poured concrete. He hummed a few bars of his song and heard the bass beat in his mind. He'd have to put it down on paper one day. Play it for the boys in the band. "But for now, let's start the fifth flight of steps, ladies and gentlemen."

Goddamn, he was tired. And his toolbox weighed what? A million pounds right about now. But on he went, humming and trying to keep the image of that pristine-white breast out of his head.

"Mr. Bowman," she said, inclining her head. A strand of blazing red hair fell across her face, sliding the length of a high arched cheekbone. He envied that lock of hair for a mind-muddying moment. What would her skin feel like under his fingers? Better than the unpleasant inside of the toilet tank, he was sure. Again he wondered why he'd allowed Uncle Dom to catch him sleeping at the construction site one too many times. Why had he been that stupid? Not having the heart to cut Zeke off, Dominic had put him in charge of maintenance for one of his buildings. Dom called it a solution. Most days, Zeke called it a punishment.

She was staring at him. He cleared his throat and nodded. "Yes. Hi, Mr. Bowman. I presume I don't need to show you the way."

"No, ma'am," he said, and wiped his feet on the doormat. He tromped through to the very, very white bathroom with black accents and set his toolbox on the bath mat. He lifted the tank lid, grabbed the lift wire, gave it a jiggle till the little links fell straight, let it go. Then he watched to confirm that the tank began to fill with water. All as she watched him. When the water was halfway up the inside, he put the lid on and replaced her tissue box. She was blocking the door.

"All done." He stated the obvious.

"But don't you want to make sure? Stay until it stops running?" She frowned just a bit and somehow that made her even prettier. She looked to him like some mythical beauty who possessed powers to infuriate and woo men simultaneously.

"I know it's fine."

He wanted to tell her never to use her toilet again. Not even to *look* at the toilet. But he knew that was the fatigue talking.

"Really. It keeps getting stuck."

"I know. We'll figure it out." Zeke tried like a champ to keep his eyes to himself, but her damn nightgown was long and sheer and white. A bit old-fashioned for his taste—but damn—on her it worked. Playing into that ethereal-being thing. An angel, a fairy, a goddess. He shook his head. But his eyes were traitors, they skated over the bodice and found the twin discs of dark mauve nipples pushing at the thin fabric. Then (oh, shit) they slid lower and lower. Taking in a shadow he thought to be her navel and then lower, a dark triangle somewhat hidden by folds of gauzy fabric. *Somewhat* hidden. He felt his cock start to respond and forced his eyes away.

Maybe if he dropped the toolbox on his foot…

Saved by the bell! Or in this case, the toilet. It stopped running with a gasping sound and the sudden silence was deafening. Thank God. "There you go, Ms. Sheridan." He forced a smile into his voice. She led him out and even though he was sad to see the end of her fair form in that nightgown, he was desperately happy to be going back down to his apartment to bed.

He was dreaming it. He had to be. There was no way in merry hell that phone was ringing. But it didn't stop and when he peeked, the clock said 2:13 a.m. In big, red demonic digital numbers. Zeke clawed around, knocked the phone off the station, finally snagged it. "Oh, dear Christ, hello?"

"*Mr.* Bowman."

He didn't. He couldn't. Nothing beyond, "I'll be right there, *Ms.* Sheridan." And up he went. Jeans, tee, boots, box, trudge. Up he went. Up, up and forever up. Past the fissure in the plaster on the first level, the graffiti that kept bleeding through that said *Josh is an ass crack* with a jagged-lightning bolt. Past level two with the spiderweb of splintered glass in the window. Level three with the pink silk flower on the sill that no one would claim. And finally—*finally!*—level four with the wad of gum stuck on the ceiling so high up even he couldn't reach it without risking life and limb. Which he would not do for gum, thank you very much.

He knocked on 444 and waited. The door opened and there she was. Pine Sheridan. Who in no way looked like it was the God-blessed middle of the night. She was gorgeous and blushing and…what *had* she been doing? Again he shook the thought off before he could get wood. Not that he hadn't woken with his morning wood, but the Andes-like trek up the flights of steps had dealt with that. And the nightgown was different. Midnight-blue, silk, it clung to every damn curve of her. Hugging her so succinctly he could see the swell of her sex at the V of her thighs. He stared counting ceiling tiles to stave off the flow of blood to his cock. "Please, come."

That was what he heard anyway. Something must have said that in the staggering step back he took. She frowned, perfect pink lips turning into an upside-down bend of confusion. "Mr. Bowman? Please, come in."

"Let me show you how to do it. Please, Ms. Sheridan. At least until the damn company sends an elevator repairman. My ass is a knot, my thighs are burning, I think I'm getting sciatica." She looked both mortified and amused. He gave a beleaguered sigh and trudged into the bathroom to fix the most cursed toilet part in the history of toilet parts.

When it was all done and filling, he took a step back, right into smooth, soft, slippery...woman. "Maybe next time, Zeke, you can show me. But thank you very much." She was standing so damn close to him he could smell her peppermint toothpaste and feel the cool blow of her breath over his stubbly chin. He took a deep heady breath of her and smelled sandalwood and lemon and some kind of spice. Maybe cinnamon. Whatever it was, she smelled good, like dessert. Like a treat. Like something he wanted to eat.

"Zeke?" he said dumbly

"Isn't that your name?" She looked flustered then and he felt his cock getting even harder. Between the blush and the hair and the full lips and the clingy nightie, he was a dead man. He had to get out and regroup.

"Yeah. Of course it is. I just didn't think you knew that. Well, off to bed. And please, I pray your toilet holds out until morning, Ms. Sheridan." He swallowed a yawn but wondered how the hell he was going to sleep with an erection he could hammer a nail with.

"Pine. Please, call me Pine. Did you know it's Latin for suffering? My parents had no idea."

"I believe it," he said, thinking of the torturous stairs, but recovered when she looked beautifully stricken. "But it's perfect and unusual. Good night. Ms.... Pine."

"Good night, Zeke."

And he swore she was leaning in to kiss him, but he was delusional. So he turned on his work boots and fled.

6:47 a.m.

"Zeke?"

"Coming, Pine."

Up, up, up he went. His heavy, useless toolbox gripped in

his weary fingers. Climbing the never-ending sets of steps. Sometimes he daydreamed (hallucinated) that they unhinged themselves and lay flush and flat like a slide. Then he would slide all the way back to his apartment door in the basement. And he would have to start over. Never knowing when they would suddenly fold in on themselves and shoot him right back to the beginning.

Had he been a weaker man, he would have cried.

Early-morning light was shyly peeking through the cracked safety glass on level two. Pinkish-yellow light that should only be enjoyed from the comfort and safety and darkness of one's own bed. "Good morning, level two," he grumped. He hadn't even had coffee and here he was on his first trip up to Pine's apartment. For her toilet. The toilet he was thinking now was possibly possessed. "Maybe a sledgehammer would fix the toilet."

Level three, he stretched, his shoulders popping, his knees crackling. He was young, but even the young could get repetitive injury to joints. Did climbing the same sets of steps perpetually and almost without interruption count as repetitive? He was pretty sure it did.

And level four. Almost there. Amen. He raised his hand to knock, looking down into the pit of crazy turns all the way down to the ground floor where he had started. No wonder he'd been eating like a horse lately. How many calories was he burning doing that much climbing every day? These were not short, compact modern steps. These were old school, spaced, steep, narrow steps from back in the day when they, according to Uncle Dom, knew how to construct a building. Whatever the case, if he got one more cramp in his ass, he was going to scream.

"Good morning, Zeke," she said, and captured his attention. White capri pants despite the frigid February chill, red-and-white-striped socks that made him think of candy canes, and a white sweater with a dipping V-neck that somehow showcased everything and revealed nothing. No bra. His brain was working well enough to spot a stunning braless woman when he saw one.

"Pine," he said, giving her a nod. His voice sounded like a gasp. Like someone was slowly constricting the air from his lungs. Someone was—Pine! "I know the way."

He brushed past her but somehow her breasts, her belly, her hip bone raked over the sleeve of his jacket and he had to close his eyes and steady his breathing. He could not throw down a tenant and have his way with her like some caveman. No matter how beautiful she was. No matter how interesting. And annoying and…

"…coffee?"

Zeke blinked. Confusion, exhaustion and horniness all at war within his skin. "Sorry?"

She smiled. An odd kind of predatory smile that made his heart beat faster and his cock grow hard. "I said, it's kind of early. Would you like some coffee?"

He nodded and soldiered on past her. "That would be great. I'll just go and untangle the chain." In the bathroom, he froze. The tank lid was off, the flapper was stuck up like it was giving him the red-rubber-toilet-tank version of the finger, and she came in right behind him. He could hear music playing. Nothing he recognized. But it was good in a heavy-metal sort of way. And he didn't peg her as a heavy-metal kind of girl.

"Sorry." She handed him a coffee mug. Long thin fingers brushed his and he felt the touch shoot straight to his crotch. Zeke pinned the toilet with his gaze. Had to focus. *Don't molest the tenants.* "It's a demo tape. Not my cup of tea…or coffee." She laughed. Where was the former stern redhead with the pinched frown? he wondered. "But I have to listen. Musical taste aside, they have talent, don't you think?"

Zeke felt a bit poleaxed. Open toilet tank, coffee, niceties and music discussions. Had he died and this was the afterlife? Now if she got naked… He laughed nervously. "Yeah. They're pretty good. Especially the drummer. Wicked rhythm." He swigged the coffee, burned his tongue, hissed and nearly dropped the mug.

Pine winced in sympathy and took the mug from him. There were those fingers again. Soft and somehow electric on his skin. He sighed without thinking and covered with another wince. "It's so hot. I should have said." She leaned in, touched his lip and that was it. Zeke threw in the towel. He had an erection and they were just going to have to deal with it. He was a breathing human male being touched by a stunning warm woman and he had wood. The end.

"I…yeah, let me get that—" Trying to move to the tank.

"Shh," she said, and pulled his lip out a bit. Green eyes flashed with concern and she licked her full pink lips which brought to mind the pale pink bud of her nipple which made his cock even harder. He was going to die. Or she would have him arrested.

"But I need to get that water to stop running for you," he babbled.

Pine released his lip but not before dropping one single gentle kiss on the lower lip alone. In his mind, he took her then. Right there up against the wall. Yanking down her little white pants and whatever (God, maybe nothing) lay underneath. Spreading her legs, draping her knee over his arm, ramming home until he just couldn't stand it and they both came in a simultaneous explosion of orgasmic glee. That happened in his head while his tired eyes watched her walk to the toilet, reach in, jiggle the lead, release the flapper ball, return the tank lid and rinse her hands. She watched him, silent and intent, in the vanity mirror.

"You…know how to do that?" His brain was trying desperately to unravel just what the hell was going on. The charley horse that erupted in his left calf didn't help. Zeke started walking in circles and panting through the pain.

"Are you angry at me?" Her eyes were wide.

"No. I'm in pain. But you knew and you made me do those steps." The step-induced cramp grew worse and he bit back a groan.

Pine came at him, fingers out, and he flinched. God only knew what this woman would do. But she pulled at his mouth and ran her finger over the still-stinging burn. Then her lips. Then her tongue. He grabbed her shoulders, kissed her, pushed her away and started to pace some more.

"You are angry," she said.

"No. I have a cramp. The granddaddy of all fucking cramps, I'd say." He moaned, walked. Watched her small shapely ass as she bent to examine his calf. She touched the muscle that now resembled a rock and he hissed.

"I'm sorry. It's my fault." Her fingers dug into the muscle and he swore he saw spots. In the living room the CD player erupted with *Kill, kill! Die, die! Love, love. Bye bye!* Zeke wanted to throw his head back and wail with the pain but couldn't. Wouldn't. "Every time I called you up…" She trailed off, dug in harder with those fingers.

He really just wanted to lie down and cry, it hurt that bad. Or stick his fist through a wall. Or scream until his head cracked open. Instead, he tried to breathe through the pain. Whatever she was doing was helping a bit. "You made me come up those steps a million times," he accused. He wanted to be angry, but that sweater had gaped open and there was that pink nipple again and dear Lord, a perfect replica to the left of it. Wonderful, small, perky breasts completely displayed to him as she stroked and kneaded and frowned.

"Well, you're not very bright, are you," she said, glaring up.

She caught him looking and twin spots of rose-red heated her pale cheeks. But she didn't stand.

"What!"

"You are not every bright. I would think after the tenth trip up here you'd make a...you know."

"No. I do not know! A what? I thought it was just some bizarre punishment from the universe or my uncle Dominic for my being into music instead of finance or travel or construction!"

"Dominic is very proud of your music. He's the one who told me to pay attention to you. And I did. And I liked what I saw. And heard. But again, you're not too quick on the uptake." Her fingers bit into his muscle and he did finally howl. Goddammit, she had done that on purpose.

"He what? Why should you pay attention. What the hell—" And then it clicked. The odd hours, being home all the time, "demo" CD. She was in the industry. She was...what?

"I'm an agent. But that isn't the point. I think that you're, you know..."

He clenched his jaw and tried not to get angry. "No. I do not know, Ms. Sheridan. Sorry. Pine."

"I think you're very...attractive," she said to his calf.

"Oh."

Genius.

"I thought that possibly, if I got you up here enough times—"

"That I would catch on."

She nodded, worked her magical finger and suddenly the cramp let go as quickly as it had come. Zeke moaned again, but this time from relief and pleasure. Blood. He had blood back in his calf. Unfortunately, it was still in his dick, too. "But you didn't."

"No. Instead, I trudged up the steps a billion times."

"And didn't notice me."

"Oh, I noticed." He let out an ironic snort and when her eyes found his hard-on, it bobbed like a tuning fork. Her fingers followed, tracing him over the fly of his khakis and he thought he might just snap right there. Make his mental movie a reality. She smiled, stroked. Waited.

"You noticed what?"

"That you are infuriating." He closed his eyes, absorbing her touch but reliving every god-awful ascent up those horrible, steep, concrete steps. Her fingers slowed, probably stricken, he thought. "And beautiful." They sped up.

Her fingers moved like liquid silver over him and he felt her lips brush his jaw. He reached out, eyes still closed, found that red flaming hair. It was softer. Softer than he'd even imagined. "Go on," she said against the hollow of his throat. Zeke could feel his pulse jumping rapidly under her lips.

"And you had the most cursed toilet in the history of plumbing." She gave a soft laugh, but Zeke smothered it with a kiss. He allowed in only a slice of reality by barely opening his eyes. He took her face in his hands, pulled her in. Her lips tasted like lemon lip balm and coffee. He licked her slowly and pulled her to him. Now the silly white pants were crushed to the front of his work pants and he could feel her soft shape mold to him. His cock pressed to the indentation between her slim thighs and he knew he was a goner.

"It's fine. The toilet. I was kinking the lead with a pin," she confessed. Her bright green eyes were filled with mischief as she pulled at his worn leather belt. "Are you angry?"

He laughed. A long, loud laugh that shook him from his insides out. "God. You have put me through seemingly endless punishment with a pin?"

She nodded. Her fingers had maneuvered the buckle and the snap and the zipper. He frowned, caught somewhere between grateful and furious. Then her long gentle fingers closed over his cock, squeezed and Zeke said, "I forgive you. God. You are so very forgiven."

"I thought you would know. I thought we'd have been here much faster, Zeke. I thought by now I'd be listening to your music, at least." She had dropped to her knees and he struggled to keep his eyes from going wide. Shocked and gobsmacked were not the emotions he wanted to exhibit.

"And at the most?"

"I'd have had you in my bed by now," she said, pink, pink lips wrapping around the tip of his cock. She took him in and then she took him in more. Her small hand tickling at his balls, her breath tearing in and out of her nose. Zeke let his head fall back and it rapped against a small Manet print on the wall.

"I'm an idiot."

"You're a gentleman," Pine said, changing her tune.

"I'm a moron."

"You're a talent. Holding down two jobs, walking up..." Her lips touched the base of his penis, her nose buried against the thatch of pubic hair, her throat a molten nirvana. He fucked her mouth slowly, watching it now. Each inch sliding into her, his anxiety and exhaustion falling away from him.

"A million steps to fix your toilet." Zeke put his hands in her hair as she sucked him, watched them tangle in the mess of red and gold and burgundy locks. Her hair was fascinating, he thought, thrusting faster into her mouth. Her hair and her eyelashes, long and dark, dark red, sweeping her white cheek when she closed her eyes. She looked like a painting. An artist's rendering of what a beautiful woman should look like.

"Pine," he said, remembering it meant suffering. He smiled then, and pulled her up. They had time for that later. Much later. He wasn't facing those stairs for days if he could help it.

She smiled when he pulled her in and parted her lips for his kiss. Lips that looked much better on his dick than in an angry scowl. Zeke played out his movie then. Dropped the tool belt, let the pants fall and pulled hers down, too, on the way. Bare under the capris, she was shapely and pale. A thatch of red between her thighs. He kissed her belly, her thighs, tested her pussy with his fingers and she gasped.

Ready. Perfect. Wet.

Up against the wall and under her Manet. Some woman on a beach with an umbrella. He lifted her leg as he'd imagined, planted her small foot on the basin and separated her with his fingers. Pushing into her slick wet cunt until her blush deepened to raspberry and her chest was flushed with arousal. "Zeke. I think you've caught on now."

He made a noncommittal noise, comfortable now. In control. He fucked her with his fingers with agonizing patience. Watched her face, watched her eyes grow darker like sea glass.

"Please," she begged. Gone was the command and demand and annoyance he had heard on the phone and in person. Now he got it, she was annoyed at his ignorance. He smiled. Pressed to her. Pressed into her and started to move.

"Sorry it took me so many trips." He wouldn't last long this time. She was a tight, wet fist around him. A velvety clamp on his cock that rippled and tightened as he moved. He wouldn't last long, but she was right there.

"It's okay," she said, coming just like that. Her fingers locked behind his neck and her head fell back against the wall. Her hips pushed up to meet him, riding out that first orgasm. Her lips opened and closed until he kissed her. Then she pulled at him tighter as he thrust. Her hips rammed the wall and Zeke gritted his teeth to hang on. "I think you've finally got it."

Her pussy tightened around him and he pulled the sweater to bare the breasts that had starred in more than one masturbatory fantasy. His lips found her, suckled one nipple, the other, until she arched up under him. Clutched. Pulled. Came again. "Please come," she said in his ear.

He heard her saying it at the front door in the dark blue nightgown. "You said that to me," he growled. His body in control now, hips moving fast. Too far gone to find finesse.

"Yeah."

"I thought I heard you wrong." He bit her throat and she sighed. Pulling him flush and cinching up her inside muscles so he lost the battle.

"I know." She laughed.

Zeke rested his forehead to hers as he came. Her red hair a fire in his peripheral vision as he emptied, moving his body to soak up every flicker of their coupling. "God, you are cruel. You are more cruel than the universe." But he laughed when he said it.

"Sorry." They stayed that way. Locked together. Tangled. Eventually, she let her leg fall and he pulled her to him, kissing her at his leisure.

Pine stuck a finger in his coffee, tasted it. "Cold. Will you stay? I can make more."

"You bet. I'm not doing those steps before I absolutely have to."

She grinned. "That could be a very long time. My toilet appears to be fixed."

"Good thing, too. But it might be broken again soon. Which would require my attention."

"An in-depth project."

"An uphill battle. Keeping a place this old working." He kissed her. "Could take me days," he said.

"Or longer." She sighed against his lips.

"Or longer."

Moonset

A.D.R. Forte

"Let's do something kinky," he told her.

She looked at him leaning on the kitchen counter. She looked at the narrow leather band with a tiny gold padlock around his wrist, looked back at him and said, "Are you nuts?"

How does one do something kinky when kinky isn't even a something, but an unconscious fact of existence, as natural as breathing? What's kinky to a freak? Especially after seven years. Seven years. She liked that, a nice round, odd number with a middle that she could divvy up into clear stages.

The first odd, awkward years where they tried to adjust their lives around each other and around the lust that pulled them together like a couple of pins dragged by a magnet. Thrown one on top of the other whether they wanted it or not. Confused still about who and what they were.

The middle years where compromises got easier and arguments got less. Where the sex was still hot and it was still so new: this thing they'd discovered about themselves, even if it had lived in them all along.

The security of now. Of this knowledge that they were

adults and could damn well do what they wanted to. That playing house could be anything they wanted. It didn't have to be the pristine, sanctified domesticity they'd been taught. It could be raw and scary and bleeding.

It was still happiness.

She folded up her newspaper and brushed crumbs from her lap. "What do you mean by kinky?"

He smiled. It still amazed her that she reacted to his smile as she did: heart beating quicker, a blush and a smile rising to her own cheeks.

"Every full-moon night," he said. And he left it there.

"Every full-moon night, *what?*" she prompted. Impatient and ready to go because she wanted to be at the office early today.

He looked down at the abandoned newspaper and his fingers rubbed the worn leather of the wristband. She could see the hint of a smile still playing around his lips.

After a heartbeat or three where she fidgeted and checked her purse twice to be sure she had everything, he looked up at her from under his brows, fifties-movie-star-style.

"I can't say what. You'll just have to agree that we'll be kinky." He tilted his head up and looked her full in the face. "Can you agree to that for me, my love?"

She felt her stomach tingle, and at the same time felt her heart thump a little nervously. Unknowns were not a good thing. Whenever they tried something new, she always had to stifle the anxious whine at the back of her mind listing every dire possibility in ugly detail.

Forget something new. She worried each and every time that he would forget to stop her soon enough. She would watch his pale, sweating face like a hawk, trusting her instincts to know when he'd had enough, in case he didn't. Taking comfort in the fact that if something went wrong, she had a plan, her first-aid training, the phone easily within reach, a carefully thought-out process to follow, mentally rehearsed a million times over. Just in case.

How could she agree to some new brainstorm of his sight unseen? But time was ticking away. He had a parent-teacher meeting this morning; she had miles of snarled traffic into the city to face. Real life didn't wait around and she had to make a decision.

"Okay," she heard herself say. "Every full-moon night. You got it."

He came to kiss her goodbye, first on her lips, then sinking to his knees and pressing his mouth to the warm triangle between her legs.

"Thank you," he told her.

She grabbed a handful of his hair, rumpling it, and yanked his head backward. He winced at the same time he smiled.

"You know there's just barely a week until full moon," she said.

His smile widened into a grin even as he squinted against the pressure on his neck and spine.

"I know."

She wasn't afraid of admitting to nerves; she was afraid of the nerves themselves. Anxiety made mistakes, possibly fatal ones. *Please, Aaron,* she thought as she pulled into the driveway and parked, please don't think of anything too insane. Did he have any idea how much she worried?

She took groceries out of the backseat, bread and eggs and veggies, weekly replacement stuff. It was Friday, it was payday, and it was full moon. Chewing her lip, she jabbed the doorbell with an elbow because her hands were full, and he opened the front door, came down the step barefoot to take the grocery bags from her with a smile. To give her a kiss on the cheek.

She followed him inside, asking about his day, talking about

ordinary things as she took off her shoes and he put groceries away. Acting as if this was just another afternoon.

Then he came to stand before her and caressed her cheek,
studying her face.

"You look tired," he said. "Why don't you take a nap and
I'll make dinner."

Always so gentle, so utterly devoted, so addicted to suffering for her sake. And she *was* tired. She needed rest before
tonight, so that she'd be alert and aware and not prone to make
mistakes.

Upstairs, she wriggled out of her clothes and lay down on
the bed in her underwear, staring at the drowsy flutter of thin
curtains in the afternoon breeze until her eyes grew heavy.
Only briefly she wondered once more what he wanted.
Kinky. But how? Unable to think of any more possibilities,
of anything that they could do, that he could want that they
hadn't already tried, she gave in to the lulling motion of the
curtains. She slept.

She was sweating. The breeze had died, stifled under the
navy blanket of evening and she opened her eyes to a world
of shadows and silver and heat. She began to sit up, to roll
over because she'd been sleeping on her stomach, and found
she couldn't. Her arms and her hands were tied behind her
back. And what had woken her was a gentle stroking along
her spine, gentle fingers exploring between her legs, rubbing
the thin material of her panties against the already wet flesh
between her legs.

"Aaron?"

"Yes, my love?"

She didn't ask the obvious question, didn't ask why. She
only lay still, her heart beating so hard her throat hurt, and
enjoyed the touch of his fingers while she came to terms with
the fact that her ankles, too, were tied. Loosely. Enough for

her to walk, but not enough for her movement to be her own. She had learned to tie those knots, to gauge that length, and he had learned with her. He knew it all as well as she did.

Tonight, all the worry, all the responsibility was in his hands. She had given it to him, knowing deep down when he asked that this was perhaps what he meant and giving it anyway.

"I've been thinking about the moon. And about were-wolves," he said in his schoolteacher's voice. Still stroking, still playing, while her sweat and her juices soaked the sheet beneath her and her nipples throbbed, caught between the cups of her bra and the weight of her body.

"They change by the light of the full moon. Werewolves," she said softly because she couldn't quite trust her voice not to squeak. She could feel him nod, his approving scholarly nod. Without seeing him, she knew his breath and his body and his mind almost as well as she knew her own.

"Yes. Change."

He fell silent and his finger slid under her panties, slid into her wet opening and then slowly out. She shuddered and clenched her muscles, wanting to feel his touch in her again. Not daring to ask.

"The moon is all about change. It affects all life on earth, the tides, the cycles of life. And, if you believe in the werewolf myth, it changes the very nature of things."

His breath was hot on her neck as his lips touched the skin over her shoulder and his finger twirled around her clit before invading her again. Moving hard in her.

"But always—whether you believe in science or magic—the power of the moon always maintains the balance."

She swallowed hard; she couldn't speak, but she was thinking. "Yes. Yes and yes and yes."

She felt his hand withdraw and knew from his satisfied intake of breath that he was sucking her juices from his fingers.

She shifted in her bonds. Her panties were a torment and she wanted them off.

"Restless already?" he asked, laughing.

"Damn it, yes. I'm uncomfortable!"

He laughed even more. Then he rolled her over and helped her to sit up. She squinted up at him while he sat next to her, his back to the window and the moonlight. A male shadow, broad shoulders and strong arms. He was naked, all except for the cuff that she saw was still on his wrist.

He reached for something on the bed behind her and then began to cut her bra straps with all-purpose scissors nicked from the kitchen. He peeled the material away and her nipples puckered in the air, seeking touch, but his attention and his scissors only moved to her panties, slicing the thin material so that he could pull it away, rubbing painfully on her flesh before he threw the knickers on the floor. She winced and swallowed and watched him stand.

His cock was erect, deliciously so, and she longed to capture him in her mouth. Wrap her tongue around his musky salt-sweet taste. But as if guessing her longing, he shook his head and smiled. He stood before her and she tried to keep her eyes on his face, half in shadow, half in moonlight, but her eyes kept straying to his cock that she so wanted in her mouth, in her pussy.

"Up here," he said, amused reprimand in his tone, and blushing, she raised her gaze.

"I know, I know. Sorry."

"No, you're not sorry one bit. But that's why you're my love."

Something clinked in his hands and she saw what he was holding now. He fit the key into the gold padlock and turned it. The cuff slipped off and he set it on her lap, on her bare, slightly sticky thighs, before he stepped back.

She looked down at the symbol of his love and obedience and pain discarded.

"According to some legends, all one had to do to take the form of the werewolf was wear its skin."

She glanced up, searching for him in the shadows.

"It won't fit," she said, thinking of the cuff, but he shook his head.

"You aren't paying attention, love. The skin, not the bonds."

The skin. The wolf's rough, broken skin. Her nipples tightened and even in the heat, she shivered. She felt like a snared creature in her binding ropes as he helped her to her feet; steps unsteady as he led her to the window.

In the heatless silvery light she felt her skin burn and she turned wildly to look at him; saw the same feral light in his eyes, the same excitement. They had changed, as surely as the tides, as the wolf. They were, tonight, creatures of the moon, and she was his to tame.

She looked out the window at the trees bathed in shimmering pearl-white, at the fields beyond the house where rabbits and raccoons roamed, restless under the moonlight.

Her heart was pattering again.

"How much does it hurt?" she heard herself ask. "Wearing the wolf skin."

She was proud at least of the fact her voice stayed strong.

For a minute, he didn't answer. She felt him move away and then return, felt his gentle hand on the back of her neck and his kiss on her shoulder.

"There is no change without pain, love."

She turned to look at the strands of braided cord dangling from his hand, at the long handle burning in the moonlight, reflecting silvery fire. She'd never seen it before; it wasn't one of hers. Something new; something he'd bought just for her.

A laugh, strangled, burst from her throat and she turned away, shaking her head in disbelief. "Oh, my God," she whispered. She closed her eyes and tensed her body, still shaking her head lightly from side to side.

Her hearing picked up the whisper of motion, the whine of air sliced through by leather and metal. She thought, with humor, of what that sound meant to her. Normally. On any night but tonight. Tonight where it meant something entirely the opposite. In the fragment of a second between sound and impact she wondered at herself for allowing this. What had he said? It all maintained the balance.

Then she knew pain.

She gasped and staggered, but his hand was under her elbow, his body was there for her to lean against. He made sure she could stand before he stepped away again. But then he gave her no quarter. Before she could make sense of the line of pain burning across her ass, the second blow came, and the third, each harder than the one before. She whimpered and ground her teeth, but she stood firm, legs planted as far apart as the rope would allow. Far enough for her to keep her balance.

The blows came soft, and then hard, raining pain on once-smooth flesh, transforming her as she wobbled and concentrated on standing, on taking deep breaths between each blow. Listening to him reminding her to stand still, to breathe. Laughing through tears of pain in the moonlight that made everything upside down. That took her words and gave them to his deep, strong baritone. That took his cries and shuddering gasps for air and gave them to her frightened voice.

She was afraid; the terror of a wild animal trapped and in pain. Her heart beat hard, sweat wormed its way down her skin, her ears rang and her limbs trembled. She pictured red lines hidden by shadows and moonlight. Livid and raised on the shivering flesh of her ass, crossed by other lines and yet more lines. Etched deeper with every blow; flaying control and thought.

Yet her body fought the pain, desperately pumping desire between her legs, into her throbbing clit. Desire jiggled heavy in her breasts and nipples with each hit, every time she rocked precariously forward on tiptoe and fought to maintain her balance. Her cries were longing as much as they were fear, and she was on fire.

But she didn't worry. For not even one instant did she think about what she should do or shouldn't do or what made sense. She had become nothing but instinct and lust and agony, and beneath it all, her anxiety, her need to be sure, slept like a beast finally tamed.

They lay in the bed, in the dark, her welted ass touching his soft cock, both sticky from their juices. The pain throbbed dully, broken now and then by a stinging twinge from a deeper bruise. She could feel strength of muscle and bone against the back of her head if she pressed it hard against his chest.

"Are you all right?" she heard him say, and she smiled again to hear him asking her questions.

"Yes. Perfect," she mumbled through tired lips that didn't want to move now that they had been kissed and bruised into laziness.

She felt him shift, arms folding tighter around her body.

"In the morning…?" she asked as his body pressed gingerly against hers, careful not to hurt wounded flesh too much.

"In the morning the change recedes. Things regain their normal shape."

She nodded sleepily and rubbed at his wrist where smooth leather usually met her fingers.

"But tonight…?" she said, forcing more words out because she had to know.

He thought a minute or two.

"The wolf still roams until moonset. Until sunrise."

"Even without his skin."

"Exactly."

Another little pause where they listened to the sounds of the night. An eighteen-wheeler on the distant freeway, the chirpings and rustlings of creatures making the most of the remaining hours of darkness.

"This is why I love you," she said.

She heard the little growl in his chest, that sound of satisfaction when he knew he'd served her well. Devoted, as loyal and long suffering as a hound. No, as a tamed wolf.

In the dark, she smiled.

Contented, she slept.

Mastering Their Dungeons

Bryn Haniver

Gabriel says the most important thing he learned in college was that a really hot cheerleader can have pretty much anything she wants. I'm not saying he's wrong, or that it's a bad thing, 'cause in 1983 I was a really hot college cheerleader. Like most of life's important lessons though, that one had implications I didn't quite understand at the time. Still, it was fun while it lasted.

My fondest memory from those days involves crashing a game of Advanced Dungeons & Dragons. You know, the fantasy game with wizards, monsters and thick volumes of instructions, the sort of thing that could only be popular amongst nerds.

Why would a hot cheerleader crash a gathering of fantasy-role-playing geeks? In a nutshell, I had recently decided my boyfriend, as gorgeous as he was, was much too annoying to keep, and I was bored to death with the football scene. I was intrigued by the idea of a group of college-age students sitting around playing a game that consisted of little more than metal figurines and silly dice with lots of sides. I knew it was based on imagination and a bunch of rule books full of elves and goblins and swords. It could not be any *less* like football. I got wind of an AD&D gathering and decided to expand my horizons. Everybody's horizons, as it turned out.

So close your eyes and picture me as a college girl in 1983. I'm fairly tall, with blond hair, icy-blue eyes and a killer, twenty-year-old athletic body. It's the eighties, so make that blond hair big, with bangs teased upward. It's winter, so include very tight jeans, leg warmers and a puffy pink vest on top of a tight sweater. Okay, the photos make me cringe a bit now, but back then, I had power…

It was damn cold out, so I jabbed the buzzer again, my breath steaming. They'd better be here—I had walked all the way across campus. After the fifth or sixth buzz, the door finally opened.

A skinny guy with long, dark hair managed to say, "What the hell do you want?" before he really noticed me. Then his jaw kind of hung open.

"You must be Gabriel," I said. No response. "Your cousin said I might find you here," I added. I'd been fishing for something different to do, and one of the girls on the squad had a cousin that played Dungeons & Dragons a lot. This guy fit the description, but if he was her cousin, he wasn't saying anything yet.

"Can I come in?" I finally asked. "It's fucking cold out here." The language jolted him enough to pull the door open more, so in I went.

"Raven," someone yelled. "What the hell are you doing? Ditch them and get back in here."

"Raven?" I asked, keeping my voice low.

He looked at his feet. "Um, we call each other by our nicknames here mostly," he told the floor.

"Well, why not?" I said. "My name's Jenny by the way."

"I know who you are," he said.

A young woman burst into the hallway, words spilling out of her. "Raven, come on! We're still waiting at the Circle of Darkness and Dominus is getting pissed off." She stopped short when she saw me and flat-out stared.

"I'm Jenny," I said brightly. When no one said anything, I asked Gabriel, or rather, Raven, "Well, aren't you going to introduce us?"

"Jenny, this is Math-Girl," he said.

I tried not to laugh. I mean, she was small and wearing Coke-bottle-thick glasses, the sort of glasses you just don't see anymore, but still: Math-Girl?

"They call you Math-Girl?" I finally said.

"We call each other by our nicknames here," she said defiantly.

I shrugged and smiled. "Well, why not?" I said. "Lead on. I can't wait to meet Dominus."

It turns out I probably could have waited. The final member of their fantasy trio was solid looking and oozed attitude, which reminded me too much of football. When we got to the room, he proceeded to browbeat both Raven and Math-Girl ferociously, telling them their characters were going to die horrible deaths if they didn't take the Circle of Darkness more seriously. He spoke like an irritable drill sergeant and clearly had control issues.

He stopped when he saw me, though. "What is SHE doing here?" he asked no one in particular.

No one answered, so I said, "I'm here to play a game."

He sneered. "This isn't checkers. You can't just jump in. These two have advanced characters, and they're about to attempt an extremely difficult challenge."

"Right," I said. "The Circle of Darkness, I presume." I smiled at his reaction. "But that's okay," I continued. "I don't want to play *that* game." I wanted to try something different, and a friend of a friend had suggested fucking someone with a strap-on. I think she was just being outrageous, but after that, I started having fantasies about it. Pretty soon I was dreaming about fucking a room full of people with a strap-on. Finally, I went out and bought a strap-on.

Now fucking a room full of people with my new attachment seemed a bit unlikely, but to tell the truth, one of the reasons I wanted to crash a D&D party was that I figured I could use my body and my popularity to get these kids to do just about whatever I wanted. And I wanted to fuck them.

Dominus, Math-Girl and Raven were all looking at me expectantly. I'm sure it was strange enough to have an A-list cheerleader in their midst, but if I didn't want to join their world of magic and multisided dice, why was I here?

"I'd like to have sex with each of you," I said, thoroughly enjoying their expressions.

"Sure!" said Dominus, probably hoping to get into me before I changed my mind. "Bedroom's right over there—I'll go first."

Raven was unreadable, but Math-Girl gave me a puzzled look. "You want to have sex with *me?*" she asked somewhat plaintively.

I stood and stretched a bit, letting my tight jeans and sweater speak for a moment or two. Then I said, "I should probably be a bit more specific." I plopped my Chanel handbag down and pulled out a harness, a medium-size pink dildo, a tube of lubricant and a box of condoms. I placed each item somewhat carelessly down in the middle of their game. My sexual accoutrements looked decidedly out of place amidst their strange dice, the little metal figurines and the rule books. All three of them stared.

"Holy shit," Raven whispered.

"You want to fuck our asses with that?" Dominus said. "That's what you mean by having sex?" His face was quite expressive, and I watched disbelief, disappointment and then anger all scroll across it. Finally, he said, "No fucking way!"

Math-Girl didn't say anything. Her eyes just went back and forth from the dildo to me.

"Tell you what," I said. "No matter what happens, I get to fuck each of you." I leaned over the table and picked up the die with the most sides, studying it for a second or two. "But afterward, if you roll, say, sixteen and up on this twenty-sided die, then *you* get to fuck me." I rolled it—it came to fourteen. I shrugged. "What do you think?"

They were all looking at me intently, their eyes betraying a variety of emotions. I wasn't a plus-four wizard, but it was time to unleash some of my magic. I pulled my sweater over my head, standing before them in tight jeans and a white bra. I shook my mane of blond hair. I unbuttoned the top of my jeans.

"I'm in," said Raven softly. I smiled at him.

I walked over to where Math-Girl was sitting. I leaned over and gently pulled her glasses off. Her eyes, still big, remained fixed on mine as I kissed her.

"What's you're real name?" I asked.

"F-Flora," she stammered softly.

I moved my lips to her ear. "Flora, will you offer your beautiful body to me?" I breathed. She shuddered.

"Yes," she whispered, her voice almost imperceptible. I slipped my tongue into her ear and she shuddered again. "Take me any way you want," she said, louder this time.

The hell with wizards, I felt like a god as I walked over to Dominus. "And what's *your* real name?" I asked him. He didn't reply, his face defiant.

I stood right in front of him and peeled off my jeans. I spun, a vision of youthful grace, beauty and power. I often wish I could watch my performance on video now, over twenty years later. I stared at him and could practically read his thoughts—while he was very unsure about letting me fuck him, he knew damn well this was his only shot at a woman like me in the real world.

"My name is Dave," he finally said, his defiance gone. I felt triumphant. My body and the force of my personality had vanquished their fantasy world. In Dave's imaginary dungeons he was the master, but here in the real world, in a dorm room in 1983, he was willing to let me fuck him. Awesome.

"So who's first?" I asked playfully. When no one answered, I picked up another one of the dice on the table. This one appeared to have twelve sides. Using as deep and serious a voice as I could, I intoned, "Dominus, 1 to 4. Math-Girl, 5 to 8. Raven, 9 to12."

I guess they were used to this sort of thing, because all three of them leaned forward and watched as I rolled, their eyes fixed on the tumbling die. A ten showed up, and everyone turned to look at Raven. He shrugged, but I could see the apprehension in his soft eyes.

"How are we going to do this?" he asked.

I walked up to him and turned around. "Undo my bra, then take off your clothes," I said. I watched the other two as Raven fumbled a bit with the hook in the back. When my breasts popped free, Dominus Dave's eyes seemed to glaze over. Math-Girl Flora tried to look away, but when I walked back to the table and began to put the harness and dildo on, she was watching just as intently as the other two.

By the time I put a condom on the dildo and turned around, Raven was completely naked. For a second, I wasn't sure what to do next, after all, I'd never done this before. I'd worn the harness and dildo at home, but I'd never actually fucked anyone with it. I was standing in the center of a strange room, wearing only white panties and a strap-on, and there was a skinny, naked young man in front of me. Nearby, his friends were watching.

Let the games begin, I thought, and motioned him to the couch. I picked up the lube and caught up with him, grabbing his shoulder and spinning him for a kiss. Up close, those dark eyes of his were quite captivating, but I wasn't about to become a captive. I spun him back around, bit the back of his neck and pushed him forward.

The other two watched me lube up as if it was the most interesting thing they'd ever seen, and how could it not be? I reveled in their attention, slopping the excess onto Raven's pale ass, grinning at his intake of breath. Holding his narrow hips, I moved in closer.

It was easier than the first time I had anal sex, that's for sure. It was like he trusted me right away. There was a brief moment of resistance, then he relaxed and in I went. Flora made the loudest noise of anyone, a long "Ooooo" as the dildo disappeared completely.

Though I was tender enough at first, I couldn't resist grabbing that long, glossy dark hair of his and pulling his head back. Keeping one hand on his hip, I gave him some deep, steady thrusts. It was kind of sweet how quickly he came. He turned to look at me as it happened, his eyes first fixing on my bouncing boobs, then meeting my own the moment his whole body began shuddering. I took him through what seemed to be a powerful orgasm, and I felt like the Queen of the World.

I was putting a fresh condom on when he recovered enough to roll the big die. He needed a sixteen or higher to fuck me, and we all watched very closely. A four came up. I have to admit, I was half relieved and half disappointed. I was on a power trip, and didn't want to relinquish a fraction of it. Still, there was something sweet and sexy about this quiet, skinny guy.

Enjoying being the center of attention again, I picked up

the twelve-sided die. "Now you're 1 to 6," I said to Flora, "and you're 7 to 12," I finished for Dave. It came up five.

Flora closed her eyes, sighed softly and began to remove her clothing. She was all curves, and under her baggy sweatshirt were surprisingly large breasts.

"Look at me, Flora," I said, standing in front of her. My panties were wet now, but I left them on. I flexed some muscle. Cheerleading can be quite demanding, and I was strong. I reached down and stroked my dildo, putting on a show.

"How—how do you want me," Flora whispered. I had a startling thought. We were all juniors or seniors in college, but was this girl a virgin? Oh, my God—I didn't want to take her virginity this way. Did I? Power trip or not, waves of conflicting emotion ran through me. I stepped right up to her and whispered in her ear.

"You're not a virgin, are you?" I asked. I put my ear to her lips.

"N-no," she whispered back. "At least, not in my—my pussy."

For some reason, the difficulty she had saying the word made me want to make sweet, gentle love to her. I stepped back. "Bedroom," I said.

Dave went in first, clearing the bed off. Gabriel followed. I knew they wanted to watch, I wanted them to watch, and I think Flora did to. She had watched me fuck Gabriel intently enough.

I grabbed her hand and led her to the bed. "On your back," I said, and she settled down. "Open your legs," I said, still standing. She opened them, quite wide, her eyes never leaving mine. I knelt on the bed and touched her—there would be no need for the lube. Moving into position, I opened her gently with my fingers and she groaned.

I took her like my best lovers had taken me, with a mix of

tender compassion and animal lust. Our skin got warm, then hot, and our fragrances mingled and filled the room. The boys were dead silent, fascinated, probably absorbing how to do it right. When I couldn't take it anymore, I lifted Flora's leg, positioned it so each of us was grinding the other's clit, and I fucked her for all I was worth. Quiet little Math-Girl got remarkably loud, yelling and thrashing as if electrified. I let myself come, just a little, as she came big for the second time.

We all walked back to the main room for the next roll. A good orgasm suited Flora well. Her skin was flushed and warm looking, her dark nipples erect. She had put her glasses back on, but didn't bother with any of her clothing. Moving to the table, she picked up the twenty-sided die.

She rolled an eighteen. Again, I had mixed feelings. Under different circumstances, I would be delighted to let her fuck me, but I really was in dominant mode. I didn't have to think about it long though, because she asked, "Can I fuck Dave instead?"

"What!" said Dave, his voice a bit hysterical. "No way!"

Flora was looking from me to him, her face defiant. There was obviously something between these two. I wondered if he was abusing his power as dungeon master. Did she like him? Or was this her way of getting some payback? Whatever it was, I wanted to make it happen.

"Sure," I said. "You can take my turn." Dave was shaking his head. "I'll jerk you as she does it," I offered. "C'mon, Dominus—two women? You can't resist that."

He looked confused. "Well, yeah, but…"

I grinned. "You won't have to tell it exactly the way it happened," I said, walking right in front of him. My nipples were stiffening. I was digging the idea of watching Flora fuck this guy. Dave's eyes went straight to my breasts and he looked mesmerized.

I unbuckled the harness and handed it to Flora. "A threesome with two babes in college," I said huskily, thumbing my nipples. "You'll be telling this story for decades." Out of the corner of my eye I saw a grinning Raven helping Flora attach the dildo.

Dave seemed paralyzed as I undid his jeans. "Well, yeah, but..." he whispered.

"Drop 'em and lean over," I said.

I felt a different sort of power as I held him in place while Flora got behind him. I positioned him right against the table that their game was on—his upper body sprawled across the map. Flora yanked his underwear down just enough—his jeans stayed pooled around his feet. Raven, still grinning, squirted some lube onto the dildo for her. She guided it to Dave's opening and he whimpered but kept still when I tightened my grip.

Slowly, firmly, she pushed.

"No," he said, squirming. "It won't fit. I can't..."

"Relax," I told him. I was feeling very strong, and held him fast. "Don't fight it. Push back, let her in."

He stopped moving, but his knuckles were white on the table. Flora kept pushing.

Dave's voice came in guttural gasps. "Careful—gently—slow—wait, oh, Christ," he said as she moved deeper and deeper.

When her hips met his ass, she stopped and said, "Who's the master now?"

"Shut up," he said, but I could see him stiffening. He changed position a bit, settling more of his weight onto the table. He moaned as she began to withdraw, but was silent as she thrust back in. Slowly, Flora picked up the pace.

It wasn't long before she was really going for it. Her eyes were intense, and she had him by the hips now, pumping hard. From his expression, he was lost somewhere in the foggy land between pain, pleasure and shame, and not sure how to get out. Little wizards and elves were bouncing onto the floor from the cluttered table. I squeezed some of the lube into my hand and reached underneath the two of them, finding his half-erect cock.

I got the rhythm pretty quick, matching my strokes to Flora's thrusts. In my fingers, Dominus Dave got harder and harder—I slowed down when I realized he was going to come.

Dave didn't look so pained or shamed anymore—he just looked blissed out. I put one hand on Flora's ass, stopping her. Moving the other slowly over his dick, I said, "Tell her you want it."

He shook his head and I squeezed, grinning as I watched Flora lick her lips. There was a sheen of sweat on her face, and her chest was flushed from the effort, but she held still.

"Tell her," I said, "and we'll finish you." To make the point, I ran my slippery fingers down the length of him, and there was considerable length now that she had stopped—he was huge and throbbing. I moved the other hand between Flora's cheeks and pressed a finger into her sopping folds. She twitched, and Dave moaned.

"I want it," he said, his voice husky.

Flora let out a low growl, grabbed his hips firmly and began to thrust. Like a traffic cop in a busy intersection, I kept a hand on each of them, directing the action. Dave came first, spurting all over the floor before collapsing onto the table. I moved behind Flora and stuck two fingers into her. She ground her clit against the base of the dildo as she fucked Dave, who had become completely passive and was making soft O sounds with each thrust. When I bent my fingers just the right way Flora came, shuddering down across Dave's back.

I stepped back to survey my handiwork. Their game table was leaning precariously underneath them, and there were books, figurines, dice and bits of paper everywhere. The room smelled of fresh sweat and a whole lot of passionate body fluids. I was very pleased with my contribution to their fantasy world.

I heard Gabriel step up beside me. "Awesome," he said, and I nodded happily. When he had recovered enough to stand, Dave ended up rolling a nine, but didn't seem to mind.

Does power corrupt? It turned out a hot cheerleader with the right attitude could do amazing things to a group of lesser mortals. I left that gathering feeling quite impressed with myself. Of course, neither cheerleading nor youthful beauty last forever, and I learned a whole lot more sobering life lessons shortly after I graduated. Still, that was a hell of a time.

I was an active woman, I still am, so I never did get into fantasy-role-playing games, at least not the kind with dice and dungeon masters. But good sex can be more powerful than a cheerleader even, and my little power trip ended up having quite an impact. More than twenty years later I'm still having good sex with Raven, though his long hair is long gone and I call him Gabriel, or dear, or Dad if the kids are in the room. We still get together with Flora and Dave, usually for dinner and a game of cards. Just the cards, no hanky-panky.

Sometimes, when the game is going my way, I'll catch all three of them looking at me, their eyes distant. I like to think they're remembering me wearing only a dildo and a pair of wet panties, rolling their colorful dice to see who's next.

A Taste for Treasure

T.C. Calligari

There once was a tailor whose only treasures were his three sons and the nanny goat that had been his long-dead wife's. The goat was fed well because it supplied the family with milk.

The eldest son, a tall lad with raven-dark hair often took the goat to pasture. James was known for his good-humored tricks and many called him Jimbo. One day Jimbo and the goat strolled to a meadow ringed with daisies, and air so crisp it nearly chimed. After grazing all day, Jimbo gathered his crook and the goat, saying, "Well, goat, have you fed enough?"

The goat answered, "Enough, enough, I'm very well stuffed. Meh, meh," and shook its silvery head.

James looked for one of his brothers pulling a trick, but when he found none he led the goat home.

When they arrived, his father looked up. "Well, son, has the goat fed well?"

James smiled. "Indeed, Father, she has."

The tailor smiled at his goat, their white beards nearly matching. "Ah, goat, you have fed well."

The goat gave a little leap, replying with its gravelly voice,

"I am not stuffed. The leaves and grass were far too rough. Meh, meh…"

The tailor glared at James and grabbed up a willow switch. "Liar!" he roared. "You would let her starve." In a rage, he beat his son and drove him from the house.

The next day, the second son, a stout lad with auburn hair and eyes that mirrored a placid lake, took the goat to feed. Jon strolled, never one to hurry, and eventually spied the same lovely meadow with the daisy circle. He led the goat within and took a long nap.

But on return, the enchanted goat proved to be as ornery and the tailor drove his second son from his home.

The next day, quite alone, the youngest son led the goat in search of a verdant pasture. Eric had hair as bright as a coin. Where the girls had teased Jimbo and laughed at Jon, they shyly eyed Eric for he was broad shouldered with green eyes that flared like emeralds and shards of topaz.

He led the goat to the same enchanted glade and watched astutely. But it was as before and Eric, too, was ousted from his home.

Jimbo traveled far and wide, taking work with a carpenter. When he was done with his apprenticeship, his master gave him a magic stick.

Jon wandered a few long miles and took work with a rancher, herding cattle and horses and learning their care. When he left, the rancher gave him a magic riding crop.

Eric traveled the farthest of all three, meeting a wiry, gray-haired tinker along the way who taught him to repair items from pots to wheels, to whittle wood, sing and play, spot a good deal from a dishonest one and many other tidbits of knowledge. When Eric reluctantly left, the tinker patted his shoulder and said, "Most of the treasures you need are in your head. But I'll give you this enchanted cot, for it may serve you well along the road."

★ ★ ★

Many folk compared Lorilei to fire. Her luxuriant coils of hair caught the russet and burnished gold tones of autumn and held them. Lorilei was a season, when the best of summer's abundance is still evident, colors growing rich and deep, bleeding together, with a hint of change hidden beneath the firmament. Any weary wayfarer sitting in her inn perked up at the scents of cinnamon and apples that seemed as much a part of her as her rich laugh. Her azure eyes reflected the nearby alpine lake, and a spray of red freckles over her nose and cheeks gave her impish charm. Many a man eyed the sensuous sweep of her hips and luscious bosom, commenting that she was meant to be loved.

Those few who knew her for more than an innkeeper saw her as far more than fire. Flame is one element, a simple dimension in itself, but Lorilei was like the earth. At times she became as tumultuous as a volcano or as unsettling as an earthquake. Yet she could be as gentle as the tender shoot lifting its head to the sun.

Traffic steadily crossed the little inn between two mountain passes. Lorilei had her pick of lovers, and had once even bedded a prince, curious to see how he compared to shepherds and farmers. When it came down to sweat and flesh there was little difference. He had pleaded with her to be his princess or at least his mistress, but Lorilei knew she was better suited to the country than a court built on coyness and demeanor. She loved hearing news from travelers passing through her small domain.

Beyond all else, Lorilei loved magic. The rarest of treasures, it was elusive in a world where few still believed and fewer found it. Her charms fulfilled most men's desires and were so memorable that with little coaxing she often gained enchanted items.

She possessed a carved ruby bird that sang in sunlight, a fan that whisked soft breezes when commanded, a magic pillow always scented with fresh-cut lavender and an enchanted rooster crowing only at the hour she wished. There were other small trinkets: a peculiar painting of a mermaid that was always wet in the morning, and one or two pieces of unknown use. Lorilei pulled them out from time to time, to gaze upon their mysteries. She grew quiet and introspective when magic became scarce and even the most handsome man might go unnoticed.

One day, Lorilei washed the linens, humming as swallows swooped over the inn. She saw a young man striding up the path, carrying a small pack. He bowed gallantly when he saw her, his sensual mouth holding a smile that reflected a humorous glint in his eyes.

"Greetings, fair lady," said Jimbo, brushing back the wings of his black hair. "I am on my way to visit my father and need a room for the night."

Like a bloodhound, Lorilei sniffed the air, sensing something different, and replied, "Come right in. I'll fix dinner soon and you can tell me of your adventures. Two ales on the house if you do."

In no time Jimbo settled in at a table with a few locals in the lanterns' golden glow. His tales had everyone laughing or giving him a friendly slap on the back. Then Lorilei quivered, alert as a hare under an eagle's glare, when Jimbo said, "When I took my leave of the carpenter, he gave me a magic stick and told me to say, 'Stick, stick, show me your tricks.' I've tried it and although the stick takes on an interesting texture and shape, I find little use for it."

Lorilei passed around some free ale, and when the last local staggered home, she closed up and was upstairs before Jimbo made it back from the privy.

Using her master key, Lorilei quietly slipped into Jimbo's room, leaving a small lamp burning by his bed. She quickly unlaced her emerald corset, pulling it, her skirt, blouse and chemise off. She draped herself over the sheets where the light's amber tongue licked along her curves.

Presently, Jimbo stumbled into the room, singing haphazardly, his hair mussed into curls. He was half-undressed, his shirt in his hands when he noticed Lorilei in his bed. "One of us has the wrong room," he slurred.

Lorilei smiled, running a hand over her hip. "There are rare occasions that I like to give my customers preferential treatment."

Jimbo laughed, plunking down on the bed to struggle off his pants. "I think it's wasted here."

She kneeled behind him, stroking his back and chest, thinking he was too drunk. "I'm very good at building appetites."

Jimbo fell backward, crooning, "I only want to make my fortune and return to the arms of my love."

Lorilei knew that loves often were forgotten when a man glimpsed her charms. "I'm sure she would not mind for you to gain some experience."

"My love is no woman, but my adoring Richard." Jimbo smiled goofily.

Lorilei rolled her eyes. Indeed, her charms would be wasted. How then to get the magic stick? She looked down at Jimbo as a snore erupted from him. After climbing over him, Lorilei pulled Jimbo's legs onto the bed and covered him up. Then she found the worn leather pack and a plain brown stick about a foot long and an inch in diameter. She wasn't fooled by its bland appearance and took both the stick and her clothes back to her room.

Standing beside her bed, she held the stick before her and said, "Stick, stick, show me your tricks."

It warmed in her hand, slowly thickening, becoming a

browny pink. The end rounded, taking on a bulbish appearance until Lorilei gasped. In her hand, she held a rather well-endowed, life-size phallus. Her muscles clenched from groin to stomach and a flush spread through her, giving a rosy glow to her skin. Then the phallus began to vibrate.

Experimentally, Lorilei turned the thrumming tip toward her pussy and touched it to her labia. The vibration sent a delicious thrill through her, wetting her with desire. Falling back on her bed, she moved the penis back and forth, rubbing it around her clit, deliciously spreading her wet lips. The thing leaped in her hands. "Oh," she squeaked out as it pushed into her, just a bit, then withdrew. Her hips moved back and forth, following the building waves of pleasure.

Lorilei thought she didn't guide the phallus, but of its own it pushed into her so that her muscular walls clamped down, drawing it farther in. Even when buried all the way in her cunt, there were still a good five inches to hang on to, but it sat for a moment, letting the thrum build through her body. Just as she thought she could stand no more, the phallus withdrew to all but the ridged knob. Then it proceeded to plunge in and out, building speed. The wooden penis gave her a good fucking until she cried out, tsunami pleasure squeezing, rolling, overlapping pulses. Five minutes went by when the toy jumped to life again and kept Lorilei heartily entertained for half the night before she gasped out, "Stick, stick, no more tricks," and fell into an exhausted slumber.

The next morning, Lorilei dragged herself from her bed, putting on a simple russet gown. Before she left the room, she looked at the stick on her bed. If only she could find a man like that.

Three people, including Jimbo sat in the tavern. They drank mulled cider and chatted quietly. When Lorilei walked in, they smiled knowingly.

Lorilei hummed as she cooked up eggs and bacon and cut

huge slabs of brown, seedy bread. How would she get the stick from Jimbo? For have it she must.

When she brought the food over and plunked it down on the sturdy oak table, everyone dug in. She sat down with a ceramic mug of cider across from the tall man who looked a tad hungover. "Your tales were of such charm and wit last night that I will not charge you for your lodgings."

Jimbo smiled and said, "And you obviously have found a better use for that magic stick than I. Keep it as payment."

Lorilei blushed but smiled and shook his hand.

A few months later, Jon wandered along. Though handsome, he had little grace, and no penchant for storytelling. Still, Lorilei asked enough questions as she served up carrots, stewed chicken and dumplings, and ample ale to find that Jon, in his training, had been given a magic riding crop by his master.

"I will see what becomes of that when I return home," Jon said around a mouthful of dumpling. He said and drank little. Lorilei closed up the kitchen and larder and went up to her room and waited. She wanted to see what the magic crop did.

When an hour had passed since Jon had gone to bed, she crept to his room in just her nightgown. She quietly opened the door. A short candle flickered on his bedside dresser and Jon's back was turned away. As Lorilei moved closer, she peered into the shadows, searching for the pack. She carefully pulled open a drawer, when Jon rolled over, his pale eyes open and watching her.

"Look what the mice have brought in."

Lorilei decided truth was best. "I came to check that your candle was out and truth be told, I was curious to see your magic crop."

Jon smiled, but it wasn't friendly. "Oh, I can show you that, but first you must remove your gown."

She eyed his bare chest and the sheet tucked around his frame. His body was sturdy and young and a man was what suited her best. She shrugged and pulled the gown over her head, her russet curls dancing as she shook her head.

Jon's gaze moved from her slender neck, over her full breasts, to her waist and along the slope of her hips. Then he said, "Crop, crop, give a fine beating until I yell stop."

The pack rustled and a long, slender brown crop wriggled loose. It shot into the air and then began to slap at Lorilei's behind. She turned from it but it kept shooting around to smack her ever harder. Squealing at the mounting pain, she tried to dodge it and ran about the room. Once she hunkered down, but then it whacked her on the back or breasts, which was worse. Jon laughed, doubling over in his bed as she scooted left and right.

Angry and beginning to hurt a great deal, Lorilei gritted her teeth and decided to take the punishment standing still. But the blows increased and drove her to her knees. Her ass, stinging fiercely, hot as a furnace, had her gripping the edge of the bed where Jon peered down at her, smiling. Gasping from the searing pain, Lorilei groaned, "Please, make it stop."

Jon gave the words and the crop stopped. Lorilei leaned her head against the bed frame, catching her breath. Then she arched back, gasping as Jon's cool hand slid over her butt. The contrast was extreme with the heat of her ass, and her nerves flared at every touch. His fingers slid down her butt until they burrowed between her pussy lips. She moaned, realizing that she was oddly turned on. He stroked her, spreading her silky wetness, and then said, "I have something to help you."

Lorilei looked up and saw him lying naked, his cock standing stiff and straight.

He smiled and said, "Take a ride on that."

Shivers of pain raced through Lorilei's body. The only way

to tamp it down was to bring equal levels of pleasure. She crawled onto the bed and straddled Jon's hips. He grinned at her arrogantly, and reached to squeeze one of her breasts. She hovered above Jon's cock for a moment, but knew she'd derive as much from this as he would. Plunging down onto his cock, she felt a slight resistance before he filled her. His cool hands continued to caress her ass cheeks, squeezing and pulling them apart. She moved at her pace, up and down, as delicious tremors overtook her, not letting Jon speed up. As she reached her crescendo, she stretched out her hand and mercilessly tweaked his nipples. He shouted, arching up as she slammed down onto him, writhing and moaning.

He fell into a deep slumber, and Lorilei stole from his room, the crop in hand. In the morning, she charged him for his stay and he went on his way. Whether he knew the crop was missing or not, he did not say.

Weeks later, Eric jauntily approached the inn. His thread-bare, saffron tunic was clean and outlined his trim frame. Lorilei stopped washing in the wooden tub to stare, noticing his finely muscled legs. He was like spring leaves rustling through the reds and golds of fall. Her breath caught as the sun gilded the waves of his hair.

He stopped and looked a Lorilei, then bowed and asked, "Do you have space for the evening meal?"

"Yes, that and a room if you need."

Eric shook his head, his emerald eyes flashing in the sun. "Ah, no, my lady. I have here a trusty cot, both magic and comfortable." He patted the bundle of sticks and leather at his back.

Lorilei's eyes grew wide. A magic cot. Now, what would that do? "Of course, my lord…"

"Eric. I heard told that my brothers, James and Jon, came this way and recommended your hospitality." They had

also mentioned her desire for their meager enchanted treasures. But Eric hoped to gain his own treasures.

Lorilei brought out her best ham, potatoes and squashes.
She poured Eric spiced wine and sat with him, listening to
his tales. But mostly she found she couldn't help but stare into
his eyes.

Eric for his part wanted to linger in her fiery radiance, soak
in Lorilei's natural joy. Eventually, he bade her good-night and
repaired to the barn. Lorilei climbed to her bedroom, vowing
that she would not trick this man, for she sensed his honest
gaiety. Pacing her room from armoire to bed and back, she
found she could not settle, and crept out to the barn. For just
a look, that was all.

Eric knew she couldn't resist and lay waiting, having not
yet used the magic words. He stared up at the loft, his arms
tucked behind his head. The barn door creaked open and he
smiled.

As Lorilei approached she was disappointed to see nothing
more than a worn cot. But the man upon it warmed her heart.
She blushed and said, "I just came to see your wondrous cot."

"Just that?" asked Eric, laughing. He patted the cot for her
to sit. And as she did, he said, "Bed, bed, show a fine spread."

Lorilei laughed as the bed rumbled, doubling in size, the
thin linen changing to sumptuous silks and a brocade coverlet
in umber and peridot. Pillows appeared, as a canopy of fine
blue muslin spread out from the posts sprouting at each corner.
She clapped her hands. "Oh, what a delightful piece of
magic."

Eric watched her and reached out to touch her face. He
began to kiss his way up her neck and nibble her ear. "You
are a better piece of magic."

Lorilei closed her eyes, sinking back as he kissed along her
arm, gently sucking her fingers. He inched her gown up,
kissing, licking, tasting along the way. Lorilei sighed and wrig-

gled, grasping his hands or his face to lay delirious kisses along his flesh. He tasted of honey, wood smoke and cedar. She breathed him in as their bodies slid along each other.

It was much later, after Eric had sucked her rosy nipple, trailing his tongue from her navel to her clit, bringing her to an apex of orgasm, that he entered her, his cock melding with Lorilei so that they moved unconsciously, tempos changing, slowing, building until they came together, passion vibrating through them, clenching them closely.

In the morning, as the first radiant rays of sun slanted through the barn door, Lorilei and Eric lay entwined and the other travelers had to fend for themselves.

Lorilei drew in a deep breath, smelling the salty musk of their lovemaking. Never had she found a man like this and she now knew her need for magic had been fulfilled, for she had found the greatest treasure.

Two brothers returned home to the tailor's house for a while. Eric only returned to invite them to the wedding.

The Broken Fiddle

Andrea Dale

"Erik, stop the car!" Phoebe shouted.

With a dramatic sigh, Erik slammed on the brakes. "Girl-friend," he said once the car halted, "you are going to give me a heart attack."

But Phoebe wasn't listening. She was already out of the car, a few hundred yards back on the narrow tarmac road through the tiny Irish town of Arderra, staring up in rapture. When Erik joined her, she breathed, "Isn't it magnificent?"

Erik grudgingly agreed that it was, although he grumbled that it wasn't on the list and he didn't even know what little Irish town they were *in,* anyway. She knew he wasn't really angry; they'd been friends since before he'd figured out that he was gay, and she knew his dramatic ways.

Besides, he'd been just as enthusiastic about this trip as she, ignoring the warning of friends that they didn't have a publishing contract and it would be a waste of money. He agreed with Phoebe: Even if they didn't sell the book, they'd have had a glorious vacation in Ireland, right?

She hoped the book would fly. She believed it would. There were enough Anglophiles in the U.S. to appreciate a coffee-table book of gorgeous photos of unique pub signs, accompanied by the stories behind the signs. No prefab Saint George and the Dragons or the King's Arms—no, they were going for local legends and exceptional original artwork.

Like this one. Phoebe shivered with excitement.

In the foreground was a fiddle, finely etched with Celtic knotwork. It was broken, however—the neckpiece split and lolling drunkenly, the snapped strings dangling so realistically that Phoebe thought she could hear their tortured death twang.

It wasn't just the lifelike artwork that had caught her eye, though. In the upper corners, faded and half-seen like ghosts, were two women.

The one on the left was a redhead, with creamy skin and sad emerald eyes. The opposing woman had black-as-night hair that glittered with diamond-like drops of water. Between them stretched a night sky, clouded and wild, a bolt of lightning sundering the picture and forever separating the women.

Which, Phoebe supposed, was probably a good thing. Somehow, instinctively, she knew the women were rivals.

"Well," Erik said, "it *is* getting late. We might as well stay here tonight, and you can pump someone for information about the sign."

"Deal. I'll get us checked in."

She asked the usual questions as she acquired rooms for them, but the desk clerk, a pretty young thing with a wild thatch of tangled black hair to her waist and a ring in her nose, said vaguely that it was about some sort of legend, and she should be asking Harry, the owner, tonight at the ceilidh. He'd be running the bar, see. They *would* be coming down for the ceilidh, wouldn't they?

Phoebe assured her that they would.

★ ★ ★

It was a gloriously traditional pub, all dark red upholstery and wood so old and scarred it looked black beneath the loving polish. A sooty stone fireplace held a low, peaty fire.

They watched the band set up as they ate (prawn cocktail and steak-and-kidney pie for Phoebe, Camembert and fresh salmon for Erik, and apple-blackberry crumble with hot custard for both of them).

"Yes, he's mighty fine," Erik said, propping his chin on his hand.

"Who, what?"

"That delicious boy you're ogling. I'd fight you for him, but I'm already sure he's as straight as a road in Iowa."

Phoebe knew it was useless to deny she'd been ogling. The young man across the room who was pulling a fiddle from its case *was* delicious. Hair as black as coal and curling silkily to his collar, eyes as blue as twilight eve. High, sharp cheekbones that looked as though they'd been chiseled out of marble. Pale skin that would have made Snow White blanch with envy. Slender but sturdy, wearing a pair of faded jeans so snug he must have had to use a shoehorn to get them on. She spooned another bite of crumble, laughing to herself. He was barely more than a boy, and at thirty-two she felt like a dirty old woman for contemplating his impressive bulge.

By the time they finished their meal the crowd was gathering for the ceilidh, and they managed to snag two chairs by the fire just in time.

The band played reels that left Phoebe breathless with melodies that leaped like cold, wild streams. Reels with boundless energy and a relentless beat that made her think of really great sex.

The fiddle player's hands flew over the strings, made a blur of the bow. He played his instrument with passion, and she imagined that passion extended to other areas in his life.

That left her breathless for another reason altogether, and with her nipples tightening beneath her shirt. She shouldn't, she told herself, be thinking about the young man's lips and how they might feel on her skin. But she squirmed in her seat all the same.

During a break in the music, Phoebe went to the bar, waiting until the crush of people cleared so she could actually get a few words in to Harry, a slender, clean-cut man with graying hair and a calm demeanor in the face of the frenzy of Saturday night at the pub. A score of taps lined the bar, glasses hanging from racks overhead and stronger spirits in bottles on the wall behind. She ordered another pint of Guinness, watched approvingly as he poured it with a deft hand to create the outline of a shamrock on the foam, and slid her coins across the bar.

"My friend and I, we're doing a book on unusual pub signs," she said. "A coffee-table book. He takes the pictures, I write the text. You've got a gorgeous sign out front—what's the story behind it?"

"A book, eh?" Harry swiped a towel across the gleaming wood between them, then leaned on the bar.

"We don't have a publisher yet," Phoebe admitted. "But I don't think we'll have a problem selling the project. It'll be good publicity for you."

Harry gazed fondly around the packed pub. "Ah, I don't think I'll be needing much of that—not that I'll ever turn it away, mind you. I'll tell you who can really spin the tale for you is Finn over there."

She tried to follow his gaze. "Finn?"

Harry indicated her sweet fiddle player. Ah, *Finn*. It suited him.

"Will he be spinning me a tale, or telling me the history of the sign?" she asked.

Harry waggled his head in a yes-and-no motion. "A little

of both, I'll warrant. But he does know the tale of the sign better than any of us. He actually did the research on it, for a school project."

"He's something of a scholar, is he?"

"A little here, a little there," Harry said. "I don't think his time at uni was wasted."

So he'd been to college. Maybe she wasn't quite as dirty or as old as she'd thought.

Someone jostled up to the bar beside her.

"Two black-and-tans and a snakebite, Harry," the man said without a glance at Phoebe.

Phoebe thanked Harry and retreated to her seat with her drink.

"Are you sure you don't want anything?" she asked Erik again.

He shook his head. "I'm fine, darling. Except I've got a headache, and I'm afraid the music isn't helping it. I'm going to abandon you for my bed and the very real possibility of a *Black Adder* rerun."

"Because I know how you feel about Rowan Atkinson."

"Especially in the Elizabethan series. Oh, honey, that codpiece."

She missed Erik, but she certainly had enough to occupy her with Finn in the corner of the room. There was no stage; the band had mostly just grabbed nearby chairs. Yet somehow they all seemed higher than the rest of the room, the music advancing them onto an unseen but very real stage.

They finished the next set with an air, a sweet sad song that made Phoebe forget about her drink. The notes curled through the air, burrowed under her skin, clouded her throat with beautiful despair.

Finn stroked the bow across the strings as if he stroked a woman, and his only thought, his only care, his only goal was to coax and tease from her the most exquisite sounds. A raven wing of hair fell across his brow as he concentrated, eyes half-lidded.

Then he set the fiddle aside and began to sing. His pure, strong tenor filled in the spaces made by the other instruments, until the pub was wrapped like a body in a linen shroud. It was as if, for a few moments, they existed only within the song.

When it ended, first there was silence. Even the locals, who presumably had heard the song before, seemed frozen by the music's spell. Then the clapping started, and the whistles and cheers, and Finn took a deep, theatrical bow that took nothing away from his performance. When she could move again, Phoebe took a long draft of her Guinness.

She looked up from it to find Finn, all gloriously lanky length of him, standing before her. She shivered, deep inside, at the smell of his spicy aftershave piercing through the scent of the peat fire, at his proximity.

"I hear you're wanting to talk to me," he said.

She smiled. "Did Harry send you over?"

"That he did." Finn easily rested a hip on the small round table between the chairs. "But your friend also put in a word before he left."

"Erik talked to you?"

"Aye. He told me that you fancied me."

Phoebe blushed. "Well, you do have a way with that fiddle of yours," she said, hoping to diffuse the subject. But Finn's eyes, twilight-blue and perceptive, held hers. There was a hint of amusement in their depths—and also a hint of desire. She was sure of it.

She caught her breath.

"Thank you," Finn said. "Although I'd be sorely disappointed if the only thing about me that interested you was my fiddle."

He had the typical Irish accent, where the "th" became a "t" or "d": "Altough I'd be sorely disappointed if de only ting about me dat interested you was me fiddle."

She loved it. She absolutely loved it.

"Well, that and your research on how The Broken Fiddle got its name," she said.

She really did care about that. But she also found herself leaning forward, revealing a bit more cleavage, putting a hand on his knee.

He put his hand over hers. She could feel the calluses on his fingertips from his fiddle playing. She imagined what those gifted, swift fingers, those rough pads, would feel like on her breasts, between her legs, and excitement skimmed through her, pooling at her groin.

"And why are you so interested in that?" he asked.

It took her a moment to realize he wasn't talking about sex. She told him about the book. He looked impressed.

"You'll be putting our little town on the map."

"It would be nice if more people could appreciate the sign—and come here to appreciate your music," she said.

Before he could reply, the squeeze-box player shouted, "Finn! Leave the bird be and get your arse back over here."

Finn squeezed her hand, then reluctantly stood. "We've got one more set to play," he said. "Will you be waiting for me afterward? I'll tell you all about the sign."

The way he said it somehow sounded like a promise of an assignation, of stolen kisses and much, much more.

"I'll be waiting," Phoebe promised.

She found out from Harry what whiskey Finn drank, and had a shot waiting for him after he stowed his fiddle in its case and got through the crowd of people, all of whom wanted to clap him on the back and say hello.

He grinned at the sight of the drink, tossed it back and said,

"I see I already told you the price of the story was a single malt and a kiss."

Phoebe raised an eyebrow. "The whiskey's the down payment," she said. She leaned closer, feeling the heat of him beneath his linen shirt, indigo like his eyes. "The kiss, though—well, I'll pay you that after I've heard the story and agree it's worth the cost."

He laughed softly. "Is that so? Then I'll have to make it worth your while." He held out his hand. "Walk with me, girl, and I'll tell you the tale of a fiddle and a heart both cleft in twain."

Despite the late hour, the sky hadn't achieved full blackness. At the height of summer, this far north, it never got past the velvet-blue of deep twilight. When she was a girl, Phoebe had believed that time of evening to be when the fairies came out. Here in Ireland, she could almost believe it again.

There was little light pollution from Arderra, and glittering stars blanketed the sky. A moon just past full gave enough light for Phoebe to see where to put her feet as Finn led her through the pub's back garden (pointing out a corner of tangled overgrowth, beneath which was a holy well, he said) and up the hill beyond. She was glad for her sturdy hiking boots and jeans as they tromped through thigh-high grass and vines and occasional bramble.

They crested the hill, and once again, she caught her breath. Maybe she *had* been transported to fairyland.

Below them, in the cup of the hills, lay a small, still lake, black as night but with a path of shimmering white laid down by the moon. Darker shapes against the gorse looked to be the ruins of a small building, possibly an ancient tower.

When they got to the bottom of the slope, it was as if the village no longer existed. Any noise from the departing pubgoers had vanished. A pair of crickets serenaded each other, or perhaps they were flirting. Beyond that, there was just the sound of hers and Finn's breathing and the brush of their feet through the undergrowth.

Irish roses, wild and untamed, tangled around the broken stones, their heady scent making Phoebe light-headed. Or maybe it was Finn's warm, strong hand resting on the small of her back, guiding her through the rough terrain.

He led her to a hip-high wall that was relatively flat.

"I'm going t' tell you a story now," Finn said, and Phoebe automatically settled herself into a comfortable position on the stones. She knew what Irish storytelling was like. They could be here till dawn.

She wondered if the lake had the popular legend that many did, that anyone who survived a full night on its shores would either go mad or become an amazing poet. If so, she crossed her fingers for the latter.

"Many years ago—no one's quite sure of how many, but they all agree that it was quite a few and then some—there was the small village of Arderra here, smaller than it is now. Farms and the like scattered around it. The pub was here, but it had a different name then, one no one remembers now."

Finn was slipping into the story, his voice rising and falling in a tale-teller's lilt. "There was a fiddle player, too, and his name is lost, as well. He was the best fiddle player anyone had ever heard. His talent was known beyond the bounds of Arderra, and that was saying something back then. These ruins are of the little house he had here by the lake.

"Of course he had a sweetheart, and it's said her name was Róisín. That means *rose,* and given the abundance of roses here, it's not a surprise that she'd be named for that. She was a wild Irish rose, you see, with the red hair and skin soft as petals."

Phoebe thought of the woman on the pub sign, and tried not to be distracted by how close Finn was sitting to her, so close that his arm brushed hers as he gestured.

"Our fiddler, well, he loved his Róisín truly," he went on. "She was beautiful and kind and strong and wise, and she had a voice that could bring grown men to tears."

She should remember that phrase for the book. It was nice to hear of a woman with brains and strength and talent, as well as looks.

"But like many men, he had a streak of pride and a streak of foolishness, and the mix of the two never ends well. His fiddle playing was renowned, but he wanted more. He wanted true fame; he wanted the world—he wanted the whole of Eire, anyway, to know his name. So he sat out here and he played his fiddle and he wished with all his heart, but more than that, he swore aloud that he'd do anything to have that fame. I doubt he had to call on the fair folk by name, because any oath like that would attract them like cats to fresh cream."

Phoebe thought of cats lapping cream, and her lapping at Finn's cock, a mental image so strong it rocked her to her core. She could see his strong profile in the moonlight as he gazed out over the water, lost in his tale.

"It was a water fae—one of the Glaistig, maybe, or an Asrai. It's hard to say now, for we've lost that connection with the faerie folk. She rose right out of the lake there." Finn pointed. A fish leaped, splashing the surface, and Phoebe jumped. She laughed at her own nervousness, but then Finn put an arm around her, and she stopped laughing.

He dug a flask out of his hip pocket, not a knotwork-decorated one like the kind she'd seen in gift shops, but plain silver. She wondered how he'd shoehorned it into those jeans. He offered it to her, and she drank. The whiskey danced like fire in her veins.

Finn took a swig and continued.

"Whatever she was, she was lovely beyond reason, dark as night just as Róisín was bright as day. She promised the fiddler his heart's desire, but there was a price, as there always is with the fae. One night with her was all she asked, one night from Midsummer's Eve to Midsummer's Morn, and in his foolish desire to fiddle to the world—or at least all of Eire—the fiddler thought it wasn't that bad of a price."

"I'm guessing Róisín thought differently," Phoebe murmured.

"That she did," Finn said, his warm breath fanning across her cheek. "She and the fiddler were to be wed, and she chose Midsummer's Day. He thought that might not be the best of ideas, and somehow she got it out of him why he hesitated so.

"So on Midsummer's Eve, she stole down to the lake, and she confronted the water fae right in front of the fiddler, claiming him as hers. The fae woman countered, and offered her a challenge. Róisín loved her fiddler above all else, and she wouldn't let him be lost to the faerie folk."

Probably not the smartest thing, Phoebe mused. But many people did foolish things for love, and even for lust.

"He would fiddle, the fae said, and she and Róisín would sing. The better singer would win. How the contest was to be judged we no longer know. But Róisín accepted, and the fae took her to the center of the lake, where she'd bespelled a rock for them to sit upon. It's said they sang until the sky began to turn light again."

Finn sighed. "Róisín's voice was so sweet that it called the sun to rise, it's said. But it took her last breath, and her last strength. She hadn't anything left, and when the fae woman left, taking the rock with her, Róisín didn't have the energy to make it back to shore. The fiddler swam out to her, but it was too late. Their fingers touched as she sank, and then she was gone.

"The fiddler, it's said, played one more song, a song for Róisín, and it went something like this."

Finn drew in a breath, and sang. The lyrics were in Gaelic,

but it didn't matter. His voice carried the tune pure and smooth, and over it she thought she could hear the original fiddle strains, what the fiddler would have played before the words were added. The tune soared and wept; it was choked with despair and desperate with love.

"And then he smashed his fiddle on that very rock you can see, there at the edge of the lake," Finn said when he finished, "and he never played again."

Phoebe took a deep breath, feeling as if she'd been holding her breath for the whole song.

"There was another song, though," Finn said, almost as a casual afterthought, although Phoebe knew better. "He'd written one for the water sprite, too, for their Midsummer's Eve meeting."

He stood before her to sing this one. His blue eyes turned black and deep in the darkness of the night, but always on her.

This song was in no way melancholy. No, Phoebe realized with a tremor of arousal, this one was all about desire. About the wanting of a wild fae, about the need to have her, just for one night. About passion and ecstasy beyond mortal comprehension.

The music pierced her straight between her legs. Wild, wanton music for a wild, wanton lover, and her nipples peaked to an almost painful hardness, her sex growing wet.

It wasn't the potent whiskey, or the resonance of the wild Irish music through her veins, although those things, and the moonlight and the heady scent of roses, all added to the spell that seemed to settle over her like a silken net. Finn's voice was a charm, and she reached for his magic with both hands.

But none of that was an excuse; she was in full control, and she knew exactly what she was doing when he finished singing and she slid her hands up under his coat, cupped his shoulder blades and drew him closer, watching until the last moment as his head tipped toward hers, soft hair brushing her cheek.

A whiskey and a kiss, the price of a story well told.

It wasn't enough. His lips were cool, but warmed swiftly as they kissed. Phoebe met his tongue with hers, tasting whiskey, drinking in the final notes of the song.

Finn murmured something about going to her room, or his, but she didn't want to wait that long, and told him.

"Then we'll have to thank the fiddler for letting us use his home," Finn said, and stripped off his long black coat to lay it on the grass near the wild Irish roses.

She plucked his shirt buttons open and ran her tongue along his smooth, hairless chest, sucking gently at his nipples and making him tremble and arch into her, his hands stroking her hair.

Kneeling, facing each other, he stripped off his shirt and then hers. He cupped her naked breasts in his hands, bit gently on her neck as he tugged and tweaked her nipples. She felt as though taut fiddle strings connected from her breasts to her clit as his fingers sent vibrations of pleasure streaking through her.

He lay back, encouraged her to straddle his face, murmuring encouragement for her to play with her own breasts, to feel the night around them. His tongue was as talented as his fingers, playing her like a fine instrument, respecting her but at the same time urging her to give him everything.

And she sang, releasing her own music to the night as she came, her thighs tensed around his face and her hips bucking in his hands.

She crawled down his body to take his penis, long and smooth and hard like the rest of him, into her mouth. She circled him with her fist and her mouth and coaxed sweet beads of moisture from the tip of him, honey to go with the whiskey they'd already shared.

She could tell he was getting close, but then he gently drew her away, urging her onto her hands and knees in front of him. He bent low, his hair brushing her back, her skin so sensitized that another small tremor rocked her before he slowly sank the length of his cock into her.

Callused fingers strummed a melody on her clit while he carried the rhythm on his steady thrusts into her.

Their song moved steadily toward a crescendo.

Blood pounded in her ears, beating like the bodhran played in the ceilidh. Her orgasm soared on the strains of wild music.

On the cusp of the dawn, he reached for her hand. "We should be getting back."

She knew better than to suggest they wait to see the sunrise.

They sold the book, and Erik's photographs and Phoebe's text received much praise. Phoebe arranged for the publisher to send a copy to Harry at the pub. She wanted to send one to Finn, but she didn't even know his last name.

"Send it to Finn, care of The Broken Fiddle, in Arderra, Ireland," she said. "It'll get to him."

Care of the broken fiddle. How appropriate. He was the one who cared for the legend, kept it alive.

And on the day the book was launched, Erik gave her a picture he'd taken of Finn, wild and sexy and fiddling.

The Cougar of Cobble Hill

Sophia Valenti

A crisp morning breeze streamed in through the window, the cool gusts of air causing the curtains to billow and part, allowing streaks of sunlight to flash across my rumpled bed. I breathed in deeply and smiled, gradually awakening to a reality that was far better than any dream could ever be.

Behind me, I felt the mattress shift. I rolled over to face the tasty morsel next to me, who was still fast asleep. Jake was lying on his stomach, both arms wrapped around a pillow. The sheet had slipped off him during the night, revealing his muscular arms and back, as well as his tight little ass that still bore faint stripes from well-placed strokes of his own leather belt.

Only a few short hours ago, I'd seen his chocolate-brown eyes wide with lust and anticipation before he lavished my stilettos with kisses. At my direction, his pouty lips traveled upward, and he nestled his face between my trembling thighs to tongue my aching sex. I wrapped my fingers in his hair and crushed his face against me. Jake had just the right touch, not too hard, not too soft. With unceasing devotion, he lapped at my pulsing button until he turned my slow-burning desire into a raging inferno of pleasure.

But at that moment, in the bright morning sun, my bad boy looked blissful, nearly angelic. His black hair was so perfectly mussed, it looked as though a stylist had snuck into the room in the middle of the night to primp and pose him just for me.

"Good morning, Cassie," said Rick, startling me from my reverie. He spoke in a hushed whisper, so as not to wake his friend. Rick was leaning against the door frame, wearing nothing but his drawstring pajama bottoms. My eyes lingered on his six-pack abs as he approached the bed with a mug of fresh-brewed coffee. I sat up and took the drink from him. I nodded my thanks, and he smiled and left the room.

I'm not one to believe in fate, but sometimes when you least expect it, life gives you exactly what you need—even if you didn't realize you needed it.

Up until last year, my life was going according to plan. I'd checked off every milestone my twenty-two-year-old self had detailed years before on her list of must-have accomplishments: MBA, marriage to a lawyer and a swanky apartment on the Upper East Side of Manhattan. But somewhere along the way, things changed. I changed. And suddenly "the list" didn't matter anymore.

For more than a dozen years, my husband, Brandon, and I had been working sixty-hour weeks and spending more time with our personal trainers than with each other. Of course, we'd penciled in weekly "sex dates," but I was dissatisfied. When I finally stopped speeding through my days, I realized I was always on the go because I was too scared to admit that I wasn't happy. It was at the start of one of our sex dates that I kept my panties on and confessed to Brandon that I didn't know what I wanted, but it wasn't the life I'd been leading. After a few moments of silence, he admitted that he felt the same way. There was no yelling or dish throwing, just a realization that we were through. Our divorce was a simple contractual arrangement, much like our marriage had been. I was closing in on forty years old, and I realized that a sensible life full of proper choices had left me feeling hollow.

I wanted—no, I *needed*—something more.

I felt as if I'd woken up from a multidecade nap. The world seemed fresh and new, and I decided to do all the things I'd been too meek to go for but had always wanted. I gave up my corporate job, got a position working for a small nonprofit and set up a new home across the river in a Brooklyn brownstone. Living in Cobble Hill was nearly like being in the country. It was the best of both worlds for me, the convenience of the city nearby and a house on a peaceful, tree-lined street.

I was happy living by myself, so I had no intention of opening up my home—especially to a couple of strangers. But one day, a business associate mentioned that a couple of her interns needed a place to stay. They would be starting their senior year in college in the fall and hadn't been able to sublet a place for the summer. Right after she inquired about my three empty bedrooms, she began the hard sell about how they were such good, industrious boys. And while I wasn't eager to give up my solitude, I agreed to do this one good deed. After all, it was only for three months.

When Jake arrived on my doorstep, I could hardly believe my eyes. After hearing about his dean's-list grades, I was expecting more of a geek. But Jake looked like nothing of the sort. Tall and muscular, his black curls rakishly disheveled, he strode into my living room with a large duffel bag tossed over his shoulder, looking like a strapping sailor heading to shore for leave.

Jake greeted me shyly and stuttered a sheepish thank-you. His cheeks flushed adorably, and he seemed barely able to meet my gaze. That was just as well because *I* was unable to stop my eyes from roaming over his beautiful physique. I stared at the muscles in his arms, which flexed as he shifted the weight of his bag from one shoulder to the other. And when he bent over to drop his belongings in the corner, I nearly swooned from how tempting his ass looked cradled in the broken-in jeans. Fortunately, I regained my composure before he turned around, feeling my face heat with embarrassment. I showed him to his room and left him to settle in. Meanwhile I headed for a warm bath and a glass of wine, wondering what had gotten into me. He was a gorgeous young man, but there was no way he'd be interested in a woman my age—or would he? In those fleeting seconds that our eyes actually met, I saw something that I couldn't quite put my finger on. It was a look laden with admiration, appreciation and a certain eagerness that I found endearing.

While I was shocked by Jake, the next morning I received yet another surprise when his friend Rick arrived. Blond, fair-skinned and lanky, Rick perfectly complemented Jake. His peaches-and-cream complexion looked delicious, and I was having a hard time not imagining eating him up. Rick was bolder than Jake. He wasn't shy about looking me in the eye, even as he deferentially expressed his gratitude to me for giving them a place to stay.

During the first two weeks, I barely saw the boys. We kept drastically different hours. But on the weekends, they were constantly underfoot. My house was in livable condition, but there were a host of home-improvement projects that needed to be completed, and the boys were quick to offer their assistance. But they wanted to do more than simply help. From the beginning, they insisted that I sit back, relax and tell them what to do.

At first, I felt uneasy about the situation, but they were so full of energy and eager to please that I easily found myself falling into the role of mistress of the house. We started with the backyard garden, and they followed my landscaping redesign to the letter, while I sat in the shade, sipping lemonade and admiring their shirtless torsos glistening with sweat as they labored in the July sun. While I enjoyed the sight, what surprised me most was how much I enjoyed telling them what to do. It seemed to give me a little charge, and I began micromanaging their household chores.

As the weeks passed, I sensed an erotic vibe growing between the three of us. At first I thought it was my imagination, but Jake began giving me a warm smile whenever he saw me, and Rick had taken to having my coffee waiting for me in the morning. Their schedules gradually changed, so that they both were in the house to greet me in the evening when I arrived home from work, and consequently we began having dinner together. While I appreciated their attention, I wondered where this was headed. Well, I finally got my answer at summer's end—and it was hotter than any fantasy I could have dreamed up on my own.

I was sitting in an easy chair in the corner of the living room, dealing with office paperwork. The day before, I'd had the boys spackle and sand the walls, which were ready to be painted. Jake had just finished taping up the edges of the ceiling and was descending a ladder. As he jumped off the last rung, he knocked over an open paint can, and the cinnamon-hued liquid quickly spread into a large puddle at his feet. Before he could grab the can, an ocean of gooey color spread across the tarp and seeped into a patch of unprotected carpet.

I jumped up in alarm. It was a knee-jerk reaction because I'd already made the decision to tear up the cream-colored wall-to-wall and purchase a deep-pile throw. "Oh, Cassie," Jake said, his eyes wide. "I'm sorry. I'll make it up to you."

Rick wandered in from the kitchen in time to hear Jake's apology. "That's one big mess, Jake." Then he turned to me with a twinkle in his eyes. "That was awfully clumsy of him. I think someone needs to be punished."

I gasped at Rick's unexpected words and saw Jake flush, his handsome face quickly going from pink to crimson as his eyes stayed glued to the spilled paint. I immediately got the impression that these boys had lived a lot more than I'd initially given them credit for. Without thinking, I instantly slid into their game.

"I think you're correct, Rick. Punishment *is* in order," I said slowly. Jake looked up at me, his brown eyes filled with a delicious mixture of fear and desire. His breathing was coming in quick little gasps, and his erection was tenting his jeans. The sight of his hard cock made my mouth water, but I forced myself to stay in character and play the game—to not give in to my hunger.

"But, Rick," I added, "you're the one who left that open paint can near the ladder. You're just as much to blame. You stay where you are until I'm ready for you." Rick tried hard to hide his smile, biting the corner of his lip, but I could still see how thrilled he was.

Feeling bold, I strode over to Jake and grabbed his belt. I quickly unfastened the buckle and slid the leather from around his waist. Jake licked his lips but said nothing. He just kept taking those deep breaths and staring at me. Holding the smooth black leather in one hand, I used the other to deftly pop open his button fly and yank down his jeans. Now it was my turn to bite my lip. Jake wasn't wearing any underwear, and his thick erection sprang up from his jeans in indecent invitation, sprouting from a nest of dark hair. I resisted the urge to stroke his cock and ordered him to turn around. Acting as though he'd done this a thousand times before, Jake grabbed the arm of the couch and bent over, presenting his bare ass.

As for me, I'd never done anything like this before, but suddenly the situation felt right. I doubled up the belt and placed one hand at the small of Jake's back to steady my target. I slapped the leather against his ass, and he let out a little moan that caused a twinge in my pussy. I lashed him again, and he whispered, "Harder, please." His urgent begging increased the ache in my sex, and with Jake's words ringing in my ears, I whipped him more soundly. As his skin blossomed, turning from lily-white to carnation-pink to rose-red, I felt my panties grow damp and my arousal skyrocketed.

After a dozen strokes, I stopped lashing him and told him to remain in position. Jake didn't move a muscle, although I could hear his ragged gasps for air as he struggled to maintain his composure. I looked over at Rick, who, as ordered, had remained in the same spot I had left him. I pointed to the opposite arms of the couch, and Rick mirrored Jake's position. I wandered over and worked my hand beneath him to open his cargo pants. When I reached for his zipper, my hand grazed his cock, and he exhaled loudly. Using two hands, I tugged his pants and boxer briefs down to his knees. His ass was even more pale than Jake's had been, and I couldn't wait to give it some color.

Whipping Jake had gotten me seriously worked up, and I'd already found my stroke, so to speak, so I had no problem laying into Rick. After all, this scene had been his idea, and I didn't want to leave his expectations unfulfilled. With rapid-fire precision, I delivered a dozen solid lashes, which only served to make me hotter. As I stared at Rick's striped ass, I squeezed my thighs together, feeling desire and hunger swell inside me. I'd never been more turned on in my life than I was at that moment, having had these two strong, handsome men so readily submit to me.

"Now, Jake. You'd said something about making it up to me?"

Jake looked up, still clutching the couch.

"Come here."

He rushed over to me, stripping off his clothes in a mad

haste. He knelt before me and placed reverential kisses on each of my high-heeled shoes before reaching underneath my skirt. He paused, his hands on my thighs, and looked at me for approval. When I nodded, he pulled my panties down my thighs. The silky garment was so wet, it left damp streaks along my flesh. Jake helped me out of my undies, and then dived underneath my skirt. He grabbed my ass, palming my cheeks roughly as he slurped up my juice. He trailed his tongue along my slit, and I jumped every time he grazed my swollen clit. I began grinding my sex down against his lips and chin. He responded to my motions by zeroing in on my button, and I tangled my fingers in his hair and held him in place. I was lost in my own world as he teased and flicked my clit until he took me over the edge. I cried out loud, shivering as I came, and glossing his face with my juice.

Once I caught my breath, I pulled away from Jake and told him to sit on the couch. He readily obeyed, and I couldn't hide my smile when I saw him wince as his well-whipped bottom hit the velvet cushion. His erection was as hard as stone, and this time I reached out to stroke it, imagining what it was going to feel like inside me.

Rick was still in position, watching us. I leaned over and rummaged around in the pockets of his pants, which were still banded around his knees. I found his wallet and was grateful to find a condom inside. I tossed his wallet to the floor and then opened the little foil package and rolled the condom over Jake's shaft. Once it was in place, I straddled his hips and slowly lowered myself onto his cock, sighing with satisfaction. I kissed him, our tongues tangling wildly, and I tasted my own musky flavor on his lips. I rose up and slammed down, repeatedly filling myself with his dick. Once I got a good rhythm going, I turned toward Rick. "Come," I gasped, waving him toward us.

Rick kicked off his pants and rested one knee on the

couch. I grabbed his cock and brought it to my parted lips. I circled my tongue around the head of his dick, and Rick closed his eyes and hissed through his teeth. I slowly slid my lips down his shaft, swallowing his entire length and savoring his flavor. By this point, Jake had grabbed my hips and was pumping upward into my pussy. Each time he hit bottom, I groaned around his friend's dick. Rick kept his hands at his sides and let me suck him at my own pace. I felt so deliciously dirty to be enjoying these two young men. As always, they followed my lead and were looking to make sure I was satisfied. That realization sparked my second orgasm of the night. It came on me suddenly in an explosion of pleasure. As I felt the ecstasy course through me, my cunt fluttered around Jake's shaft. His hips rose off the cushions one last time, and he groaned loudly. I felt his shaft pulse inside the condom as he reached his own peak seconds after me.

Moaning around a mouthful of cock, I redoubled my efforts on Rick. His groans blended into one long, erotic chant as he struggled to reach his climax. To help him out, I reached around and scratched my nails over his ass. He jerked his cock from my mouth, and with a shout, shot his load across the tarp on the floor and then collapsed next to us on the couch.

They never did paint the living room that night; they were far too busy with an entirely different set of tasks.

Who knew? It took tossing away all my carefully detailed plans to find my own happy ending, and I trust my boys to come up with plenty of bedtime stories to keep me satisfied.

Wolff's Tavern

Bella Dean

I barely rolled into the parking lot. Barely. And though I was totally grateful to the Big Guy in the sky for making it to "civilization," I was also letting a long string of very bad words fly. This was not the first time Father Bill had broken down recently, just the most inconvenient. That's right, Father Bill. Yes, my car is a boy.

"You couldn't have made it twenty-five more miles, you piece of shit?" I barked. I slammed my open palm against the dashboard and fought the urge to scream. Gravel crackled under my barely moving wheels until we finally came to a complete halt. Guilt got the better of me. "Fine, fine. I am sorry, baby. You're not a piece of shit. You're old. I'm not being fair."

Father Bill was over forty, in fact. A 1966-and-a-half Mustang coupe. Ash-gray. Black interior. Left-right-quarter panel a lovely primer gray for accent. The engine ticked and popped and I ran my hands through my short red bob. My bangs stood up in spikes, and when I tried to tame them, they stood right back up.

"Lovely," I muttered, and put him in Park. The dark

wooden sign that swung over my head was so dirty and faded I had to squint to read it. "Wolff's Tavern. Well, I'll say this for you, Father Bill, you know where to break down. At least I can have a drink while I wait for my tow."

Another soft click from the engine. I swear, the car was laughing. I grabbed my cell phone and checked again. No luck and NO SERVICE. Beautiful. Dead car, dead cell phone, out in the middle of nowhere. A strange place, no, a strange *bar* that could possibly be full of all kinds of crazed lunatics who would see a single woman alone and—

"Enough of that bullshit, Ruby. Jesus. It's a tavern, not the state correctional facility." I flung open the car door and the wind caught it. The rusty hinge let out an ear-splitting shriek, and I snagged the handle before the frigging thing ripped off and sailed away. "And what bonus is this? A storm!" I chirped and stomped noisily to the huge wooden tavern door and wrenched it open.

The inside of the tavern was cavernous and dark. Black wooden bar, black wooden stools, black ceiling beams. I felt like I was in the Black Forest. Four heads turned to regard me. Four! The place could house a 747 and there were three patrons. Also, the bartender. He had shaggy blond hair, a face full of stubble and was roughly the size of a tree.

"Yo, Red, what can I do for you?"

Red. Ah, so original. When he leveled his azure-blue gaze my way, my breath stopped. It froze the pithy comeback halfway up my throat. I nervously tried to paste my bangs down with my fingers. I felt them spring up and I sighed. "Got a phone and a martini? Not necessarily in that order." Good for me, my voice only wavered a touch. Not normal for me. Normally, I don't get flustered, but the bartender was looking at me like I was on the menu and I liked it. A lot.

"You don't have a cell phone? City girl like you?" he said. His voice was deep and raspy and I felt my skin tighten into goose bumps. He handed me a phone. It was quickly followed by a martini. Three olives. The glass was opaque from the chilled liquid.

I picked up the glass, knocked back half the drink, then ate all three olives at once. Fortified, I picked up the phone and punched in the number I knew by heart. She answered on the third ring. Her voice was strong but not as strong as usual. There was an underlying exhaustion and frustration that only a few would notice.

"Grandma? It's me, Ruby. Father Bill broke down. I'll be there soon. I have to call for a tow. You okay until I get there? Should I call someone else to come?"

"Ruby, darling, I'll be fine. I'm tougher than you think. I have my remote, my medicine, and don't tell anyone, but I have a glass of wine."

"You rebel." I laughed. I could breathe a little. She sounded pretty good and she'd be fine. "I'll be there as soon as I can get a truck to get me there."

"Don't drive yourself crazy and be careful!"

"I will, I will. How's the hip?"

"The hip is a pain in my ass but I'll live now, God willing, another twenty years just to drive you all crazy. Now, I have to go, *Jeopardy!* will be on any moment and I feel lucky tonight."

I grinned. "I'll be there as soon as I can."

"I know you will, Ruby. Be careful!" she repeated.

"Yes, ma'am." I hung up to the sound of *This is Jeopardy!*

"Everything okay with Grandma?" the gigantic man said and leaned in. He grinned at me when I frowned. His teeth were white and even and, in the low light of the bar, looked wickedly sharp for some reason.

"My grandmother could kick your ass with one foot tied behind her back," I snorted. I sucked down the rest of the martini and he replaced it with a fresh one, like a magic trick.

The best magic trick ever. "But she just had a hip replace-ment and since I recently lost my job, I am going to go play nursemaid and possibly some pinochle."

Hmm. Apparently the alcohol had loosened my lips.

"Is that so?" Mr. Humongous ran his fingernail down the modest but visible seam of my cleavage. Instinct said to ram him upside the head with my empty, but instead I made a soft needy sound in the back of my throat.

"Yes. She could. Kick your ass," I stammered. "Phone. Where is that phone? I need to call a tow."

The bartender pointed to the phone still on the bar. He had never taken it back. My scrambled brain and overactive nether regions had done a number on my perception. I squeezed my thighs tight and my pussy flexed. I could feel a hot line along the tender skin of my breasts where his finger had been. I wanted him to put it back. I wanted to feel him touch me again. Instead, I said, "The owner would have your head if he knew you'd done that."

I gave him my best evil eye and completely ignored the vivid mental flash of wrapping my thighs around his waist while he fucked me.

"I *am* the owner," he said, and grinned. "Wolff. Ryan Wolff, at your service. What can I *do* you for?"

I blew out a long, exhausted sigh. Then I gave in and said, "Tow truck. I need a tow."

"I could drive you to Grandma's when the bar closes. Wouldn't that be easier?"

"And be alone with you?" *And beg you to do things to me. And do things to you. We could do things together. I wonder what you taste like.* I shook my head to clear my thoughts. "That's okay. Thanks ever so much but I'll stick with a pro."

"Fine by me," he said, and handed me a business card. Then he disappeared. His big wide shoulders, his fine chiseled jaw, his hot fingers.

I punched in the number on the card and it was answered by a gruff and rude man. "Yeah?"

"I need a tow."

"No kidding. What a surprise. Since we are a towing company."

I frowned. Jerk. It also said "mechanics" on the card, but I wasn't going to argue. "I am at Wolff's Tavern. How soon can you be here?"

"About two."

"Two!"

"Did I stutter?"

"Fine. I'll just call another tow company," I threatened. I sipped my cold martini and thought it might be a good idea to get some food. Food would be brilliant.

Quiet laughter snaked into my ear through the phone cord. Forget the fact that I could not remember the last time I had held a phone that actually had a cord. "Good luck with that. The closest one besides us is about four hours away. That would put you at about four in the morning."

Very bad words fluttered to my lips and I swallowed them. "Fine," I said between gritted teeth. "I will wait for you. It's a sixty-six-and-a-half Mustang."

"Good for you. You riding with me?"

"I have to."

"Right. See you at two. What's your name?"

"Ruby Brunner."

He sang a bar of the old Drifters song, *Ruby Baby,* softly. And then he hung up.

"Weirdo."

Wolff came back wiping his hands on a bar rag. "Who's a weirdo?"

"Where do I start?" I sighed and finished martini number two. "I need slumfwood," I said. I blinked and tried again. "I meet some food."

"You need some food, babe," he said, and leaned in and kissed me. Hard. Like the cretin he was, he forced his lips against mine almost angrily. I felt my lips plump up from the rough pressure and before disengaging, he bit my bottom lip so that I hissed in pain. In direct contrast my pussy went wet for him. I felt warm fluid pleasure and wanted to tell him to forget the food. Let's go in the back room.

I didn't. Instead, I said, "Got any hot dogs?"

"Boy, you like to eat," he said. He was watching my lips as I finished my fourth dog. I licked my lips just to mess with him and he clenched his big stubbly jaw. "Careful, Red, don't think I don't know you did that on purpose. Be careful how you taunt me. I'm a bit of an animal."

I rolled my eyes and finished my Coke. I was ready for another drink. "Ooh, I'm so scared, Wolff. What time is it?"

He glanced at his watch. The watchband was a leather cuff. Battered and busted brown leather that somehow turned me on to the point of panting. "It's a quarter to two."

"And you are bare-ass empty in here," I said. "So, you should lock up." I coughed softly. He was staring at my breasts. The sensation I felt from his gaze was similar to having his hand on my throat. Gently squeezing my breath into submission.

"I guess I'll lock up in a minute." He disappeared again and I dug in my hobo bag for my wallet. Four hot dogs, two martinis, two Cokes. Christ, I hoped I had enough cash to pay him.

Maybe you could barter with him if you don't. Maybe you could offer him a service for his hospitality.

Before I could even consider the voice in my head, I heard a blaring air horn and hopped off the stool. Part of me was thrilled to be headed to Grandma's, part of me was bummed that nothing had come of the animal attraction between me and Wolff.

"Wolff! The tow truck is here! Come out and let me pay you."

Nothing.

Another long blast of the horn and my head felt like someone was ringing the Liberty Bell in there. "Christ. How does that guy not go deaf?" I pushed the heavy door open. I would just tell the driver to hold on while I found Ryan and paid him. Maybe get just one more kiss—

"Come on, Red," he said, leaning out the driver's side of the huge tow truck. Father Bill was still in the parking lot, and he was grinning like a predator who smelled good vittles. His sharp white teeth glowing in the sodium streetlamps.

Wolff was the tow-truck driver. The door read AW Mechanics and Towing. Was this a one-man town? Tavern owner, mechanic, tow-truck service. Was he the mayor and the sheriff, too? I caught the keys he tossed my way a split second before they could smack me in the forehead. I locked the door and made my way to him. This should be interesting.

"I brought that out of the car." He nodded toward the floorboard. His big hand settled on my thigh. I jumped. I felt my body jolt. There was no hiding it. But on the inside, oh dear, on the inside I felt like I was being shocked with the most decadent electricity. My body was humming with attraction and excitement. His big mitt traveled farther up until his pinkie stretched out and for the briefest of moments traced the slit of my pussy. I sighed and shifted in my seat.

"Thank you. And why isn't my car on the truck?" I squawked. I noticed my lone suitcase was shoved behind the bench seat.

"It needs work, babe. I'll fix it for you. What's in the basket?" He was clearly changing the subject.

I regarded the basket covered in red gingham fabric and

tried to recall. It was for Grandma. A bunch of things to make her feel better and cheer her up. That much I recalled. Beyond that, I was drawing a blank because now he had spread his entire palm over my mound and his middle finger was rhythmically flexing against me. Stroke, stroke, stroke it went against my swollen clit. "Uh—"

"Food? Dirty magazines? Metamucil?" he asked, and laughed softly. It was an entirely sinister sound. "Come on, Red, surely you know what's in your own present."

His gruff, deep voice set the hair on the back of my neck on edge. I sucked in a great breath of air and recited. "Her favorites. Cinnamon thins, almond cookies, butter creams. A nice bottle of wine, which she shouldn't have. A book of crosswords and a bottle of her favorite shower gel."

"Good girl," he said, and reached down. He slid my long black skirt up. The calluses on his palm made a hissing sound on my skin. Heat trails bloomed under his firm touch and I slid lower in the seat. He wormed his finger under my blue silk panties and stroked me firmly until I moaned.

"You're afraid of me," he said. "I can smell it."

I nodded. Sinking a bit lower, letting his big brutal fingers invade me as the truck rumbled and swayed under my bottom.

"And you like that. You're wet, Red." He flexed his fingers deep in my pussy. Stroked the greediest parts of me with a come-hither motion until I squirmed on the red pleather seat like a whore.

I nodded again. Verbal communication skills had deserted me.

The white-yellow headlights split the black night, and that storm I had felt coming lit up the sky with sickly yellow flashes of lighting. Booming filled my ears as Wolff propelled the truck with one big hand. The other big hand fondled me roughly between the thighs as I arched up to welcome more. Another harsh crack of thunder and I jumped.

"Red?"

"I don't like storms," I managed to say. I spread my legs wider to give him better access. I was willing to take the hit morally. I mean, I wasn't supposed to be spread out before him and practically begging him to make me come, but in my defense, he knew what he was doing. And my body was already flirting with orgasm. And I wanted one. I really, really wanted a nice mind-numbing orgasm to take the bite out of a really bad day.

Wind buffeted the truck and the hand disappeared. "Whoa," Wolff growled and I bit my tongue to keep from balking. It was unreasonable to expect him to maneuver the truck through the sudden deluge with one hand. Unreasonable. Really.

"Oh, it's flooding," I said, and then blushed. Yes. My panties were positively soaked, but what I meant was the road. Water gushed over the macadam and swirled around the debris the high winds propelled. Sticks and rocks and debris from the nearby highway. I held my breath. I did not like storms in general. I liked violent storms even less.

"This road is a bitch on wheels," he said. His voice was like busted glass and gravel and barbed wire all rolled into one. I fought the urge to slither across the seat and put his hand back in my lap. I had clearly lost my mind.

"No, it's pheromones you're feeling," he said as if he was reading the mind I had lost. "I have to pull over. This section is infamous for completely flooding out. More cars and motorists have been lost along this stretch than any other." He nudged the giant black truck over to the shoulder and we sat. The truck vibrated and grumbled beneath us. I wanted to grumble, too.

"So, we just sit here?" I grumped.

"What else do you suggest?" he asked. When he turned to me his eyes flared white and green in the low light. I told myself it was the dashboard lights illuminating his naturally feral face.

"I—um—I was just—"

Wolff turned to me and shoved both hands up under my skirt. He hiked it up even farther, exposing the tops of my motorcycle boots and the thin scrap of my panties. "I say, snack time."

I swallowed hard. Somehow I knew I was the snack. "I was just—" What? Was I really going to argue with him?

"Red, you know there's no fighting me. I'm the Big, Bad Wolff," he whispered, and my nipples peaked, hard little points in my soft gray sweater. Without thinking, I arched my hips up in his general direction. A silent, shameless plea for him to carry through with his threat.

He fought his way over the gearshift, and pushed his hand under my seat. The seat slid back quickly and I let out a surprised little whoop. He held my skirt back and ate me with his eyes first. "Well, look what we have here. Dessert," he said, and ran his red, red tongue over his full lips.

Between my thighs, I was hot and wet and ready. Ready beyond comprehension. He tugged my panties roughly and I shimmied to help him along. When his shaggy head lowered, my heart stopped, or so it seemed. When his tongue lapped at me, hot and wet and slick, I fisted my hands in his hair. I tugged. Hard. I didn't care if I hurt him. "Oh, please," I said mindlessly.

"Please what? Please don't, Mr. Wolff? Please do? Please don't stop? Please go faster?" He pushed his fingers deep inside me and my hips jerked up on their own. I mewed softly, ashamed of my shamelessness.

"All of it," I said.

He fucked me hard with his fingers but soft with his tongue. For every brutal thrust of his digits, his lips adored me. I felt myself hovering right there on the edge. Right on the cusp of letting go and christening him with my juices. "Do it for me. I'm far from done, sweet thing. We have time for a mating, if you will, and then when the storm passes, we'll get you to Grandma's house all safe and sound."

He thrust higher with his big fingers and sucked my clit firmly between his lips. I came with a plea, but I couldn't tell you what I was pleading for. Most likely it was for more.

I couldn't see his hands but I heard his zipper. Even over the pounding rain, my ears picked up that sound. He pushed my thighs wide and muttered, "Open." I opened as far as I could as the velvety hard head of his cock pushed against me. My body split wide and accepted him. He rocked into me as deep as he could go. Just as I had fantasized at the tavern, I wrapped my legs around his hips as he sank his teeth into the sweetest spot where my neck met my shoulder.

"You are tender, I'll give you that," he teased, and bit me again.

I dug my nails into his hips as far as I could and yanked my heels hard against his hips. Maybe I wanted to hurt him a little, too. Maybe I just wanted his cock as deep as it would go. Either way, a brutal flash of lightning flared and his face, darkly stubbled and somewhat lupine, lit up with an eerie light. He grinned at me and those teeth flashed again one more time before sinking into my flesh right above my collarbone. I came with a breathy little cry that evened out his deep animal growl as he emptied into me.

Just like that, the rain went from downpour to mist. He took a deep breath of me and I listened to his panting. He smelled like sweat and smoke and earth. My cunt flickered lazily around his cock. When he pulled free of me, he licked my lower lip before kissing me.

"Jesus," I said.

"Ryan." He laughed softly. "But thanks for the compliment."

"We'd better go. My grandmother will be worried. I don't know what I'll tell her."

"Tell her the Big, Bad Wolff stopped you on your way."

"And?"

He shrugged and raised an eyebrow. I felt my body go soft and ready for him again. "And it was good?" he said. He got himself back behind the wheel.

I nodded. "Fair enough." Good didn't even begin to cover it.

"How long will you be visiting Grandma?" He took a right and I recognized my grandmother's street. She would have waited up. She would want to make sure I was safe and sound.

"Until she's healed."

"Does she have a car?"

"No," I said slowly, not understanding.

"And the Mustang is your only car?"

"Yes."

"It's a real piece of shit, you know that?"

I felt a smile come to my face and his hand was back on my thigh. His finger traced the still-slick seam of my pussy and I had to take a deep breath to steady myself. "I know," I breathed.

"You'll need lots of help with that. With patience and regular trips to town, we can get her running good again in no time."

"She's a him," I said.

"Of course he is," Wolff said, and pulled in front of Grandma's cottage.

"I hear the local mechanic serves free hot dogs," I teased as he slid a finger into me and flexed. Pleasure unfurled in my pelvis and I sighed.

The front door opened and Wolff withdrew his finger. I smoothed my skirt. "Only if you provide dessert, Red," he said against my ear. He nipped my lobe hard enough to make spots bloom before my eyes. My cunt went fluid, aching for him all over again. Grandma waved. I waved back. "I can do that," I said. "No problem."

Slutty Cinderella

Jacqueline Applebee

Kazimir was still undressed when I called round that night. He answered the door with a small white bath towel draped around his hips that drew my eyes to his groin. I'd never known a man to be so unconcerned about his appearance, but still manage to be effortlessly handsome. He moved a lock of damp hair from his hazel eyes and winked.

"You're early, Lisa," he drawled. "What's the hurry?"

I went to check my watch, and then remembered that I didn't have it tonight. Instead, I wore a pretty silver timepiece that dangled from a chain in my waistcoat. The watch was the finishing touch to my outfit. This was the first time I'd dressed completely in men's clothing; a fetish charity ball was the perfect opportunity for me to explore cross-dressing. I wore a formal pinstripe suit, complete with bowler hat and umbrella—a throwback to the old *Avengers* TV show. I'd discovered the alternative scene rather late in the day; I'd married very young, and had spent twenty years as an obedient little housewife. One divorce later, I was a free woman, determined to make up for lost time—that's where Kazimir came in.

"We've only got fifteen minutes before the ball starts," I

complained as Kazimir ushered me inside. "Don't you think you should get dressed?"

I stepped over strewn clothes that lay on the floor of his apartment, making my way to his bedroom. Once there, he pressed me against a wall. He gyrated against me, and the towel slipped away. He removed my bowler hat and flung it on the bed. I felt his hot cock growing harder with every movement he made against me. His hands went to my breasts, but I captured his wrists, and held them at his sides.

"I thought you said I had to get dressed?" Kazimir asked with a smile. "But we could always stay here and have some fun of our own."

I released him, patted his bare backside and stepped away. It's not that I don't like the idea of restraint, but I knew where it would lead. If we started doing that now, we'd never get to the ball. On our second date, Kazimir had tied me to his bed; it was just supposed to be a little naughty fun, but it soon evolved into more when he refused to release me until I'd admitted my secret desires. After so many years bottling things up in a stale marriage, I was only too ready to spill. One of my wishes was that I could be more forceful during sex. My admission had only served to arouse my new man—we swapped places, I cuffed him to the bed and then proceeded to screw him through the mattress. I'm not usually that bold, but now that I was dressed like a man, I could feel some of my hidden power start to rise to the surface. I idly wondered where I had last seen the leather wrist cuffs, just in case things got interesting, but it was impossible to locate anything in Kazimir's untidy room.

I opened his wardrobe and pulled out the dress he was going to wear tonight, still in its plastic dry-cleaning cover. The frilly pink-and-white creation looked like a cream cake, with layers of lace and full wide skirts. Kazimir took the gown from me and started pulling it over his head. I stopped him quickly.

"You can't just put that on without any underwear!" I explained. "That dress needs some foundation garments."

Kazimir looked at me as if I were mad.

"What the hell are those?"

"Bras and knickers," I replied patiently.

He rummaged around in a pile on the floor, and I was dismayed to see him hold up a pair of my black knickers and a red push-up bra. Funny, but I didn't remember leaving them after my last visit.

"Don't worry, babe, they were just mementos." He answered my unspoken question with a guilty smile. He pulled on the bra, and then tried to do up the fastening at the back. Luckily we were a similar build, although Kazimir's much taller than I.

"Don't you move," I commanded, and he arched an eyebrow. I twisted him around, pulled the bra in place and secured the hook-and-eye fastening. The padded bra gave him a pair of nice little tits. I reached inside, and pinched one of his nipples until he gasped.

"Now everyone can see this peeping out the top of the dress." He ran his hands over the lacy cups, squeezing the imaginary breasts inside. "I'll look like a slutty Cinderella." As Kazimir spoke, I trailed my hand down his back and lower to his ass. My fingers tickled his crack, massaged the globes of his cheeks, and then I pinched him hard enough to make him yelp.

"Shoes!" he suddenly exclaimed, jumping out of my reach. "A girl's got to have some heels." He scampered into a corner of the messy room, and then produced a pair of black patent-leather shoes. He tried and failed to step into them, stumbling. I sighed, knelt at his feet, and gently lifted first one and then the other foot into the shoes. He wobbled for a moment, but then he straightened his back, jutted his hip and stood up tall. The sight of a half-naked man wearing only heels and a bra was something else. My mouth went slack.

"Do you like?" he purred. He walked carefully over to his bedside table, and produced his camera. "Why don't you take a photo of me." He handed me the camera, a high-tech model with lots of features. I'd used it once before, and I knew it had a timer, so we could both be in the shot. I set the device, and ran to Kazimir's side. I only came to his shoulders, now he was wearing his shoes, but I didn't care. I could still reach over to pinch one of his nipples. He made a gentle "Oh!" as the flash came to life. I knew the picture would be hot.

"Now kneel down, Cinderella, and let me stand behind you." Kazimir did as I said, and as the camera flashed, he gripped my thighs and buried his head in my crotch. The camera continued to flash every few seconds whilst Kazimir unzipped me slowly. A flicker of light made me look up as he nuzzled my open fly. His long fingers slipped past the barrier of the boxer shorts I wore, and he finally spread my labia wide. The flash went off at the exact moment that Kazimir's lips touched my clit. He craned his neck to reach me, and with every flick of his tongue, the flash sparkled, il-luminating us. He unbuttoned me, and then tugged down my trousers. The flash went off once my legs were bare. I couldn't open my legs as wide as I would have liked, with the trousers bunched around my ankles, but Kazimir didn't need much room. He mouthed my pussy, licking hungrily around my clitoris. His goatee beard grew wetter from my juices—the pulsing light reflected on his shiny face. I gripped his head with both my hands, steadying myself as I thrust against him. I felt the heat build inside my pussy, and every nerve ending tingle as my whole being centered on Kazimir's lips. My heart pounded in my chest as I came, and I leaned on his shoulders to stop myself from falling over. He stood to kiss me. I could taste myself on his hot face, could feel his bruised lips and his sticky beard from where I had used him for my pleasure.

"Kazimir, we've got to stop, or we'll never get to the ball." I sighed, staggering back. He sauntered over to the camera and switched the machine off. Our photo album was certainly going to be interesting.

I helped him into his dress, and carefully pulled the zipper up the back, dotting a kiss to Kazimir's skin as I did so. The dress really did suit him. Once he had shaved, his look would be perfect, but he had no such plans.

"You can't go out wearing a bright pink dress and a goatee," I explained as rationally as I could. Kazimir only pouted, pulled out a hairbrush and started combing his hair. There was no way I would turn up to the ball with him looking this way. I had a hard enough time hailing a cab dressed as I was, and I didn't want to walk. I felt my face burn with frustration at being ignored, so in a fit of outright defiance, I grabbed the hairbrush out of his hand, midstroke. I tapped the wooden back against my thigh, making loud slapping noises.

"What are you going to do with that?" he asked quietly.

"I'm going to teach you to listen." I had no idea where this had come from—maybe the clothes I was wearing, or maybe Kazimir's outfit, but I felt a rush of power at my words, a rush that went straight to my still-sensitive crotch.

Kazimir swiveled in his chair, looked me right in the eye, before saying, "You wouldn't dare." I clutched a handful of his hair, and pulled his head back roughly. The sound he made was a surprise to me—there was pleasure in his groans, and not a drop of pain.

"Oh, God, that feels so good," he gasped. I released him, and stepped away to sit on the edge of the bed, trying to figure out how I was going to harness the power that lay inside me.

"Get over here," I said, though I could hear the tremor in

my voice. Kazimir shuffled over on his knees until he knelt at my side. "Bend over my lap," I whispered, and he swiftly moved to drape himself over my thighs. I pushed all the frills and layers of his dress upward, bunching them into the waistband. My ex-husband loved to threaten me with something like this, but he never followed through. I, on the other hand, had more balls than he ever did. My palm slapped Kazimir's ass with a loud clap. He shivered beneath me, and then arched up for more. This wasn't punishment—this was instruction, and Kazimir was a willing student.

"Next time I come round, I expect the place to be tidy." I followed my words with three tentative slaps from the hairbrush. His skin went pink instantly—I could see the clear outline of the brush on his flesh.

"Of course," Kazimir said breathlessly.

"When I give you some advice, you damn well do what I say." The hand holding the hairbrush was sweaty, but I wasn't about to stop. The brush landed on his ass with a solid thump.

"Yes!" And then, "More, please!"

I could feel his cock hard against me. The slippery fabric of the dress rubbed against my thighs, but his length poked through the folds. I took off my pocket watch, and dangled the cold metal case against his heated skin. He jerked against me, but stayed on my lap once I pushed him firmly down. When I slipped the fob chain between his ass cheeks, he flinched, but I held him firmly in place. I ran the length of chain up and down his crack. He stifled a moan, and pressed his cock harder against me. Up and down, over and over, I ran the silver chain between his cheeks, slowly teasing him. I was starting to become aroused at my actions. The boxers I wore rubbed against my pussy. I knew I was getting deliciously wet again. I could smell my own scent rise to my nostrils, and I knew that Kazimir could smell me, too.

"Next time we go to a party, we will be on time, am I understood?" I asked, using my gruffest voice. "We're already fifteen minutes late."

I wiped my palms on my trousers, and then delivered fifteen harder whacks to Kazimir's backside. He counted every one of them, his voice going rough near the end.

After that, I felt a little at a loss. I had never done anything like that before. In fact, I would never even have dreamed of this, if not for the threats my ex used to make. Hell, I suppose he was good for something after all. Kazimir remained panting beneath me. His hair obscured part of his face, but I could still make out a wide smile. I soothed his stressed skin, gently rubbed my hands over the hot flesh.

Then I spotted a small bottle of moisturizer on his bedside table. I just about managed to lean over to grab the tube without dislodging Kazimir. I smeared some of the cream over his skin, massaging in the lotion. He sighed contentedly as I worked, but then his sighs became more urgent as I dribbled some of the cold liquid between his cheeks. I circled a finger over his asshole, gently pressing as I went.

My index finger slipped in, quickly joined by my middle finger. He was hot there, so hot and tight that he practically sucked me inside. Kazimir humped my lap. I pushed the full fabric of the dress higher until the ruffles covered his face. I didn't want him to see how nervous I was. I slowly worked my fingers deep inside him. I twisted them, and he panted loudly. More cream, and I could slide in and out quickly. My fingers rubbed up against a magic spot inside him, and he almost leaped off my lap.

"Do that again!" he yelled.

"Excuse me?" I purred. "What would you like?"

"Please," he wailed. "Please do it again." I complied with his request, and soon he was grunting and thrusting against me with force.

"Are you going to come all over your pretty dress?" I

crooned, tapping his special spot, the place I began to suspect was his prostate.

"Yes, I'm gonna come!" he yelled from beneath the pile of pink fabric.

"Then get off me."

Kazimir rolled off my lap, and stood, lifting the skirts of his dress to place his hard cock flat in his palm. I wiped my hands on a discarded bath towel, picked up his camera and centered him in the view screen.

"Stroke yourself for me," I whispered. I could see his pupils dilate from where I stood, could hear the painful gasp as his hands touched his cock. I snapped a photograph, capturing the moment forever. Kazimir looked away from me as he ran his fingers over his cock. I had never known him to be even remotely shy before. He bit his lip, hesitantly peeking back at me.

"Look at me," I said, but he turned away even more. I followed him with the camera. "Look at me, Kazimir."

"I don't know about this, Lisa," he said quietly. His hand hovered above his dress, not touching, but longing to.

"You look so good, Kaz. Do it, do it for me." He nodded slightly, and then gasped when he held himself once more. I took a string of shots as he stroked himself. I zoomed in on his crotch—I could just about see the tip of his cock squeezing through his fingers, all surrounded by pink-and-white fabric. His face was open to me. His usually wicked eyes were soft, and his skin was flushed. I set the timer on the camera, before placing the expensive plaything on the bed. When I moved behind him, I could feel the tremors his body made. I angled us so we were facing the camera, and then stretched my arms around to cradle his cock. I heard the flash flutter to life, felt the lacy dress tickle my wrist, and I inhaled the smell of sex. Kazimir's cock was like a rod of steel in my hands as he moved faster.

"Come on, princess," I growled, "Do it, do it now!"

Kazimir's hand sped up around his cock. He cried out and jerked as he came in a gush. Then he sagged against me, breathless and sweaty, before hugging me hard. He stumbled into the chair by the dresser, and fumbled for a discarded T-shirt on the floor to wipe his face. I looked around at the room, now even messier than usual—he'd managed to splatter the pillows with the force of his orgasm, and the room looked depraved, debauched and absolutely fantastic.

"Oh, babe, you're a natural. I just have a favor to ask."

"Yeah? What?" I hoped it wasn't a request to have me dress up in black PVC or something strange—at least something stranger than a man's three-piece suit.

"Could you use the hairbrush handle inside me the next time? At least, until we buy a dildo."

I hadn't planned on repeating this performance, but something in Kazimir's bright hazel eyes made me melt. I wanted to make him happy, plus I wanted him to tidy up his pigsty of an apartment, too.

"Come here, slut," I said, crooking a finger in his direction. He quickly scooted over to me, and then he crouched down so I could kiss him. This time, I held his hands, rubbing them over my breasts. "I think I can do that, Cinderella," I whispered into his ear. "Now, have a shave, so we can go to the ball."

Kiss It

Saskia Walker

"They say if you kiss it, you'll get the gift of the gab."

It was the man's seductive brogue that caught my attention, rather than what he said. I knew all about the Blarney stone already. I'd flown from England and then covered the breadth of Ireland on a bus full of tourists to get to the castle where it was located.

I paused on the woodland path I'd been strolling along and glanced in his direction, wondering where he'd appeared from. He was a couple of inches taller than me, and built solid. His features were rugged, his eyes filled with whimsical charm. Thick, dark hair and bold blue eyes reflected his nationality. He was a local, and he had a wild gypsy look about him that captured my attention. Was that what he was, a gypsy in the woods?

"The Blarney stone." He nodded in the direction of the castle that housed the legendary Irish stone, and lifted his eyebrows. "Did you want to kiss it?"

For some reason, the way he said "kiss it" didn't make me think of kissing the rock that was currently surrounded by tourists. Instead, it made me want to kiss something else.

Him? Embarrassed, I clasped my hands around my arms and glanced back along the path. The crowd of people gathered outside the castle was growing all the time. That's why I'd wandered away into the forest instead, my attention strangely lured by the pretty woods. And now I was being strangely lured by a man who looked like a gypsy. When I looked back at him, he was smiling at me as if he knew what I was thinking. The sun was bright behind his head and I shielded my eyes as I replied.

"Yes, I thought I would—" I paused "—kiss it…" Oh, for some odd reason, saying that aloud made me feel as if I'd been embraced and fondled by the words. "But there were so many people up there." My explanation dwindled off as self-awareness gathered inside me. Where had he appeared from? Faded blue jeans encased strong thighs. The jeans were worn with heavy boots, and the dark, open-necked shirt he had on exaggerated both his coloring and his stature. Broad shouldered, shirtsleeves rolled up over muscular forearms. He had large, masculine hands, and I could scarcely look away for wanting him to touch me.

"You came here for some Irish magic, didn't you?"

I shrugged and smiled, trying to be nonchalant about his question. It sounded more like a come-on than a serious suggestion. But, yes, I had made the journey in the hope of some of Ireland's magic rubbing off on me. As I was crammed in the queue of tourists, the magic seemed too far away.

Stepping across my path, he grinned. "An adventure, maybe?"

There was speed and lightness about the way he moved. It was almost dancelike. He began to wend his way along the stepping-stones that made a path through the trees and bluebells. The trees had grown dense, and the smell of summer was heavy in the air under their canopy. I realized he was now leading me as we continued along the way. But we were within shouting distance of other people, and I felt safe with him.

"Yes, I suppose you're right." The self-awareness I'd felt when he first spoke to me was shaping into something else, something that was making me bolder.

"Tell me, now. If you had three wishes, what would they be?"

I laughed softly. "Three wishes?"

"You're on the Irish Myth and Magic tour, are you not?"

"Well, yes." He must have seen me getting off the bus. Perhaps he worked here. Yes, he had the look of a caretaker, earthy and rugged.

He chuckled, and there was a ribald quality to the sound. "Did you want to kiss the Blarney?"

I was mesmerized by the way his mouth moved, slow and seductive, as he said that. He'd stepped closer, and my body responded. He locked eyes with me, demanding my response.

"Yes, I did want that." A warm breeze moved in and wrapped itself around us as I spoke. I swayed, my senses suddenly filled with the scent and the atmosphere of the woodland.

"I've kissed the stone," he said, his voice low, his breath warm on my face. "Kissing me would be just as good as kissing it yourself."

He made me want him. Badly. Squeezing my thighs together, I nodded. "Maybe it would."

My breath condensed in my chest as the space between us vanished, and his mouth brushed over mine. It was the subtlest of kisses, but it set free a wild thread of excitement—a thread that electrified my body and made my center clench and melt.

"Tell me your wishes," he breathed as he moved to kiss my earlobe. His body was hard and demanding against mine, his breath hot on my skin.

"Confidence," I found myself responding, strangely intoxicated by his blatant approach.

He lifted his eyebrows suggestively, eyes twinkling as he assessed me. "Confidence to do what, exactly?"

There was something so immensely appealing about his naughty approach that I was affected by it. Well, I was affected by some damn thing, because I laughed and wrapped one hand round the back of his head, my fingers moving into his thick dark hair. "Confident enough to do this?"

I returned his kiss, savoring the way he moved against me when I did.

He held me tightly to him, teased the tip of his tongue against mine and then thrust it deep into my mouth, moving in and out in a direct suggestion of raunchy sex. The sensation made me squirm, my body clenching, my pussy growing slicker by the moment. What was happening to me? Not only did I feel empowered, I was acting on it. I ran my hands over his chest and then down, around his hips, and grasped his buttocks. They were firm, muscular, and when I squeezed them, he rubbed against me and I could feel his cock through our clothing—big, and hard. My head dropped back, a sigh of longing escaping me.

"What else?" He continued to explore me with his hands as he asked the question, squeezing my breasts roughly through my top and bra. "What would your second wish be?"

Heavily aroused by his touches, and under the spell of his powerfully persuasive suggestions, I found my mind filled with fantasies—the fantasies I entertained in my private moments, the things that turned me on but I wasn't brave enough to share—to use a sexy, aroused and willing man, to work his body with my own, to tell him to do me hard and do me well, and revel in every decadent moment. A man like him? I stared at him, unable to voice it, but wanting him to know.

His intense gaze made me sway, and he grabbed me in against him, holding me steady. I shuddered in his arms, heady with arousal.

"Come on," he whispered, his Irish brogue lifting on the summer breeze as he took my hand and pulled me away from the path and into the thick bed of bluebells.

I had to jog through the flowers to keep up with him, and the scent of them rising up from beneath my feet was almost overpowering. When he drew me to a halt I was panting, my senses reeling. It was deliciously dusky and yet warm beneath the trees, the summer heat haze mellowing under the shifting pattern of shadow and light there. He turned to me and tipped his head to one side.

I saw the question in his eyes, and I nodded.

He lifted my top, pulling it over my head and dropping it into the flowers. With one finger he flipped my bra strap from one shoulder and, as it lowered, he cupped my breast with his hand, lifting it from the bra and bending to take my nipple in his mouth, his free hand clasping me around the hip, holding me upright. He sucked heavily on my nipple. A red haze of pleasure shot from his mouth to my cunt, where I was hungry for a man. The sunlight darted over my eyes as I shut my eyelids, melding my senses in a wild frenzy of awareness. I moaned aloud, shocked, yet willing, wanting more.

He drew me down, lying on the ground, pulling me down with him.

I climbed over him, suddenly knowing what I wanted. Panting, I grabbed for my bra, pulling it off. I stretched my arms above my head, reveling in my bare breasts, reveling in the bacchanalian magic of the moment.

He was smiling at me, a wicked gleam in his eyes. "Show me," he whispered. "Show me what you're thinking about."

I growled, lustful, and unleashed. Pushing against his chest with my hands, I closed my eyes and inhaled the wild forest. Even while I did, my hips were moving, my inner thighs squeezing his flanks. I wanted to pull off his belt, undo those buttons on his jeans and check him out. Images exploded through my mind, images of proud women, women who reveled in their sexual confidence. I took his hands to my hips, and my eyes opened.

His expression told me he knew what I was thinking. He pushed my skirt up around my waist. Grasping the band of my knickers, he paused and flashed me a dark look, then tore them apart, exposing the slit of my pussy in one powerful movement.

I gasped aloud, thrilled.

He ran his thumb over my clit and flashed me an appreciative glance. "You have a beautiful pussy," he breathed. "Show me what you're made of. Do it. I want you to." He had a hungry gaze, and there was no mistaking what he wanted.

I laughed decadently, amazed at my own response to him. "Why don't you kiss it," I said, moving closer to his face. Where had the words come from? Deep inside me I recognized them, yes, but never had I said such a thing before.

Oh, but he did what I wanted, and how!

He grinned and then moved right under me, kissing me right on the clit.

I nearly passed out, it was too good.

He teased me, alternated, caressing my pussy with long, slow strokes of his tongue and then pressing back and forth over my sensitive clit, stroking every inch of my intimate places. I had to fight for my breath, gasping between the words as I urged him on. "That's good, so good."

He drove me to distraction and then sought the juicy center of me, probing me with the strong muscle of his tongue, shoving it in and out, over and over.

"Yes, yes," I murmured, strung out and panting. Pressure built, my clit buzzing. He probed deeper still, then returned to my clit, circling it. I cried out, shuddering with release. My groin was heavy and hot, my core in spasm. His hands on my hips kept me upright, but I was fast coming back. I pulled free of his grip, desperate for more. "Take me. Fuck me hard, right here."

Rolling onto my back, I breathed deep the smell of the flowers crushed beneath me, a decadent bed upon which I was going to be fucked. My body was hot and pleasure-filled, and still I wanted more. I wanted to feel his hard cock inside me, filling me up. I opened my legs to him, beckoning to him as he climbed over me. His eyes were dark with lust, and I knew I was going to get what I wanted. He unzipped his jeans and I moaned aloud when I saw the thick shaft of his cock in his hand. The glistening head—so slick and ready to be inside me—made me lift my hips.

The look he gave me then was wicked, and his cock nudged against me. So hard, so large. A shiver ran through me, a shiver of longing. I wanted it. I nodded, my hands clutching at his shoulders. He pushed, opened me up and entered me. Moving slowly at first, he made me feel and appreciate every inch of him. Then he began working deeper, his hands on my hips as he pushed home and met my center. My core burned, the pressure of his cock there sending shock waves right through me. My head rolled from side to side, my breath was trapped in my throat.

He drew out, thrust again. I tried to speak, to urge him on, but all that I could get out was a low, guttural sound. He nodded, understanding. Rising up onto his arms, he began to work me harder.

Each thrust sent me into a spasm of ecstasy, the thick, long shaft of his cock stretching me to my very limits, making my body writhe. Oh, but he had stamina, riding me back and forth until every bit of me vibrated with pleasure, and I was almost gone. I arched my back, plucked my nipples hard, driven by instinct and seeking my release. I thrust my hips against his, ground on him. "Give it to me, give me more!"

He grinned, his brow lowering and his breathing audible as he thrust into me harder still. Then his cock seemed to swell and I cried out, my center burning, my legs clutching at his hips as I hit my peak.

"Oh, yes," he grunted, and his cock stiffened, jerked.

His orgasm kept me floating there at my peak for some time, pleasure rolling through me, until he slid free and I melted away, sank into the very earth itself, sated and mellow.

Even as my erratic pulse settled, I began to wonder what had happened. What had come over me? I'd never done anything like that before. I watched the canopy overhead moving on the breeze. The sun winked at me through the leaves, and I felt a deep sense of happiness. I pushed my fingers out against the ground. That's when it dawned on me—he wasn't there anymore.

He'd gone. Sitting up, I looked for him. I was alone. Had he ever been there at all? I grabbed my top and bra, pulling them on hurriedly, constantly glancing around as I made myself decent. It occurred to me that it was the first time I was worried about anyone seeing me. It was as if I'd lost all my inhibitions.

He'd done that to me. Yes, he had. And it was good.

If only he was real, I thought wryly. It was likely that he'd been a figment of my imagination. Wishful thinking, after too long traveling? The thought unnerved me, and for a moment I covered my face with my hands, relieved, because my sensitive, pleasured pussy attested to the fact that it had been real. Standing up, somewhat reassured, I brushed leaves and petals from my skirt, and peered at the great big telltale green smudges on my knees and down the front of my skirt. "Damn, I look a sight."

It meant that it *had* happened, though. I even had the torn knickers to prove it. Yes, a man had ripped the pants right off me. They were barely clinging around the top of my thighs and I pulled the shredded remains off, balled them and shoved them in the pocket of my skirt. I'd never gone out without undies before, but as I began to wend my way back through the bluebells I found that I liked the feel of the air against my sensitive pussy and my juices sticky against my thighs. This felt earthy and natural. He'd introduced me to that. All that blarney about the three wishes, he'd got the gift of the gab, all right. I couldn't help laughing to myself. Whatever, it sure had helped boost my confidence. I weaved my way quickly through the bluebells and relocated the path. Three wishes indeed! I felt as if I'd had several wishes granted, and I couldn't help teasing myself about another one. What would I wish for now? That he was still here, that he was real? He had to be real!

I shrugged off the feeling that I'd been under some spell. It was just some guy who wanted to get his leg over and saw the opportunity for mutual pleasure. And who could blame him? Not me, and I was glad of it. As I retraced my way along the path, I wondered how long I had been gone. What if I had missed the bus? I walked faster, and then broke into a run. When I got to the parking area, I was relieved to see my bus was still there, and no one else was around. I hadn't been away as long as I thought.

The driver didn't seem to be on board, but when I got to the entrance the door swished open. I climbed the steps. As I did, a shiver went down my spine. There was someone else on the bus. I stared down the aisle at him.

The man from the forest was right there, sitting in the center seat at the end of the aisle, right at the very back of the bus. He had his legs cheekily sprawled, and he was beckoning to me. The quintessential bad boy at the back of the bus. Had my third wish come true, or had he been on the bus all along? My cheeks warmed when I realized that he might well have been on the bus. I hadn't taken much notice, and yet…I was pretty sure I'd never seen him before. Besides, he was a local.

I remembered the way I'd acted after he'd asked me what I wanted. I fought off the embarrassment, wanting to be cool. What had I thought? That he was a granter of wishes, or— more likely—a figment of my imagination? He'd known which tour I was on. If he was the driver, that would explain why. Even so, I wasn't able to keep the silly grin off my face as I closed on him. "Are you the driver?"

"Maybe," he replied somewhat quizzically. "For the next leg of the journey, at the very least." Humor twinkled in his eyes. He reached out and grabbed my hand, pulling me over to sit on his lap. With one hand under my skirt, he ran his hand over my bare pussy, reminding me of what he'd done.

"Cheeky," I breathed, secretly thrilled.

His warm smile went right through me. "When we get to Cork," he said, "would you like to get together and make some more magic?"

Joyous laughter bubbled up inside me. I could feel his cock through his jeans, right there against my hip. I could also hear the door of the bus swishing open again, and the noise of happy tourists approaching.

I didn't care whether he was the bus driver, or the devil himself. What I did care about was that I didn't want the moment to escape. I didn't want this to end. "Yes, let's make more magic tonight," I said, and bent to seal the wish with a kiss.

Let Down Your Libido

Rachel Kramer Bussel

This is ridiculous, I thought, pacing around the room that I'd now been confined to for almost a month.

I'm a grown woman; I ought to be able to go in and out as I pleased. At least for a breath of fresh air. Who knew that the boring aisles of a drugstore would hold so much appeal after being deprived of them for weeks? I missed the click of my heels on the sidewalk, the dash of pedestrians all around me, the way in a moment a pair of eyes could seize mine and I'd feel the sexual heat right down to my toes. New York is a voyeur's paradise, and being alone in a room with only a mirror was wearing real thin. Deal or no deal, I was going stir-crazy, which perhaps was the point of the experiment I'd signed up to be part of six weeks ago without really thinking through the consequences. I'd just gotten laid off, and was combing the papers for a job, *any* job. I answered ads, plenty of them, but they yielded nothing but impersonal form rejections, if anything at all.

Finally, desperate, I'd started answering ads for studies, offering myself up as a human guinea pig, for everything from market research to scientific experiments. The first few gigs

I'd landed were easy: taste test several vodkas and say which was the strongest. Look at ads for sports cars and proclaim which one I'd be most likely to buy. Read copy for laundry detergent and determine which was the most friendly to young, single women like me.

And I'd gotten paid cash.

Perhaps the ease had made me greedy, or selfish or a little too full of myself. I thought I knew the tricks, knew the right words to say to make the employers think I was an obedient subject. But it's one thing to sit in a room and answer questions for a few hours, quite another to agree to be locked up in solitary confinement for two months for a study on sex drives. I was given room and board—if you can call it "given" when you pretty much sign your life away—in order for them to study my response when forced to go from nonstop cock to my own means.

These particular scientists were trying to develop a pill to cure women who were "too horny," though *oversexed* was the word they chose.

"Do you have sexual intercourse more than five times per week?"

"Do you think about sex more than ten times a day?"

"Have you *never* gone longer than two weeks without sex since becoming sexually active?"

Yes, yes, and *Thank God, yes,* I'd answered. I don't really think I'm abnormal. I'm a woman with a libido, and I exercise it as often as the fancy strikes me. I've had boyfriends, sure, but at the moment I was single, which shouldn't mean I had to rely on a battery-operated friend, right?

Instead, I made do with a rotating cast of overnight guests, the type who can be found in bars around the world—all of them looking for one thing: a woman just like me. The kind who want it fast and quick, who don't want to go through the wooing process. I'd had a steady diet of cock for years, sometimes even two in one night. Sometimes a woman would join us for a circle of triple the pleasure.

But desperate times call for desperate measures, and the hosts of this study were offering twenty thousand dollars if I could go the full two months. The catch was that, like on a game show, if I messed up, I would leave empty-handed. These people weren't messing around, either. They had my room monitored so that I couldn't flee. I was given menus where I could check off whatever I wanted, up to a hundred dollars a day worth of room service. I had cable, and they'd bring me all the books and magazines I desired. I had some stimulation, but not the kind that matters. In preparation, I'd even fucked my way through my local bar in the little over two weeks I had before the experiment started, figuring that the memories would keep me going, but they hadn't. I felt lost, even though I could tell you which celebrity marriages were breaking up and all about the latest crimes and political happenings. None of that information is worth anything without someone to share it with. I would rather my mind been blank and my pussy been filled—that's just the kind of girl I am. I was feeling like Rapunzel, from the old fairy tale, but instead of my hair being let down, I needed my legs to be spread wide. At least, my reactions provided good fodder for those studying me and my libido.

What I lacked, though, was human contact. I couldn't even go online; the researchers felt that interacting with my fellow humans via the Internet, or heaven forbid, looking at porn, would interfere with what they were trying to study. Which was, in my own words, how to drive a woman mad by drying up her pussy. I was into week three and my libido was definitely on the wane, although I still could use my hand. But I didn't mind them watching me; in fact, I got a kick out of the fact that otherwise staid lab-coat wearers were now getting big bucks (at least, I hoped it was big bucks) to watch me jerk off.

But nothing compares to a real-live cock to satisfy my carnal cravings.

Contrary to popular belief, for me it's not the size of the dick so much as the way a man uses it, what he says, how turned on he is. Hardness is only one measure of arousal, and taking in the full measure of a man, feeling him up and down, kissing him all over, hearing his breathing change from steady to staggered, is what drives me wild, what I was missing each night as I slid between the decadently high-thread-count sheets and tried to approximate what I was missing with my fingertips.

I'm sure I was offering much to the scientific community, but I was starting to feel like I was going crazy, like when I got out I wouldn't remember how to interact with men, wouldn't recall how to sink down onto a man's dick and welcome him inside. Even more, I wasn't sure I'd want to. They say your libido is a use-it-or-lose-it type of thing, and I was beginning to think that on that score, conventional wisdom was right on the money. My libido was dying, and I wasn't sure if twenty thousand dollars was a high enough selling price.

So when the first note was slipped under my door, I grabbed it. The only human contact I'd had was from the researchers during their weekly questioning. They made sure to dress as seriously as possible, not giving off any hints of eroticism, lest they skew their results. I answered as honestly as I could, trying not to whine as I reported how my tendency to wake up and need to put my hand between my legs (I'm like a guy in that sense) had diminished considerably. I was no longer a horny-all-the-time girl, and it was doing a number on my self-esteem. They listened and nodded and took notes, but didn't seem to truly grasp the severity of the situation.

The note was unsigned, but it made my heart sing and my

pussy…well, my pussy started to pound like it had just seen an old friend.

Iris, I couldn't hold back any longer. You are so fucking sexy I cannot stop thinking of you. I want to see you, touch you, make you come with my tongue followed by my fingers and then with my cock. I have a feeling you'll like it; I'm big and thick, the way you've described the perfect dick, and I can last a long time. I want to bend you over the bed, spread those long legs of yours, then sink so far inside you…

I took the note and rubbed it against my breasts; this was as close as I'd come to flirting, to a sexual interaction with another human being, in longer than I could remember. To some women, that would be no big deal—in fact, it might be a relief, a two-month sex vacation—but for me it was starting to feel like a slow death. The note brought me back to life, even if I couldn't answer it. The writer went on to say that he was one of the researchers who was in the background, one of dozens who were studying my every move. This made sense; watching me so intimately had to have an effect on those doing the study. Even though they could see what I was doing, nobody had to know what the note said, but for good measure, I ripped it up and placed the scraps in different wastebaskets, keeping a few in my private box for safekeeping.

But there would be no way to "sneak out." The researchers had made sure of that when they'd devised the study. The money was nothing to sneeze at, and I couldn't afford to fuck things up, even for a fuck that sounded so damn juicy I had to make myself come right then and there. The next morning, there was another letter, this one even more graphic.

I see you haven't deigned to respond, but that I've gotten to you. I didn't expect much more yet, but you have five more weeks. Five times seven is thirty-five; imagine that many more notes, maybe I'll up them to twice a day. What if I told you I was going to stand outside your door with my dick in my hand, jerking off?

He was killing me. I knew what he described was impossible; someone would surely notice. I was surprised they didn't have cameras in the hallway, but I think you have to pass some special security clearance to get to be part of the study. When the day of my next evaluation arrived, I stared at my questioners, wondering if they knew. "So, Iris, please tell us about your mental state and how it's affecting your...desires."

I wanted to lie, but I was also starved for conversation, so I shared some of what I was feeling. "I'm not sure I can go through with this, especially when there's so much temptation. I don't have a job lined up or any way to pay my bills, but this feels like being a whore, only in reverse. I'm selling myself by not having sex, and that feels wrong, like it's going against my nature."

"What do you feel will happen if you don't have sex soon?" one woman asked, her pen dancing along the edge of her lips. Even an only vaguely phallic object like an ordinary pen was enough to have me imagining her sliding the pen into my pussy; once a lover had inserted a lipstick, just a small, simple tube, but he'd gotten me so turned on beforehand that I had come like a shot. I was even willing to switch teams if that's what it took.

"I feel like I'm going to explode. This is different than a typical dry spell—not that I've had one of those in a long time—because it's not that I lack the ability to get a man. That

I know for sure." I paused and stared at each of them significantly, hoping one might cough or blush or otherwise reveal himself. Maybe he wasn't even in the room, but I knew that everyone on the project watched these taped sessions.

"Being with a man, one who's hard for me, who wants me, wants to do things to me and have me do things to him, when he whispers in my ear…it doesn't just make me come. It makes me feel alive. Powerful. Like I can conquer the world. Sex is better than caffeine, better than getting high, better even than skydiving, which I've done. There's nothing that rivals the feeling and right now I basically feel like I'm starving to death, slowly, like I'm shriveling up."

They all nodded intently, their expressions unchanged, while I was starting to feel even more depressed about my situation. Would I have subjected myself to an experiment where my food intake was drastically reduced? Was I letting them assume that "oversexed" women were inferior in some way? I wanted to make a statement, but even more, I just wanted to get fucked.

That night, another note arrived. This one held more urgency, and was also tender in its way.

The way you talked about sex as a matter of life or death was so poetic. I know exactly how you feel, Iris. It's not just that I want to fuck you so hard that you scream, want to feel your juices spurt all over my cock, want to tie your hands above your head, straddle your face and sink my dick deep into your mouth because I know you love swallowing as much cock as you can. It's all of that…and more. I've never met a woman like you, who knows exactly what she wants and goes after it. Who talks about cock and sex like they're life affirming, rather than just something fun to do. I jerked off while I watched you speak. I pictured myself shooting all over your skin.

His words made my breath come fast and furious, my clit swelling up.

"I bet if you snuck out at three in the morning, they wouldn't notice." He was starting to make me angry. I had a month to go and he was asking me to sabotage my livelihood, all over a good fuck? I mean, would he really be worth sacrificing twenty thousand dollars? What about my rent? He hadn't mentioned stepping in to pay my expenses himself, though I guess that would've turned me into a more traditional kind of whore.

I ripped up the note angrily and vowed not to read the next one. Except the next one came the next day, and it was a photograph. Of his dick. Unsigned and untouched, because what more did I need to know? It was so beautiful, so perfect, that I held the photo to my lips and kissed the shiny surface, then quickly shoved it into my jeans pocket. Would I be disqualified for receiving these communications? From then on, the messages came every day, sometimes twice a day. My mystery man spun elaborate fantasies about what he wanted to do with me, about where we'd fuck, who he'd show me off to, how he wanted to dress me, about taking me to get pierced, about spanking me in front of a roomful of people. I wound up telling the researchers at our next meeting.

"These—these letters have started arriving," I said. "The writer claims to be someone involved in the project and says that he wants to fuck me. How twisted is that, right?" The researchers just let me talk and talk, and then listened as I read a few out loud. When nobody seemed to be shocked, I started to wonder if maybe there was no man after all. Was this just a trick to get me to leave and save them all some cash?

Yet that couldn't be true. I shook my head, then ushered them out and climbed into bed. I was getting my period, thankfully, and knew that should take some of the edge off.

Except that unlike usually, when all I want is hot chocolate and Chex Mix and fluffy pillows, now I wanted sex, hot, mad, messy sex that would make me forget I even knew what a cramp was. I fell asleep early, and my dreams were vivid. There were a variety of men, different looks, shapes and sizes. One had long hair, like he was in a metal band, and he was extra talented with his tongue. Another was built short and bald, but with a giant cock. They kept coming, literally and figuratively, and when I woke up, I was so turned on I was barely aware that it was the middle of the night.

I was almost ready to take the risk. My pussy was telling me to do one thing while every other part of me was telling me to do something else: the right thing. I stood up, not caring that I was naked; the people watching me had seen me in the buff plenty of times. I slipped on a purple silk robe, then tied the belt around my waist. I turned on the lights and checked myself out in the mirror, making sure I still looked good. They'd set me up with a jump rope and exercise bands so I could get some exercise, but nothing beats walking around New York.

Then I heard the sound, a soft knock on my door, so quiet I would've thought the noise was coming from my imagination if it wasn't the middle of the night. But the wee hours had arrived, and noise was scarce even in Manhattan. I wasn't scared, because none of my friends even knew precisely where I was. I had sent them a mass e-mail letting them know I'd be MIA for two months. I walked over to the door, but instead of looking out the peephole, I pressed my ear to the door, then whispered against the crack. "Who's there?"

"You know exactly who it is."

"No, actually, I don't."

"But you still want me, don't you? Without even knowing what I look like or anything. You've been thinking about me. I can tell."

"Why are you torturing me like this? Is this a twisted kind of test to see just how horny I really am?"

"No, Iris, I swear. I just saw you and felt this instant connection that went beyond my job or responsibilities, beyond right and wrong. And I know I told you all about my cock, but really, it's about more than that. I think I'm meant to be with you."

His voice sounded anguished, and finally, I couldn't take it anymore. I undid the latch above the door and then turned the knob. The man standing there was pretty much the man of my dreams—tall, probably about six feet, bald (that's my thing), big and strong. He was wearing jeans and a white long-sleeved shirt, and had some stubble on his chin. I just stood there, though. If I let him in, everyone would see, and if I left the room, everyone would see.

"You're even more gorgeous in person, Iris."

"What's your name?" I had to know at least that.

"Raymond," he said, then just stared at me. Suddenly, this wasn't just about his cock or my dirty dreams. I could feel the air between us becoming even more charged. Without thinking too much more about it, I grabbed my key and slipped into the hallway, knowing I was likely closing the door on my chance for twenty thousand dollars. That would mean the past month had been wasted, too.

He led me to another room and there the tenderness stopped. "I know exactly how you like it, Iris, probably better than you know yourself," he said as he slipped two fingers inside me. I shut my eyes and floated on his voice, his touch, because if I pondered it too much, I'd realize I was with a complete stranger, one who'd been watching me intently for weeks. It wasn't like picking someone up at a bar, where you're both blank slates.

He did, indeed, know exactly what he was doing. He not

only bent me over the bed, but shackled my wrists together with padded cuffs. When my whimpering got too loud, he taped my mouth shut. As many kinky things as I'd done before, no one had ever done that. I could make noise, but no sounds come out, staying trapped inside me, with only the music of his belt whipping across my bottom and my heavy breathing, in and out of my nose, and the sound of his cock entering and leaving my pussy filling my ears. I cried, but they were happy tears, tears of release, tears that told me the price I'd been asked to pay was too much. I couldn't sell my sexuality short like that, and after five (I think) orgasms for me, Raymond switched things around, uncuffing me and removing the tape so I could suck his extra-hard, ready-to-burst cock.

His fingers stroked through my hair and I played with my sore but still throbbing pussy as I knelt before him. "You're so beautiful, I'm going to take good care of you, Iris." I sucked harder, and was rewarded with a burst of his salty fluid in my mouth, a sign that he'd enjoyed this as much as I had.

I slept fitfully, knowing I wasn't going to return to the study. There was a knock on Raymond's door at seven, and I didn't even bother putting on the robe. "Iris, we know you're in there," I heard when Raymond didn't open the door fast enough.

He flung it open, and we were faced with the entire committee staring disapprovingly. "The experiment is over. You can go. You'll get your check in the mail," the lead scientist said in a clipped voice.

"Thank you," I said, not wanting to ask more. I was going to get my money *and* this sexy man who wanted me as often as I wanted him?

I only found out later, when I got a copy of the report, that they'd concluded that "oversexed" women like me simply couldn't resist the temptation of cock. As it turned out, the notes had started as part of the experiment, but Raymond had gone rogue. And thank goodness for that.

Now we do our own form of experimenting, but it's not for money, and it's just between us. I live with him, and don't have to worry about anything…especially where my next orgasm is coming from.

Dancing Shoes

Tsaurah Litzky

When I was little, about seven or eight, my favorite fairy tale was "Cinderella." That was because my two older sisters, Claudia and Patricia, were always picking on me. My mother sent me off to school with them in the morning, thinking I would be safe, but as soon as we turned the corner of our block they would start razzing me.

Claudia, who was two years older than me, would run a few steps in front of me. "You're so little," she taunted, "if someone saw you behind us they would think you were our dog." They would then both cackle uproariously like the little witches they were. Trying to hold back the tears, I would struggle to keep up with them, catch my shoe in a crack in the sidewalk, stumble and fall. I would fantasize that a handsome prince would come and rescue me, and whenever I was alone I would practice dancing so he would notice me at the ball.

As I grew up, I became fascinated by shoes, maybe because I saw every new pair as the ones he would find me in. I did meet many handsome princes, and while some of them rescued me, none of them ever rescued me for long. My hope of meeting a prince who will stick around is still with me, as is my fascination with footwear. I own maybe thirty pairs. When I first moved to this neighborhood twenty-five years ago, I was delighted to find the local shoemaker only a few blocks away.

Natasha Shoe Repair is the name of the shoemaker's shop up on Clark Street. The owner, a bald man with steel teeth, looks the same as he did when I came to the neighborhood. Once I asked him the secret of his youthful appearance and he said he drank vodka for breakfast. His steel teeth make his smile quite scary, but actually he is a genial man. He has been calling me Miss Moscow all this time because he thinks I'm Russian, too.

Das vadanya is how he always greets me. I keep telling him that my grandparents were born in Russia, but not my parents, not me. I'm as American as popcorn at the movies and Mickey Mouse, but he persists. *"Das vadanya, das vadanya,"* he keeps repeating until finally I respond with what Russian I know. *"Balalaika, beluga, Baryshnikov,"* I answer. This usually calms him down, and he then rings the little silver bell that stands on the counter because he is not a fixer of shoes. He spends the day standing behind the long counter at the front of the store where he repairs watches and sells the knockoff designer handbags that are in a glass showcase below the counter. When he rings the bell, he summons the real cobbler from a small room in the rear of the store where the cobbler, who is his employee, mends the shoes. These back-room cobblers usually stay a year or two and then they are replaced. I think some of them must leave to open their own shoe-repair shops, but I don't really know.

The soles of my orthopedic sneakers—they are called MBTs—are all worn out. I decide to bring them in to Natasha Shoe Repair. These sneakers were so expensive, I lived on tofu and spinach for three months to afford them. It was worth it.

Not only do they make me two inches taller, walking in them is like walking on helium.

When I get there, the bald Russian is nowhere to be seen, so I ring the bell myself. The man who comes out from the back of the store is not the pale, squat, tubby guy I am used to seeing. This man is slender with a wiry build and big dark eyes like a faun. His thick, brown hair is close-cropped and curly like a Brillo pad. He wears a black T-shirt, black jeans and a white canvas apron. Even behind the thick canvas of the apron, I can make out a bulge between his legs. He is wiping his hands on the sides of the apron, long powerful hands with thick but graceful fingers. The sight of them makes the inside of my thighs shake, and I think about his upper lip tickling my clit while those fingers grasp my ass, caressing it. Because I am immediately thinking like this makes me realize how lonely I am, how hungry for hot cock inside me.

"What you need?" he asks in a foreign accent I cannot place. What I need is those fingers ripping off my blouse, my skirt, pulling down my panties, but I cannot tell him that. I show him the sneakers.

"Hard job?" I ask apprehensively. "Too much work?"

"No problem," he answers, giving me a crooked, zigzag smile. "Come back Tuesday, ten dollars."

"Ten dollars?" I can't help exclaiming. The fancy shoe store where I brought the sneakers had told me when the soles wore out they could be repaired there for one hundred and thirty dollars. "Sure," the shoemaker says. "You nice pretty lady." He fishes a yellow ticket out of the pocket of his apron and tears it in half, puts half in one of the sneakers and hands the other half to me. His admiration surprises and confuses me. He looks to be in his early thirties, at least twenty years younger I am. I nearly bolt out the door, but then I remember I haven't even thanked him. I am wearing my brown alligator pumps and orange fishnet stockings. When I turn to say

thank-you, he is still standing there, and—do I imagine it?—
he is looking at my legs.

When I come back to pick up the sneakers, once again the
bald Russian isn't there. I ring the bell, and the shoemaker
comes out to greet me. His hands and wrists are all stained
with black dye, which makes them look even sexier, as though
he is wearing high leather gloves. "Your shoes ready," he says,
and takes the ticket I hold out to him. Our fingers touch and
a warm jolt of electricity runs through my body.

He vanishes back into the interior. I can just make out a
large sewing machine, a rack of steel hammers of various sizes,
rolls of leather on a shelf. He rummages below the shelf and
pulls out a white plastic bag. He brings it to me, opens it and
pulls out the sneakers to show me. When he upends them to
display the soles, they look better than new; the seamless rubber gleams dark as the mysterious night.

"Perfect," I say. He puts the sneakers back in the bag. His
luminous eyes shine like jet and he is looking at me, smiling
happily as if he finds me beautiful. Shyly, I return his gaze
and our eyes lock and hold in a warm embrace. I remember
I have to pay him and get out the ten I have folded in my jeans
pocket for this purpose and hand it to him. Once again our
fingers touch and this time the heat that passes between us is
even stronger, insistent, like the steam rising from a pot.

Just then, the bald Russian stomps in, carrying a bag from
Forever Bagels up the block. I look down and the shoemaker
turns away. "*Das vadanya,*" says the bald Russian, and then,
more insistently, he says it again, "*Das vadanya.*" A few Russian
words float up from the bottom of my consciousness.
"*Smirnoff, Stroganoff, Stolichnaya,*" I say as I grab my sneakers
and flee the store.

Out on the street, I cradle the sneakers between my breasts.
When I put up a hand to brush my unruly bangs from my
eyes, my fingers smell like leather. I imagine I am dancing

with the sexy shoemaker. I am wearing a strapless white dress with a wide skirt and the sneakers. His hand is firm on my waist as he whirls me around and round.

After I get home, I take the sneakers from the bag and handle them, knowing he touched them. I imagine his fine fingers clasping a silver knife, carefully cutting away the old worn sole with sure movements. I want those fingers on my back and pulling me to him with the same intensity with which he grips the knife. I want his big tool deep inside me. I am getting wet.

I kick off my shoes; take off my clothes, my fishnet tights, my bra and panties, and put them on the kitchen chair. Then I put on my sneakers because I know that he has held them in his hands. I lace them up and head into my bedroom, go to my bed and lie down on top of the covers. I think of his fingers, taking pride in their handiwork, proudly patting the soles of the sneakers. Then I see those fingers move up, brushing my ankles, stroking the muscles of my calves, holding my knees open. He parts my thighs, looks inside. He licks his lips at what he sees and then buries his mouth inside me. His supple tongue laces its way up to find my clit and then he is sucking me slowly, methodically, showing me the way a master cobbler works with extreme patience. My clit swells, throbs, my cunt quivers and my whole body shouts, *Yes, yes, yes!* My flesh softens, becomes more pliable. He can stretch me; mold me any way he wants.

He reaches up, and his hands envelop my breasts, his fingers rub my nipples, with the same rhythm with which he is sucking the tender button between my legs. I feel the quickening inside that means I am about to come. How I want him to fuck me! The metal buckle of his belt presses into my belly. Below it, through the fabric of his jeans I can feel something else, the solid proof he wants me.

I reach down, unbuckle the belt, fumble with his zipper

and pull it down. But then I hesitate, shy about touching him. He helps, puts his hand inside and pulls it out. It is a deep purple color, and so long it reaches to my navel. He is uncut, my preference. When he leans his body on top of mine, his master tool, hard as steel, presses into my vulva.

It is only then I lean over and get my giant Blue Rabbit vibrator out of the drawer in my bedside table. I don't need any lube because I'm so wet from my imaginings that my juice is flooding out of me, running down my legs. I lie on my back, put a pillow under my hips and close my eyes. The cobbler is standing over me, his pointy cock combing through my pubic hair. He is my prince who knows just how to find the way inside. My legs spread even wider. I flip on the switch to the vibrator, loving the sultry purr. Easily, it slides into me and I imagine my prince moving in me with a steady rhythm. The joyful friction between us makes sparks fly. I push the speed button on the vibrator up to high. The pulse between my legs quickens into a roar and then I am opening up, turning inside out, flooding with waves of bliss that carry me out to a calm warm sea.

I don't know how long I drift there. My bladder is full and the dildo still inside me. Reluctantly I pull out the dildo, imagining it is his thumb sliding out of me. I hold it as I swing my legs over the bed and stand.

I dash out of the bedroom down the hall to the bathroom but am stopped short by the vision I see in the mirror on my bathroom door. An old hag carrying a brilliant blue sex toy, its bright, happy color a mockery. My legs are still shapely but my small breasts hang down, having lost all their bounce. What would the shoemaker think if he saw my body? Would he laugh, feel sorry for me? Maybe he is just being nice to an old lady? Maybe he looks at all women with desire no matter their age? Some men are like that. I know I'm driving myself crazy. I seem to be doing this a lot lately. At least he has inspired a delightful fantasy. I make use of the toilet and then, in the bathroom sink, I lovingly give the Rabbit vibrator a little bath. It will never laugh at me or mock me.

When I wake up the next morning, I feel loose and free. It's been cold; a lot of rain; today is the first sunny day. The temperature check on my computer says 72 degrees, in April no less! If the polar ice caps continue to melt, maybe there will be no spring this year, but I'm in a springtime mood. Today, I will put away my winter clothes and get out my spring things.

I go to my closet, sort through my skirts, blouses and jackets. I decide to give away my old beige trench coat and get a new one, maybe in a flower pattern. I sort through the great pile of shoes in the bottom of the closet. I pick up one of my torn red leather pirate's boots and see the shoemaker holding it, then, his fingers flashing, he uses a big pointy needle to sew up the rip in the side. As I put them back in the pile, I see a flash of silver, my dancing shoes.

I got them for five dollars at the Salvation Army years ago when I first moved to the neighborhood. They were black, lace-up vintage shoes with a low stack heel. As soon as I tried them on I knew they would be my dancing shoes. I wanted to make them dressier. I went up to Natasha Shoe Repair and got shoe spray paint and sprayed them silver.

I did the salsa in those shoes, the tango, lindy hop, waltz, rumba and the cha-cha-cha. I never lacked for partners and many were the nights I danced my way into a fine gentleman's bed.

Now the shoes are worn and shabby. The silver paint is chipped off and the holes in the leather over the big toes seem to gape even wider than before. If anyone can fix them, my cobbler can.

I apply lipstick and fix my hair. I put on my favorite maroon velvet blazer. I wrap the dancing shoes in a bag and go up at noon. I hope the bald Russian will be out to lunch. I am in luck. He is playing chess at one of the tables outside at the Chess Classic Café, a few doors down from his store. He is so involved in his game, he wouldn't notice if the entire Bolshoi Ballet whirled past.

I enter the store and ring the bell. My shoemaker seems to grin when he sees me. but maybe it is only my own wistful thinking. "Yes?" he says.

I feel embarrassed like a shy Cinderella who wants to run away. I try not to look at his crotch but am not successful. I take the shoes out of the bag and put them on the counter.

"Can you fix these shoes?" I ask him.

"Sure," he says, "but why you paint them silver? I see they used to be black."

I tell him. they are my dancing shoes. "I wanted to make them special," I say.

"How long you have these shoes?" he asks. I wonder if this is an oblique way of asking my age. I decide to go for broke and tell him the truth. "Twenty-five years," I answer. His expression does not change. "You have good times in these shoes?" is his next question.

"Oh, yes," I answer. "I love to dance."

"Me, too," he says.

Gold, On Snow

Janine Ashbless

You wouldn't think, to see me crouched here among the rocks in my black rags musty from the damp, the hems heavy with mud, that I am a queen. I have made sure of that. I will not be recognized. My hair is white, my back hunched and my sunken mouth almost toothless—though my limbs are still strong, as I've had miles to walk to reach this place in the black heart of the forest. Not that anyone will see me, because I've made sure of that, too. Sprinkled with fern seed, I will pass unnoticed unless I draw attention to myself, which at this moment I have no intention of doing. I've scrambled up the outside of the hollow limestone outcrop that serves my stepdaughter as a home, squeezed under the roots of a birch clinging to a cleft in the stone and positioned myself so I can look in through one of the window holes.

There she is, asleep. She looks so innocent, doesn't she? But don't be fooled; there is no innocence in her. She lies on a bed of bearskins, her head thrown back, one arm crooked over her eyes to ward off any sunlight that might creep into her stone house. Her long hair looks as glossy and black as split charcoal, even against the dark pelts. She's wearing a dress of doeskin—very well made, I imagine, considering who she got it from, but laughably rustic.

No real peasant girl would be asleep at this time of day, not with the sun setting and the evening meal not yet prepared.

When I married her father, the girl was already notorious. Beautiful beyond the norm, she'd broken the heart and nerve of every page boy and stable lad and done the rounds of the squires; she was working her way through the grown men, those not wise enough to resist her games. Ungovernable, they called her; a sly and shameless tease. Or more candidly: the royal slut. They wondered why her father the king didn't put a stop to it, but all he did was execute or exile any man he found to have succumbed to his daughter's appetites. Nor did he seek to find her a husband and rid himself of the problem.

I tolerated it, more fool me. Newly married, I was not yet come into my full power over her father or the realm. These things grow slowly, like the roots of ivy that cling to a wall and work their way into the cracks, eating the mortar—until those roots are the only thing holding the wall together. I recognized in the girl the signs: the old blood burns hot in those of us who carry it. And I knew that it was not only her bad reputation that kept her in the parental home and not only her rank that protected her from punishment. She had, perhaps without knowing it, worked an enchantment that ensured the king kept her close and safe. So I tolerated her behavior for years, until the day I saw that she had turned her eyes upon her own father, my husband.

That was when I determined to do away with the girl.

Uncomfortable, I shift my withered body against the stone and glance about the clearing. It is tempting to accede to my impatience and take the opportunity now, while she sleeps and is alone. But I've learned to be more careful than that. I've come across her late in the day and I doubt she will be alone for much longer. She didn't build this house herself—this parody of a human dwelling, carved from the living forest rock. And from what I saw in my mirror, her protectors are not to be treated with contempt.

Almost a year ago I picked a soldier with, I thought, the right temperament and told him to take her secretly deep into the forest, into that trackless gloomy labyrinth of needles and moss under the canopy that blocks all sunlight, and there cut out her heart. He failed. To mask his failure he brought me back the heart of a hind, and it was many months before I realized my error and extracted from him the true story.

Shadows are lengthening from the tall firs that hem this lonely clearing. Only the tops of the trees are still touched with light.

When my stepdaughter had realized what he intended, she'd wept and opened her clothes and begged him to let her live and promised him her neat little furrow or her sweet pale rump to plow in exchange for mercy. He'd laughed at that— Do you think I would have chosen a softer-hearted man for such a task?—saying that he could and would take those things just as easily after slipping the knife into her. Then she'd promised him the pleasure of her mouth, pleasure beyond imagining, just for a few moments' delay. He'd fallen to that trap. I imagine she did keep her side of the bargain, at least for a little while; certainly he'd dropped his guard at some point.

She'd bitten off his ball-sac entire. I made him show me the ruination that she'd made of his manhood. And while he'd screamed and thrashed about on the ground she'd run off into the forest, naked and spitting out his blood and laughing.

I made the soldier hang himself, not for his failure—I am not unreasonable—but for having lied to me.

See her lying there, her lips still crimson as if painted with a man's blood. But now she stirs and wakes, cocking her head as she rises, and she's right: there is a noise, a faint sound as if of slow drums, thrumming through the rock to my finger-tips. The girl stands and stirs the fire and lays on more wood, moves the pot of yesterday's stew to the heat, then looks to the door expectantly. The soft leather of her dress, I note with some corner of my mind, clings to her form in a manner flattering her already obvious loveliness.

And here they come, her protectors. Her saviors. They haul themselves up from deep cracks in the earth, from barely visible fissures in the shadows of boulders, and slink toward the house. Despite my disguise I shiver. Ignorant people call them dwarfs, but that is not what they are. Their name in the old tongue is *svartalfar,* which means *dark elf.* Certainly they are shorter than most men, but no shorter than my step-daughter. They are creatures of the deep places and of the shadows. They are the gray of snow that has been trampled underfoot, or black as the shadows under the unending firs or sheened with the oily colors of the dead water that collects among the needles in the hollows where trees have fallen. They dress in leathers that are crusted with dirt. Their faces are lean and hard, but their eyes shine with the colors of gems; blue like sapphires or green as emeralds or red as rubies. They are lithe in the body but muscular across the shoulders, almost top-heavy, from digging and from forge work. Because the *svartalfar* are artisans. They make objects of peerless cunning and craft, and they prize beauty above everything else in the world.

There are seven of them in all.

One by one they converge upon the house, upon my step-daughter. I turn my gaze back through the window hole, to see what happens inside. It seems domestic enough at first. Each of the *svartalfar* goes up to the girl and looks her up and down, without touching or speaking, almost as if inspecting her. She stands demurely, her eyes downcast but glittering through her long dark lashes and the fall of her fringe. Then they turn aside and go about their tasks. Occasionally one will mutter to another, but they are otherwise almost silent. They light lamps and set them about the center of the room, they clean the tools they have brought home. The wiriest of them stirs the cooking pot, then he chops up and adds ground-elder and a brace of rabbits that have been hanging behind the door. He is the cook; there seems to be no question of the girl doing any chores. When she has been looked over by each of her seven hosts she simply sits again and waits to be fed.

I ignore the insects that whine in my ears as the world darkens at my back. I am all patience. Haven't I been patient many years? I watch as they eat their stew and lay the bowls aside. Then the girl lifts her eyes to the oldest, broadest and most knotted of the *svartalfar*. He nods, and two of the others hurry to take an iron chest from the shadows and lay it before him. From his belt he brings out a key upon a thong, and unlocks the chest, setting back the lid.

It is full of gold. Not coin, but jewelry of extraordinary delicacy and beauty. The girl stands. See how the tip of her tongue wets her plump berry-colored lips: she is trembling with anticipation. She moves into the center of the room, the circle formed by the *svartalfar* on their stools. Then one of them, his eyes the yellow of topaz, comes forward and unlaces her dress, dropping it to her feet then helping her step out.

Skin as white as snow. It is very nearly no exaggeration; in the lamplight she seems to glow. I squirm with envy and with trepidation; the blood of the *ljosalfar* must run strong in her, and if the *svartalfar* have given the world wonders then the light elves have bequeathed it witchery. She is absolutely beautiful. Perfect breasts, twin-tipped with pink. Perfectly curved hips. Perfect, flawless thighs. She is as smooth as marble taken from a riverbed, as a polished moonstone, as new-fallen snow. The only colors about her are in the soot-black hair upon her head, her gleaming dark eyes, her blood-red lips. I hear the *svartalfar* sigh.

They dress her from the treasure box. They come forward all at once, and work with the patient care of true craftsmen, neither getting in each other's way nor fumbling, their dark hands delicate and sure on her pale skin: a pair of elaborate earrings, filigree greaves that embrace her shins and calves, wristlets that attach to finger rings by a web of golden links, spiraling armlets. They catch up her hair in a crown of gold lace and drape her cheekbones in a mask of finely pointed mail. Then a collar of gold, and chains that hang down from it to rings that go through her nipples, pulling them up. Rings through her labia and her clitoris. She does not flinch; the invisible holes in her flesh must be old, and she well used to the jewelry. Her whole body is hung with arcs of delicate gold chain, pinned to her flanks by fine wires. Filigree wings attach flat to her shoulder blades. A plug is inserted deep between the snowy globes of her bottom and she bends and takes it with equanimity: when it is in place a gold tail stands in a curve like a cat's behind her, gleaming in the light of the fire.

See how they admire their own handiwork when they are done, standing back to revel in the full effect? They love artifice and they love beauty; she is now the perfect combination of both. Her lips curve with satisfaction under her chain-mail half veil. She runs her hands gently, gently down her own body, plucking at the wires that pierce her flesh, circling her breasts and hefting their orbs to make the pendant beads dance. She rolls her rear to make her tail twitch. She shimmies her hips. She loves her own body, dressed only in gold. She loves what they have made of her: a pagan idol.

To show her gratitude, she begins to dance for them. The *svartalfar* kneel back in their circle, eyes aglow, transfixed by her slender glittering form, and they beat time for her upon their thighs, the seats of their stools, an upturned bucket. This dance is one she never learned in her father's ballroom. It is all pride and taunting, pleasure and lasciviousness. It is slow like the ooze of cream, then urgent as the shudder of an arrow striking home. She writhes her hips and rolls her buttocks and shakes her breasts until the dark elves look entranced, half-witless with desire. Even from my spyhole I can see the moist gleam on her inner thighs, the swelling petals of her secret rose peeking out when she bends to tease each of them in turn. They must be able to smell the perfume of her lust.

Finally one of them—it is the cook, the one I think of as the youngest—breaks. He pitches forward, grabbing her legs, planting hot kisses on her bare thighs. He drops his breeches and pumps the swollen member that rises from it frantically in his fist. The girl signals to the leader with a flash of her eyes, and suddenly they are all on their feet again.

There are treasures still waiting in the jewelry box, you see. They prise the youngest of their number from her, and clip more and longer chains to her nipple rings and to the piercings through her sex—and the ends of these chains they keep in their hands, taut. Then they dress her in a harness such as I have never seen before; a device that straps about her thighs and stands proud from her mound: a phallus of gleaming gold, rendered in perfect detail to every fold and vein, horrifyingly oversize and twice as obscene arising from the narrow hips of this pretty girl.

She laughs. Then they bend their young cook on hands and knees and she crouches to impale him up the fundament. And as she rides him—and she is not gentle, she is not kindly, she buggers him like a soldier in a long war rutting his whore—the others hold the chains tight and pluck upon them, stretching her nipples and labia out and sending repeated stabs of sensation to torment them. Her breasts quiver, sweet prisoners of nipples that have turned dark and swollen. She slaps the muscular rump beneath her hands and squeals. The youngest *svartalfar* holds his own pintle and jerks it, groaning, the muscles standing up on his arm and shoulder—until she comes, shrieking and tearing at his arse cheeks with her nails, and he spurts the thick jets of his seed over the floor.

That is too much for the other six. They release her from the harness, leaving their comrade to collapse with the golden phallus still buried to the hilt in his bowels. They unclip the long chains to make sure she will not become entangled and pull the cat's tail from her anus. Then they ravish her, each desperate to take possession of their goddess.

They are too impatient to each wait their turn, but take her two or three at a time, impaling her in the arse and the coynte and the mouth or simply humping her exquisite breasts. Their dark bodies knot around her pale one. Watching from my vantage point, I learn a number of things about the *svartalfar;* for example, that their virile members are by human standards very large, very thick and gnarled like tree roots. That their spend is prodigious in quantity. And that unlike men they are not exhausted by their first shot from the bow; each of them takes his pleasure of her three or four times. Even the cook recovers sufficiently to stuff her throat and ram her until she chokes on his cream.

You might think such a slip of a girl could not take such a riving, but she does. She receives the most brutal hammer blows of their thrusting pricks eagerly and her spasms of pleasure are unmistakable though her screams are usually muffled by cock. You'd imagine she has no bones in her body, so swiftly does it accommodate those thick and glistening tools. She spreads herself wide with her hands to ease their entry, and through her tears she searches blindly with her mouth for more.

But she is a mess by the time they are finished; flushed, tear-stained, slack-jawed, swollen, scratched and bedecked with the sticky white tracks of their seed, as well as her golden chains.

No longer perfect, for the moment. Afterward they bring basins of water and clean her and the jewelry with great care and patience, returning the latter to the iron box, wrapping her in furs and laying her upon the bed of bear pelts. She falls unconscious almost at once, a smile still lingering on her lush, bruised lips.

I turn away.

Almost I am tempted to leave her here, to her lovers and her forest idyll. Even these old bones feel the urge to return to my palace and my husband and my own diversions. I understand her appetites—I, better than most. We share the old blood, she and I.

But it cannot last, this truce. Right now she is still a girl, filled with green sap and an all-consuming self-adoration, but sooner or later these games will not be enough. She will grow restless. Then her mind will inevitably turn to thoughts of her future. Then it will turn to thoughts of revenge.

There's no room for more than one witch in a kingdom.

So I must deal with her, quickly and cleanly, by my own hand and without the *svartalfar* knowing there has been foul play. Poison is best I think. But I'm not sure how to administer it. Obviously I must wait until she is on her own during the day, and then offer her... What? A golden hair comb? Yet there's nothing I could fashion that would match the consummate artifices of the *svartalfar*. A bodice that tightens until it cuts off the breath, perhaps? But she has no need of fine clothes out here.

An apple, I think. She must be fed up with a diet of game and pine nuts and herbs.

Yes, an apple will work best.

After the
Happily Ever After

Heidi Champa

Sometimes, I wish the glass slipper didn't fit. I wish I hadn't become a modern-day princess, living in the castle on the hill. Sure, I was the envy of every girl in town; every other girl who had secretly dreamed of marrying Mr. Charles Channing III. He had gotten the name Prince Charming many years ago in the business world, for his ability to charm the money out of the men and the pants off the women.

And, now here I was, staring out my leaded-glass window at the city below, feeling just as empty as I had in my studio apartment in that basement on the other side of the tracks. I was supposed to be over-the-moon happy, perfectly content with my new surroundings. But something just didn't feel right. The love that had grown between us before our nuptials was now replaced by something else. Every aspect of my life felt like a job, like a duty. I always had to say the right thing, dress the right way, act like the perfect princess everywhere I went. Being Mrs. Cynthia Channing was not an easy task.

It was a complete accident that I had even met Charles. My friend Teresa had dragged me to the charity ball at the Channing house. She knew I had always wanted to see inside the mansion, and she had an extra ticket. Of course, she had to loan me an outfit, right down to the shoes. We just had to make sure to be home by midnight, so she could relieve her babysitter.

Pretending, for a night, to be someone I wasn't, felt as if I was acting a part in a play. I didn't even recognize Charles when he first approached me. I had never seen him before. When the tall, dark and handsome stranger started chatting me up at the bar, it never occurred to me I was speaking to the most powerful man in the room.

I had forgotten myself, forgotten who I was supposed to be. I talked to him as I would have any other man. He laughed at my jokes, made me feel so at ease. After two drinks and some rather interesting conversation, we were interrupted by an older man.

"Well, Charles, I have to commend you on this event. It is just splendid."

"Thank you, Judge. It is always nice to see you."

The old man collected his scotch and made his way back to the stuffed leather chair from which he came. I nearly swallowed the shrimp I was snacking on, toothpick and all.

"You're Charles Channing?"

"Yes, I am. I'm sorry. I just assumed you knew. Does it matter?"

"I guess not. It's just, if I'm being honest, I never thought you'd actually be here. I thought you'd write a check and call it a day."

"That's not exactly how I like to do things. Especially when I know the room is going to be full of beautiful women. Like you. Could I interest you in a tour?"

I couldn't help but accept his offer. He was so easy to talk to, so down-to-earth for someone in his position. So incredibly good-looking. We walked out of the grand room, and started up the carpeted staircase. He was busy explaining things, pointing at paintings and sculptures that lined the hallways. I couldn't pay attention. I was too busy concentrating on the fact that his fingers were laced with mine; that every time we stopped to admire some priceless work of art his hand would drop to the small of my back.

We came to a beautiful piece of stained glass that filled a small alcove floor to ceiling. He pulled me into the relative privacy of the space, his face right in front of mine. He was shadowed in colors; blues, greens and reds marking all over his skin. My body pressed against him almost by instinct; a sudden rush of dizziness shot through me. His hands steadied me, resting on either side of my flushed cheeks. His fingertips moved slowly, sliding like pads of silk over my neck and down to my bare shoulders. His thumb ran back and forth over the length of my collarbone, sweeping lower with each pass. It came to rest right over my pounding heartbeat, his hand inches from my breast.

"You're not nervous, are you, Cindy?"

"No, I'm not nervous."

"Good, then your heart must be pounding because you're excited."

Before I could open my mouth, he was kissing me. The tender first touch of his lips quickly gave way to a ravaging, forceful taking of my mouth. I hadn't expected passion like this from such a buttoned-up guy. Something told me this was the most action that alcove had seen in all of its years. His hands slipped down, taking the top of my dress down with them. My nipples now exposed to the cool air around us, I felt his thumbs strum over them in unison, my flesh contracting under his touch. His mouth reluctantly released mine, and a small moan escaped his lips before they latched around my stiff nipple. I could feel his hard cock pressing against my leg.

But just as my hand started rubbing his impressive erection, the old grandfather clock that stood in the hall started to strike, startling the two of us apart. I hadn't even realized the time. Midnight. Teresa was going to kill me.

"I'm sorry, Charles. I have to go."

I started down the stairs, trying desperately to remember which way we had come from, while straightening my dress. Luckily, I only made one wrong turn, and the party noise made it easy for me to find my way. I spotted Teresa, who had clearly been looking for me. "Where did you disappear to? I *told* you I had to be home by now. My babysitter is going to be furious."

"I'm sorry. I got caught up. Charles Channing was giving me a tour."

"Right, and I was chatting with the queen of England. Come on, let's get out of here. I think we've had enough of the blue bloods for tonight."

I turned to take one last look at the room, and saw Charles emerging from the hallway, his face a mixture of lust and anger. I caught his eye one last time before Teresa dragged me out into the real world again.

Charles didn't waste any time finding me after the night of the charity ball. He tracked me down easily, calling my work and home numbers, making his intentions very clear. I had piqued his interest and he wanted to get to know me better. At first I wasn't sure I wanted to get involved with someone so prominent and important. But I soon realized that Charles wasn't going to take no for an answer. I relented. His dates weren't just dates. They were elaborate events straight out of a storybook. One night we enjoyed dinner on a yacht; the next week, a limo-driven trip to the opera.

The romance unfolded like some kind of dream. After he had hooked me with the dazzle of fabulous dates, the gifts started pouring in. The biggest thing I had ever received from a man before Charles was flowers. But Charles even managed to make flowers an extravagant purchase. Jewelry, clothing, shoes, everything a woman could ever ask for. The luxury started to feel like too much, but every protest I put up was met with a quick dismissal.

"This is just who I am, Cindy. It's the Channing way. Trust me, you'll get used to it."

The sad part was, he was right. I *did* get used to it. I allowed myself to be caught up in the world of glamour that Charles offered. I stopped balking at the gifts, stopped being concerned about how much things cost. When he asked me to move in with him, I didn't hesitate. How could I turn down the chance to live in a mansion when I had spent the last four years living underground in a crappy apartment? The old Cindy was slowly being replaced with the new-and-improved version that would make Charles Channing proud. I kept telling myself I wanted this world, that I wanted to change. I didn't leave any room in my mind for doubt. I just said yes, and accepted the three-carat diamond ring on the spot.

To say the wedding had been straight out of a fairy tale would have been an understatement. Every last detail, right down to the horse-drawn carriage, was selected for maximum effect. This "wedding of the year" was being held to a slightly higher standard than most. For my part, I did nearly nothing as wedding planners, coordinators and my future mother-in-law took over. All that was expected of me was to show up for dress fittings, ooh and aah at the shower, and smile a lot. The real me didn't have to do a thing except keep quiet.

In my heart, I had always wanted a simple wedding. Just me, my fiancé and a few close friends. I had dreamed about getting married outdoors, in nature, with no shoes on. But the Channing family would never hear of anything so common.

"Come on, honey. Who wants to get married with a bunch of bugs flying all over the place? Saint Mark's is amazing. You'll love it."

After the wedding, we quickly fell into a routine. Charles insisted I quit my job.

"It wouldn't look right for me to have a wife who works. You understand, don't you?"

Of course I understood. I didn't really like my job that much anyway. I was sure I could find something to pass the time. But the truth was, there wasn't much for me to do. There were maids, drivers, gardeners, cooks. Every whim I had could easily be taken care of by someone else. At first, having people do things for me was a joy. I had never in my life had someone do my laundry. I had never had someone make me exactly what I wanted for dinner, right down to the number of ice cubes in my drink.

But ultimately everything that had been so amazing in the beginning started to lose its luster. Being a pampered woman didn't come easily to me. I started sneaking my own laundry to the basement, and I planted a small garden of my own on the side of the house. I was so bored doing nothing, so bored of being just another society woman who had turned useless. And it had only been six months.

To make matters worse, Charles was always working, even when he was at home. He spent hours in his study and some nights he barely came to bed. I missed him, even when he and I were in the same place. Our sex life that had started out so promising soon dwindled to barely twice a month. One night, I scrolled through the memories of recent days and realized nearly three weeks had passed since Charles and I'd made love. I decided to be bold, something I hadn't done since we had been together.

I walked into the study, listening to his voice echo off the walls. It was still so hard to believe he was my husband. Sometimes, I felt like I was watching a movie of someone else's life. I approached him slowly, quietly, and put my hands on his shoulders. He held up the customary finger, the "hold on a

second" sign he had perfected. I ignored his hand, and leaned
down to kiss him on the cheek. His lips pulled into a smile,
despite the serious tone of his voice. I turned the chair around,
twisting the phone cord around him, and straddled his lap. His
attempts to push me off quickly stopped as I kissed his neck,
just below the ear. His voice never changed, but his hand went
to my back, and his hips rose up slightly under me. I waited
for him to stop me, but he didn't.

Soon, Charles was hanging up the phone, and put a hand
on either side of my face. Just like he had that first night we
met. His kiss was so familiar, so comforting. He slid his hands
down to my breasts and his fingers had my nipples at attention in no time. He could still flood me with desire, even
when I felt so distant from him. I was surprised by his insis-
tence, but happy. My shirt soon landed on the floor, as did
his. The couch across the room seemed the most logical
choice, and our pants joined the pile as we made our way over
to the brown leather.

I moved to lie down, but Charles pulled me onto his lap.
The look on his face took me back to the beginning, to the
man who couldn't wait to get into my pants. I eased myself
down onto him, his hard length fitting into me like we were
made for each other. His mouth, the mouth I fell in love with,
covered my nipple and sucked hard until I gasped. I rocked
on top of him, feeling his body press against my clit.

God, he felt so good.

His hands held on to my hips, trying to make me slow
down. But I didn't want him to slow down. I rolled my hips
harder against him, my mouth crushing his. I was so close,
and I could tell he was, too. Just then, his phone rang from
across the room. I tried to ignore the sound, but I could tell
Charles had no intention of doing so.

"I have to get that."

"Charles, no. You can call them back."

I kissed him again, pleading with him not to go. He picked me up, pulling me off his cock, and set me down on the couch. Walking quickly across our clothes, he answered the phone, his voice normal again. I whispered his name, and he put up one finger, wanting me to wait. Thirty seconds turned into five minutes and I watched with disbelief as he pulled on his boxer shorts and sat down at this desk. He opened a file, and I could tell that I was gone again from his mind.

Silently, I picked up my own clothes, and walked out of the room. The fury in me didn't stop the heat pulsing between my legs. I went to our bedroom and pulled the covers back on the bed. I lay down, pulling my vibrator from the bedside table. The all-too-familiar hum was the sum total of the love I got that night.

For days, I tried to put the night in the study out of my head, but I remained angry. Charles hadn't tried to touch me since. I barely got a kiss on the cheek as he headed out the door in the morning. It seemed impossible to feel so lonely in a house full of so many people. But I was alone. I hadn't seen my family since the wedding; my friends didn't want to hear any more about my perfect life. Now my ideal husband was too busy to spend time with his princess bride. My perfect storybook life seemed to be missing a few pages.

I walked through the halls of the house, the night air trapped behind all the big, beautiful windows. I decided to let in some fresh air, let the cool breeze clean out some of my bad feelings. None of the windows would budge. The only way I could get any ventilation was to open the French doors at the back of the house. There weren't any lights on, but I could see the tennis courts and the pool. Mostly unused, these luxurious items were put in for show. The cool water looked more inviting than ever before. Before I could go to the bedroom to change, I heard a scrape and a splash coming from the open door.

Despite the initial fear that leaped into my throat, I headed downstairs. Walking quietly toward the back of the grounds, I heard the rhythmic slap of water getting closer and closer. I froze next to the pool house, trying to see who was enjoying a late-night swim. My first thought was that Charles had come home and needed some exercise. But as I watched the wet brown head of my guest surface, I realized this was Charles's slightly delinquent but handsome brother, Ted. I hadn't heard him come in, and I certainly hadn't invited him.

Emboldened by my fresh anger, I walked straight up to the edge of the pool and waited for Ted to surface. He came up, shaking his wet head, splashing water all over my silk pajamas.

"Hey, Cindy. How are you?"

"Ted, I thought you were done breaking in." We'd had words about this before.

"It's not breaking in when you know the code. Besides, I didn't want to bother you. It's not like anyone uses this thing anyway. How did you even know I was here?"

"I had the doors open."

"Oh, well, sorry. God forbid you're not in bed by ten."

He snickered as he swam to the steps, sitting on the concrete edge. My frustration had come to a simmering boil, but all I could think to do was pace. Ted watched me for a few minutes, not saying anything.

"Trouble in paradise? Don't tell me, it turns out your glass slippers are a little too tight? I could have told you that."

"Not that it is any of your business, but no. Things aren't perfect right now."

"Charles is a good guy. But he looks at everything like it's a business. Hell, he treated your wedding like some kind of corporate takeover."

"Things will calm down once work calms down."

"I hate to break this to you, sweetie, but work never calms down. This is it. And something tells me you already know that."

I sat near the edge of the pool, tired of walking, tired of everything. Ted was right. Damn him. Charles wasn't going to change. This was my trade-off. The perfect life that wasn't nearly as perfect as it seemed. But how could I walk away now?

As if reading my mind, Ted said, "Divorce wouldn't be the end of the world, you know."

"I'm not sure your brother would see it that way," I responded sarcastically.

"Well, then, you'll just have to do what rich people have always done. Discreet cheating."

Ted was staring straight at me, but I couldn't look at him. There was a part of me that didn't really believe Charles was working late all the time. I had my suspicions about his real motives for staying away so much. But I had never really thought he was with anyone else. Until that moment.

"Is that your subtle way of letting me know what Charles is really up to?"

"No. It is my way of telling you this."

I waited for some sagelike words of wisdom, but instead Ted splashed water from the pool all over me. My eyes stung and my mouth opened in shock at the cool water soaking straight to my skin. When I opened my eyes, Ted was smiling, floating back into the middle of the water.

"Come on, Cindy. Get in. Take a break from perfection for a minute and just have a swim."

"I don't feel like putting on my bathing suit."

"So, don't. I don't mind. When was the last time you did anything you shouldn't? How long has it been since you were bad?"

His provocation should have bothered me, but instead

something inside me shifted. Why shouldn't I have some fun? Charles would never have to know, and nothing would happen.

"Fine, I'll come in. Turn around."

Ted spun around while I stripped out of my silk pajamas, leaving my bra and panties on. Not that the white fabric would provide much coverage when wet. I gingerly stepped into the water, letting the cool fluid dissipate the heat that was bubbling under my skin. I eased my head under the surface, opening my eyes to the blurry world underneath. It was so quiet, the only sound the hum of the filter. I saw Ted's legs coming closer to me, and I popped back out of the water. I watched him moving toward me until he was so close I could feel the heat from his body in the water.

"Was that so hard, Cindy?"

"I guess not."

"You still seem really tense. Don't trust me?"

I was nervous, I didn't trust him. But, more important, I was beginning to wonder if I could trust myself.

"Maybe you shouldn't trust me. After all, you have to know what I want to do to you right now."

I shook my head, not wanting to admit that I did know. At least I hoped I knew what he wanted. I hoped it was the same thing I wanted. I looked into his eyes, and stopped thinking. I took his hand with both of mine, and slid it up to my neck. He ran his big hand down my neck, following my lead, until he was right above my breast. I could feel my heart pounding under my ribs. He hesitated, not letting me move him any farther.

"You sure about this, Cindy?"

"No, but don't stop."

His hand relaxed and I slid it down on to my breast. His palm slid over my bra-covered flesh. He stopped moving, his breath fast and hard, his eyes locked on mine. I moved his hand until his thumb slid over my nipple, now hard as a rock. I motioned him to gently squeeze my flesh, and soon I let go, letting him move all on his own. He brought up his other hand, moving them over me in unison. His thumbs and fingers toyed with my nipples until I was stifling a moan in my throat.

"You don't have to be perfect all the time, Cindy. Nobody is. Not even Charles."

I couldn't speak, couldn't form coherent thoughts. There was no guilt, no shame. Just the pressure of his fingers running over the wet fabric that shielded my nipples. I took one of his hands and slipped it below the water. He ran his fingers over my stomach, and this time, I could feel him tremble. He dipped his fingers inside the waistband of my panties, until he was touching my curls. Again he stopped. I moved a little closer to him, and pressed his fingers onward. He parted my lips with two fingers, and I guided his middle finger to my clit. He let out a small gasp when he felt my hard, hot clit under his finger.

I moved his finger over me in a circle, and then lightly up and down. I was just about to let go of his hand, to let him move on his own. But I pushed his hand one last time and eased his finger inside my cunt. He shuddered, and I could feel his hard cock against my leg. Letting go of him, I reached into his shorts and felt his cock throbbing against my hand. I jerked him gently under the water, his fingers and mine moving in time with each other.

"How long has it been since you've come, Cindy?"

"Too long."

He leaned his forehead against me, a second finger sliding into my wet pussy. I grabbed his wrist as he finger fucked me right there in my husband's pool. I should have been ashamed of myself, but I wasn't. I couldn't think about anything but coming all over Ted's hand. One thumb toyed with my clit, and his other thumb was back torturing my puckered nipple. I could feel his dick pulsing and twitching as I slid my fingers up the underside of his shaft. I gave him one last twist of my wrist and I heard him cry out into the empty night. His hot come hit my hand and mixed with the cool water all around us. My body shook and I moaned deep in my throat as I tightened around his fingers, coming all over him.

Ted gasped one last breath and pulled me to him, the water cloudy from our come. He pulled his hand from between my legs, and I worried that he would run away from me screaming. Instead, he smiled at me, breathing heavy, sweat on his forehead. He kissed me on the cheek before heading out of the water. I watched as he grabbed his towel and headed toward the dark house. I thought he was going to leave without saying a word, but at the last second he turned to me. I was still floating in the pool, unable to move.

"I have to go. It's almost midnight. Good night, Princess."

Cupid Has Signed Off

Thomas S. Roche

It all started so innocently, really. Just a little anonymous online sex on a Saturday night, in a chat room called *Filthy Submission for Sluts in Training*.

Sarah had been there so many times, ever since she'd decided to indulge her kinky fantasies in a way that wouldn't require her to actually, you know, meet up with anyone. What could be safer than cybersex under an assumed name, Psyche, with photos that showed pink but no peach?

Most Fridays and Saturdays, Sarah had her dorm room to herself while her roommate, Annie, partied over in B dorm, as she was so fond of doing—"where the men are men and the women carry condoms and lube," as Annie was fond of putting it, which made Sarah want to hide over here in the all-female A dorm. Friday and Saturday nights were when Sarah would take her only real breaks from studying with a few hours of living her weird fantasies in back-and-forth storytelling with some random stranger twice her age and half her IQ.

Despite her proclivity for online sex, Sarah was far from a player in real life (IRL). When guys tried to flirt with her,

Sarah usually pretended to be a foreign-exchange student and not to speak a word of English, though only one guy so far had clued in to the fact that she was in fact speaking medieval Latin and therefore, barring foreign-exchange time travel, was almost certainly fucking with him.

Making it even more unlikely that she would fuck around was the fact that Sarah lived in the dorms despite being a junior; her scholarship included on-campus housing through all four years but no allowance for off-campus housing.

Sarah's sex life settled into a thrilling routine of twice-weekly Friday-and-Saturday-night cybersex in online chat rooms and the application of her favorite vibrator to her nether regions only on those nights. She gravitated toward AltFet because while it was quite possibly the crappiest social-networking engine known, the chat rooms were usually pretty lively.

That Saturday night, Sarah had been sorely bored by the boneheaded conversation in the chat room. She actually had her cursor over the Logout button when an Instant Message popped up.

CUPID: Psyche, eh? Cute. Bet you like blindfolds.

Sarah stared at the screen in disbelief. Before responding, she quickly hit the View Profile and looked at the guy's stats. No age. No real photo—just shadowy outlines of a guy in poor lighting. Role: Top. Kinky: Very. Experience: Very. Looking for: LTR. Location: Sonoma, California.

Sarah had an absolute rule against dirty-chatting with guys from her own area because sooner or later—usually within ten minutes, often within five—they were begging her to hop in a cab and come over and service them "IRL."

Despite this rule, she found herself typing.

PSYCHE: I LURVE blindfolds. Preferably ones with pad-locks.
CUPID: And gags? Cuffs? Ropes? Whips? Chains? Pad-dles? Canes, little whore?
PSYCHE: :-)

Lord have mercy, responding with a smiley face? She hated that, but there it was, and she'd typed it.

CUPID: I'd like to send you a dirty picture, Psyche.

Sarah had recovered enough to type:

PSYCHE: Hopefully not of your dick. LOL LOL LOL LOL ROFL

Spewing LOLs was at least as stupid, in fact far stupider, than typing another happy face. But that's what spilled out of her. At times, typing a hundred words a minute was a huge disadvantage in online chatting. Sara tended to be a little trigger-happy on the Enter key.

CUPID: No, Psyche. It's not a picture of my dick.

Cupid has sent you a picture. Do you want to accept?
What could it hurt, right? Some picture of a pretty girl on her knees in chains wearing a dog collar... Sarah had seen a million of them, but oh, how she liked them.
She clicked Accept and watched with widening eyes as the photo came into view line by line. A hot wave went through her. Her nipples went instantly hard with an ache that made her grit her teeth. She could feel the swell of her clit. She stared at the picture for a long hot minute.

CUPID: Hot?
PSYCHE: Way to use Wikipedia, dude.

The picture on Sarah's screen was *The Abduction of Psyche* by William-Adolphe Bouguereau, an 1895 painting in which Cupid himself is caught in the act of carrying off his true love Psyche after jabbing himself with his own arrows of love. The painting and the story were, in fact, the reason Sarah had chosen Psyche as her nom-de-chat. She couldn't say why the arrival of the image on her screen made her so wet—she had a JPEG of it elsewhere on her laptop, but this one did something filthy to her. Her hand dipped down past the loose waistband of her sweatpants and she felt herself—wow.

Her hand came out and left a smear of wet across her keyboard as she typed.

Almost without knowing what she was doing, Sarah went to her Photos folder and grabbed the one photo she had of herself in black leather wrist-and-ankle restraints with her skirt and shirt both pulled up, nothing underneath. The filename was "The Abduction of Psyche."

PSYCHE: Tit for tat.

This was utterly unheard of for Sarah; normally if she deigned to send guys online pictures, they were photos of porn stars downloaded from the Net; if she actually sent pictures of herself, it was always "pink but no peach." Her body, maybe bikini-clad, from the neck down, maybe seminude in underwear, from behind. But her photos never showed her face. This one did.

CUPID: Natural blonde?
PSYCHE: Sure. LOL.

For fuck's sake, what was going on? She was reverting to pathetic online speak… Normally she avoided LOLs and happy faces like the plague, but here they were spilling unbidden from her fingers while she squirmed around, wondering why she'd sent a stranger a photo of herself after chatting with him for three minutes. What the fuck was wrong with her?

CUPID: Nice restraints. Are they yours?
PSYCHE: No, I'm poor. I took it in a changing room at a leather store in the city so I could have something to send perverted guys like you.
CUPID: What are you wearing now?
PSYCHE: Sweats, tank top. Nope, no panties, no bra.
CUPID: Take off your clothes, Psyche.

Sarah's hands trembled, as if they were fighting not to reach for her tank top of their own accord.

PSYCHE: Don't I get to see a pic of you first?
CUPID: No. Take off your clothes.

She did. She sat naked in her desk chair. She'd done it a hundred times, and she did it like a dance she knew well. The chat went from naughty to dirty, edging toward filthy. Cupid told her to spread her legs. She did. He told her to feel if she was wet. She did; she was. She rubbed her clit and slipped her fingers inside and pinched her nipples. He told her she was a filthy little slut, in stunningly creative terms.

She liked that. She liked that a lot.

When her excitement mounted, she begged him, as was her habit.

PSYCHE: Please, Sir, my vibrator. I need to cum. Please, Sir, may this little slut cum?

CUPID: Spell it "come," please, for the love of Venus. Not yet, Psyche. First, tell me what you want to happen to you when you do things like put on restraints in a changing room in public.
PSYCHE: You mean, tell you a fantasy, Sir?
CUPID: That'll do.

Sarah took a deep breath; she was well past ready to come, but she would happily put that off for a few minutes in order to tell Cupid something filthy, something terribly filthy and impossibly titillating, the sort of thing that turned men (and Sarah) into ravening, drooling, fuck-hungry beasts. This part, she was very, very good at.

She told him what she wanted to happen when she stripped down and restrained herself and snapped pictures in a changing room in the city. The details spilled savagely from her fingers, exploding in long columns down the chat window. She wanted four big rough cops to discover her taking dirty pictures of herself in a changing room in a leather store in the city, and to tell her that such a thing constituted shoplifting.

"Do you know what we do to shoplifters here in the big city, little girl?"

Sarah knew, all right. It involved bondage, spanking and a padlocking blindfold. She described it in excruciating detail in about five minutes' worth of frenzied typing, with Cupid asking questions when it steered her toward still filthier territory.

CUPID: You are a very dirty girl. Do you have a dildo?
PSYCHE: Yes, Sir.
CUPID: Fuck yourself.
PSYCHE: I'd like to go to bed first, Sir. I am on a laptop.
CUPID: Then do it.

She went to the bed, propped herself up on one arm, lifted her ass in the air and fucked herself.

PSYCHE: What position, Sir?
CUPID: Doggy style. Always doggy style. Fuck yourself from behind.

Far be it from Sarah to refuse an order. Actually, she refused orders every time she chatted, but this time—oh, Lord, have mercy, that was good!

PSYCHE: It's in, Sir. I'm fucking myself. Fuck, it feels good. Sir, may I cum?
CUPID: Not if you spell it that way.
PSYCHE: Sorry, Sir. May I come?
CUPID: Yes, without your vibrator.
PSYCHE: Sir, I can't. I never do.

Sarah reached for her vibe, but her hand hovered over it, uncommitted.

CUPID: You can come without it. You're about to.

Sarah took her hand away.

PSYCHE: Yes, Sir. I'll try. Close. Very close.
CUPID: Ask first. Ask permission.
PSYCHE: Yes, Sir.

Several long minutes passed as Sarah had worked the dildo into her pussy, repeatedly, in increasing thrusts, feeling herself relax, feeling the tautness turn to shuddering pleasure, wishing all of a sudden she'd selected the longer dildo, the fatter dildo, the one with the thicker head—maybe then she could come…

Whoa, wait a minute. Oh, wow, holy shit, that was, wow, she was actually going to—

PSYCHE: Adfsjjdfk;lasdfkj;ladfskj;lfsdj;lfadskjl;dfs
PSYCHE: adfskj;ladfskj;ladsfkj;ldafskj;ladfskj;lfadskj;lkjadfs;l
PSYCHE: fkj
CUPID: Well put.

Another long minute passed as Sarah panted and bit her lip and contracted rhythmically around the dildo, trying hard not to moan too loud—the anarchists next door always pounded on the walls and cheered with shameless obscenity when they could hear her making sex noises.

PSYCHE: OMG I came so hard, Sir. I'm still kinda cumming!!!!
CUPID: Say "OMG" again and you'll be sorry. And don't call it "cumming."
PSYCHE: Sorry, Sir.
CUPID: You did not ask permission first.
PSYCHE: OMG, Sir, I forgot.
CUPID: Spanking.
PSYCHE: Sir?
CUPID: Time for your spanking, disobedient girl.

Sarah went all gooey inside, her clit still sensitive from her orgasm but her pleasure mounting at the order for a spanking.

PSYCHE: Sir?
CUPID: Spank yourself. A dozen times. Hard.
PSYCHE: Yes, Sir.

She obeyed, lifting her ass and smacking herself hard enough to make the shuddering go through her body and deep into her clit. How many guys had told her to do this? Had she ever wanted even one of them to actually do it in person?

PSYCHE: Um…
CUPID: Yes?
PSYCHE: Do I get to see a picture of you, Sir?
CUPID: No. Be here tomorrow night, same time.

Sarah felt a twinge of guilt: She wanted to, badly; she wanted more of this, *lots* more of this. But her boundaries—

PSYCHE: I can't, Sir. I have to study.
CUPID: Tsk, tsk. When, then?
PSYCHE: Next Friday, Sir. Same time.
CUPID: See you then. Good night, Psyche.

Sarah couldn't believe she typed it, then, hastily, hands wet with lube and her juices. She got the question in before Cupid signed off.

PSYCHE: Do u play IRL, Sir?

There was a long pause, and Sarah feared she had lost him.

CUPID: What an interesting question, Psyche. Do something for me.
PSYCHE: Anything, Sir.
CUPID: Do you have a blindfold?
PSYCHE: Two, Sir. One that padlocks. It attaches to my slave collar and my ball gag. I stole them. I also have a regular sleep mask.
CUPID: You have a roommate?
PSYCHE: Yes, Sir. :-(

CUPID: Wear the sleep mask.
PSYCHE: I won't be able to read what u write, Sir.
CUPID: After I'm gone. Wear it while you sleep. From now on, wear it whenever you can.
PSYCHE: Sir?

Cupid Has Signed Off.

Sarah wore the sleep mask that night, and woke up a dozen times hot and hungry in the darkness, the blindfold a tight caress across her unseeing eyes. If Annie had an opinion on the sudden appearance of the sleep mask when she stumbled home drunk at 4:00 a.m., she didn't say a thing. Sarah had never worn it to sleep in before, but the affectation apparently flew under the roommate radar.

It should not have seemed such a strange start to a kinky love affair, but since before meeting Cupid Sarah had no real interest in having a kinky love affair, that made it strange from the get-go.

She took naked pictures of herself for Cupid that week, including many with the blindfold padlocked on her pretty face. Sarah logged in on Friday for a long filthy chat in which she confessed a fantasy, and he gave her sweet soft rough nasty orders corresponding to it—*Spank yourself, fuck yourself, put the dildo in your ass, put the clothes on your nipples*—that would lead her to come, never "cum," like crazy.

Saturday was the same, and after that she no longer pled study time when Cupid told her to be there the next night. She chatted with Annie in the room, the intensity of possible exposure making it that much hotter for her. Whenever Annie was gone, Sarah was on the computer, looking for Cupid. Often she'd sit there idle for hours, invisible to everyone but him. They'd chat, she'd spin filth for him, and he'd direct her in a tightly scripted fandango of sensation and submission. She became quite acquainted with the feel of her several dildos inside her, with the smack of her hand, of a textbook, of a Ping-Pong paddle from the rec room, and finally of a wire coat hanger on her bare ass and splayed thighs. And one thing he kept coming back to, at the end of each session: *Blindfold yourself while you sleep.*

If we did voice chat or talked on the phone, she typed once when he gave her the order, three weeks to the day after they'd first chatted, I could blindfold myself while we talk.

CUPID: Interesting idea. Dangerously close to meeting IRL.
PSYCHE: Would Sir be open to that idea?
CUPID: What an interesting question, Psyche.
PSYCHE: You are on the North Coast, yes?
CUPID: I will consider your proposal, Psyche. Good night.

The next morning she logged in, as she always did four or five or eight or ten times each day—just to check, just to verify, just to make sure that Cupid hadn't left any messages for her in her AltFet mailbox. This time, Cupid had.

CUPID: Your proposal is accepted, Psyche. Meet me at the Venus Motel on Highway 35 at midnight tonight. Room 216. Follow these instructions—

Sarah's heart pounded as she read the detailed instructions. She couldn't. She just couldn't. She couldn't do something like this—not really. Not IRL.

But she could, and she would, and she was about to. Eleven came quickly, and midnight thundered on as she followed his instructions exactly and rode the bus out to the Venus Motel on Highway 35—talk about inauspicious. The very sleaze of it excited her.

But too much about the onrushing encounter scared her.

She'd heard stories, of course. Single women should not meet men from the Internet. Bad things would happen. Worse things, even, than she was hoping and praying were about to happen to her, in the Venus Motel on Highway 35…

She stepped off the bus in front of the motel and felt a surge of excitement. She found room 216, discovered the door very slightly ajar. She went inside; a dozen candles shed a soft light. The crusty polyester bedspread had been folded up and stuffed into the corner. In its place was a lush black silk bedcover.

Sarah's heart pounded. She closed the door behind her and left it locked but did not shoot the dead bolt, per Cupid's instructions.

Sarah took off her clothes.

When her coat, dress, bra, thong and combat boots were piled in the closet, Sarah took out three items: a collar, a blindfold and a ball gag. The blindfold went soft and tight around her head, and leather straps leading from it locked in four places to the ball gag that she spread her lips around, and in two places to the collar she buckled around her throat. She panicked and took the blindfold off before she could close the padlock.

Bad things happen to girls who meet men on the Internet.

Sarah put the key to the padlock under the pillow on the bed, within easy reach. Then she donned the blindfold again, locked it to the collar and lay down on the bed, legs spread, arms slack alongside her. She ran her fingers up her thighs and felt how wet she was. Her nipples were so hard they hurt. She was breathing hard through her nose, and she moaned softly behind her ball gag.

The door clicked open; heavy footsteps came inside.

"Hello, Psyche," came his voice, deep and rich like chocolate: a man she'd never seen, whose voice she'd never heard, a man who was about to touch and spank and fuck her, a man to whom she'd pledged obedience.

Sarah felt her heart racing ever faster. She tried to nod, but even that was difficult with the blindfold and the ball gag and the collar. She managed a whimper, deep behind the ball gag, which sounded scared and, frankly, kind of hot.

She heard zippers, she heard buttons, she heard his clothing hitting the floor. He was upon her, his heat all over her, his weight between her legs and on her belly and pressed firm against her naked breasts, bearing her hard into the bed. His sounds sang in her ears: there was the bestial growl of savage lust, the sound of the bedsprings creaking under his weight, the soft shushing sound of his skin against hers as he slid over her, mouth hot and teasing, his tongue behind her ears and then down her neck and over her breasts—she tried to scream, it felt so fucking good when he suckled her hard nipples, but it came out as nothing more than a gurgle when her tongue hit the ball gag filling her mouth. Then she felt the head of his cock grazing her moist sex and nuzzling her clitoris, and she attempted to moan, *Please, fuck me!*—because she wanted to be fucked so bad that to be teased by Cupid was tantamount to being tortured.

As his cock moved from her sex to her belly, she arched her back and tried to guide him into her—unsuccessfully. She bit hard into the ball gag and drew a deep breath. His smell— God! His smell was all over her, a smell that made her wet to her core, made every cell in her body sing, made her thighs burn without the weight of his body on them, pinning them open as he fucked her. She drew great deep shuddering breaths of him, like the smell of his body was a drug.

Foreplay? No, thank you. Fuck me. Just fuck me. Every instant he wasn't inside her was agony.

She tried to hook her legs around him and pull him onto her, into her. He pinned her thighs open with his weight, held her down. She reached for him, and he caught her wrists easily, forcing them over her head and holding her there. She writhed helplessly, back arched, tits high in the air, legs spread, ass hard against the silk bedspread. Suspended between heaven and earth.

"No," she tried to cry, squirming back and forth. "No! No! No! Fuck me now!" But it was just a whimper and a whine and a moan and a grunt behind the gag, and Cupid grabbed her wrists and pinned them over her head easily with one hand, holding Sarah tight and immobile under him as he ran his other hand slowly from thigh to sex to belly to breast to neck, taking long minutes on each one, coaxing her quickly into a writhing, desperate mass, moaning behind the gag. He pinned her legs with his weight and held her wrists firmly, and implacably made her wait.

"Patience, Psyche," he said. "You didn't just come here to get fucked. Any man could do that to you. You're here to get what you deserve."

Sarah was not a large girl, but neither was she exceptionally petite. Nonetheless, Cupid seemed to exert no effort whatsoever as he grabbed her and f lipped her and held her down, bringing both her arms into the small of her back and pinning her wrists.

"Count, Psyche," he growled. "In your head. Say, 'Thank you, Sir, may I have another.'"

He spanked her. Hard at first, making her jolt and surge and writhe. Then softer, now that he'd established she was his to spank in a manner he desired. He warmed her well— firmly but slowly, building the pressure of his blows as the heat of her round ass mounted. The shuddering smack of his naked palm against her ass sent throbbing pulses into her clitoris.

Sarah had never been spanked before. She had spanked herself, yes, more times than she could count—but she had never been spanked before. She was totally unprepared for it, especially after Cupid lifted her, effortlessly, and folded her over his lap. He felt her sex, teased her clit and then began the regular, rhythmic spanking motions, building with harder and harder blows until Sarah realized what he was doing—her clit pulsed, her muscled tightened, and—

Sarah came, hard, over Cupid's knee. He caressed her sex as the afterglow warmed its way through her... She tried to squirm and look up at him, but all she could see was darkness.

Cupid effortlessly turned Sarah onto her belly. With his knees, Cupid forced Sarah's knees wide, exposing her. He put his big firm hands on her hips and lifted them. He grabbed a pair of pillows and stuffed them under her stomach, forcing her ass up high and her back into an arch; with her legs spread like that and his weight hard against her thighs, Sarah had never felt so exposed.

He pinned her there under him; his big hands went around one wrist, then the other, and he collected her wrists like a pair of errant pets. He held them tight with one hand in the small of her back. His other hand traveled with poisonous slowness up Sarah's back, tickling her shoulders until his fingers snaked into the great sweep of Sarah's long hair, and with a fierce implacability he seized her hair tight, making her shriek behind the ball gag.

Immobilized with his hands at her hair and wrists, his weight on her thighs, her back arched impossibly and her legs spread so wide she was all but paralyzed, Sarah knew what was coming. Just the knowledge of it was enough to make her cum—not "come" (respectable, positive, beautiful), but "cum" (filthy, uncouth, sordid, dirty). Exhilarating.

Cupid made her beg for it. Not with her mouth—she was still gagged, effectively, her pleas and protests reduced to groans and whimpers. He made her beg with her body, squirming and thrashing and trying to get her sex onto his cock, which she could feel lying smooth and hard and wet at the tip in the cleft between her ass cheeks. When she'd struggled and fought and could almost not stand the torture of waiting—then, Cupid gave it to her, teasing his cock head between the swollen lips of her smooth-shaved sex, holding her down hard and firm when she tried to push back onto him, and making her wait while he let go of her wrists—she brought them suddenly to her sides and tried to push herself back, for the sole purpose that she knew he would collect her wrists again, and she liked that.

While Sarah struggled, Cupid spanked her so hard she froze in an instant, shocked at the sharp sudden pain. Then he meticulously parted her sexual lips, fitted his cockhead into her entrance, and before she could even come to her senses and fuck herself onto him, he'd collected her wrists, pinned them in the small of her back, and pulled her hair so hard it sent a wave of heat through her naked body.

Then he entered her.

It went in slow at first and then fast, hard. The first moments stretched her sex so that she squealed behind the gag. Then the thickness of his head popped into her, and with a great thrust of his hips, Cupid opened her up with one long, firm, slow, sweet stroke.

He fucked her, slow then fast, then fast, faster, harder. He put one foot on her thigh and drove into her savagely, making her cry out as she mounted toward orgasm.

She came fast—twenty strokes, or thirty. He pulled out and entered her again. She heard the buzzing of a vibrator; he pressed it to her clit and behind the blindfold her eyes rolled far back in her head. She came a second time. He'd released her wrists, but she could do nothing with them; she was incapacitated by her hunger, her pleasure, the delicious sense that she was utterly out of control. Her arms stretched limp over her head, useless. He ran his hand through her hair, over her neck, down her back. He reached beneath and pinched her nipples, stroked her belly, ran nails down her back leaving great hot furrows of sensation. She heard a gurgling sound, felt a cool slick sensation in her cleft, felt the stretch of his finger going into her ass. More slickness, then two. Cupid parted her cheeks. She felt his cockhead at her rear hole and tried to say "Yes," but neither "Yes" nor "No" were hers to say, just a long low moan of pleasure behind the gag as Cupid fucked her again, this time a way she'd never been fucked— thought, at least partly, that she *would* never be fucked.

It was exquisite. She probably could have come without the vibrator—cum! Definitely cum, being fucked in the ass on a cheap motel bed by a man she'd never seen, and she was going to fucking cum harder than she ever had in her life. But when Cupid decided there was another orgasm in her, Sarah didn't have a choice about that, either.

She came, powerfully, and felt Cupid pinning her under his weight as he pressed the vibrator to her clit. She came and came, and felt his essence flooding deep inside her. Her orgasm continued for what felt like minutes, as his slickness seeped into her, and his breathing went from fast to slow, gradually.

It was at that very moment that Sarah decided she was in love.

There were long delicious moments of his fingers all over her, over her neck, in her hair, over her back, across her hips where she was normally so fucking ticklish, the weight and the touch and the scent of him enveloping her.

But he never turned her over; he never positioned her to face him. His breathing went slowly dark, and soon he was snoring, still atop her.

She wanted to ask him questions. She wanted to know things. She wanted to see him.

Their scene was over, right? She could see him now. She could look at her lover.

She delicately pried herself out of Cupid's embrace; she

reached under the pillow; the key was still there. She fumbled with the padlock, opened it. She took out the ball gag first; her jaw ached. She unfastened the collar. She gingerly took off the blindfold, running her fingers through her blond hair.

The candles had burned down. Cupid had drawn the blackout curtains. It was not long until dawn, but there was not a hint of light in the room yet, and Sarah stared into darkness at the unseen body of the man she'd come to love.

Sarah had not slept. She was punchy; when the thin strings of light began to seep through the blackout curtains, she thought she saw—

She leaped off the bed. Sarah looked into the steadily lightening gray of the cheap motel room. It was impossible.

She stumbled to the window and threw back the curtains.

Cupid awakened in an instant and threw his hands up, letting out a scream. He sat up, then, and Sarah understood why he had only fucked her from behind—great silver wings rose from naked Cupid's back, behind him, knocking over lamps, nightstands, spilling a cheap white hotel phone with a huge ringing crashing sound. Cupid's eyes went wide, and as he wakened, light burst from his every contour.

Sarah screamed. She stumbled back against the wall, staring aghast—it was impossible. But then, so many things were impossible.

Her jaw still ached and her tongue felt swollen from the long hours wearing the ball gag. That's why it seemed impossible that she managed to speak:

"I love you."

The light burst everywhere. And Sarah covered her eyes, blinded. She cowered against the wall and a great wind seared her naked body; there was a crash, almost an explosion—and when she peeked out terrified from behind her hands, the motel-room door had been wrenched from its hinges, and a great molten illumination poured through it onto an empty bed. It was dawn.

Sobbing, Sarah groped for her dress, for her coat, for her combat boots; she had never dressed so fast, and was gone long before the sheriff's cars got there.

On the longest week of her life, Sarah blew a Latin midterm, got a C on a Greek test and pleaded illness to put off having to write her poetry paper. She cried almost constantly and checked AltFet six, eight, ten, twenty times a day. She told her concerned roommate, Annie, that she'd just had an online relationship that went bad. "He broke up with me, I guess," she said, shrugging. "No big deal." She tried hard not to burst into tears.

"You should come out with me tonight," said Annie on Friday. "Come over to B dorm. Things are going to get pretty wild. I guarantee that you can find a new boyfriend, a *real* boyfriend."

"IRL," said Sarah vaguely.

"Huh?"

"Nothing," said Sarah. "I think I'll sit this one out."

The second Annie was gone, Sarah signed in to AltFet, the elaborate blindfold-gag-collar combination piled close to her left hand. She stared blankly at the screen.

VENUS: Hello, Psyche.

Christ, another one of those stupid FemDom bitches. Sarah had absolutely no interest in that shit, and she was not in the mood. It was only the minimum standards of politeness that made her type:

PSYCHE: Hello.
VENUS: I think you've failed greatly and need to be punished—isn't that right, Psyche?

Sarah gritted her teeth and almost hit the Ignore button.

She paused at the last instant. She felt as if she had basically blown it on heterosexuality, and was probably schizophrenic to boot. She may as well try girls; it was worth a shot, wasn't it?

Besides, she was too depressed to care. Decently creative online sex with a woman would be a lot better than another night freaking out and wondering what she really saw in that motel on Highway 35.

PSYCHE: Yes, ma'am. I fucked up. At your motel, actually. LOL.
VENUS: Don't say "LOL."

Sarah caught her breath.

PSYCHE: Yes, ma'am.
VENUS: Don't demote me. It's "Goddess."
PSYCHE: Srsly?
VENUS: You tell me.

Sarah could still feel the sting where her unseen lover had spanked her. She shifted on her chair, reached back to touch the soft dark yellowing bruises, took a deep breath and typed:

PSYCHE: Do you know him?

There was a long pause, during which Sarah held her breath.

VENUS: Say his name.
PSYCHE: I can't. It hurts.
VENUS: Not as much as it's going to. Shall we begin your expiation?

Sarah felt hot, her nipples hard, her pussy going wet. She'd never gotten turned on like this chatting with a woman—but then, she'd never had a woman promise her "expiation."

PSYCHE: I like that word. Expiation.
VENUS: Shall we begin it? There is hope for you and Cupid...if you suffer beautifully. I make all things possible, Psyche. Do you believe that?

Sarah took a deep breath, ran her hand through her hair, and remembered the sting of Cupid pulling it.

PSYCHE: Yes, Goddess.
VENUS: Shall we begin, then?
PSYCHE: Yes, pls.
VENUS: :-)

Sarah spread her legs.

The Walking Wheel

Georgia E. Jones

London, 1483

Madchen Sprynger slid her hands into her hair and pressed them against the hard warmth of her scalp. This helped with the cold and shaking in her hands, but did little for the breathless ache in her chest. Outside her meagerly appointed chamber, the raucous street life of London had been under way for hours, the continual clamor so familiar it was like breathing.

What had he been thinking?

However agonizing the question, Madchen knew she did not have far to look for the answer. Her father was an ambitious man, canny in business, but a poor drinker. Spirits brought out his worst qualities and trebled them. He must have been deep in his cups to have made the bet he made last night: that she could spin nine pounds of roving into yarn over the course of three nights. Her stomach lurched painfully.

Three pounds a night.

She was an excellent spinner, her yarns strong, even and lustrous. And she was quick. Where it normally took five spinners to keep one weaver occupied, with Madchen it took only three others because she did the work of two in the time of one. In seven or eight hours, she could easily spin two pounds of roving into a one-ply yarn. But after eight hours, no matter who you were, you were tired.

Pushing away from the desk, Madchen stood and began to pace the small room, as if by doing so she could escape the ugly knowledge lodged under her breastbone: the task her father had set for her was impossible, and drunk or not he must have known it. A member of the Mercer's Company, he lacked the funds and position to rise in the guild, which led her to one solitary conclusion. Her father had sold her virginity to Anthony Wydeville, Earl Rivers, for silver.

Madchen went to her wheel and began, picking up the draft in her left hand, letting it out with her right, guiding it to one of three spindles. When one was full, she began with the other, the age-old motions easing her agitation. The long-staple wool was her favorite, Border Leicester, a creamy moonlight-gray of which she never tired. She skipped dinner, not wanting to face her father. As long as she worked, she could avoid thinking, but she went in for tea late in the afternoon because she was tired and thirsty. Blessedly, he was out, but he appeared not too long a while later, bounding into the room with a fanatic light in his eyes and a joyous step. Madchen's heart sank. He was a stolid man, her father. The only thing that pleased him was achieving his own pecuniary ends, which in this case was bound to bear ill tidings for her.

Face flushed, he spoke quickly, the words tumbling over one another in a rush to be spoken. "The king's got wind of it, Maddie!" He was exultant. "The contest is to be held at the Tower, with Queen Elizabeth and all the court in attendance! At the *Tower*, Maddie, imagine it!"

He's truly thrilled, she thought. The ramifications of all this to her seemed to impinge in no way upon his good spirits. Madchen felt the first surreptitious twinges of anger. She waited until he was at the door. "Father?" She spoke softly. "What do I receive if I win?"

He turned, his eyes wide. "Why, Maddie-girl, didn't I tell you? You become the bride of the earl's son. Lord Scales is his name, I believe."

It was true, then. He had sold her. No one in their right mind would risk marrying the heir of an earl, who was brother to the queen of England, to a penniless wool spinner from Saint Laurence Lane. The real thing, the awful coldness of what he had done, circled around her in the cooling air of the room. But finally, Madchen drank the last, bitter dregs of it standing there, a thoughtful look on her face. She was the best spinner in England. There was nothing to do but try.

At two o'clock the next day, the Tower green was emerald in the clear March light. There had been a banquet, to which she and her father were not invited. This had not bothered Madchen in the least, but it had put her father grimly out of sorts and he had complained the entire way from Saint Laurence Lane to the Tower. They had come on foot through the noisy, fulsome streets of the City. Everyone else either lived at court or had come by private barge on the river, being let out at Traitor's Gate, which led through the old portcullis directly onto the green.

Madchen watched the richest, most privileged people England had to offer. They tumbled onto the green like gems tipped out of a casket, and moved to and fro to little apparent purpose. Madchen thought of her wheel. There was a reason they called it the walking wheel. You walked to and fro, back and forth, always with the purpose of spinning out the draft and winding the yarn onto the spindles. The ladies and gentlemen of Edward's court fluttered and wafted. She thought about the kind of yarn their movements would produce and afforded herself a smile. They would think her poor and plain and worth less than the expensive leather on the soles of their shoes. So she did what she always did. She made it not matter. She thought briefly of Judas and his thirty pieces of silver, and went out among them.

From a distance, she looked like sand. Hair, skin, eyes, lips; everything just beige. Lord Scales watched the girl, not because he was unduly interested in her, but because it was unique in his experience to be betrothed, however disingenuously, to two women at the same time. Also because, though it pricked his pride to admit it, neither woman seemed interested in the outcome. Eleanor appeared to think the whole affair beneath her notice, and the little spinster had hardly spared a glance in his direction, though she must know who he was. She moved among them, a brown moth amongst butterflies. She was acting, he thought only like herself (though he did not know or pretend to care who that was) and it was a sight he was beholding for the first time in his life. At the court of Edward the Fourth and Queen Elizabeth Wydeville, the price of acting simply as oneself was always too high to pay. Following like hounds on a hare was the perturbing thought, presented in whole cloth, as if God had sent down a note borne on a silver platter and left it hovering in midair at elbow height, was that she saw herself as somehow among equals. Equals of a different proficiency, perhaps, but equals nonetheless. There was no reverse snobbery in it that he could detect, which meant it did not exist. He was the nephew of Elizabeth Wydeville, the commoner queen, and had come across enough snobbery, even in the exalted circles in which he moved, to know when he was in its presence.

That was when he began to be intrigued.

★ ★ ★

Madchen tinkered with the wheel, checking the tension, making sure the maidens were in alignment, ensuring that the leather parts were oiled and flexible. The room was warm. A fire burned in the grate and a brazier of coals was set near the wheel. Her hands would not bother her for hours. The roving had been delivered, prepared exactly as she had specified. Heaped in nine balls, each the size of a ram's head, it was an intimidating sight. Madchen moved the pyramid out of sight behind her and kept one ball next to her. Picking out the first draft, she began to spin, the gray Leicester moving through her hands with its wavy, familiar crimp.

Spinning did not require thought, or even sight. Madchen took in her surroundings; grander than those at home, of course, but not by a lot. They did not care enough to try to impress her. There was one tapestry, thin and faded, no doubt moved here to unravel in solitude. She gazed at it with a critical eye; a hunting scene with hounds and roebuck and archers with longbows.

Her thoughts wandered. The fire burned down, the coals elapsed to a bed of red embers, the light made strange shadows on the walls and ceiling. She went on spinning. She found herself thinking about Lord Scales, though she didn't care to. Someone had pointed him out that afternoon, eager to be part of the drama and, looking, Madchen had felt a trickle of disappointment. She would have at least liked for him to look like the prince of her girlhood dreams: slim and golden and sweetly tempered. This man, Piers they called him, was taller than she by two feet or more, black-haired and green-eyed, physically substantial to the point of burliness, with lips of such a sensual bent that she felt embarrassed on his behalf. He seemed in no way affectionate or friendly, acknowledging one or two people, but in the main keeping to himself. Of his father, Earl Rivers, she refused to think at all.

The night wound down, and near dawn she stopped to rest by the fire, warming her hands and rubbing her neck. She had spun more than two pounds of roving and every part of her ached. By seven, the official time they would come to fetch her to the hall for breakfast, she would not have completed the last three-quarter pounds of wool. One part of her mind insisted she could make it up on the two successive nights, while the other part chided her for foolishness and demanded she come up with a better way to avoid being a midnight morsel for the earl. She climbed to her feet, every muscle protesting. As she did, a latch snicked deep in the stone, a section of the wall slid open and a small, unkempt man stepped forth into the room, bringing with him a cloud of dust and a great many cobwebs trailing from his clothing and beard. "Bertram Rumpolzey," he said, bowing, as if it were entirely normal to spring from nowhere. It was impossible to guess his age. Behind the beard he might be thirty or three hundred, but the beard was almost full gray and his eyes had creases around and under them, so she judged him to be older. Having never met one, it took Madchen a fraught moment to perceive the truth. He was, in fact, a dwarf. The night, indeed the whole preceding two days, began to take on a surreal, dreamlike quality which was not entirely unpleasant. Not sure of the best way to proceed, Madchen fell back on good manners.

"Can I help you?" she asked politely. The dwarf had gone immediately to her wheel and was examining it and the skeins of completed yarn in a basket on the floor.

He straightened at her question. "I would like a child."

"Oh," Madchen said agreeably. "I would, as well. But I'm afraid I haven't got any here at the moment."

"Of course not," he said, as if she were a little daft. "I mean later, after you're married."

"Am I to be married?" Madchen asked.

"Of course you are. To the earl's son."

Madchen laughed. It was very amusing, the way he spoke to her, but gradually Madchen came to understand that the strange little man wanted *her* child, the union of her marriage to Piers Wydeville, Lord Scales. This was less amusing, but as he had been in no way rude in his request, Madchen explained the situation.

"But you will win the bet," he countered. "I have your yarn. In there." And he gestured to the cobwebby passage behind her.

Madchen shook her head to clear it. "Are you telling me," she began. "Are you suggesting that I *trick* them, that I cheat to win the bet and that in return I'm to give you my firstborn son?"

"Exactly," he said, satisfied that at last she understood the parameters of the problem.

There were a lot of things Madchen could have said at that point, but in the end she chose the simplest. "Why?"

"Any child of my body runs the risk of being as I am. I want a man-child that will grow to full height and have full weight in the affairs of men."

Madchen weighed her options. If she was honest, she would lose, and the rewards (herself among them) would go to those who were unscrupulous. That didn't seem fair. If she lied, that wasn't right, either, but she would have escaped the snare. She didn't believe for a moment that Piers Wydeville was going to marry her. He was engaged to the Duke of Somerset's daughter, Eleanor, a girl so in love with herself and so secure of her position in the world, that she needed little other regard. As for the future child…Madchen stood, brushing dust off her skirts. She felt bad for lying, but if she didn't marry Lord Scales, there would be no child for the dwarf to claim. It would be a moot point. She held out one hand. "I accept your terms," she said, and they shook hands firmly, his hand small and strong in hers.

Bertram spent several unpardoned minutes jumping up and down with an unholy glee before retreating into the passage. He returned presently, handing the wool out to her in several wicker baskets. The Border Leicester was the most beautiful worsted Madchen had ever seen, more accomplished even than her own, and this gave her a deep twinge of alarm. There was no work more accomplished than hers, so where had this come from? "What have you done?" she said aloud, not sure if she was asking the dwarf or herself. But when she looked up he was gone, the secret door moving so quietly she had not even heard it close.

The little spinster looked appropriately tired, Piers noted the next morning at breakfast in the great hall. But his idle interest turned to suspicion after the announcement, accompanied by a smattering of applause, that she had successfully completed the first night's task. He ignored it. They had no earthly idea what they were celebrating, but Piers knew the difference between a pound of roving and a pipe of wine and what she had done shouldn't have been possible, even for a very accomplished spinner. He chewed his bacon and kept one eye on Edward and his father, practically arm in arm at the high table. The fact that Tony Wydeville was the queen's elder brother did not mean she condoned the constant amusements with which they entertained themselves. They had whored and drunk themselves into equal states of dissolution and corpulence. Downing the last of his ale, Piers wondered if she was the sole reason the spinning contest had been held at the Tower, which functioned both as a prison and royal residence. Not so easy to do in youthful, robust form, Edward was less of a challenge to keep under her thumb now. Wiping his mouth, Piers rose from the table. The girl had been escorted to another chamber to rest, and he thought he might take the opportunity to examine the spinning room more closely.

At the feast, Piers kept one eye on the girl, one eye on his father and a third eye—the invisible one in the back of his head—on her father. If the man was any more toadying, he would begin to croak before the day was out. When the meal was at long last complete, and Edward and his cronies had reeled off to the next amusement, Piers followed her outside. She went in the opposite direction from the crowd, and he closed with her where she had come to a stop by the fountain and the air was redolent of the rosemary and lavender neatly contained in the herbaceous borders.

"Ah," she said without a trace of irony. "My betrothed." He inclined his head graciously. Up close she was extremely fair. Not sandy, just faintly gold all over. Pretty, in fact. But her hands were astounding, as if God had bestowed this one great extravagance upon her with unstinting generosity. They were classical in perfection of proportion, and the unbidden thought of those hands on his skin made his body jerk in response.

"May I?" he asked, reaching out. She had imbibed a great deal of wine. She gave him her left hand, languid and curious. He explored it as he would any instrument of detailed engineering—an astrolabe, or something of its like—turning it over in his and deftly tracing all the delicate connections. He released her hand reluctantly, like a woman who puts down an expensive jewel she knows her husband will not purchase for her. She was looking up at him now, with nothing but acceptance in her face. Of the moment? Of him? He didn't know. He bent his head and kissed her.

The instant he touched her, everything changed. Madchen had been kissed several times, enough to know how. But this was heaven, his full, soft lips against hers, once, and then when she did not protest, but reached up to meet him, again and again. And he kept speaking to her in between, as if he remembered it was her he was kissing, as if to say, *See? We aren't behaving scandalously.* Madchen kissed him back, her body coming alive, melting, catching fire. She answered him, in words and with her lips, though later she did not remember any of the words. Her arm crept up around his neck, where it fit perfectly, despite his greater height.

"I love your skin," he said, and she smiled, her cheek against his as he explored her neck. His next kiss was firmer, with just a hint of slick, inner lip, and the next gave her the barest tip of his tongue, as if he was asking permission. She would have given it gladly, but he pulled away.

"We have to go back," he said. And what else could she do, the poor girl, except agree?

Madchen spun that night, partly from force of habit, partly because she wasn't sure if the bizarre events of the previous night would repeat themselves and partly to calm herself. She could think of nothing but Piers Wydeville. She hadn't known a man existed who could kiss like that. The golden prince of her youth was gone; in his place was a living man, infinitely more complicated and just as unavailable. Every time she remembered his mouth on her own, her body fell into a stupor of desire. How long would it last? A week? A day?

The dwarf broke into her reverie, earlier this time, but brought with him the same amount of finished wool and took away the unspun roving with him, stuffing it into a large sack that he could barely squeeze through the narrow tunnel. He looked slightly more dapper, his hair combed, his beard trimmed. He did not linger. "This will overset them!" he crowed. And then, "Mind you don't forget your promise, girl." Madchen assured him she would not. After that, there was nothing to do but sleep.

★ ★ ★

In the morning, Madchen Sprynger did not look tired at all. Indeed, her face had taken on a rosy glow and her mien was of good cheer, as well it should be. Somehow in the night she had managed to spin three more pounds of roving into yarn. Sometime during the same night, Piers had been beset by a feeling that the bet had not been fair to begin with. Her father and his had colluded so she could not win, to the benefit of everyone but her. Madchen was simply the pawn in their game. The fact that she was winning did not alter this feeling. The fact that she was cheating did not even alter it.

For she was cheating.

He just couldn't figure out how.

Madchen. It was how he thought of her now. Madchen, the one word containing how the whole of her felt in his arms. He wanted to absorb all of her through his lips: every part of her body and her breath, and not stop at kissing, not stop at anything until she was his. He was going to be married. A man in his position could not afford to stay single, even did he want to. The thought of being tied to Madchen for life held infinitely more appeal than the thought of being tied to Eleanor, whose charms had never held much appeal in the first place. She had been his father's choice, as was the custom.

Piers sought out his father before dinner that day; early enough that Anthony would not be insensible with drink, and while he was with Edward. It was not hard to find him with Edward. They were always together. After greeting the two men, Piers inquired whether his father had given any thought to what he would do should he lose the bet. Tony Wydeville looked up from his cards. A losing hand, but he was going to bluff. Edward sometimes fell for that. "Do?" he said. He was drunk, but not very. "Do!" he said again, as if his son had made a witty remark.

"If you lose," Piers repeated patiently.

The earl waved him away. "She can't win. Can't. Not possible." He threw some gold carelessly onto the table. Edward matched it and raised. He had a good hand.

"She might, though," Piers insisted. "She's done it two nights running. Why not a third?"

"No," his father said, as if sheer obstinacy could make it so.

"You won't honor it?" Piers made his tone merely curious, and watched Edwards's fingers, clinking his gold pieces together, go still.

"What's this?" Edward said, straightening in his chair. He gazed at his best friend blearily, through eyes red-rimmed and bloodshot. They had not slept. But there was nothing compromised in the mind behind those eyes. "You won't honor your bet, Tony?" He looked grave, then leaned back in his chair, laughing. "You'll honor it," he said with certainty, "because I'm your king and I say you will." That simply, it was done. Piers hid his sigh of relief. He had planned for it to go that way. He had hoped for it to go that way, but he could not be certain it would. His father sat slack-faced, cards in hand. "Damn you," he said to Piers, but the words were vacant of anger. He was too busy trying to find a way out of this new predicament.

There were no secrets at court. Before the noon meal was served, every person, from the lowliest servant to the queen, knew what had passed between the king and his dearest friend. This made Madchen the cynosure of more pairs of eyes than the two on either side of her, which she failed to enjoy, but she remained calm, mostly because she was not silly enough to believe she was going to be enjoined in a state of wedded bliss with Lord Scales in the near future. She would cheat to save herself, but she refused to cheat to gain a husband, even one who kissed like Piers. If it came to that, he would have to be told. She shuddered to think about the consequences of that, pushing her food around on the plate with her knife. Spinning in itself was pure simplicity. That was one of the things she loved about it. To have it tangled in such a farcical plot was a painfully ironic juxtaposition.

The day passed. She retired to the spinning chamber as soon as they allowed her, embracing the silence with gratitude. There seemed little point in spinning. She was certain now that the dwarf would appear. He had seemed almost delirious the previous night, with the fruition of his plan so nearly in his grasp.

She fell to pacing, but kept forgetting the walking part, coming to herself in this corner of the room, or that, with no sense of how long she had been standing there. A noise made her look up. Instead of a dwarf through the wall, she got Piers Wydeville through the door—a small, personal miracle that felt infinite. He had brought with him, clever man, a bottle of Bordeaux and two silver goblets.

Twenty minutes later, Madchen knew it wasn't the Bordeaux, because they hadn't got around to opening it. Kissing him straight sober was even better in a way. The urgency built so fast, cresting like a fever in her blood. He was kissing her neck again. "I could do this for hours," he crooned, breathing her in.

"I can't." She was definite. "I'll split my skin."

"Good," he said. "You're supposed to." Madchen forgot to be afraid of the unknown, because the knowing was such pure, drenching pleasure, every new thing sublime. *Who taught you this?* she wanted to ask. *How did you know to do this?* But touching him was saturation enough. He was taken by everything about her; infatuated, smitten. Her body was strong and supple to his touch in a way that was wildly arousing.

When it became clear that hours was stretching it for him, as well, he stopped long enough to fashion the last three balls of roving into a pallet and covered it with his cloak. He divested them of their clothing and lay Madchen down, and he knew from watching her face that her trembling was from eagerness rather than fear. He touched her first between her legs, knowing she would be wet there. He touched her flesh, and she pulled her legs up, opening them wide. He took the slick moisture and rubbed it on her lips, kissing it off. He glazed it over her nipples, sucking it off. He spread it in her navel, licking it out.

She could please this man. The knowledge broke over Madchen like light. She pleased him by being herself. He didn't know why, but Piers felt the moment a kind of shivering rapture took hold of her. He entered her then, with one sure thrust, not afraid of the pain he was causing her. Then he kissed her and kissed her and kissed her, willing to wait but not to stop. She touched him everywhere she could reach, those gorgeous hands so sweetly inflammatory. She didn't care about the pain, only that it kept him still when she ached for him to move. "Let go," she said. "Bring me with you." But she carried him with her, climaxing first, before he could touch the small nub of flesh that would bring her the greatest pleasure.

"I have so much to tell you, Madchen," he gasped, before releasing himself to her body.

Much later, when he was near sleep, she began collecting bits of her clothing. "What are you doing?" he asked, his eyes closed.

"Um," she said, her voice muffled as she wrestled with her drawers under her cloak, which he had spread over them, "just getting a little bit dressed."

She got as far as her shift before he confiscated the rest of her clothing. "I like you naked. Lie down or I'll make love to you again."

"That's not a very effective threat. You do know that?" But she was worried about the time. "We're going to have a visitor," she confessed. "You may be birth-day naked, but I would prefer to be clothed."

"We're not having visitors." He pulled her down. "I made the guard a wealthy man and I have the key."

"He's not coming through that door." Madchen refused to subside. She pointed. "He's coming through that one." Piers looked understandably baffled, but Madchen was saved from further explanations by the advent of the dwarf himself, popping through the door in undiminished high spirits. The sight of them brought him up short, but recovering quickly, he rubbed his hands together in a strictly mercenary gesture. "Well, well," he said. "This is going better than I thought." And he executed a little bow to Piers, complete with flourishes.

"Where is my tunic?" Madchen got one severe look from Piers when he took it from her hand.

"A little warning would have been nice."

"Here, here, here." Bertram was dragging the baskets of yarn from the tunnel and handing them to Piers, who had slipped his tunic over his head and dragged on his hose. "Where is the old roving? Oh, for Lord's sake!" he exclaimed, upon realizing where it was. "Get up, you silly girl," he ordered, barely waiting for Madchen to wrap herself in her cloak before gathering it up. "Don't forget," were his last instructions to her, and he whisked himself and the wool through the door and had it closed behind him before Piers had time to formulate a single question. In the little pool of silence left behind by the dwarf, Piers and Madchen contemplated one another.

"You knew I was cheating," she offered.

"Yes, I knew you were cheating. I just couldn't figure out how." He glanced musingly at the hidden door. "I had no idea that was there. I don't know of anyone who does." Picking up the new yarn, he began to remake the bed.

Madchen watched him, her brow knit. "You don't mind?"

"Well," he said reasonably, "they were cheating. And you weren't facing a very pleasant consequence. Stop looking so worried and come back to bed."

Curled up with him, near sleep herself, Madchen's thoughts escaped and made their way to her tongue. "You'll leave me in the morning."

"Don't be ridiculous. I'll marry you in the morning." Madchen sat straight up, an arrow jerked from its quiver. "Are we going to sleep at all?" he asked, but his eyes were soft, lambent in the firelight. She just shook her head, speechless. "Fine," he went on, stroking the skin of her belly; he'd gotten her naked again. "Hang me on a technicality. We'll be married in three weeks. Marry me, Madchen," he encouraged softly, when she was silent.

"Never call me Maddie," she said. "I hate it."

"Agreed." He waited for her other demands. She was negotiating her marriage contract, after all, for all that she was sitting naked on a pile of yarn and her virginity was gone. "I'll keep you safe," he vowed, and seeing her face, perceived the cause of her hesitation. "Do you mean safe from me? Well no, then, I won't. I'm going to have you. But don't worry," he added, "you're going to like it."

Still, she said nothing, but there was a smile creeping to the corners of her mouth. "I have no experience with happiness," she warned him. "It frightens me a little."

"Only a little every day, I promise," he said. "Come here."

This time she let him pull her down, but when his hand slid immediately to the juncture of her thighs, she said, "If we really are to be married, there's one more thing I have to tell you."

Elizabeth Wydeville's mother-in-law, the dowager queen, took her seat at the high table. She was ancient and rheumy-eyed, but anyone who judged her incapable was in danger of making a grave error. Her daughter-in-law, a commoner and a widow with three children when Edward met her under the old oak tree in the forest, had not become the queen of England by accident. The court was abuzz with the latest rumors: the Duke of Somerset paid a fortune to annul his daughter's betrothal to Earl Rivers's son, and that son, Lord Scales, was now to be wed to a spinner from the City. The dowager approved. Why leave it all for the nobility? No one knew better than she that you took your happiness where you found it. And she had. She had, and she did not regret any of it for a single instant.

The benches had been moved to clear the hall for dancing, and the musicians were tuning their instruments. The court was in a merry mood. Edward had spared no expense at dinner; the match pleased him, no one knew quite why. But a contented king meant a happy court. The musicians struck up the first number. Everyone waited politely for Edward and Elizabeth to take the floor, but he waved them away. He was too fat to dance. He indicated Lord Scales, who bowed to the girl and led her to the middle of the floor. They had found a proper dress for her. It was palest rose, shot through with gold thread and even to the dowager's old eyes, she glowed like sunrise. Before they had danced a measure, a disruption at the front of the hall drew everyone's attention.

A disembodied voice rose up to the beamed ceiling. "An audience! I have an audience with the lady affianced to Lord Scales." When the servants moved aside and he strode forward, he was revealed as the dwarf, only not the scraggly little man who had made Madchen's acquaintance. This dwarf wore a tiny, immaculate suit tailored of cloth-of-gold with brocade edging and gilt shoes, turned up at the toes, on his little feet. Reaching Madchen, he bowed, low and grand. "I have come to claim my prize—the firstborn son of Madchen Sprynger and Piers Wydeville!" He made his announcement triumphantly, the culmination of a lifetime of planning.

A shocked hush descended upon the room, surprise lighting every face except that of Piers Wydeville. Madchen only looked sorrowful. She stepped forward. "I'm sorry," she said, bending down to the little man, and she meant it. "I didn't know that I would marry him."

"You were supposed to marry him," the dwarf answered. "I've come to claim the child. My child." Madchen only shook her head. "Come with me. I have something to tell you."

All eyes were riveted to the play. Into this hush came her father's voice, loud and bewildered. "What child? She had the scarlet fever when she was seven. She's barren."

The dwarf stared at Madchen, a dull red rising into his features. "Barren? Barren? Childless, barren, horrible girl!" Piers stepped forward at that, but Madchen stopped him, a hand on his arm. The dwarf began to stamp his feet in uncontrollable, inchoate anger, his voice rising to a shriek. A low murmur began in the room, rising like a hive of bees about to swarm.

"Be silent!" The dowager had pulled herself to her feet and stepped down from the dais. Reaching the relative safety of the floor, she advanced on the dwarf. "You thorn in my side," she hissed. "You insolent little man. I thought I was rid of you years ago."

"Little man!" he screeched. "*Little* is the only insult I ever hear! Why not evil, why not insufferable, why not traitorous? No one ever—" he pointed wildly at Piers "—accuses him of being *tall!*" The look of shocked wonder on Piers's face changed to delight and he began to laugh. The dwarf was nearly apoplectic. "My father loved you, and you banished him because he was a dwarf. You stole him from me. You broke him. My mother never saw him again. And for that, you deserve to pay."

"All right, you evil, insufferable, traitorous *little* man," the dowager said. "I'll tell you the truth, if you can bear to hear it. I never banished your father from this court. I took your father as my lover and he was the best lover I've had, then or ever. He would lay between my legs for hours, giving me the most unspeakable pleasure and taking what I gave him willingly in return. He never asked me for anything other than my body and my affections. In a way you could never fathom, he was wealthy beyond measure."

"What about me?" the dwarf said.

The court held its collective breath. She would either give quarter or she would not.

"He had to choose," the dowager said. "You were the price he paid for me." Giving the awestruck crowd a fierce, haughty glance, she turned, gathering the train of her gown in one hand, and surged back up the dais. Throwing herself into her gilt chair, she sat glowering like Methuselah on the throne.

There was another ten seconds of impeccable restraint, then a rising babble of voices broke out as one. The secret! The court did not like secrets. Everyone present felt tremendously buoyed by its exposure.

Ignoring the chaos, Piers gave Madchen a charming, lopsided grin. He put his arms around her. "Is there a place to begin?" he asked. "And would you know where it is? You're so lovely."

She smiled up at him, her head tilted back, exposing the pale column of her throat, so he could not resist bending to kiss it.

She said, "I think we begin here."

Rings on My Fingers

Alison Tyler

Most women I know linger over the diamond rings shimmering in jewelry-store windows. They spend their lunch hours designing their own engagement rings online, whether or not there's a fiancé in sight. And they can't help but drool during those sappy "Diamonds are Forever" commercials that tend to pop up oh so innocently during reruns of *Friends*.

But not me.

That doesn't mean I don't swoon over carefully crafted window displays—simply not the ones at Tiffany & Co. My fantasy fodder can be found in a slightly seedier part of town, on Sunset Boulevard, in a window filled with emeralds and sapphires and deep hearty rubies, just like any exclusive jewelry haven. But the items for sale in this neon-encrusted store aren't gems, but hues. Pigments. Images on paper to be transferred to willing, waiting flesh.

Recently, diamond merchants have tried to sell women on expensive jewelry for the right hand. Left hand equals married. Right equals independence. *Buy more diamonds,* the ads suggest, *to show what a strong, brave woman you are.*

Tattoo stores don't go in for similar campaigns. *Anyone* can get adorned, if your wallet holds the cash and your soul possesses the appropriate appetite for pain. But that's not what I wanted. I didn't need to prove my strength, my confidence, my independence. I wanted to be tattooed for a reason. I craved the commitment accompanying the ink. The permanence of artwork as tribal, as traditional, as a ring on my finger. One that would never come off.

So I watched the windows every time I passed by.

And I waited.

My friends married up. They settled into their lives. Not white-picket-fence lives—not in Los Angeles, where fences tend to be chain-link and heavily padlocked—but cojoined, smug, satisfied lives. My buddies sported rings on their fingers that sparkled even in the dimmest light over cocktails at our favorite shady little place in Hollywood.

"Don't you *want* to get married?" Cassie cooed to me during one girls' night out. We were four high-school friends nestled into a blood-red leather booth—three married girlies and me. Which of these things was not like the others? That was obvious on sight. I felt as if I had a nobody-loves-me aura permanently stapled to my slender frame.

"I don't know what I want," I said, lying.

Of course, I knew. Yet it wasn't a what that I desired, but a who.

Janelle twirled her princess-cut ring, and rainbows shot on the walls. It was a sick habit, in my opinion, one she'd invented as soon as Blake slipped the engagement ring on her finger. I stared at the dizzying, dancing swirl of colors, and thought immediately of Brody.

Brody, the handsome tattoo artist who worked on Sunset Boulevard. Brody, with the heavy sand-colored hair that fell to his shoulders, the dark blue eyes that looked black in the right light. During his breaks, he always came into the bookstore where I worked, and I liked to try to guess which genre he was going to read next. No matter what I bet on, I was always surprised. He started with noir, which suited him, the old-school detective mysteries: Chandler, Hammett, Spillane. Then he moved to some coffee-table art books, especially those featuring artists from the early 1900s, such as Klimt and Egon Schiele, before choosing a recent best seller, in French. He was quiet, but not sullen or shaky like some of the rockers who came in to buy the latest copies of *Spin* and *Rolling Stone*. And every so often he'd give me a stare that made me want to melt away into a pool of liquid lust.

What color would lust be? Gold-streaked crimson, for sure. Brody could dip his needle into me, paint with the color I'd become.

When I walked home, I'd pass by the window of his parlor and peer in. I couldn't see the tattoo rooms from the street. Only the pictures in the window, and sometimes Brody behind the counter, reading his most recent purchase.

Read me, I wanted to beg him. Or, more accurately: *Write on me. Draw on me. Make me your own.*

Cassie tried to set me up. She felt that married life was vastly superior to singlehood, and she wanted me to be as happy as she was. That's what she said, anyway. But I could guess the truth. She wanted to understand me.

How could she, if I didn't understand myself?

"It's different," she claimed. "Being married, I mean. You're not desperate anymore. You've got a whole part of your brain back. You no longer have to lose sleep over whether someone else will be sharing your bed."

That wasn't something I *ever* lost sleep over. There were plenty of men who wanted to share my bed. And when there weren't—well, I had the whole damn bed to myself. Company wasn't what I craved.

What I wanted was Brody. And not just Brody, himself. But

Brody's intensity. I wanted him to look at me the way he looked at his books. To focus his attention fully on me, not in stolen little glances over the tops of paperbacks. I wanted Brody to spread me out on his tattoo table and mark me up. To claim me, to find me, to make me his own.

Truly? I wanted rings on my fingers, but not the diamond kind.

The next time he slid into the store, I was ready. I had the latest four-color tattoo magazine out and open on the counter, and when he reached the front of the line, I made sure that the image I liked the best was the one facing him. The photograph of the girl with pale skin like mine, long dark hair and ravenous purple-blue eyes. The one with the girl showing off her latest adornment, a visual design by Klimt. Swirls of colors. Like rainbows dancing on a barroom wall. A tapestry. A painting. Done on skin with a needle rather than on canvas with a brush.

Brody raised his eyebrows. "You like that?" He seemed surprised.

"And *this*," I said, pointing specifically to the close-up inset photo of the woman's hands. The rings on her fingers. Rings that would never come off. There were people behind Brody in line, but he didn't seem in the slightest bit of a hurry. I liked that about him. He refused to rush.

"Have you ever been inked?"

I shook my head and he grinned. "A virgin," and I felt my breath catch. Wasn't that the name of the Klimt piece? The same one he'd been looking at in one of those high-end art books. The same one as the image on the girl's back in the magazine. A shudder ran through me, and Brody's smile broadened, wolfish and hungry.

"I've seen you looking," he said softly, and I felt as if the rest of the store had disappeared. Vanished in a magical puff of L.A. smog. "Window-shopping," he continued, a taunt in his voice. "When are you going to work up the nerve to come inside?"

I had an instant answer for that. "When you work up the nerve to ask me out."

We locked eyes for a moment, and his grin faded, but the force of his expression remained. I could have touched the power between us, held it in my hands, electric and hot.

"After work," he said, his voice low and dark. "We'll have a drink."

I nodded, feeling as if every minute would last an hour. Every hour a day.

Time crawled, yes, as I'd known it would. But ultimately, I was able to clock out. And when I finally snagged my thrift-store leather jacket from the back room and made my way to his store, I felt as if I'd been set free. He was waiting for me. Sitting on the chipped front steps of the tattoo parlor. A paperback in his hands that he was clearly not reading. The tension hovered in the air between us—ripe and ready.

"Where to?" I murmured as he stood up to greet me. But I didn't have to ask. We went to my place, because that was closest. Went to my bed. Or *almost* to my bed. To the wall outside my bedroom, where he waited for me to kick off my boots before he tore my clothes off me: the black T-shirt with Blondie's face on the front, the indigo stovepipe jeans, the plum-colored satin bikinis. His hands moved fast for once. I'd misread him. He *did* rush. When it was necessary, he rushed.

But once he'd gotten me naked, he stopped and stared.

I could feel him drinking me in—my skin, so pale, so fresh. He seemed in awe for a moment, but only a moment, because then he was in motion once more, and his own clothes were quickly shed, a rumpled pile of denim and black, like mine. And I could see the colors on his skin. The waves of blues and gold and reds. The fish on his forearm. The mermaid on his back, when he turned for a moment, her tail a deep serpentine green. As he seemed in awe of my blank canvas, I was in love with the designs on his body, and I watched him with the reverence of an art student at the Louvre. A hush had fallen on us. A wave of respect.

We touched each other slowly at first, each tracing, each learning, my fingertips following the lines of every piece of artwork, his hands caressing the muscles and sinews beneath my naked skin. And then suddenly we were fucking, hard, the type of fucking that leaves you breathless and wanting more. His body on mine, firm hands lifting me, legs balancing my weight. He was strong, maneuvering me exactly how he craved. Turning me this way and that, so that first I was astride him, atop him, and then I was faced away, hands on the wall, hips arched.

"I want to be the one," he said against the nape of my neck, a rush of air, an ebony whisper. "I want to be the one to do it."

I shivered all over, knowing what he meant, seeing my future, spread out on his table. The way he'd look at me, the way he'd focus.

"Yes," I echoed. "Yes."

He fucked me until I came, crying out, biting on my bottom lip to stifle the sound. But he didn't stop. He merely spun me once more and gripped me up in his arms, hands cradling my ass. Then he pushed through my bedroom door, so that we were in my tiny space and up on the bed, fucking again, this time slower, more carefully. The mirror reflected us: his tattooed skin, my naked flesh. Brody on top this time. My black sheets beneath us. Rumpled. Wrinkled. His mouth on my neck, and then down, lower, to my breasts, and lower still, to my pussy.

"I want to mark you," he murmured. Fingers tracing every-where. "Here." A heart shape drawn effortlessly on my hip. "And here." A butterfly outline flickering to flight on my lower belly. "And here." A dagger on my thigh, blade pointed down, drips of crimson blood trailing along my tender skin. And then his mouth became sealed to my nether lips, so that he couldn't speak anymore, and I could no longer think.

In my head, he'd already done the deed.

In my mind, I was as decorated, as adorned, as he was. Freshly inked. Colored like a painting, a living, breathing work of art.

We didn't sleep afterward. We talked in crazy whispers. With him confessing how he'd tried for months to impress me. Choosing his titles carefully. Which books would make him stand out from the crowd? The noir was cliché, he felt. The art books too pompous. The French one a gimmick, just to throw me off my guard.

He'd been window-shopping, too. Craving something be-hind the glass, something just out of reach. And that some-thing was me.

When Janelle twirled her ring on the following Thursday night, for once I didn't feel sick with longing. Instead, I watched transfixed as the light hit the walls in crazy spirals of color, watched the colors dance and gleam, watched the way my friends' faces appeared smug and satisfied in the blood-red booth.

Did they truly have what they wanted?

Diamonds are forever—the ads proclaim this as truth. But a diamond ring can twist and turn. The metal band can wear away. The stone can come loose and fall free, leaving a hollow space behind, an empty hole, a gaping wound.

I looked down at my hand, under the table, slid my silver ring aside to see the band of ink Brody had intricately designed.

"You know what you need," Cassie began in her regular Thursday-night mantra, but I tuned her out easily.

I had what I needed.

Or if not a what, then a who.

The Princess

Elspeth Potter

The sun beat down and the sea roared. "Aren't you too short to be a prince?"

"*Princess,* not prince. I've come to save you to escape my evil stepfather! Gold is the reward!"

"Save me? You can't 'kiss the lips no man has kissed.' It's too late! The huntsman kissed me before he stuck me on this rock! The dragon will be here any minute!"

The princess in trousers scrambled onto the rock and pushed aside chains, gathering silk skirts in her hands. "I didn't say I was going to kiss the lips on your *face,*" she said.

⁂about the authors⁂

Jacqueline Applebee is a black British woman, who breaks down barriers with smut. Jacqueline's stories have appeared in various anthologies and on Web sites, including, Cleansheets, *Best Women's Erotica 2008* and *2009, Ultimate Lesbian Erotica 2008* and *2009,* and *Best Lesbian Erotica 2008.* Jacqueline's favorite fairy tale is "Three Little Pigs" because she has a thing for adventurous bacon. Jacqueline's Web site is http://www.writing-in-shadows.co.uk.

Janine Ashbless started her erotica career with her single-author collection of fairy and fantasy stories, *Cruel Enchantment,* published by Black Lace in 2000. Her follow-up collection, *Dark Enchantment,* appeared in 2009. In between came three erotic novels and various short stories, including one that made it into *Best Women's Erotica 2009.* Her favorite fairy tales are "East of the Sun and West of the Moon" (which she retold as *Bearskin* in the novella collection *Enchanted*) and the horribly creepy "Mr. Fox." She lives in the U.K. and blogs at www.janineashbless.blogspot.com where she enthuses about mythology, Victorian art and minotaurs.

Rachel Kramer Bussel (www.rachelkramerbussel.com) is an author, editor, blogger and reading-series host. She has edited more than twenty anthologies, including *Tasting Him, Tasting Her, Spanked, Dirty Girls* and *Best Sex Writing 2008* and *2009.* She is senior editor at *Penthouse Variations,* writes the "Dating Drama" column for the *Frisky,* and hosts *In The Flesh Reading Series.* Her writing has been published in more than a hundred anthologies, including *Best American Erotica 2004* and *2006,* as well as *Cosmopolitan, Fresh Yarn, Huffington Post, Newsday, the New York Post,* the *San Francisco Chronicle, Time Out New York,* the *Village Voice* and *Zink,* and she has appeared on *NY1, The Berman and Berman Show* and *The Martha Stewart Show.* Her favorite fairy tale is "Cinderella," with whom she shares a shoe fetish (high heels especially), though she also envies Rapunzel's long hair.

T. C. Calligari lives in British Columbia, writing in many worlds of what-if. She grew up reading fairy tales and fables from the children's series *My Book House.* Her favorite though is "East of the Sun and West of the Moon," a Norwegian fairy tale based on the Eros and Psyche myth where the woman must rescue her prince. T.C.'s stories have appeared in *E Is for Exotic, B Is for Bondage,* as well as *Open for Business, Naughty or Nice* and *Guilty Pleasures.* "Stocking Stuffers" is featured in the *Mammoth Book of Best New Erotica.*

Heidi Champa is a typical last-born child. Snarky, attention-seeking and rebellious, she chooses to write dirty stories to keep out of real trouble. Her work appears in *Tasting Him* and *Frenzy.* She has also steamed up the pages of *Bust* magazine. If you prefer your erotica in electronic form, look for her at Clean-Sheets, Ravenous Romance and The Erotic Woman. Despite her latent cynicism, her favorite fairy tale will always be "Beauty and the Beast." Find her online at heidichampa.blogspot.com.

Portia Da Costa is a British author of romance, erotic romance and romantic fiction, specializing in intense, character-driven contemporary novels, and praised for the vivid emotional depth of her writing. Since 1990, she has had more than twenty titles published, as well as around a hundred short stories, and her work has been translated into many languages including German, Spanish, Italian, Dutch, Norwegian and Japanese. Always a lover of fantasy and fairy tale, she adores the stories of "Cinderella" and "Sleeping Beauty." Portia lives in West Yorkshire with her husband and her cats and she enjoys reading and watching television.

Andrea Dale's stories have appeared in *Do Not Disturb: Hotel Sex Stories, Frenzy,* the *Mammoth Book of the Kama Sutra* and *Dirty Girls,* among many others. With coauthors, she has sold novels to Cheek Books (*A Little Night Music,* Sarah Dale) and Black Lace Books (*Cat Scratch Fever,* Sophie Mouette) and even more short stories. In other incarnations she writes SFF and media tie-in. A lover of fantasy, mythology and the fae folk since a young age, her favorite tale is that of Tam Lin, because the heroine rescues the hero for once. For more information, check out her Web site at www.cyvarwydd.com.

Bella Dean is new to the business of dirty stories. She still blushes when she types, but has no plans to give it up. Her work has appeared in *Afternoon Delight.* She lives with her small family in her small house in her small town. Her favorite fairy tale growing up was "Cinderella." Even then she had a thing for shoes and hot men.

Once upon a time, a playwright scarred by her first lover's betrayal and an actor who lost his love in the 9/11 conflagration came together in a shabby off-Broadway theater. Though this is not **Erica DeQuaya's** background, it formed the backbone for her critically acclaimed first erotic romance novel, *Backstage Affair.* Five novels and many short stories later, Erica continues living her own happily-ever-after as she pens erotic and mainstream books (including her well-received hockey romance series) from her middle-class castle in Texas. Erica shares her royal surroundings with her beloved handsome prince and soul mate of more than two decades, a princeling of a son, two loyal, if somewhat neurotic, dogs and a collection of geckos in the backyard.

Benjamin Eliot is a stay-at-home dad and a WWII freak. He has a huge collection of memorabilia and books and has been known to trap unsuspecting people for impromptu historical lectures. He loves his wife, his kids and his old-piece-of-crap car. For the record, he can fix a toilet and even install a faucet. Benjamin was never one for fairy tales, but in college he found he could really get into a good meaty greek myth. Look for more of his work in the future. He's just getting started with his storytelling.

A. D. R. Forte's erotic short fiction appears in various anthologies including collections from Black Lace, Cleis Press and Circlet Press. Her favorite fairy tale, of course, is "Beauty and the Beast." Visit her at www.adrforte.com.

Lana Fox's erotic stories have appeared in anthologies by Xcite, and she also publishes literary fiction under a different name. She started writing erotica when she gave a reading and members of the audience came up afterward saying, "Your work is all about sex," when she didn't think it was! Her favorite fairy tale is "Little Red Riding Hood," especially when it's turned on its head and Red has a feisty side.

Shanna Germain's work has appeared in places like *Best American Erotica, Best Bondage Erotica, Best Gay Romance, Frenzy* and *Luscious.* She's obsessed with the wolf and the girl in the red cloak, and often sings a darker version of "Li'l Red Riding Hood," by Sam the Sham. Visit her at www.shannagermain.com.

Bryn Haniver, a nature lover and sexy B-movie aficionado, writes fiction from islands and peninsulas whenever possible, and prefers fairy tales with menacing mermaids, like "The Mermaid and the Boy." Bryn's work has appeared in *Red Hot Erotica* and *B Is for Bondage.*

Georgia E. Jones graduated with an MFA from Mills College. Her stories have appeared in the *Santa Barbara Review* and the literary magazine *Estero.* She lives in northern California. Her favorite fairy tale is "Snow White and the Seven Dwarfs" because the heroine is smart and resourceful.

Tsaurah Litzky is an internationally known writer of erotica whose work has appeared in more than seventy-five publications, including *Best American Erotica* (eight times), *Best International Erotica* (twice), *X: the Erotic Treasury, Penthouse,* the *New York Times, Sex For America, K is For Kinky, Got A Minute, The Merry XXXmas Book of Erotica, Politically Inspired, The Urban Bizarre, Dirty Girls, Evergreen Review 12.* Simon & Schuster published her erotic novella, *The Motion of the Ocean,* as part of *Three the Hard Way,* a series of erotic novellas edited by Susie Bright. Tsaurah Litzky's groundbreaking erotic writing class, Silk Sheets: Writing Erotica, is now in its eleventh year at the New School in Manhattan. Tsaurah believes that great sex often is inspired by a pair of shoes and that fairy tales do come true.

Kristina Lloyd is the author of three erotic novels, *Darker Than Love, Asking for Trouble* and *Split,* all published by Black Lace. Her short stories have appeared in numerous anthologies and magazines in both the U.K. and U.S., and her novels have been translated into German, Dutch and Japanese. She has a master's degree in twentieth-century literature, and has been described as "a fresh literary talent" who "writes sex with a formidable force." She lives in Brighton on the south coast of England and her favorite fairy tale is "Little Red Riding Hood" because it's dark, sinister and short on princesses. For more, visit http://kristinalloyd.wordpress.com.

Nikki Magennis is a Scottish author of erotica and erotic romance. She grew up on fairy tales and has always loved "The Red Shoes." Lily takes her name from a song on Kate Bush's *Red Shoes* album. In folklore, lilies are used to break spells or enchantments. Nikki's second novel, *The New Rakes,* is published by Black Lace, and you can find her work in many anthologies. She is currently working on a collection of short stories and could use a spot of lily juice to break her procrastination habit. Read more at: http://nikkimagennis.blogspot.com.

Sommer Marsden writes her naughty fiction from a small town near the Chesapeake Bay. Her work has appeared in dozens of print anthologies and magazines, and her stories haunt many Internet sites on a regular basis. When she was a little girl, she loved the tale of "The Princess and the Pea," mostly because she is a complainer at heart. You can see what she's up to at www.SmutGirl.blogspot.com.

N. T. Morley is the author of sixteen published novels of erotic dominance and submission, including *The Visitor, The Nightclub, The Appointment* and the trilogies *The Castle, The*

Library and *The Office.* Morley has also edited two anthologies, *MASTER and slave,* and has contributed to many erotic anthologies, including the *Naughty Stories from A to Z* series, the *Sweet Life* series, the *Best New Erotica* series, and many other anthologies. Morley's favorite fairy tale is unquestionably *Pretty Woman,* though there's something strangely hot about *Leaving Las Vegas.* That said, there's lots to love about "Sleeping Beauty," the Anne Rice version. Visit www.ntmorley.com for more information.

Elspeth Potter's stories have appeared in *The Mammoth Book of Best New Erotica, Periphery: Erotic Lesbian Futures, Best Lesbian Romance 2009, Best Lesbian Erotica* and *Best Women's Erotica.* Her erotic novel *The Duchess, Her Maid, the Groom, and their Lover,* by Victoria Janssen, was a 2008 release from Harlequin Spice. *The Moonlight Mistress* was released in December 2009. Her favorite fairy tale is "The Tinderbox." Read more at www.victoriajanssen.com.

Thomas S. Roche is the author of more than two hundred published stories that fall into the horror, fantasy, crime, paranormal and erotica genres—frequently all at once. His books include *His* and *Hers,* two short-story collections written with Alison Tyler, and *Dark Matter,* a collection of his own stories, as well as four anthologies of fantasy/horror and three books of erotic crime stories. Roche has always had a love-hate relationship with fairy tales. He hated them as a child because there were rarely any spaceships in them. As an adult, he has adapted dozens of fairy tales for various projects, starting with a rewrite of *A Midsummer Night's Dream* he did in the mid-1990s. He's very fond of "The Little Match Girl," probably due to his lingering goth damage from the eighties. He blogs about such topics as ghosts, aliens, sex and politics at www.thomasroche.com.

Donna George Storey is the author of *Amorous Woman,* a semi-autobiographical tale of an American's steamy love affair with Japan. Her short fiction has been published in over ninety journals and anthologies, including *X: The Erotic Treasury, Naughty or Nice, Frenzy, Best Women's Erotica,* and *The Mammoth Book of Best New Erotica.* Her favorite fairy tale is "The Twelve Dancing Princesses," not only because she played the role of Angelica in a summer-theater production in high school, but because she can really relate to the story of girls who are perfect ladies by day sneaking off to a magical land every night to dance Freudian holes in their slippers with charming princes. Read more of her work at www.DonnaGeorgeStorey.com.

Sophia Valenti's erotica has appeared in *Afternoon Delight* and *Playing with Fire.* She believes in happily-ever-afters, but thinks that sometimes fate needs a little push in the right direction. Her favorite fairy tale is "The Ugly Duckling" because coming into your own is as important as finding your place. Visit her at www.sophiavalenti.blogspot.com.

Saskia Walker loves to read and write stories where magic and passion are found in unexpected situations. Her favorite fairy tales reflect this, stories like "Cinderella," and the tales of "Scheherazade" and the "Arabian Nights." Saskia began writing in 1996 and her fiction has now been published in more than fifty anthologies. Her novel-length work spans from contemporary erotic romance to exotic fantasy. Saskia lives in the north of England on the windswept Yorkshire moors, where she happily spends her days spinning yarns. She has lots more stories to tell, so be sure to visit www.saskiawalker.co.uk.

Allison Wonderland has a B.A. in women's studies, a weakness for lollipops and a fondness for rubber ducks. Her favorite sound is Fran Drescher's voice, and her cocktail of choice is a Shirley Temple. On the fairy-tale front, she is quite fond of Jane Yolen's collection, *Not One Damsel in Distress*. (She finds the dearth of distressed damsels very refreshing.) Allison has contributed to numerous anthologies, including *Island Girls, Hurts So Good, Coming Together: At Last* and *Visible: A Femmethology*. See what she's up to at http://aisforallison.blogspot.com.

✺about the editor✺

Once upon a time, Alison Tyler was a shy girl with a dirty mind. Then a magical fairy godmother (also known as the editor of *Playgirl Magazine*) handed over a pen, and all of her fantasies began to spill out onto lined notebook paper. Over twenty-five racy novels, forty-five explicit anthologies and a thousand stories later, Alison gives thanks every day to that very first editor who showed her the way.

Called a "Trollop with a Laptop" by *East Bay Express,* a "Literary Siren" by *Good Vibrations,* and "over caffeinated" by her favorite local barista, Alison has made being naughty a full-time job. Her sultry short stories have appeared in more than a hundred anthologies including *Sex for America, Liaisons* and *Bedding Down.*

Ms. Tyler is loyal to coffee (black), lipstick (red) and tequila (straight). She has tattoos, but no piercings; a wicked tongue, but a quick smile; and bittersweet memories, but no regrets. She believes the rain won't fall if she doesn't bring an umbrella, prefers hot and dry to cold and wet, and loves to spout her favorite motto: You can sleep when you're dead. She chooses Led Zeppelin over the Beatles, the Cure over the

Smiths, and the Stones over everyone—yet although she appreciates good rock, she has a pitiful weakness for eighties hair bands.

In all things important, she remains faithful to her partner of fifteen years, but she still can't choose just one perfume. Anyone who's met her would understand immediately when she says "Goldilocks" is her favorite fairy tale. There is a subtle art to being naughty—and to trying out a lot of beds.

Find her on the web 24/7 at alisontyler.blogspot.com.

BESTSELLING AUTHOR

AMANDA McINTYRE

They are his inspiration.
He is their obsession.

Icon, rebel, unabashed romantic...
with a single look painter
Thomas Rodin conveys the
ecstasy of creativity—the
pleasures awaiting the woman
who can fuel his artistry.

the Innocent

What did this master artist see in
me? Genius abided in his soul,
rapture in his flesh, I doubted
not. To refuse him...my folly; to
surrender...my sensual salvation.

the Upstart

I chafed at the bonds of servitude
until he set me free. I turned my
back on all that I knew to follow him and found myself between two
men—master and student. One whom I loved with my heart...the
other with my body.

the Courtesan

I understood his needs, perhaps better than any. I stoked the fires of
his soul, the spark of his creativity—he made me a legend. But never
could I forget his searing touch....

Three transcendent tales of women bewitched by a master of
seduction—a slave as much to his art as to his boundless passion.

the Master & the Muses

Available now wherever books are sold!

Spice

www.Spice-Books.com

SAM60544TR

An erotic novel by

CHARLOTTE FEATHERSTONE

He must find redemption in the most unlikely bedchamber…

In Victorian England, vice of every kind can be purchased and Matthew, the Earl of Wallingford, makes certain he avails himself of every possible pleasure. Bored and jaded, he is as well-known for his coldness as for his licentious affairs with beautiful women.

While these numerous dalliances fulfill Matthew's every physical need, they secretly leave him numb and emotionally void. Until one night when he finds himself beaten, eyes bandaged and in the care of a nurse with the voice of an angel—and a gentle touch that soothes the darkness in him and makes him yearn for more.

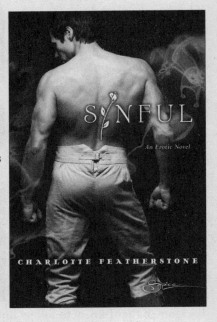

Yet, Jane Rankin is a lowly nurse, considered shy and plain by most. There is no place for her among the lords and ladies of the aristocracy—despite Matthew's growing craving for the fire that burns behind her earnest facade. And then there is Matthew's secret. A secret so humiliating and scandalous it could destroy everyone he loves. A sin, he fears, not even the love of a good woman can take away.…

SYNFUL

Available wherever books are sold!

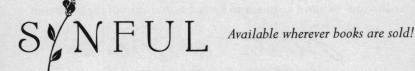

www.Spice-Books.com

SCF60543TR

From award-winning author

Saskia Walker

possession
IS ONLY
HALF THE FUN....

The moment she arrives at her rented vacation cottage nestled in northern Scotland, Zoë Daniels feels it—an arousal so powerful she's compelled to surrender to the unusually forceful carnal desires...with nearly anyone who crosses her path.

Yet there's something unsettling about the way the locals watch her, something eerie about these overwhelming encounters. Zoë knows she's not quite in control of herself and begins to wonder if there's any truth to the legend of Annabel McGraw, a powerful, promiscuous eighteenth-century witch who once owned the cottage, and whose spirit is rumored to affect anyone who stays there. Zoë doesn't believe in anything that even hints at the occult, but now strange visions are becoming frightening...and only one man's touch can bring her back to earth.

"[Walker is] one of the top erotic writers of the millennium."
—Alison Tyler

Available wherever books are sold!

Spice

www.Spice-Books.com

SSW60542TR

naughty bits 2, the highly anticipated sequel to the successful debut volume from the editors of Spice Briefs, delivers nine new unapologetically raunchy and romantic tales that promise to spark the libido. In this collection of first-rate short erotic literature, lusty selections by such provocative authors as Megan Hart, Lillian Feisty, Saskia Walker and Portia Da Costa will pique, tease and satisfy any appetite, and prove that good things do come in small packages.

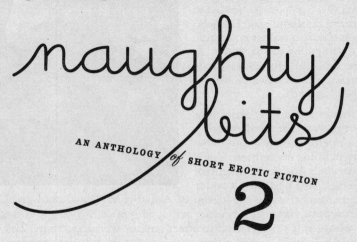

naughty bits

AN ANTHOLOGY *of* SHORT EROTIC FICTION

2

on sale now wherever books are sold!

Since launching in 2007, Spice Briefs has become the hot eBook destination for the sauciest erotic fiction on the Web. Want more of what we've got?
Visit www.SpiceBriefs.com.

Spice

www.Spice-Books.com

SV60541TR

From the bestselling author of *The Blonde Geisha*

JINA BACARR

SPRING 1873: I ARRIVED IN JAPAN
A VIRGIN BRIDE, HEARTSICK AND
ANXIOUS BEYOND MEASURE. YET I
EMBRACED THIS PERPLEXING
WORLD WITH MY SOUL LAID BARE
AFTER UNCOVERING AN EROTIC,
INTOXICATING POWER I HARDLY
KNEW THAT I, KATIE O'ROARKE,
POSSESSED.

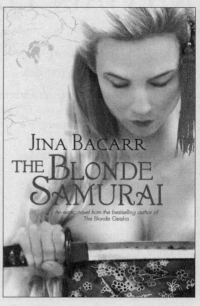

Japan was a world away from my
tedious Western existence, a welcome
distraction from my recent marriage to
a cold and cruel husband. But when
James attacked me in a drunken rage,
I could tolerate it no longer.... I had
no choice but to escape into the
surrounding hills. I awoke in the arms
of Akira, a young Samurai, and it
was he who took me to Shintaro, the
head of the powerful Samurai clan.

At first distrustful, Shintaro came to me every day for a fortnight until my
need for him made my heart race at the very sound of his feet upon the
wooden floor. He taught me the way of the Samurai—loyalty, honor, self-
respect—and the erotic possibilities of inner beauty unleashed. It is his touch
that shatters my virginal reserve, evoking danger and physical pleasures
that linger beyond our fervent encounters. But James means to find me, to
make me pay for his humiliation. I can no longer hide amongst the orange
blossoms as rebellions rage, and as my own secret continues to grow....

THE BLONDE SAMURAI

Available now
wherever books are sold!

Spice

www.Spice-Books.com

SJC60540TR

FROM THE BESTSELLING AUTHOR
OF *DIRTY* AND *TEMPTED*

MEGAN HART

Don't think.
Don't question.
Just do.

The anonymous note wasn't for me. Don't get me wrong, I'm not in the habit of reading other people's mail, but it was just a piece of paper with a few lines scrawled on it, clearly meant for the apartment upstairs. It looked so innocent but decidedly— *deliciously*—it was not.

Before replacing the note—and the ones that followed—in its rightful slot, I devoured its contents: suggestions, instructions, summonses, commands. Each was more daring, more intricate and more arousing than the last…and I followed them all to the letter.

Submission is an art, and there's something oddly freeing about doing someone's bidding…especially when it feels so very, *very* good. But I find that the more I surrender, the more powerful I feel—so it's time to switch up roles.

We play by my rules now.

Switch

Available now
wherever books are sold!

Spice

www.Spice-Books.com

SMH60539TR

AN EROTIC NOVEL
BY THE
BESTSELLING
AUTHOR OF
DIRTY AND TEMPTED

Switch
MEGAN HART

VICTORIA JANSSEN

In the throes of war, lust transforms us all....

It is the eve of the Great War, and English chemist Lucilla Osbourne finds herself trapped on hostile German soil. Panicked and alone, she turns to a young Frenchman for shelter. Together they spend a night of intense passion, but their dangerous circumstances won't allow more than a brief affair.

Even with the memory of Lucilla's lushness ever present, scientist Pascal Fournier is distracted by his reason for being in enemy territory—Tanneken Claes has information Pascal could use against the enemy but, even more extraordinary…she's a werewolf. After entrusting Pascal with her secret, Tanneken and her mate, Noel, are captured.

As war rages, Pascal and Lucilla combine efforts to rescue Tanneken and Noel, struggling with danger, power and secret desires transformed by the unyielding hunger for the beating of a lover's heart.

The MOONLIGHT MISTRESS

Available now wherever books are sold!

Spice

www.Spice-Books.com

SVJ536TR

Delve into the season's most pleasurable
erotic tales of carnal desire from

AMANDA McINTYRE, CHARLOTTE FEATHERSTONE and KRISTI ASTOR

On a solstice eve long ago,
a Druid priestess and Norse
warrior succumbed to
forbidden, erotic desire.
Their passion was one that
neither death, decree nor
time could tear asunder.

Now, three women of later
centuries begin their own
sensual journeys, awakened
by the ancient power of the
priestess's words: *"Burn
bright of winter's desire."*

WINTER'S DESIRE

Available wherever books are sold!

www.Spice-Books.com

SMFA535TR